Janet Inglis [...] w
up in Winnipeg, [...] a
director of a London stockbroking [...] is
married to a painter and they have two sons. Her
previous novels, *Daddy's Girl* and *Father of Lies*, are
also published by Transworld.

Also by Janet Inglis

DADDY'S GIRL
FATHER OF LIES

and published by Corgi Books

The Colour of Sin

Janet Inglis

CORGI BOOKS

THE COLOUR OF SIN
A CORGI BOOK : 0 552 14543 2

First publication in Great Britain

PRINTING HISTORY
Corgi edition published 1998

Material from *Poetical Works of Robert Bridges* (Oxford University
Press, 1936) reproduced by permission of Oxford University Press.

Set in 11/12pt Plantin by
Phoenix Typesetting, Ilkley, West Yorkshire.

Corgi Books are published by Transworld Publishers Ltd,
61-63 Uxbridge Road, London W5 5SA,
in Australia by Transworld Publishers (Australia) Pty Ltd,
15-25 Helles Avenue, Moorebank, NSW 2170
and in New Zealand by Transworld Publishers (NZ) Ltd,
3 William Pickering Drive, Albany, Auckland.

Reproduced, printed and bound in Great Britain by
Mackays of Chatham plc, Chatham, Kent.

Beautiful must be the mountains whence ye come,
And bright in the fruitful valleys the streams wherefrom
Ye learn your song . . .

Nay, barren are those mountains, and spent the streams:
Our voice is the voice of desire, that haunts our dreams . . .

Robert Bridges, 'Nightingales'

1952

I'm looking for Miss Right.

She could be anywhere, couldn't she? The colour of her eyes, the size of her tits, the size of her eyes and the colour of her tits, none of that matters. The kind of thing that will make her Miss Right, it's not that kind of thing. I'll know her when I see her.

Everybody wants to be Miss Right. They come up to me on the sidewalk. They follow me down the road. They whisper their clichéd come-ons at me: *Fancy a bit of it, darling? I'll give you a good time, love. Hey, handsome, I've got something special for you.*

They don't say it the way it sounds. They slur it, like they're ashamed of what they have to say. They rub themselves against me, cats begging for scraps, making a purr of their pleas.

They don't want me. They want my money.

Miss Right will be looking for something more. She'll be wanting to make something meaningful of her pointless little life.

That's where I come in.

I'm an artist. I make things meaningful.

MALACHY HAWKE
1930–1997

Though highly successful and widely admired, Malachy Hawke never moved in the mainstream of contemporary art. He pursued his own idiosyncratic path, without regard for trends and fashions or the prevailing schools of art theory. As a result he produced one of the most consistent and compelling bodies of work in post-war American art.

A tall man of striking appearance, he had little formal education. At sixteen he left his native Montana to hitchhike around America. Two years in the Navy gave him a glimpse of the world beyond, and led to further travels in Europe. Eventually he landed in New York, where with characteristic single-mindedness he embarked on what was to prove a prolific and successful career.

The work which first brought him to prominence featured three-dimensional geometric forms on monochromatic canvases, though he later moved to a less formalized and slightly more figurative style.

He sought neither critical nor commercial approval, regarding the former as being enslaved to fads and novelty, and the latter as smacking of prostitution. He refused to discuss his work, observing only that painting was a visual art, not a verbal one. Yet by the mid-1960s his strongly individual and readily identifiable style had won him considerable recognition.

He never married, though not for the usual reason.

1

To be carnally minded is death.

Ged Hawke swung his left foot out of the car, and set it down in a foreign country.

His father's country.

The scale of it was astounding. The city of Portland had nestled in a bowl of heavily forested foothills. Now, not an hour from the airport, they were in a landscape that denied the very existence of hills. In the middle of a valley so flat, so wide, that the mountains on either side had to be taken on trust.

Wheat fields spread as far as the eye could see: as far as the sunset, but not so far as the mountains. Enormous oaks reared up at random, like memories of another time, another season, a cooler, greener otherwhere.

The sky was huge and unconfined. A prairie sky, a pale immensity created on an American scale, like the valley. The sort of heaven that made sky gods.

And here, on a more mundane level, was Calum. He was returning empty-handed from his foray into the only building in sight, a petrol station cum convenience store. 'Hey, Dad, I need a dollar to buy a Coke. I've only got pounds.'

Ged gave him a dollar bill. A ten-dollar bill, actually, as he realized when it was too late to retrieve it. Damned Yankee money, all the same size and colour. 'So what do you think?'

'About what?'

'This part of the world.'

Calum glanced around with a vague mixture of surprise and suspicion. 'Flat,' he decided at last. 'Looks pretty rural.'

'Very perceptive.'

As soon as the words were out of his mouth, Ged regretted them. Regretted the words, and the sardonic tone. Regretted even more the look Calum gave him, which said *eff off* in any language.

Part of the point of this trip had been an attempt to make friends. Well, not exactly friends. Other things being equal, Ged was unlikely to get matey with a nineteen-year-old unemployed layabout who flaunted his attitude to the world in spiky face jewellery. And Calum, to be fair, was equally unlikely to seek a soul mate in the man who had abandoned him and his sister and his mother. So let's just say, something a little warmer than the purely legal and theoretical relationship they had enjoyed – endured – these last three years.

Calum wasn't wasting much time on either regret or resentment. He took the ten dollars and disappeared inside for a second assault on the drinks cooler.

Ged shoved Calum and guilt and irritation into the skeleton cupboard at the back of his head. His real reason for being here had nothing to do with his son. Well, in a tangential way it did, since Calum had been included in the invitation, if you could call it that. He fished the tattered scrap of newsprint out of his pocket and read it again.

The advertisement had an old-fashioned flavour to it. The gist was that if any male descendants of Malachy Hawke (deceased) were to present themselves, with proof of their identity, at the offices of Messrs Daud, Deforte & Makepeace, Barristers, Solicitors, and Attorneys at Law, of Corvallis, Oregon, on or before 15 August, they might hear something to their advantage.

'Male descendants' meant Calum as much as Ged. But

the ad had arrived in a letter from these lawyers. A letter addressed to Ged, with no mention of Calum. The letter had suggested that it would be more to his advantage to come *after* the 15th. To avoid the crush, perhaps.

In a spasm of anger he crumpled the paper into a pea-sized pellet and flicked it away as if it were some irritating insect. Then he leaned against the rented car to continue his survey of the surroundings, this time in more critical mood.

American petrol stations – *gas* stations, when in Rome – were the wayside shrines of the dominant religion, and they came in one format only. Along with the battered pick-ups and the weathered faces driving them, this place could have been anywhere in America.

Another sort of pick-up appeared. This one had no wheels at all. She wore thong sandals and a very short skirt.

Ged watched her come out of the building, behind Calum. Watched her pause to survey her prospects, catch his eye, and saunter towards him.

That surprised and alarmed him. He would have expected her usual customers here on the freeway to be lorry drivers. Was he as obvious to her as she was to him?

The notion unsettled him. Unsettled his views about hunter and prey. Was Calum the victim of conglomerate America, because he was thirsty and bought a Coke? Did it make any difference that the Coke machine couldn't see him coming?

The girl was taking her time, trying to look like a lady of leisure rather than a working girl. She was chewing gum, of course. Her hair was kinked and frosted, or possibly even frozen: it scarcely shuddered when the wind struck. She managed to look both pasty-faced and tanned, an all-American creature of the night. But not bad looking, all the same. If she was a trifle plump, that only emphasized her cleavage in the sleeveless top.

Her breasts did her hustling for her, swaying from side to side and bouncing up and down as she walked, shouting for attention with naïve bravado. It was the tits, he decided, that prompted his initial physical response.

And also, maybe, the fact that it was nearly three months since Elie had walked out on him. Three years of Elie every day, and then three months of nothing. Almost anything would have looked better than nothing. Maybe even the ghost of a murky past that he thought to have laid with Elie.

The breasts sashayed over to Calum, who was standing by the car, one hand on the door handle, gazing into the distant atmosphere. 'You guys going to California?'

Ged was appalled, and relieved, that she had selected Calum. Neither past sins nor present arousal had put a visible mark on him after all. On the other hand, a man must be truly past it when even the hookers ignored him in favour of his son.

She wasn't really ignoring him. She was giving him significant sideways glances as she repeated her question. 'Are you headin' for California?'

Calum was still staring into twilit nothingness. He hadn't taken his eyes from the horizon. 'What's that?'

The girl looked much as Calum had earlier, surprised and suspicious. 'Whatcha mean, what's California?'

Ged glanced past her. He saw what Calum was seeing.

A mountain floated in the eastern sky just above the horizon. A dream mountain, a child's image of a mountain, a perfect white inverted cone. No foothills, no forests, no evidence of any contact with earth; no sign that mankind had ever sullied that snow with mucky boot-prints. The icy slopes glowed with the light of the vanished sun.

Calum had been staring at a heavenly mountain, while Ged's attention had been derailed much lower down. To paraphrase Oscar Wilde, all of us are lying in the gutter, but some of us are looking at the whores.

The girl turned to see what was so much more eye-catching than her cleavage.

'Oh, that.' The miraculous mountain did not appear to

13

interest her. After all, she must see it every night of her life. 'It's Mount Hood.'

'That's the coolest thing I've ever seen. Where's my camera?' Calum stuck the upper half of his body into the back seat of the car and rummaged in his luggage, which consisted of a small but experienced canvas knapsack and a tatty plastic carry bag.

Ged went on gazing at the miraculous mountain. He was vaguely aware of the girl staring at him with some faint hope. 'Did you want a lift? We're not going very far, I'm afraid.'

'How far?'

'Corvallis.'

'The university?'

She must have mistaken Calum for a student. Something to do with the dark-blond dreadlocks and the nose-stud, no doubt, or the five earrings (per ear), or maybe even the ring that pierced his lower lip. Since no-one would have hired a person who went about looking like that, he must have been a student.

If only. In fact Calum's scholarly career had ended in the sixth form, when he had been thrown out of the local comprehensive for what must have been, even by the school's minimal standards, appalling behaviour; and then parted company after a month with the private school Polly had scrapped her egalitarian principles to get him into.

Calum had found his camera and started to photograph the mountain. He was cursing because the flash insisted on firing itself off. With the hubris of the mechanically minded, it was trying to illuminate the sky.

'Family business,' Ged found himself explaining to the girl, for no reason. 'My father died.'

Her small hope had also died by now; her gaze was drifting towards a lorry pulling up to the pumps. But she was polite enough to pause before walking away, to offer some pointless and impersonal sympathy. 'Gee, I'm sorry. That's too bad.'

'Is it? I don't know. I didn't know him.'

She didn't hear. She was already gone, moving in on the lorry driver.

The mountain was gone too, when he looked up again. Within those few moments of inattention the world had turned an infinitesimal fraction, enough to take the sunset out of reach of even that heavenly peak. Now it was lost in the night.

2

'Where the hell is this place?' Calum demanded, rousing himself from a comatose state and tugging off his earphones. 'That lawyer said it was on the coast. We've been driving for an hour without a sniff of the sea, let alone any place called Yakuts.'

'Yakuts Mountain,' Ged corrected mildly. 'I got the impression that it's not actually a place. Not a town, I mean.'

'Just a village?'

'Not even that.'

'What, then? A mountain? Your father lived on a *mountain*?'

'We haven't seen anything else for the last fifty miles, have we?'

'The back of bloody beyond,' muttered Calum. From behind the security of sunglasses he scowled through his open window at the breathtakingly beautiful scenery.

The mountains that had hidden themselves beyond the sunset last night were all around them now. Evergreen giants crowded the slopes and crowned the peaks, while broad-limbed willows wept over the lively little river that ran beside the road. The farmsteads in this narrow valley looked comfortable and prosperous, fat with ripe apples and meadow-fed cattle.

A calm and pleasant life in a lovely setting, no doubt,

but hardly the place one would expect to find a millionaire artist with thirteen illegitimate sons.

This startling information about his father had been sprung on Ged only a few hours before, in the offices of Daud, Deforte & Makepeace, solicitors to the late Malachy Hawke. Rene Deforte, the senior partner – he pronounced it Rennie, in a cheerfully flat American accent – had added with a drawl, 'The real crazy thing is, every one of those thirteen guys had a different mother.'

And Ged had once believed himself to be an only child. Now he felt more like a pebble on the beach. 'Are you serious?'

'Well, sure. We knew about you, of course. You're the eldest son.' The lawyer had glanced down at the birth certificate Ged had brought with him. 'The others all turned up on account of that ad. That was Mal's idea. Crazy idea, if you ask me, but he wasn't.

'He got it into his head that all his kids should have a share of his money. The sons, that is, not the daughters. He thought the girls didn't count, for some reason, and I couldn't persuade him different. Somewhat old-fashioned in his ways, old Mal. He had this bee in his bonnet. It's only fair, he said. They're all my sons, aren't they, whoever the hell they are? Funny way to talk about your kids, but maybe it's understandable in his case. A man could easily lose track before he got as far as thirteen. Tell me, Ged—'

Rene had pronounced the name with a hard G. Scarcely surprising, considering the way he mispronounced his own name. But Ged corrected him, quite gently. His birth certificate and his book jackets said Gerard Hawke, but the letter he had written in reply to Deforte's had been signed in his usual way, with the short form of his name.

Deforte had seemed pleased to stand corrected. 'Jed, OK,' he agreed genially. 'Tell me, did you ever meet your old man?'

'Once. That I remember, anyway.'

'Well, that's once more than most of those guys.' The lawyer cleared his throat, by way of underlining his remarks. 'The plain fact is, Mal was irresistible to women, and they were irresistible to him. No resistance whatever, on either side. But it never lasted, on account of he wasn't properly housebroken.

'He seemed to think it was just one of those things, like having red hair or being wall-eyed. It went with being an artist, he said. He claimed all artists were like that, and the homosexual ones were even worse. I don't know that I entirely believed him, but I guess there had to be *some* reason for it. He was a handsome man, sure, but the world is full of good-looking guys.

'You, for instance, Jed. I'd have known you were your father's son the moment I clapped eyes on you. You don't have his eyes or that beak of a nose, but it's plain to see you have his genes in the bone. Now do *you* carry on like that?'

'Unfortunately not,' Ged conceded. 'But then I'm not an artist.'

'No, you're a writer, aren't you?'

Deforte knew that, of course. He had written to Ged care of his publishers. Either these lawyers were enterprising detectives, or Malachy had remembered, from their one meeting, his son's confessed ambition to be a writer. Had maybe even read some of his novels.

In which case, Malachy had known more of Ged than Ged would ever know of Malachy.

Calum was still feeling tetchy. 'That Deforte guy is like something off of American telly,' he muttered. 'Lawyers must get paid by the word. What did he say you were supposed to be? The executive?'

'Executor.'

'What's that mean?'

'I think it means I hire somebody like Rene Deforte to calculate the bank balance and send me all the official forms to sign.'

'So if you're the eldest son and the exec— executor,

how come all the other blokes split the dosh and you only get the house?'

'And contents.'

'Big deal. A house in the middle of nowhere, with a few sticks of furniture? That doesn't sound much of a legacy to me.' Calum brooded over this apparent injustice, glowering at the mountains. 'Did you know your old man was loaded?'

'Let's say I wasn't hugely surprised to hear it.'

'You told me you didn't even know him.'

'I didn't need to know him, to know that much. I knew he was commercially successful.'

'Is that why you decided to come?' Calum turned to look at Ged, his eyes unreadable behind the dark lenses. 'You guessed there'd be something in it for you?'

The truth was that Ged hadn't given any consideration to Malachy's money when the letter arrived. All he had had in his head was the thought of his father, lost for ever, dead beyond recovery. What he was here for was personal archaeology. 'No, I didn't think about that.'

He half expected Calum to disbelieve him. He half disbelieved himself. It seemed too naïve, too unworldly, for a man who made his living by putting himself inside other people's heads.

But Calum's only response was, 'Mum always said you had no sense when it came to money.'

'Your mother is the most extravagantly sensible woman I've ever met.'

Financial fecklessness was hardly the worst sin Polly had accused him of. The letter from Deforte had arrived on the same day as a letter from his ex-wife. After three years of relative silence, she had taken to writing him letters. To sending him letters, at least; he had an idea that some of them had been written quite a while ago. The reason for this sudden change in behaviour came out between the lines. Especially those lines that began, 'My therapist says . . .' A social worker in therapy was a dangerous weapon.

This letter was obviously one of those older ones.

I still can't believe you've done this [she wrote], walked out of our lives like that, just so you can shag some silly girl. What gives you the right to do something like that? What gives you the right to ruin other people's lives? What are your children supposed to think about how a man ought to behave?

Maybe you think it's OK for you because you're a writer. Maybe you think you need to Experience Life. Well, I have news for you. A callous bastard is a callous bastard, and Art is no excuse.

An American could have replied that Ged had a constitutional right to the pursuit of happiness. The right to run off with Elie, if that was where his happiness lay. A corresponding right – not to be made unhappy by other people who were exercising their constitutional rights – didn't exist (though the lawyers seemed to be working on it).

He felt entitled to think like this, cold and logical, because he was now in the same boat as Polly. Elie had left him.

Polly would say he deserved it.

What else did he deserve? A father who had abandoned him, a father he never knew? After all, this trip was the first contact he had had with his own son since . . . well, since abandoning him three years ago. Could you have punishment first and crime later? Or was that confusing cause and effect?

He hadn't meant to abandon his children. He had made some attempts, however feeble and doomed, to keep in touch with them. *Keep in touch*, that was what you said to acquaintances. And then it was usually a lie.

But Calum had refused to see or speak to him. At least that was what Polly said, when Ged rang up a few weeks after moving out, to ask for his son.

That had not been completely unexpected. Calum had always been Polly's favourite, however much she dutifully tried to hide her feelings. He might have felt obliged to take her side. He took after her physically, sharing her fair colouring and pleasant open features – the very things that made it however slightly harder for Ged to see himself in his son. Whereas his daughter, Louise, was dark, clever, intense. To her father, the only alien aspect of her was her femaleness.

Just in case Polly was lying, Ged had sent a note to Calum with his new address and phone number, inviting some response. The invitation was vague, if only because he couldn't quite envisage what one did with one's sixteen-year-old son by way of exercising paternal visiting rights. Did a father have any rights with a child of sixteen? And how, in any case, did one turn a casual, everyday, familial relationship into a more formal arrangement, structured around pre-arranged meetings and specific events?

He had never had to find an answer to that one. Polly had not been lying. And to his everlasting shame he had made no further effort. Until Deforte's letter arrived.

He had been staring at that extraordinary letter, and the equally extraordinary advertisement, for the hundredth time, trying to decide what if anything he was going to do about it, when he had a thought. A plan.

This plan was one of those brilliant ideas that strike you under the influence. The sort of idea that offers to transform your life or achieve some great thing. The kind of idea that you're usually grateful for not having put into action when you wake up sober next morning – even though that's as often an expression of cowardice as an assertion of common sense.

This time he hadn't left it till the morning. He had rung up Calum right then. And Polly answered.

For some reason he hadn't been expecting that. The sound of her voice flustered him.

'Polly?'

'Yes?'

'It's Ged.'

'I know.' In two words she made it clear that having

identified himself was a wounding and deliberate insult. Implying . . . what? That she was too dim to recognize him? That she might have forgotten the sound of his voice, after nearly twenty years of marriage? God knew.

'Listen, Polly, I want to speak to Calum.'

'What makes you think he wants to speak to you?'

'Just go and tell him, will you?'

She sniffed. An expression of disdain, or maybe something else: checking his breath down the telephone line. 'Are you drunk?'

He hadn't thought he was anywhere near drunk, until she asked. He made a stab at assessing his state of sobriety. Since Elie left, he had tended to fall asleep on the sofa every night, at least on those nights when he wasn't out with Rufus. But he obviously hadn't reached the falling-asleep stage yet tonight, so the answer had to be no. He said so. 'No.'

'You sound drunk.'

'Polly, for Christ's sake, go and get Calum.'

'He's not here.'

'But it's—' He squinted at his watch. 'It's midnight.'

'And he's nineteen.' She paused. 'He should be home soon. If he's coming home at all, that is.'

'Where does he go, if he doesn't come home?'

'God knows.'

'What's he doing with himself now? Studying, working, what?'

'What.'

'What do you mean, what?'

'I mean he's not studying or working, so he must be doing – "what?"' Another pause. 'I just hope he hasn't got himself locked up again.'

'Locked up?' He was beginning to wonder how sober Polly was. 'What do you mean, locked up *again*?'

'He was up in court for assault last month.'

'*What?*'

'It didn't come to anything in the end,' she explained briskly, as if her son had been one of her so-called clients.

'When it got to court, the boy who'd been beaten up couldn't testify absolutely that it was Calum who'd done it. Might have been one of his friends, you see, who were mixing in at the time as well. Everybody blind drunk, needless to say. It happened just after closing time.'

Even in his whisky-induced state of dishibition, Ged didn't know what to say. Boys will be boys, was the obvious thing. Except that he hadn't raised – hadn't *meant* to raise – his son as the sort of mob-yob who got mixed up in mindless mêlées outside the pub.

'Do you want to hear about Louise, as long as I'm sharing my troubles? They're not your troubles any more, are they? I suppose you think you're well out of it.' *You bloody bastard*, her tone of voice apostrophized.

'All right, Polly, just tell me about Louise.' How old was she now? He did some vague calculations. Sixteen.

Jesus Christ. He had a sixteen-year-old daughter. That wasn't supposed to happen. It wasn't fair. Sixteen-year-old girls were . . . well, they were supposed to be approximately his own age.

'It was appallingly embarrassing, I can tell you. One of my colleagues rang up to say they'd been cracking down on truancy in the borough and my daughter was on the list. Talk about taking in each other's laundry, and physicians healing themselves, and pots calling kettles black.'

'Forget the original imagery, Polly. Are you telling me Louise has been skipping school?'

'On a very regular basis. She was vague when I asked her what on earth she'd been doing instead. Hanging around, was all I could get out of her. I didn't dare to ask, Hanging around with whom?'

'Why not?'

'Because I know very well whom.'

Polly paused significantly. Obviously Ged was going to be forced to play the straight man. 'OK, whom?'

'His name is Hezekiah. He's a sweet boy really, only he never had much of a chance. Young single mother, five kids by four fathers, not to mention the institutional prejudice that boys like him have to face—'

'Boys like what?'

'Well.' Polly took a breath, in the way that Ged might have taken a large gulp of whisky. 'Well, he's a Rastafarian. I think that's a good sign,' she added, picking up speed. 'It shows he has values, has commitment, has a sense of community. Obviously they have some unusual beliefs—'

'Polly, you're the one with unusual beliefs. You mean Lulu is going out with one of those black guys with the big woolly hats?'

'Don't say black. It's racist to define people by their pigmentation.'

'OK, one of those West Indian guys.'

'It's just as bad to stigmatize people by their geographical origins.'

'Polly, I am not being racist. Truly I am not. I'm just trying to define a social phenomenon by reference to the real world. Do you understand me?' He paused for effect, and tried again. 'One of those people with knitted woolly hats in pastel colours.'

'They tuck their braids into them. It's quite practical, really,' Polly said brightly.

Ged considered this scenario. It wasn't exactly Sidney Poitier. On the other hand, from personal experience, he could sympathize with anyone who had had to grow up with an improper mother. 'I thought West Indians were big on traditional values. Education, for instance.'

'Well, he's not really West Indian himself,' Polly explained, reluctantly conceding that such a place existed, and that some people might actually hail from there. 'His grandparents came over from Trinidad. Anyway, we're talking about Louise's education, not her boyfriend's.'

'I thought he might have taken an interest, that's all. What does he do for a living?'

'Are you joking? Do you know what the unemployment rate is among young inner-city men from visible minorities?'

'OK, OK, I get the picture.'

He brooded over that picture, not knowing what to say or do. In some primeval core of his brain, the notion of some yob screwing his pretty, witty, naïve young daughter was enough to drive him to contemplate violence. Polly would accuse him of racism, but he didn't think it had anything to do with skin colour. Maybe he couldn't help taking it as an insult that his daughter should be attracted to somebody thick and shiftless. One way or another, that had to reflect badly on him.

But it wasn't really his business any more. He had walked out of Louise's life.

He didn't even have any advice to give Polly. Not that she would have taken any from him. After all, she was supposed to be the expert, the social worker with all the qualifications, the person who told other people what to do with their errant children.

'I suppose it's her life, after all,' he said at last. 'She's sixteen now, isn't she?'

'Good guess,' Polly allowed with an audible sneer. 'And thanks for the help.'

'Well, if she doesn't want to talk to me, there's not much I can do, is there?'

'When did you last try to talk to her?'

'I sent her a Christmas present.'

'Give the man a medal.' The sneer was even louder now. 'And it only arrived a week late. Why don't you ring back when you're ready to start venturing into real life?'

'Listen, Polly, I admit I'm a bastard and all of that,' he had said wearily. 'Could you just tell Calum to call me?'

The official excuse for the invitation had been the ad's reference to male descendants: grandsons as well as sons. But as they had just learned, a grandson would only get a direct share if his father had predeceased Malachy. In other words, Calum's share was Ged's share.

And even now, after two days of travelling together, Ged didn't know why his son had agreed to bring him back from Coventry by coming on this trip. Curiosity? A

25

freebie? Calum's attitude at times suggested an urge to get revenge on the old man by behaving badly. But it was plain from his remarks that he had no more idea himself why he had been invited along, and was even more inclined to suspect his father's motives.

Mutual suspicion and resentment, embroidered with bewilderment. The classic father-son relationship.

3

The mountains that had shouldered them along on their journey now parted abruptly, revealing . . . nothing. No sky, no sea, no land, just a nebulous white nothingness. And no forewarning but a sudden shift in temperature and a whiff of salt.

On this side of the nothingness, this side of the sea, there squatted a small and rather tatty town. The little mountain river had suddenly grown very grand, spreading itself over half the valley and sprouting a fairly exotic bridge.

Deforte had said to turn left at the bridge. Ged turned and drove south.

To the right, as far as he could see, a wall of impenetrable whiteness reared up like the edge of the world. Down there, out there, *somewhere*, invisible breakers smashed incessantly upon unseen rocks, a noise from nowhere. If not the edge of the world, it was at least the marches of another universe.

Calum had more practical concerns. 'What happened to the heat? It was forty degrees back there in the mountains. Now I'm getting goose bumps.' He waved his afflicted arm, which happened to be hanging out of the window. 'Where'd the sun go?'

Ged was inclined to think it must have fallen off the edge of the world. After all, proof that the earth was flat had been made dramatically obvious to him last night. But the explanation he offered Calum was not so scientifically controversial. 'Sea fog.'

'Weird sort of fog. It's just sitting out there, brooding. The road ahead is perfectly clear.'

So were the mountains to their left. The road skirted a narrow hem between the cliffs and the sea, obliged to follow every fold in the coastline. There was little sign of human presence, aside from the road itself.

The next instruction was another left turn, this time at a signpost for a small campground. The campground was off to the right, hidden in the fog; Ged turned the car in the opposite direction, heading inland.

This road was much narrower, and quickly degenerated into gravel. It wound steeply up the mountainside, hoisting itself through a series of hairpin curves. The path of their progress closed in behind them, swathed in trees. They were well above the fog by now, but the trees crowded alongside, shrinking the scope of their view. Occasional flashes of sunlight and sky were more disorienting than comforting, since they struck from a different direction each time.

They were going up: that was all Ged could tell. Sometimes he could tell by the fact that he was tilted back in his seat at a fairly dramatic angle.

'Hey, this is cool.' Calum was impressed at last. He hung out of the window to peer down an alarming drop at the edge of the track. 'I wonder what it's like up here when it snows?'

'I hope I never find out,' muttered Ged, resisting the urge to duck as a low branch swept the windscreen.

'I'll bet you could ski all the way down to the sea.'

'And climb all the way back up on foot.'

Calum settled back into his seat with a shrug. 'Some thrills are worth a bit of hassle.'

Ged didn't bother to answer. He knew about those thrills. The trouble was, they didn't come with a price tag attached: labelled, for example, a bit of hassle, or a small disaster, or utter ruin. You just took what you wanted and ended up paying for it, whatever the price turned out to be.

They came upon the house as suddenly and dramatically as they had earlier come upon the sea. Up a slope, around a bend, and the forest simply stopped. Whatever was here was the point of their journey, the whole journey, all the way from London. They had arrived.

Calum was impressed again. 'Wow.'

Ged was impressed too. Anyone would have been. They had debouched on to a flat shoulder of the mountain, jutting like an epaulette from the main body of the mountain-mass. It was surrounded on three sides by sky, but fringed with the tips of fir trees springing up from the lower slopes.

On the western edge of the plateau two buildings angled towards each other, making a V-shape with part of the lower right side missing. The upper arms of the V were linked by a large wooden platform. The southern building sprawled rather than sat, an incongruous example of what in this part of the world would be called a ranch house. Its single saving aesthetic grace was the cladding of unpainted timber, weathered to a subtle, silky grey. The other building was taller and much more compact, but covered with that same well-weathered timber.

Off to the left was a vegetable patch, to the right a small wooden shed. A stable, Ged guessed, noting the timber-fenced paddock alongside it. No sign of a horse, though an elderly pick-up rested with its nose to the fence.

Another car had reversed into the space beside the pick-up, one of those enormous boat-like vehicles that Americans were so inexplicably fond of. Rene Deforte climbed out and came over. He was a small, wiry man in his late fifties, with lined face and dusty hair. His vaguely beige suit looked as if it had spent some time squashed inside a small wardrobe, and he himself had something of the same look. 'You made it OK, I see.'

'We didn't plummet to a painful death, no,' Ged agreed.

Another man emerged from the far side of Deforte's car. The lawyer waved a hand at him. 'This here is your dad's agent. He's come from New York to meet you.'

'Hi.' The agent made a remarkable contrast to Deforte. He was about as well pressed as a man could conceivably be, and his exquisitely manicured hair flashed in the sun. He made some brief but hearty contact with Ged's right hand. 'Pleased to meet you. I'm Brad Welles.'

Calum ignored the introductions. He was staring at the house, with much the same air of gormless rapture as he had devoted to the vision of Mount Hood last night. So it happened that with the rumpled lawyer and the immaculate agent facing the mountain, and Calum off somewhere in space, Ged was the only one looking at the deck between the two buildings. The only one to see the girl come out of the house.

The girl with the shotgun.

She was a pretty girl, maybe Calum's age. Her russet-brown hair had been braided into a plait that reached to her waist. Along with the obligatory Doc Marten boots, she was wearing a long, sleeveless, navy blue dress, cut high at the neck, which made her look taller than she really was. Also slimmer than she really was. Not that there was anything wrong with her actual figure, in Ged's opinion. He had plenty of time to form an opinion as she came up towards them, across the space between the buildings.

The shotgun was double-barrelled. There was nothing else to distinguish it from any other gun, except the fact that the girl was pointing it in his direction. Not really aiming it, she wasn't holding it quite that high, but the look on her face suggested that might be the next move in her plan of action.

The man from New York was saying something enthusiastic about the scenery and location, waving his arms in every direction but the right one. Ged opened his mouth to interrupt, raised his hand to point out the approaching gun.

The girl beat him to it. 'You snoopers can pack right up and get out of here.'

She hadn't raised her voice. But they all heard her, even the enthusiastic agent, who stopped in mid-stride, lowered his eloquent arms, and carefully turned his head without moving his body. Calum merely transformed his open-mouthed amazement from the house to the girl.

Deforte didn't even bother to look. He fixed his gaze halfway up the mountainside as he spoke. 'Angie, honey, these folks have come a hell of a long way to see you. Is that any way to say hello?'

The girl didn't look surprised or abashed. She didn't even lower the gun. 'You could have warned me, Rene.'

'I tried. I rang. Couldn't get an answer.' He turned to look at her then. 'What's all this with the shotgun?'

'I've had some funny characters sniffing around. Reporters and such, I guess.' She allowed the muzzle of the gun to droop towards the dry earth. 'Beats me how they find this place.'

'It's not like it was a secret, is it? Everybody around here knew Mal.'

'But we never had any trouble like this while he was alive. A flock of vultures, I call it.' She stared at the three strangers significantly.

'You should have told me, Angie.' Deforte's tone ran a finely judged line between soothing and reproach. 'I'd have sent somebody over to keep an eye on things for you.'

'I'm all right. Charles keeps a good eye on things, only he's asleep right now. This heat knocks the stuffing out of him. Aren't you going to introduce me to your friends?'

The lawyer made short work of that. 'This is Cal, Ged, Brad. You'll be pleased to see them, once you hear what they've come for.'

Calum stirred like a statue roused to life. He gave no sign of having heard any of the conversation, but went right up to the house and thumped his palm against a plank, as if to confirm that it was not a mirage. 'This is brilliant.' He turned to Rene Deforte. 'And this guy Malachy really lived here? The whole year round?'

'For the last ten years or so, yeah, he did. He was big on peace and quiet, so he said.'

'What was he, a hermit?'

'Heck, no. He just liked to choose his company.' Deforte set a hand on the girl's bare shoulder. 'Angie here, for instance.'

The girl pulled away from his touch, looking rosy and flustered. 'I was only the housekeeper.'

'And I was only joking. No need to get riled, honey.'

Ignoring his apology, she turned to face her visitors. Her grey eyes, a little lighter than the weathered sheen on the house behind her, surveyed them coolly.

'I'm Angelina Rudniki.' The questing gaze settled on Ged. 'You must be Malachy's son.'

'Only one of many, or so I've been told.'

'The firstborn son, I meant.' On her lips, the archaic phrase sounded natural. Unlike the general run of Americans, she had a faintly formal air about her. It was maybe the long plait, maybe the long dark dress, maybe the clear light in her eyes. There was something exotic about those eyes; he couldn't quite put his finger on it. 'I'm glad Rene managed to track you down. Once he'd gotten the notion into his head, Malachy was dead set on you being his executioner.'

'Executor.'

'Yeah, I know, but he kept calling it an executioner, because he'd have to be dead for it to happen. He had a funny sense of humour sometimes.' She turned her head to fix a full-frontal gaze on Calum, who was still examining the exterior of the house with a lively, and in him remarkable, interest. 'Is that your son?'

'Yes.' Ged was surprised that she should have guessed, seeing there wasn't much resemblance in features or colouring.

Maybe she guessed his surprise as well, because she added, 'He doesn't look much like you, does he? You look

32

a lot like Malachy, and he doesn't. But you have the same . . .' She hesitated just a fraction. 'The same aura.'

An unfortunate choice of word. It put him in mind of his mother, who had been a New Ager while the rest of the world was still back in the Stone Age. Any mention of 'auras' instantly provoked boredom and irritation in him, even if uttered by a pretty brunette with extraordinary eyes. He edged away from her, back towards the lawyer and the agent.

Deforte made a move in the opposite direction, towards the girl. 'Angie, honey, would you mind showing these gents around the place? That's what they're here for, after all.'

'Why ask me, Rene? It isn't my house.' She looked directly at Ged, and spoke to him. 'I guess it's yours now, isn't it?'

4

From the western edge of the deck, you could look down the precipitous mountainside to the sea. In theory. Today the view was only of fluffy white nothingness, shrouding the rocks and the water. From this high vantage-point, the edge of the world gleamed with reflected sunlight.

Angelina had supplied them all with cold beer from somewhere in the recesses of the house. American beer, of course, fizzy and sour, its only discernible flavour the taste of cold itself. The first time Ged had drunk this beer was the day he met his father.

'Fine place Mal built for himself here,' Deforte observed. 'Only trouble with this coast is that dratted fog. When it gets to a hundred degrees back in the valley and you're dying for a nice cool swim, you come out here. And soon as you hit the beach, there's the fog rolling in and it's thirty–forty degrees cooler, not real swimming weather at all. But this place is high enough up that the fog can't reach it, warm enough to relax, cool enough not to work up too much of a sweat. You can't really beat it.'

'And so wonderfully remote,' Welles chimed in. 'I don't believe Mal ever really took to civilization. He was not well suited to urban life. At heart he was an intensely private and reserved man.'

An intensely private man with thirteen illegitimate sons by thirteen different women. Evidently the concept of reserve had a different definition here in America. Ged speculated sarcastically, 'Maybe his intense need for privacy made it too hard for him to hang about and help to bring up his own children.'

'You might not regret that so much when you see the state of his studio,' drawled Deforte. 'Why don't we take a look?'

The studio, of course, was the tall building on the far side of the deck. Its south-western wall was virtually all glass. The topmost panes tilted to let the sea breeze inside. The roof had been pitched gently backwards, to encourage the rain to run off towards the forest. It was laid with cedar shingles, showing the same silver-grey patina as the walls. Nothing of the inside could be seen from outside; the wall of glass was a wall of reflected sky.

The door was glass as well, of course. Angelina slid back a panel in the seaward corner to let them through.

The interior was even more remarkable: a single room, two storeys high. The south-west wall was transparent, of course. An enormous fieldstone fireplace dominated the north-east wall. The walls at either end were of unpainted timber, open beams revealing the unweathered innards of the weatherboard cladding.

Revealed it only in shards and slivers, because those walls were hung from side to side and top to bottom with paintings. Canvas squares, each one a single primary colour, skilfully shaded to give some illusion of form and depth, in the trademark style of Malachy Hawke. They were arranged in no apparent aesthetic order, hung as haphazardly as one might sling a hat on a hook, casually, crookedly, all the way up to the roof.

No-one spoke for a long, astonished minute. There was too much to take in. With sunlight blazing along the length of the room, Ged's first impression was a blur of brightness: a disorienting dazzle of almost insolent colour on either side of him, and a milder, earthier, golder glow from the fieldstone wall in front of him.

He blinked, and took a look at the paintings on the walls.

Each one a primary colour, but each one also a subtly different shade. One red square was best compared to poppies, the yellow one next to it might have been woven of ripe cornstalks, while the blue above them both had been inspired by some tropical lagoon. A different red was darker, denser, more immediately sensual: fit for lips, fit for kissing. This yellow was pale and creamy, primrosy perhaps, compared to the sharper, more translucent, lemon-yellow painting two squares over, while a canvas elsewhere evoked the sleepy sunlight of December. There were cornflower blues and larkspur blues, the vivid zenith of a midsummer sky and the ice-pale hem of a snowy twilight. Cherries, and blood, and rust, and glowing embers. The colours of primary things.

But colour was only the starting point of Malachy's art. Every one of these coloured squares held some sculptural shape within its taut, flat depths. Some of the forms had crisply geometric outlines, but most were somewhat shadowy.

Mesmerized by this astonishing display, Ged moved forward to examine the paintings more closely. The forms intrigued him as much as the colours. But he found his way blocked by some large object.

For the first time he lowered his gaze, and saw what else was in the room.

What else was in the room? Hard to say, at first glance. Or even after looking about very carefully.

There were a couple of armchairs, old and overstuffed, one occupied by a heap of cats and the other by a dog much too large for the chair. There was a motorbike, half dismantled. Several bicycles, ditto. A large tropical fish tank, filled with large tropical fish. A filing cabinet, the drawers veiled by ivy. Two potted palms. A stack of canvas-stretchers propped against the wall. A guitar with a broken string. Books strewn everywhere, open or closed, stacked in precarious columns or splayed out like a hand of cards. An enormous terracotta urn. Cardboard boxes full of what might or might not have been rubbish. A long workbench, its surface completely hidden by . . .

Well, by things. Objects. Hand-fired clay pots. A marble bust of some one-eared pharaoh with a broken nose. Several small wire sculptures. Empty beer cans, some half squashed. A tool kit, virtually empty, since most of the tools were strewn across the bench. Rolls and rolls of drawing paper. Jars jammed with paint brushes. A paint-smeared carafe holding desiccated orange and yellow California poppies. Rolled-up tubes of paint. More books. A wine bottle with a candle stub wedged into its mouth. Another wine bottle with a cork, holding maybe a glassful of California claret. The case for a laptop computer (but no sign of the computer). Jar lids and coffee mugs perched everywhere, showing signs of heavy use as ashtrays . . .

And that was only what a first glance revealed.

House and contents, Rene Deforte had said. A few sticks of furniture, Calum had sneered. But to Ged it looked more like he had been bequeathed the remains of his father's life.

'Christ.' This time Calum spoke for Ged as well. 'What a God-awful mess.'

'I haven't touched a thing.' The girl, Angelina, spoke up from behind them. 'It's just the way it was when he died.'

Again it was Calum who voiced the thought in his father's head. 'Was he senile, or off his head, or what?'

'Of course not.' Angelina came around to face him, her tone indignant, her arms folded. 'He was totally sane. Just a little eccentric, that's all. I thought you English people were famous for being eccentric.'

'Even when we're stark raving bonkers, we don't usually live in a rubbish tip.' Calum was still staring at his surroundings in frank disbelief. 'I thought you said you were his housekeeper. What the hell was he paying you for?'

Given what Rene Deforte had said about Malachy and women, Ged thought it was fairly obvious what he had been paying her for. But Angelina, naturally enough, was insisting on her role as domestic employee.

'He wouldn't let me touch a thing,' she explained defensively. 'He said he liked it just the way it was. Whenever he couldn't find something, he used to accuse me of tidying up. But I never did.' She made a sweeping visual survey of the chaos, turning in a circle where she stood. 'It drove me crazy, but I never did get to tidy up.'

'I'm sure you did your best, my dear.' That was the agent from New York, Bradford Welles. His name sounded more like a place than a person. Bradford Welles IV, it said on his card, and he certainly looked like the sort who could readily be replicated. He had a well-trimmed moustache, an excessive amount of immaculate teeth, gold-rimmed glasses, a suit so sharp he must have been in some danger when dressing, and a smooth, self-regarding manner. 'It's a well-known fact that all artists are out of their tiny minds, and a less well-known fact that they do their damnedest to send the rest of us around the bend as well.'

He picked his way fastidiously through the rubble of his client's life, with the air of a man negotiating a bog, where the slightest misstep might prove fatal, or at least disastrous to one's trousers. When he was near enough to touch the lowest canvas on the west wall, he gave an audible sigh of pleasure and relief.

'Well, well. So Mal's been busy. I did wonder. It's been the best part of ten years since his last major exhibition. We've had very little from him since he packed up and left New York.'

'He was always busy.' Angelina seemed to feel that one of the things she had been paid for was to defend her employer from implied slights. 'He never stopped working, not even when he was so sick he could hardly get out of bed. He just couldn't stand sitting around doing nothing.'

Her comment reminded Ged of a glaring gap in his knowledge. An embarrassing gap as well, since it was invariably the first thing anyone asked about the newly dead, and he hadn't asked yet. 'What did he die of?'

'Heart.' Deforte thumped his own chest.

'So it was sudden?'

'No, no, he'd been sick for a long time. His ticker wasn't doing its thing properly. That's partly what made him decide to move out here for good. Life's too short to waste it in New York, he told me. And he wouldn't give up smoking, which didn't help, of course, nor the booze either, but I can't blame him for any of that. A man has to have his pleasures, or life's not worth living.'

'It was congestive heart failure,' Angelina chipped in, with a slightly more scientific spirit. 'Same as my grandma, but she's not too bad yet. He had some pills to drain the water off, but he had to keep upping the dose, and after a while the pills didn't work any more. He was drowning in his own body.'

She said this in a dreamy, melancholy way. Not as if she didn't mourn for Malachy, but as if his death had been a romantic tragedy. 'He died right here, in this house,' she added. 'He wouldn't go anywhere else. That's partly why he came out here, to get away from all the things he hated.'

'What things?' Ged wondered. 'Modern medicine?'

'No, not particularly. But he had a lot of . . . um . . . unusual ideas.' She cast glances at Deforte and Welles in a wary way, as if she might be giving away somebody's secrets, and lowered her voice. 'He wouldn't go into the hospital, for instance. I told him it was the best place for him, but he said he wasn't going to be just another statistic. I'm going to die in my own bed, Angie, he said. And he wouldn't let me—'

She broke off abruptly, as if she had said too much.

'We know you did your best for him, Angie,' Deforte assured her. 'All artists are crackers. Brad said so just now. We all heard him say so.' He glanced slyly at Ged. 'How'd you like to be brought up in this? Do you reckon your mother could have stood it?'

To say that Ged's mother was not house-proud would

have been euphemism on a grand scale. 'I doubt if she would have noticed. She's never really taken to civilization either.'

He decided to have a cigarette. Americans were supposed to be pathological about smoking, but what the hell, he was only going to do what his father had obviously been in the habit of doing.

To his surprise, when he produced his packet of duty-frees, both Deforte and Bradford Welles took the opportunity to light up a piece of their own private tobacco store. A nation of secret smokers, apparently.

He took a drag and tackled the lawyer. 'Now look, I agree that this is a spectacular place, but I didn't come all the way from London to admire the scenery. So what *have* I come for?'

Deforte shrugged. 'Should have thought it was plain enough. Why d'you think he wanted you to be the executor? This place has to be sorted out.'

Ged waved his cigarette at the studio filled with sunlight and junk. 'You want me to sort out this shambles?'

'Oh, it isn't me that's wanting anything out of you, Mr Gerard Hawke. It was your dad who wanted you to do it. There's nothing funny about that, is there? You're his eldest son. It's only right that you should take care of his affairs.'

'And what if I say he can stuff his affairs?'

'Well, I thought you might say that. I said so to Mal.' Rene tapped his enormous cigar, depositing a lump of ash the size of a Great Dane's droppings on a paint-encrusted china plate. 'I said to him, "Mal," I said, "maybe this guy won't want anything to do with you and your lousy estate. Why should he care about you, if you didn't care about him? If I were him," I said, "I think I might tell you to go to hell."'

This guy is a lawyer, Ged reminded himself. If he sounds stupid, it's because he wants to sound stupid. He wants me to step into his stupid little trap. None the less he stepped into it, because there wasn't anything else to do. 'And what did my father say to that?'

'"Well," he said, "Rene," he said, "here's my whole life in this place, and I don't want it falling into the hands of strangers. My son ain't a stranger, whoever he is."'

'Wait a minute, wait a minute. What exactly does it say in the will? Does it say *my eldest son*, or does it say *my eldest son, Gerard Hawke*?'

'I told you, he had to allow for miscalculations. He told me your name, showed me one of your books, wrote down the publisher's name and so forth. But just in case, he said, the will should read—'

'*My eldest son, whoever the hell he is*,' Ged finished grimly. He finished his cigarette as well, and stubbed it out in the nearest jar lid. Then he swallowed the last of his beer. It was warmer and flatter by now, and therefore almost entirely tasteless. 'But you still haven't said what happens if I tell you he and his house can go to hell.'

There was, as it turned out, provision for this in the will. Rene Deforte and Brad Welles were to be appointed joint executors, while Ged would become just another one of the thirteen sons, with a thirteenth share in the estate.

Ged took a long look at the maelstrom of disorder surrounding him. He took another, longer look at the riot of colour on the walls. Here he had an unexpected opportunity to reject his father as his father had rejected him. Not that Malachy would ever know or care.

And what was holding him back from taking that opportunity? Curiosity. That was all.

'I'll need to read the will before I make up my mind,' he decided. Making a decision out of postponing a decision. 'And I'm not deciding anything today. I'll have to give this some thought.'

'Sure, right, that's perfectly OK. Why don't you and Cal hang around here for a day or two? You can put up right here in Mal's house. I don't reckon Angie would mind.'

'It's nothing to do with me, Rene,' Angelina pointed out. 'I've only stayed on because you've been paying me to keep an eye on the place – and a good thing too, what with all those strangers nosing around. But if these two gentlemen are going to be minding the premises, I think I'll go back to my grandma's house.'

'No, no, Angie, we need you.'

'So does my grandma.'

'She's doing just fine. I spoke to her the other day, and she said she was fine. You can't leave Mal's kinfolk to fend for themselves, Angie, they'd starve for sure, and Mal wouldn't have wanted that. I'll pay you double if you stay on and look after them. Just for a few days.'

Angelina looked mutinous.

'Rene, maybe you and the lady could step outside to settle things,' Bradford Welles suggested. 'I'd like to have a chat with Ged here, if you and Angie don't mind.'

'It's not my place to mind,' Angelina said repressively. 'Malachy wasn't *my* dad. Or my client.' She swept out of the studio, followed by Rene and Calum and a bustle and clatter that turned out to be the enormous dog, roused from his nap in the armchair.

'What a splendid young woman,' Welles remarked, apparently without a trace of sarcasm, as soon as Angelina and her retinue were out of earshot. 'Extraordinary eyes.'

She did have extraordinary eyes. Ged had taken particular notice of them, among her other charms. They were pale and clear and full of light, the colour and quality of the evening sky, before it had reconciled itself to the loss of the sun and the inevitability of darkness. But Ged was more taken with her ability to impress her will on everyone, even without the aid of a shotgun.

Except Malachy, as he was reminded by the chaos surrounding him. You had to admire a man who could successfully resist Angelina's urge to tidy up.

'Amazing.' Welles was gazing at the paintings with a greedy fascination. 'Some early-period paintings I've never seen before. Possibly he kept them because they were favourites.'

The early ones had the geometric figures, Ged recalled

from the obituary. He felt an obscure sense of shame at the idea of learning about his father's work from a newspaper article, and tried to compensate by waving a hand in the direction of a canvas with clean and simple lines. 'That one, for instance?'

'That's right. It was typical of Mal that he developed in the opposite way to most painters. They usually start with realism and switch to formalism, but Mal did it the other way, from the abstract to the actual. That was typical, in more ways than one. He always had his own ideas.'

Brad Welles's attention moved from the paintings to Ged himself. 'Do you understand the value of what he's left you? There's the cultural value, of course, and whatever sentimental value these might hold for you personally, but I mean the actual market value.'

Well, what else? That was what agents were for: to put a price tag on creativity. 'Give me a clue.'

'Well, let's see, there are at least a couple of dozen paintings here, and his work is coming back into vogue right now, and of course the price jumps when they die, so it's possible that your share of the estate is about equal to what your half-brothers will be dividing twelve ways.'

Was that possible? Rene had said Malachy was a multimillionaire, but admitted he was only guessing. Bradford Welles was only guessing, too.

And I am not, swore Ged to himself, about to let the old bastard buy me.

'Just a couple of things I thought you might want to be clear on,' Brad was saying. 'My firm has acted as Mal's agents for more than twenty-five years, but of course his death invalidates any contract we had with him. Assuming you agree to act as executor – and assuming you intend to sell any or all of these paintings – it's up to you to appoint whoever you choose to act on your behalf. Rene says Mal didn't specify anything about that in the will. He left it entirely up to your discretion.' He glanced around significantly at the cluttered walls. 'A great honour, I should think. A great compliment to you.'

Ged shrugged one shoulder, a minimal acknowledge-ment. He was not inclined to be much moved by compliments from a father who couldn't be bothered to make or keep his acquaintance. 'If he was happy with what you did for him, I don't see why I should rock the boat now.'

'You might like to have a look at this, then.' The agent produced a document from his inside breast pocket.

Ged was faintly surprised: that a suit so plainly designed for show should even possess such a pocket, and that a man so plainly obsessed with his image would risk spoiling the cut of his jacket by carrying a bulky piece of paper.

'It's pretty much our standard contract, but rephrased to allow for the fact that it's Malachy's work rather than your own that we'd be dealing with.' Welles flashed a smile with too many teeth for comfort, neither his own comfort nor Ged's. 'We haven't gotten around to expanding into the literary field yet.'

Ged took the paper without opening it. 'I'll have to look at this later. Along with the will.'

'Naturally, naturally. Make sure you know what you're getting into, that's the best advice I can give.'

Advice impossible to follow, of course. Who ever knew what they were getting into, even with the least conse-quential actions? Like stopping to ask a girl for a light . . .

No, he wasn't going to think about Elie now.

Bradford was still admiring the paintings, with a vaguely proprietary air. 'What do you think of these?'

'I don't know anything about art.'

'That's OK.' Brad smiled again, this time a sign of real amusement, with hardly any teeth at all. 'Just say if you like them.'

'I do, yes. Though I get the impression that he wouldn't have cared if anyone liked them or not.'

'No, I don't guess he did. He knew his own mind, like no-one I've ever met. On the other hand, he used to say the only thing that ever reconciled him to selling his paintings was the thought that somebody else liked them enough to want to have them around. If he was going to give them up, he said, he wanted them to go to good homes. You'd have thought they were his children. Artists get funny ideas sometimes,' Brad observed, in a judiciously disapproving tone. 'Did you ever meet your father?'

'A long time ago. I was Calum's age.'

'And?'

Ged shrugged again. He didn't know what he felt about his father.

Or maybe he was just afraid to let himself feel it. He could recognize the feelings if he thought about them. Could even consider them as if they belonged to someone else. Blind rage, inconsolable grief, the resourceless despair of abandonment. All over a man he had scarcely known.

He didn't let himself feel any of that, of course. He simply noted and catalogued the phenomena for possible future reference. After all, they were useless, since the focus of them was dead. They were infantile emotions that had never found another focus, another father.

5

One thing about having a famous parent, you were bound to hear about it when they died. Even if it was only by reading his obituary in the newspapers.

His mother saw it, and rang to tell him. More likely she had it pointed out to her, since she had never been a great reader of newspapers, except for the horoscopes. She claimed to be more concerned with the *Zeitgeist* than with petty tragedies or the doings of politicians.

'Your father's dead, did you see? I couldn't believe it. He was only my age. People my age are too young to die.' She pondered this impossibility. 'It doesn't say how he died. An accident, maybe. Poor thing.'

She said that in a tone she might have used over a dead blackbird in the garden. Though to do her justice, she was perfectly capable of genuine tears over dead songbirds. Just as Ged was about to ask her if she found the news distressing, she said, 'Does it distress you, darling?'

He had to consult with himself about that. He found it easier to deal with life by leaving emotions – especially his own – out of the picture as much as possible, unacknowledged and unexamined, on the theory that if you ignore anything long enough, it either goes away or becomes irrelevant. In his experience, any emotions strong enough to force themselves on his attention were liable to lead to disaster. Obsession, jealousy, anger, guilt – even happiness, unearned and peremptory – such

46

were the furies that had lately ruined his life.

Thoughts, views, ideas, opinions were a different matter, of course. One could think about them in a productive way. Trying to think about feelings was impossible, and usually painful as well.

But distress was not a symptom he would have entertained under any circumstances, so he rephrased the question. Did it bother him?

In a general, impersonal sense, it did. His father's death had moved him one step closer to the grave. He was in the front row now, with no generation between him and death.

All of which was only a slightly different slant on his mother's reaction, a shiver at the thought of someone walking over your grave. Not grief, just mild self-pity.

'I don't know,' he said to Melissa. 'Why should it bother me? I barely knew him. You should be more upset than me.'

'But he was your father, darling, and you only get one of them. Lovers are two a penny. I did love him madly, but that was a long time ago. I haven't seen him for over forty years.' She added with a wistful touch, 'If I'd known he was going to die, I'd have liked to see him again.'

If he'd known he was going to die, he would have had more pressing matters on his mind than entertaining old lovers, Ged expected. 'Why didn't you know? You're supposed to be a fortune-teller, aren't you?'

'Oh, no, darling, I've told you before, I don't tell fortunes. It's against the law to do that. Anyway, the Tarot is much too complex and venerable to use for anything as vulgar as telling fortunes. It's more like – well, I call it a focus for counselling. It allows seekers to see the patterns of their life more clearly, to understand where they've come from and where they're going.'

Everybody knows that already, he thought. They just don't want to know it. Earth to earth, ashes to ashes, dust to dust; a simple, pointless story, and the same for everyone.

At nineteen, just arrived in New York, he had seen his father's name on a poster. 'MALACHY HAWKE AT THE TURPENTINE GALLERY', that was all it said.

The poster was red, with black lettering at the bottom. In the upper right section a three-sided pyramid appeared to be rising out of the depths; different densities of red gave it the illusion of a three-dimensional shape. He took a moment to realize that it must be a reproduction of one of his father's paintings.

He found the gallery, a very posh establishment just off Fifth Avenue. But he didn't find the exhibition. That was last month, the woman told him.

He was too disappointed and too disoriented to know how to respond. He simply stood there, staring around him at the paintings that were not his father's. You didn't wander into a commercial art gallery without some particular reason for being there. But just walking out again seemed rude, especially since the woman was standing there, watching him.

'Do you mind if I have . . .' He waved at the walls. '. . . If I look around, since I'm here?'

'Go ahead.'

He moved away. She followed him. Maybe she had nothing better to do.

He stared resolutely at the first painting he encountered, a maelstrom of colour with no apparent design, wondering what he was meant to make of it.

'Are you particularly interested in Malachy Hawke's work?'

He didn't know what to say. He knew nothing about his father's work. The only Hawke painting he had ever seen was on the poster. 'I suppose so.'

'You're English, aren't you? I didn't realize he was so well known over there.'

Now he felt more than ever like a fraud, picking his way around some sort of explanation. 'I saw the poster,' he muttered. 'I didn't notice the dates.'

'That was a brilliant poster, wasn't it?' She managed to be soothing and patronizing all at once, as if she were talking to her pet dog. 'A brilliant painting, I mean. What was it in particular that attracted you?'

Since he knew absolutely nothing about art, he couldn't even come up with a convincing lie. So he had to tell her the truth. 'His name.'

'What about his name?'

'It's the same as mine.'

She lifted her sharp nose, like a hound striking a likely scent. 'Malachy, that's a very unusual name. He tells me it's Irish. Are you Irish?'

'Not as far as I know. And my name's not Malachy. It's Hawke.'

'What a coincidence.' Her nostrils flared again. She was staring harder than ever now. Her tone had thrown down a silence into the space between them, a silence that began to nudge and prod him uncomfortably. Then she added, 'Is it a coincidence?'

He would have walked out then, but she was standing between him and the door. 'Look, it doesn't matter. I just came to see his paintings. If they're not here, I might as well go.'

'I have a few of his works in the back. I always keep some special treasures to show my best clients when they come to town.' She paused, challenging him. 'Would you like to see them?'

He didn't want to tell her the truth, but also he didn't want her to misunderstand. 'I can't buy anything. I have no money.'

'Yes, I know.' Of course she knew. He was so plainly an impoverished student. Except he wasn't a student, just impoverished. 'Sit down and I'll bring them out. Can I get you a coffee?'

She brought him coffee and the paintings, four of them. All vivid colours, all monochromatic. The figures in them were realized only through a change in the quality of the colour, designed to simulate shadow and light around

49

some three-dimensional thing. Most of the figures were geometric, like the one on the poster. One other was more amorphous, an unknown object hidden under a cloth.

He went down on his knees to study them.

They intrigued him visually, and also imaginatively: they implied another world behind the surface of tangible reality, a world that could only be experienced indirectly, through its effects on our own world. He had no idea how they rated as art, except through the prices the woman quoted him, which were astonishing. He'd have thought an artist would have to be long dead to command money like that.

She watched him looking at the paintings, though he was barely aware of her. 'Do you like them?'

'Yes.' He paused to see how he felt about that pat answer, and confirmed it. 'Yes, I do like them.'

'You're his son, aren't you?'

He stared at his father's paintings, and said nothing.

She took no notice of his silence, or maybe took it for an answer. 'I thought there was something very familiar about you when you walked in the door, but I couldn't quite place it. Then when you asked about his exhibition, I started wondering. Your accent threw me off for a while. But I was watching you, the way you moved, the way you stood still. It has to be, I thought, it just has to be.' Now she was looking at the paintings too, kneeling down beside him. 'Did you come over here to see him?'

'I don't know him.'

It was a terrible humiliation to have to say that, especially to this woman. She knew his father, and he did not. His father had not thought him worthy of acquaintance.

'Does he know about you?'

'So my mother says.' Without looking up, he added bitterly, 'He gave me his name, after all.'

'Then you're luckier than some. Do you want to meet him?'

He had to think about that. What if his father didn't want to see him? How did one go about ringing up a stranger and saying, Hi, you won't remember me, but I'm your son?

'I could fix something up for you,' she said, reading his mind. 'Arrange for you to meet somewhere.'

Somewhere was one of those demotic New York restaurants that provide anything, from a hot dog and a Coke to sirloin steak with a bottle of burgundy.

Nervousness about meeting his father was temporarily swamped by the potential embarrassment of telling the waiter he was looking for his father, and then being asked what his father looked like. And it really did happen just like that, except that as he was opening his mouth to confess that he didn't know his own father, he saw him. And knew him.

Not everything was the same, of course. Malachy's nose was an altogether grander affair, entirely worthy of a man with the name of Hawke. And his eyes were black instead of blue, though he must have harboured blue-eyed genes, since he had passed them on to his son. But enough was alike to make Ged understand the gallery manager's response to his appearance. Each feature in himself was less extreme, less prominent, than in his father: the height, the sharp-bladed bones angling over long cheeks, the vigorous black hair and swarthy skin. Even the wary way he held his mouth, like a warning about the words that might come out of it.

Ged sat down and let his father look him over. It felt like a real examination, with the real possibility that he might fail the test. Eventually his father smiled, and that felt like a real accomplishment. Beta plus, at least.

'Sylvia warned me you sound like a Limey.'

'Well, I am a Limey, I suppose.'

They were both smiling broadly now, because it was more polite than laughing. It was like hearing yourself speaking with a foreign accent. To his father he must have sounded like someone from the BBC. To him his father sounded like the white hat in a western, speaking at a more leisurely pace than these hasty New Yorkers, in a gentle drawl, with broad vowels. But at heart the pair of them had the same voice, light in tone, dark in resonance.

Which was maybe why his father amended, 'Only half a Limey.'

Ged had never really considered the American half of himself. It had been useful for impressing children at school, when they taunted him with having no father and he could say, My father is American. America then had been a fabulous, far-away place, and in his mind the image of his unknown father had borrowed that air of improbable glamour.

Now here was his flesh and blood father, and the magic had not quite evaporated. Had turned into something else, in fact, something much more personal, transmuted from America to Hawke. He watched his father light a cigarette – plain tip, none of your prissy filters – and everything about him seemed miraculous, from the deftly precise movements of his big hands in striking a match and touching it to the tip, down to the weight of his heavy hair, dead black, falling aslant over his forehead as he bent his head to meet the flame. And when Malachy looked up again to see his son watching him, the slow smile, the visible relaxing of reserve signalled they were no longer strangers. All these things ensured that he could never be an ordinary man.

'Sorry, I forgot,' said Malachy. 'I keep expecting you to be a kid. It's a real shock to see somebody the same size as me sitting on the other side of the table. Have a smoke?'

Ged was more into grass than weed at the time, but accepting the invitation seemed to be the only possible response. The consequences of inconsequential acts . . . He had been smoking ever since.

'How come you're over here?'

'Just looking around.' He wondered how to make it clear that this was all an accident. That he hadn't come looking for his father. He didn't want to make things any heavier than they had to be. 'I happened to see a poster advertising your exhibition. I was . . . just curious.'

'Yeah, I know. Sylvie told me all about it.' Malachy put a shocking amount of sugar into his coffee and stirred it diligently. 'She was all excited. Like she was playing Cupid. Funny woman. Hard as nails and romantic as hell. But I guess that's what most women are like.' He said it as if remarking on the peculiar habits of cats. 'Where are you off to next?'

'I don't know. I thought I'd see . . . well, I thought I'd see. What would you recommend?'

Malachy gave him a long, considering look, heavy-lidded, unblinking. 'Depends what you like.'

'What would *you* do?'

'Well, this is a funny country to get hold of. It ain't like touring Europe. You want to see Europe, you go from city to city, seeing the sights. They've got famous places, famous buildings, famous people, famous events, all laid out like in the history books.'

'And here?'

'Well, I won't say there's no history here, but it's not that kind. American cities are pretty much alike, because they're all so new, and they were all built by Americans. But the land is as old as any place on earth. You want to see America, you go and look at the land. Buy a bus ticket and take a big trip.' Malachy's finger described a square in the air, an outline of America. 'That's what I did. But I was too broke for a bus, I had to use my thumb. I wouldn't recommend that now, there's too many crazies around.' He was smiling slightly as he ground out his cigarette. 'In them days people usually had some reason for killing one another, but now they do it just for fun.'

He picked up his coffee cup, ignoring the handle, cradling it like a goblet in his big brown hand. The smile had gone by the time his glance slid back to his son. 'You want to come back and have a look at my place?'

Ged remembered oddly little of that visit, afterwards.

He remembered the skylighted studio, the high

windows looking down on a tree-lined street in Greenwich Village. A very un-New Yorkish setting, it had seemed to him at the time. New York was skyscrapers banked up over streets like canyons, the ultimate urban landscape. New York was not, he would have thought, terraced Victorian brownstone houses, dowdily domestic, with enormous plane trees springing up from the pavement to out-top the roofs. But then, as his father pointed out, once upon a time and not all that long a time ago, a hundred years or so, the city had been a much smaller and homelier place.

He remembered the heat. It had been continentally hot that day, even with the windows open and the skylights raised to catch the sea breeze. They drank cold beer straight from the bottle, American beer, fizzy and thin.

He remembered telling his father, after the third or fourth beer, that he wanted to write. The first time he had told anyone that. After all, it was the adolescent equivalent of announcing that you want to be a cowboy or a fireman. But his father didn't laugh or look sceptical, just nodded approval.

He remembered the paintings, their blatant primary colours at odds with the subtle manipulation of density that gave them shape. The shape of genius, according to Sylvia, the gallery manager. If not genius, then near enough to make his father wealthy.

He remembered that his father wouldn't talk about the paintings – artists talk through their asshole when they talk about art, he said – and that he never asked about Ged's mother. He referred to her once, calling her Missy, instead of Melly as everyone else did. But he didn't ask after her.

And also, of course, Ged remembered that it was the last time he saw his father.

6

After the two suits had gone away down the mountain, Angelina shooed the sleepy cats out of the studio, and locked the door.

Ged was not sure how much good that would do. 'Don't you have a burglar alarm? Rene says everyone knows where Malachy's place is.'

'They've known that all along, and we've never had no trouble. Malachy always said there's nothing here worth stealing.'

'There's a fortune in paint on canvas. Or didn't he count that?'

'I don't guess he did, come to think of it. But it's different now he's dead. Before that, they were just his work. Now they've turned into things.' She considered this idea. 'He would've hated that.'

He watched her go down the wooden steps ahead of him. He didn't like the idea of her being alone here with the lure of Malachy's leavings. No matter what he decided to do about the will, the sooner those paintings were packed up and sent to safety in New York, the better.

Angelina laid out their dinner on the deck: spaghetti bolognese and California claret, both surprisingly good.

'I noticed some empty bottles of this in the studio.' Ged held up his wine glass. 'Malachy's favourite, was it?'

'He wouldn't have drunk it if he didn't like it. But the reason we had so much of it was because he got it for free.'

'Free?'

'Yeah. You know how vineyards offer tastings? Well, Malachy happened to stop off at this place once. What he really wanted was one of those gnarled old grape stocks to bring back to his studio, and when they gave him one, he felt sort of obligated to buy some of their wine. But when the guy found out who Malachy was, he refused to take any money. Well, Malachy wasn't going to let him get away with that. He went home and painted the stock in one of his pictures, and sent it to the vineyard. And ever since, every year, he's been getting a free case of wine. It was a kind of battle for honour, like the Indians used to go in for. The last case arrived just after he died.'

Another thing the next-of-kin eldest son didn't know: 'When did he die?'

'Fifth of July. Just after sunset. But I didn't bother anybody about it until morning, seeing it was Sunday, and nothing they could do for him anyhow.'

Calum was staring at her in amazement. 'Didn't it feel weird, having a dead body in the house?'

Angelina returned his look calmly. 'That's what people used to do in the old days, before everybody started dying in the hospital. My grandma told me what they did in Poland, so that's what I did. I lit a candle and sat up with him all night. It was the last thing I could do for him, wasn't it? And that reminds me' – she turned to Ged – 'his ashes are in the studio. In one of those big clay pots. You don't want to throw him out by mistake.'

Ged was disconcerted to learn that Malachy's legacy included Malachy himself. Not knowing how to think about that, he changed the subject. 'You were going to tell me something earlier. Something he wouldn't let you do.'

'I didn't think I should say it in front of those guys.' Angelina frowned. 'It wouldn't sound respectful. But he was your dad, so that's different. I was going to tell you how when he was real bad, the doctor said he should get in a nurse, and Malachy wouldn't hear of it. He just would not budge. It finally turned out that he didn't want any woman seeing him in such an un-macho condition.' She giggled. 'Would you say that was pride, or just plain vanity? I know they're both sins, but I thought it was kind of sweet.'

'You're a woman,' Calum pointed out, 'and he didn't mind having you around.'

'It was way too late to be worrying about me. If you don't want all that spaghetti, Ged, feel free to leave it. I'll give it to the dog.'

The change of subject without a change of tone was startling, but not as startling as finding the dog itself suddenly lurking at his shoulder, eyeing the spaghetti, as if it had understood what she had said.

'Just tell him to get lost,' Angelina advised. 'Beat it, Charles. Get down off the deck.' She pointed to the steps leading down to the ground.

Grudgingly, the dog took the hint and disappeared around the corner of the house. Ged hastily finished up his pasta, before the creature could change its mind.

'Charles?' Calum echoed. 'Charles is the dog?'

'What's wrong with that?'

'Seems like a funny name for a dog.'

'Malachy told me he tried out dozens of names and that's the only one the critter would answer to. I guess even a dog has to know its own name when he hears it. Here, give me your plates and I'll go make coffee.'

When she had gone inside, Calum came over to sit down on the bench beside Ged. He glanced across his father's shoulder at the open patio doors. 'She doesn't look the type, does she?'

'What type is that?'

'Whatever type of girl would go to bed with an old man.'

He was right, she didn't look the type. She looked old-fashioned, somehow. Not unfashionable; simply better suited to some other time.

'But Malachy was an unusual type of old man,' Ged pointed out. 'He was rich, for one thing. And irresistible

57

to women, according to Rene Deforte. And he wasn't really very old. Only sixty-six.'

'You're just saying that to fool yourself into thinking you're still young,' Calum announced brutally. 'It's the plain fact, as that folksy lawyer would say, that forty-four is middle-aged. And sixty-six sounds excruciatingly old to me.'

Angelina returned with a tray full of coffee paraphernalia. 'You guys should bring your gear inside before it gets dark. You don't want to be stumbling around with a flashlight in the middle of the night.'

Calum, a Londoner born and bred, tried to make sense of this alien idea of darkness. 'Don't you have, you know, an outside lamp?'

'A yard light, you mean? No, Malachy didn't hold with lights out of doors. Stealing the night, he called it.' She shrugged in a businesslike way. 'He didn't hold with all kinds of things. He was a real funny guy.'

A funny guy with a funny house. Ged couldn't make up his mind about exactly what sort of dwelling-place would have been most appropriate to this spectacular site, but what was possibly least appropriate was what Malachy had actually built. It looked as if some native god with a kinky sense of humour had picked up a scrap of southern California suburb and plunked it down on the side of the mountain.

'Where's the swimming pool?' Calum had demanded, to be met with a look of shocked disapproval from Angelina.

'We haven't got that amount of water to waste, especially not this time of year,' she informed him. 'Didn't you read the sign down on the highway, about the forest-fire risk? They've just put the danger level over to red because it's been so dry.'

Calum craned his neck to survey the vast ranks of Douglas firs, marching over the mountains for as far as he could see. 'So how do these trees get to be so tall?'

'It rains all winter. Just like in England, or so I hear.'

When they returned with their luggage, Angelina ushered Ged to the bedroom in the south-east corner. 'I thought you might like to sleep in your dad's room. He never bothered with curtains or blinds. He said he liked to let the moonlight in, and anyways there's nobody out there to peek in at you. You've got your own bathroom, through that door over there.'

She hauled Calum away, leaving Ged to survey his quarters. They were pleasant enough, but far from luxurious. Spare was the word that sprang to mind. It made a surprising contrast with the cluttered eccentricity of the studio.

The furniture consisted of a big pine bedstead, an old pine chest, and a small built-in wardrobe that shared the same wall as the bathroom. The walls themselves were utterly bare. The only concession to colour and cosiness was a couple of Navaho rugs scattered over the pine floor, and a patchwork quilt on the bed.

The wardrobe and the chest proved to be still full of his father's clothes. Angelina's story implied that Malachy was vain about the physical image he presented to the world, but that vanity had obviously not extended to his wardrobe. Most of the clothing was so well worn that Oxfam would have rejected it.

And everything, even the underwear, had got paint on it. Maybe it put you off spending money on new clothes, if you knew you were doomed to get paint on them.

Seeing his father's clothes *in situ* like this gave Ged an eerie feeling. The battered garments were so unmistakably a part of the life of Malachy. It was as if some shreds of him still lived on in this room, a secret immortality lurking in the familiar darkness of chest and wardrobe.

This sense of strangeness increased enormously when he noticed something else, beside the bed. A pair of cowboy boots. They had a utilitarian air about them, without concession to country-and-western-style glitz. One sat upright and one lay on its side, exposing the irregularly worn heel and a hole in the sole. The uppers were in just the state he would have expected by now. They looked as if they had barely survived getting trapped in a stampede.

What kind of man wore cowboy boots? If he had uncovered proof that Malachy was from outer space, it could hardly have made his father seem more alien.

On the other hand, the man had come from Montana, a place apparently chock-full of cows and horses and, presumably, cowboys. Maybe everybody in Montana wore cowboy boots. And then there was the evidence of stable and paddock beside the studio. He might even have kept a horse.

Tossed beside the bed like that, where Malachy must have left them when he last took them off, maybe just before he lay down on that bed to die, the boots were even more unnerving than the tattered clothes.

Ged considered putting them away out of sight in the wardrobe. In the end he simply kicked them under the bed. It seemed the more Malachian solution.

7

There were pictures hanging in the living room, none of them Malachy's. They were mostly Picassos, as a matter of fact; lithographs in sepia tones, with flashes of pale blue. The subject matter was sex: a bacchanal, a sleeping nude, a minotaur rutting with a woman held between struggle and swoon.

The chaos of the studio seemed to have infected this room. As in the studio, every available surface was occupied by *things*. A bookshelf stood half denuded of its contents. They lay scattered about the floor, open or closed, or stacked up at random, while the space they had once occupied on the shelves had been usurped by irrelevant objects: a jar of feathers, a coffee tin jammed with pencils, a pair of binoculars. A desk had been tucked into the corner by the window. Alongside the clutter perched an open laptop computer, the only evidence of contemporary gadgetry that Ged had seen anywhere in the house.

'I didn't touch anything in here either,' Angelina said with virtuous regret. 'You'll have to tell me what you want me to do with all this. Some of it might be valuable,' she added dubiously. 'Do you want dessert? It's my grandma's apple pie. And there's vanilla ice cream, if you like it à la mode.'

Ged settled himself into the nearest armchair. 'Angelina, you are an angel.'

She giggled. 'Malachy always used to say that.'

'When you offered him your grandmother's apple pie?'

'Then for sure, but other times too. You look so much like him, and when you said that . . . I shouldn't have laughed. It's sad.'

'Sad that he's dead?'

She perched companionably on the arm of his chair. 'Sad that he never knew you, when you're so much like him.'

'Am I?'

'On the outside. I don't know what your insides look like yet.'

She looked at him with her clear, frank, penetrating gaze. It made him uncomfortable, thinking what she might be able to see within him. Wondering what his insides looked like.

What if they looked like the worst things he had ever done?

This girl came up to him while he was walking down Bayswater Road, after dark. She had the multi-layered dress style of a street person, rather than the blatant body-flashing of the streetwalker. She looked OK, she sounded OK, at least not drunk or crazy. She had a dark triangular face with big dark eyes.

She sidled up to him shyly, touching his arm. Why him? Who knows? He was the only one around just then.

Or maybe she could smell it on him, the cheap scent of whores. The sweetly nauseating odour of sexual immorality. Maybe she was alerted by that, without quite knowing what it was.

'Mister, I need money. Have you got any money?'

She was whispering, maybe ashamed to beg. As that sort of approach went, it was distinctly amateur. He glanced down at her as she scrambled to keep pace with him. 'Are you begging, or is this attempted robbery?'

She looked appalled. 'No, no, nothing like that. Please. Have you got a pound?'

He stopped. She stopped. Her face lit up with poorly suppressed hope.

He looked around. Hundreds of cars, but no-one on foot, not on this side of the road. An idea came into his head. A truly wicked idea.

It was one thing to buy something that was up for sale. It was another and much more depraved thing to tempt someone into selling herself.

No-one would know . . . except the one who always knew. Fucking takes two. He had mortgaged his conscience to whores.

The idea had found its way to his tongue. 'You can have ten pounds, if you want to work for it.'

He heard himself say it, as if he were another man. Or another sort of creature altogether. Maybe some kind of demon.

'Work?'

She licked her lips, the light of hope flickering uncertainly. She took her hand from his arm. The hand was shaking. Now he could guess why she needed the money so badly. Maybe what he was doing wasn't quite as wicked as he had imagined, not if she would have come down to that in the end anyway.

'What do you mean, work?'

'If you don't know what I mean, forget it.'

Now it was her turn to look around. Looking for some saviour, some alternative to him. Or maybe looking for the same reason he had, to see if anyone else was around to overhear the transaction. 'If you mean – I mean – you know – well, I've never done that before.'

'You'll have to get used to it, won't you, if you want to support a habit.'

He started to walk away again. She followed him, protesting, denying. Lying. 'It's not like that. I'm OK, really. I only need the money for food. Honest.'

He stopped again. This time he made one last chance to save her. To save himself. 'Why don't you quit right now? You'll be OK again in a few days.'

Her whole body started to shake like her hands. She grabbed his arm again. 'Please.'

He lost his last chance. 'Ten pounds.'

She was whispering again. 'Ten pounds.'

She didn't have a condom, of course, and neither did he, so he took his ten pounds in fellatio because it seemed safest. They went down a side street. He took her into the deeply recessed and shadowed doorway of a house with no lights showing, and pushed her down on to her knees.

She wasn't very good at it, but that scarcely mattered. She wasn't a pro. That was the point of it, after all. He was paying her to do something she had never done before.

It was his first experience of raw street sex, no car to cushion the exposure. Or the intensity. Or the knowledge of exactly what it was he was doing.

What he was doing was corrupting a stranger.

Afterwards she scrubbed her mouth with the back of one hand to take away the taste of him, and scrubbed her eyes with the knuckles of her other hand to keep the tears from coming. At that point, as always, he was flooded with shame. It never touched him beforehand. Before, he was only concerned with getting what he wanted. After, he could afford the luxury of guilt.

This time, guilt was truly a luxury, because it prompted him to give her two ten-pound notes instead of one.

She stared at them as if she suspected he was trying to put something over on her. 'You said ten. Why'd you give me twenty?'

'Because I wasn't very nice to you.'

She stared at the money a moment longer, before stuffing it away in the recesses of her baggy clothing. Then she stared at him. 'Why did you do that?'

'I just told you why.'

'No, I mean the whole thing. Offering me money to . . . you know.'

'I told you. I'm not very nice.'

Maybe that was how his insides looked. Not very nice at all.

He turned away from Angelina's gaze, so compelling

and disconcerting. 'He could have known me if he'd wanted to,' he said coldly. 'He knew where to find me when it came to the will.'

'I know. I knew how you'd feel about that.' She paused, not for effect but to collect her thoughts. 'I asked Rene how come, if Malachy knew all about you, he hadn't tried to find you while he was still alive. Why didn't he try to give himself a chance to know the man he was leaving so much behind for?'

'What did Rene say?'

'He said, "Mal was a simple man, Angie. He could only cope with one thing at a time."'

'And what do you think he meant by that?'

This time she glanced at Calum, who was stretched out in the other armchair. He must have picked Angelina's chair; he was festooned with cats, all purring madly. Calum didn't seem to mind. He might even have been enjoying it.

Angelina glanced at him, then turned back to Ged and lowered her voice, as adults might converse of adult matters in the presence of a child.

'He was dying. Malachy, I mean. He knew he was dying. He had a hard time dealing with that. He didn't believe in any kind of afterlife, and he was scared of dying. He'd spent all his life trying to become immortal, as an artist, as a man. Thirteen sons, what d'you think that was all about? He used to point to his paintings and say to me, That's what'll be left of me when I die.

'But in the end he didn't really believe it. He was just plain scared that he'd wasted his life. Scared of becoming nothing.'

In a few words she had sketched his own life, Ged realized with an awful shock. Striving to make an indelible, individual mark. Scared of being nothing. He had to take a deep breath before responding. 'Wouldn't the survival of a son make some difference?'

'But you're not him, are you?' She said it so simply. 'The Devil doesn't take substitutes.'

65

*   *   *

Calum rapped on the bedroom door and came in immediately, without waiting for a response.

Three years without a word between them, and now the kid comes along and starts acting as if he were still ten years old and his father had never gone anywhere. Ged didn't know whether to be relieved or annoyed. He decided to be relieved, because it was less trouble. And less likely to make trouble.

Whatever his mission, Calum took time out from it to admire his surroundings. 'What a cool room. Mine is boring compared to this.'

'At least your wardrobe isn't full of somebody else's clothes.'

'You mean his stuff is still in here?'

'As Angie keeps telling us, she hasn't touched a thing.'

Calum mooched about the room, prodding the bright rugs with his bare toes. Abruptly he said, 'So what are you going to do about this will?'

Ged had thrown up the sash on the window that faced south-ish. Now he leaned out into the darkness. The house was surrounded by an ocean of stars and a mountain of night. Somewhere down there, in absolute darkness, the waves were still waging their eternal war against the land. The surge and suck of the ponderous rollers made a rhythm like the slow tick of a cosmic clock, or the persistent thump-thud of the living heart.

'What do you think I should do?'

'Why not take him up on it? The money, Christ. That bloke Brad said every one of those paintings is worth umpteen thousands of dollars.' Calum came over to the window and leaned out alongside his father. 'It's too bloody dark out there. Shouldn't there be ships or something? When I was down in Hastings you could see their lights moving back and forth, away out to sea.'

'This is the Pacific Ocean, not the English Channel.'

'Does that make a difference?'

'Apparently so. Things aren't quite so cosy and domes-

66

ticated here. This is a cold, rocky coastline, with nothing out there until you hit China.'

Calum squinted into the starlight. 'China's out there?'

'No, it's not. That's what I meant.'

'You mean there's nothing out there.'

'Yes.'

There was a pause, while Calum contemplated nothingness. 'That's scary.'

Ged found himself abruptly overwhelmed with weariness. He pulled his head back inside and stretched out on top of the quilt. Since Calum still showed no sign of leaving, he dropped a hint by turning out the light.

Calum didn't move from the window. 'So are you going to do it?'

Ged answered with another question. 'Why should I?'

'He was your father, wasn't he?'

'He was also the father of twelve other fools.'

'But they only get a little bit. The same as you'll get, if you don't do it.'

'And you'll only get a little bit, too. Is that what you mean?'

Silence for a minute. Then, in flat tones, 'No, I didn't mean that.'

Ged didn't mean that either. Only there wasn't anything else he could have meant.

In absolute darkness he saw, sensed, his son rising from his knees. Heard him move towards the door, then halt at the foot of the bed to say coldly, 'It's you who needs money, not me.'

'Do I need money?'

Christ, did he need money. The cost of this trip was going on to his credit cards, and he had no idea how he would pay it back. His current book was nowhere near ready for publication and payoff, and looked like never getting there. He had already torn up two drafts, and the painfully slow and unsatisfactory progress of the third attempt had come to a standstill even before Elie walked out. Since Elie had left, he could hardly get organized enough to write a cheque, let alone serious prose.

Not writing at all was even more painful than writing badly. As long as he could recall, he had compulsively scribbled down poems, stories, fragments and sketches, whatever was in him that wanted to come out. And worse than the loss of self-expression was the failure of that inner world where scenes and characters grew. Playing god in that private world was an integral part of his psyche. Without it he felt lobotomized.

Maybe it had been the boredom of life with Polly that had enabled him to become a novelist in the first place. Maybe the intense happiness of having Elie had numbed his subconscious. Maybe his brain couldn't handle the volatile, energy-intensive pleasures of dwelling in his own imagination, on top of the all-engaging excitement of sexual obsession.

Calum had a different view of Elie. 'You've got to keep your bimbo happy, haven't you? They burn money, don't they, these high-class whores?'

He had moved closer to the door by now, but he was still only a few feet away. Reachable distance, even in the dark. The temptation for Ged to get up and hit him was very strong.

Hit him for what? For insulting the woman who had displaced his mother? The woman who had taken his father away from him? The woman who was, or at any rate had been, just what he said?

The woman who was nowhere now.

It was suddenly important, for all sorts of reasons, not to lie to Calum. Not even by implication. 'She's not . . . We're not . . . together any more.'

Calum turned towards him. Turned to look at someone he couldn't see. 'You gave her the push?'

'She . . . disappeared.'

'She's buggered off?' Incredulity was the dominant response, which made Ged feel better. 'Your grand passion is kaput? When did this happen?'

'A few months ago.'

Silence, except for the distant hiss and boom of the sea. It went on so long that he began to think Calum had gone away. Until he heard Calum's voice.

The tone was tentative. 'Dad?'

'What?'

'Mum doesn't have a bloke or anything.'

PICK-UP

Caught in that sensual music, all neglect
Monuments of unageing intellect.

The first time he saw Elie . . .

She was sitting on a bench in Hyde Park, head bowed, sunlight glinting in the shadows of her hair.

Hyde Park was where the high-class whores used to parade their wares in Regency and Victorian times, hoping to catch the eye of some swell out for a ride. But though the cigarette she was smoking and the skirt she was wearing would have shocked even the whores of earlier days, they were nowadays no cause for comment whatever. And she was reading a book: a blameless activity, commendable even, at any time in human history.

As he came along the path towards her, she looked up from her book. Her eyes were distracted, full of her own thoughts, or the events in the book. At that moment she was wholly unselfconscious, and he saw her as he was seldom to see her again: herself alone, without any awareness of his presence and regard. He could never afterwards decide whether he had fallen for her under false pretences, or in a rare moment of truth.

She had made herself up meticulously, artfully, tastefully, like a model in a cosmetics advertisement. Despite the artifice – or because of it? after all, it was very well done – he saw the shape of her face clearly. The length of the nose, perfect to one-tenth of a millimetre. The insistent delicacy of the cheekbones, almost enough to take away terror from thoughts of the skull beneath the skin. The welcoming width of the mouth, tempered by a hint of sensitivity in the exquisitely moulded upper lip, and a storm warning in the dominant lower lip. But above all he saw the eyes, wide and dark, shining with a luminous clarity that must have bestowed some tangential beauty to anything they lit upon. Even to him, maybe.

He came alongside her, slowing up, his head dragged round involuntarily. All in order not to lose sight of her a split second sooner than necessary.

Those eyes lost their abstraction, became aware of him. Turning heads must have been a commonplace to her, but she showed no sign of amusement or boredom. Her eyes widened, fleetingly, fractionally. Her mouth tightened at some points and relaxed at others, the ghost of a hint of a smile.

He never knew what made him do what he did next. In mid-stride he changed direction, brought his foot down towards her instead of following the path. He did it as smoothly as if that was what he had intended all along. And maybe it was, at least for as long as he'd been looking at her.

Without any conscious intent he opened his mouth, and was faintly ashamed to hear himself say what he said then. 'Do you have a light on you?'

That wasn't quite as grotesquely clumsy as it might have been, since she was actually smoking.

Strictly speaking, he wasn't. He had given it up at the New Year, a sacrifice to virtue and Polly's harassment. For six months he had been walking in the smoke-free paths of righteousness, and now he was going astray . . .

Without a word she set her book upside down on the bench, and dug into her small bag for a lighter. She found it, flicked it, offered it up to him, an unseen flame in the sunlight.

He put his hands into his pockets, then brought them

out, open, empty. He hoped his smile came across as apologetic rather than sheepish. 'I'm sorry, I've troubled you for nothing. I'm out of cigarettes.'

Her amazing eyes appeared to narrow in annoyance. But that might have only been squinting into the sun, because she snuffed the lighter and produced a packet of cigarettes from the magically capacious recesses of her bag. One of those silly women's brands, unnaturally long and slim like the models who supposedly smoked them.

He took one anyway.

This time she handed him the lighter. He lit the cigarette and gave the lighter back to her. She tucked it away, along with the packet of cigarettes. The whole affair had the aura of ritual. An introductory ritual, with cigarettes playing the role of a mutual friend. There was an etiquette attached to such matters, even in these casual times.

He sucked in smoke, let it roll down inside him, savoured the shamefaced pleasure of post-modern sin. When she leaned back against the bench and took a drag on her own cigarette, instead of returning to her book, he read it as an invitation.

'May I sit down?'

Again she answered without a word, by picking up the book and closing it on her lap. Without marking the place, he noticed. And no wonder: it was one of those mindless romances, each one so much like all the others that an experienced reader could no doubt open any one at any page and find herself *au courant* with events in the plot.

The cover was the classic one. He stands behind She. He looks dark and brooding. She looks blonde and vulnerable. Her bosom is clearly meant to be heaving with emotion, while He is eyeing it as if contemplating some serious physical engagement.

Keeping his own expression more opaque of intent, Ged sat down on the bench, leaving as much room as if the book had still been between them. 'Sorry to be such a twit. I'd given it up – for the fourteenth time – but when

I saw you . . . when I caught a whiff of your cigarette, I mean . . . a terrible craving came over me.'

Again that subterranean smile, or rather that sense of smiling. She shifted imperceptibly, turning very slightly towards him. Opening up to him.

'Don't let me keep you from your book,' he said dryly. 'There's nothing worse than being dragged away from a book you can't put down.'

She dropped a glance at the clichéd cover, then turned her gaze full on him. 'You're making fun of me, aren't you?'

The first time he had heard her voice. It was clear, light, faintly breathless. It went with the artless light in the eyes, rather than the made-up face or the seductive mini-skirted body. As for the tone, it sounded more like she was making fun of him.

'Now why would I go to all that trouble, just to make fun of a stranger? And why are you reading the book, if it's dull?'

'It's not really dull. Only predictable.'

'Just like real life, then. I thought that sort of book dealt in romantic fantasy.'

'It's only because it's in a book that it seems boring and predictable,' she explained as if to the simple-minded. 'Things always happen the same way in books. If they happened like that in real life, it wouldn't be boring at all. But of course they never do.'

'What are these boring things that happen in books?'

'Oh, you know.' She glanced at him sidelong, her luminous eyes no longer so innocent – infected, perhaps, by the mascara and eyeliner. 'A tall dark handsome stranger comes along, and you get swept off your feet and carried away to live happily ever after.'

He considered this novel scenario. 'Carried away literally or metaphorically?'

She looked down at the book again, smoking thoughtfully. 'Either would do. Both would be best.'

He looked where she was looking, at the blonde woman on the cover. 'Maybe it's just another case of blondes having more fun.'

'No, because quite often the man is fair and the woman is dark.'

'Then one of us is still the wrong colour. It would never work.'

She set the book aside, tucking it under her bag. She leaned back again and closed her eyes to the sun, giving him a fine view of her fine profile. She pursed her lips to blow out smoke, then kept them like that a little while longer, like someone about to whistle or kiss.

'Sometimes,' she said in that breathless, almost childish voice, 'once or twice, I think, they both had dark hair.'

He went away when he had finished his cigarette. He didn't bother to add to the clichés by asking her if she came there often. He didn't even get her name. As she pointed out, people in books always managed to meet again.

In real life they did, too. The very next day.

He went back at the same time to the same place and she was there, on the same bench, reading what appeared to be the same book. When he sat down at the other end of the bench, she looked up with a smile as much amused as welcoming.

She set the book down between them, front cover up. She patted the cover, to draw his attention to it.

Not the same book, he realized. It was one of those rare ones, the kind with a black-haired He and a brunette She.

He took out his own cigarette this time, low tar but a suitably macho brand. He offered them to her and she took one. He lit them both, his and hers. Another ritual, as rigidly prescribed as for any couple of courting bower-birds. But the bower-birds would at least have been confident of what each other had in mind.

What did he have in mind?

He wasn't looking for true romance. He wasn't even

looking for a mistress. He had an idea that mistresses, like wives and trashy romantic novels, grew dull from predictability. The scenario he was mapping out for her probably only happened between chapters, at least in the sort of books she read.

This time he felt free to assess her more openly. She had come back, therefore there could be no possibility of misunderstanding mere courtesy, of casual kindness inviting imposition. So he studied her, with as much cold blood as he could muster when looking at her.

Twenty to twenty-five, he guessed. At least fifteen years younger than him, to put it in another and infinitely more depressing way. But she had chosen to come back. So he couldn't be past it yet.

She really was extraordinarily beautiful. So beautiful that she should have been able to make a living out of the way she looked.

Maybe she did. The carefully applied cosmetics, the up-to-the-minute outfit, the elaborately casual hairstyle, suggested an attention to appearance that went beyond simple vanity. Not that she needed any such props: shaven-headed, dressed in rags, she would still have turned his head.

She looked at him looking at her. 'I was going to feed the ducks,' she said, just as if he had asked her what she wanted to do, now that he was here to do it with her.

'Why don't we do that, then?'

'We can't. I forgot and ate the crusts on my sandwich.' The breathlessness spilled over into a giggle. 'Anyway, I don't have time now. I have to go back to work.'

'Where's work? What work?'

'Over there.' She flapped a hand southwards, towards Knightsbridge, and giggled again. 'I'm a rip-off artist. I work on a perfume counter.'

She surveyed him in turn, making God knew what out of the sight of his worn jeans, overgrown haircut and forty-year-old face. Maybe it was true, what he always told himself when he looked into a mirror; maybe he really didn't look a day over thirty-five.

At any rate, whatever she saw didn't seem to put her off. 'What do you do? Do you work around here?'

'I work from home. Over there.' He waved to the north, Bayswater and Notting Hill. 'I'm a writer.'

'I knew it.'

'How could you know that?'

'Because of the way you talked about books.' She smiled, pleased with her guess, or else with his profession. 'What kind of books do you write?'

'Unpredictable ones.'

'That's the best kind.' She leaned forward slightly, looking up at him with her guileless artificed eyes. He saw for the first time the secret of their inner light. The depths of dark brown velvet were streaked with glints of gold. 'I like it when I really can't guess what's going to happen next, and I just can't wait to find out.'

'That's what I like too.' He leaned a little towards her – maybe swaying, maybe dizzied by her nearness and the scent of her perfume. 'Shall we find out tonight?'

That must have been a mistake. She stood up and looked away.

He stood up too. Close to her, as it happened. If he had taken her by the arms and stared down at her breasts, they might have been the couple on the cover of her book.

He should have spoken then. Said something – Goodbye, Wait a minute, What about a fuck? – something, anything. Nothing got as far as his mouth.

She put up a hand to her throat, to a wide gold chain that ran around it, more like a collar than a necklace. She touched her lips with a nervous flicker of her tongue.

Now he could smell something else. Not her perfume. Her fear.

'I have to go now.'

'You've forgotten your book.'

He picked it up and held it out to her. She stared at it as if she had never seen it before. Then at him – with more justification – in the same way. 'That's OK, I know how

76

it ends. They always end the same way.'

'Maybe it ends differently this time.'

She was still shying, still scared of something. 'What's your name?'

'Ged.'

She repeated it to herself, the way a cat might explore the taste and scent of some new intriguing thing. 'Jed?'

'G-E-D. For Gerard. What about you?'

'I'm Elie.'

'Ellie for Ellen or Eleanor?'

'Neither. And you spell it with only one L.'

He took out a pen and wrote on the inside cover of her stupid little book. Her name, Elie. His name, Ged. The name of a pub down in Chelsea. Today's date. A time. Then he closed the book and offered it to her again.

This time she took it.

They sat in semi-darkness outside the pub. Officially enjoying the mild evening air, in reality maintaining their protective anonymity a little while longer. Soon, within an hour by his reckoning, soon they would be intimate, though strangers still.

All they knew of each other now was a few syllables: you Elie, me Ged. Just enough to attract the right person's attention in a crowded pub or a park. But before he went home tonight, he would have had carnal knowledge of her. He knew that because otherwise she wouldn't have agreed to meet him here.

He had bought sex from strangers many times – too many times – but never had an assignation like this. And she was beautiful, not like the scrawny little tarts who were the best the streets had to offer.

What was in it for her? Excitement, maybe, just like him.

And maybe something else. She kept glancing at her watch, repeating that she had to be home by eleven. Every time she said it, she touched the gold chain. An automatic, unconscious gesture. Perhaps it really was a collar, and she on a long invisible lead.

'Why do you have to be back?'

'My boyfriend's going to ring me then.'

'Does he live here in London?'

For some reason this simple question could not be answered immediately. 'Yes,' she decided at last, 'but he's in Beirut right now.'

It didn't surprise him that she was attached. He wouldn't have believed her if she had claimed she wasn't. A girl like her couldn't go unattached for five minutes, no more than a fifty-pound note could have lain untouched on the pavement.

He decided to even the score. 'My wife is only over the other side of the park.'

Now she couldn't say he hadn't warned her. She stared at him, more surprised than dismayed. 'What time do you have to be home?'

So he had a collar and lead as well. The thought caught at his throat, as if someone had jerked that lead: the thought of his life closing in on him. His death closing in on him.

'Let's go,' he said abruptly. The closer it came to eleven, the more nervous and distracted she would grow. And he wanted her full attention.

They walked up Brompton Road to Knightsbridge. She asked artlessly, 'Are you going to walk home across the park?'

'Are you?'

'Yes, but I go the other way, towards Park Lane.'

'I'll walk with you. Keep you safe.'

She looked at him wide-eyed. Even in the garish, sulphurous lighting, he could barely make out the movement of her mouth that suggested the possibility of a smile.

He took her hand to lead her through the gate, into the grassy darkness where everything was permitted. He kissed her in the safety of the middle of the path. Kissed her gently, to test her willingness.

She was willing enough.

78

He kissed her again, nibbling her lower lip to scratch off some scales of her lipstick armour. He caught the lip between his teeth, bit down a little bit harder. Testing again.

She made a sound, a sigh or whimper. Not what he would have called an objection.

'Let's find somewhere a little more private.'

She surprised him by giggling against his shoulder. 'But we're only in Chapter Three.'

'I thought we'd skip the boring bits and go right to the interesting part.'

He drew her across the grass to the wrought-iron railing, away from the lights along the path. A few yards south of them, the traffic roared through Knightsbridge as if night had been abolished.

Rather than unbutton it, he pulled her blouse free of her skirt and reached behind her, up the back of her blouse, to unfasten her bra. Then he pushed up blouse and bra at the front, to see exactly what he had got.

She was slim enough to give her average-sized breasts a slight suggestion of voluptuous excess: just a hint, nothing vulgar. Perfect in that respect as well, he thought. It wasn't really a thought, more a sense of pleasure in uncovering and discovering her, which mingled with the greater pleasure of covering her breasts with his hands. Taking possession of them.

He stroked her for a brief eternity, feeling those lovely breasts swell and grow warmer. That was the only response he had from her, subtle as it was. Instead of embracing him, she held her arms down on either side of her. Her hands were pressed against the fence, spanning and clutching the width of two rails. Her eyes were huge, dark as the grass; her mouth a little agape.

He kissed her again, open-mouthed, and tasted a tinge of blood. He must have bitten harder than he'd thought. He ran his tongue along her lip to staunch the bleeding.

His hands abandoned her breasts now for more intimate territory. When he lifted her skirt, he felt the impermeable sheen of nylon. Tights in this weather? Maybe it wasn't respectable, in her book, to go bare-legged. Or maybe they frowned on it at the perfume counter. For him, it was another bloody layer of armour to be prised loose.

He did that roughly, hauling tights and knickers down together, halfway to her knees, leaving her bare from hip to mid-thigh. She didn't move, either to object or to approve.

He ran his hands upwards over the exposed flesh, which was almost as silky-smooth as the tights. When they reached her groin, he discovered that even her pubic hair had been trimmed and tamed. It covered the mount of Venus and nothing more, like an ice-cap on a tropical peak: no luxuriant tendrils creeping across her belly, no unruly outriders straggling down her thighs.

Until that moment he had been concentrating on the notion of possession. Now he had a different determination, to make her sweat that god-damned make-up off. Mere possession could come later. Could even be saved to savour another time.

He had learned long ago that the best way to give a woman pleasure was to use his body to let her please herself. Only this time it wasn't so easy. Her bottom tensed against the rail, resisting the sensual stroke of his hand. Her pussy was as prim as a plucked eyebrow, he thought in frustration, even as it grew warmer and wetter. Her body declined to connive in its own seduction until almost the end, when she startled and exhilarated him by grabbing his hand in both of hers and holding it captive at her crotch while her pelvis made a few frantic stabs across it. Her climax came suddenly, noisily, in short sobbing gasps.

It was the sexiest thing he had ever seen. He almost came on the spot.

It seemed to shake the stuffing out of her. She wilted, clung to him, was briefly in tears. But she didn't say a thing, neither then nor when she had restored her clothing to something like its previous immaculate state.

He walked her all the way down to Hyde Park Corner, his arm around her. Keeping her safe. He was gratified to observe, by the light of the lamps at the entrance, that her lipstick was smudged and her mascara had melted.

By that same revealing light, she glanced at her watch and uttered a squeak. 'I've got to run!'

And she ran, right through the churning streams of traffic, like Eliza leaping from floe to floe towards freedom, across the winter Mississippi. He stood helpless, watching her flight from the nether bank, the shore of slavery.

At least he hadn't frightened her off. She was sitting on the bench, with a magazine this time. One of those glossy-trendy-trashy women's rags, that dealt in fantasy and fairy tales just as much as the books she read.

With his first glimpse of her came a flood of emotion. Excitement, pleasure, a tinge of terror, enormous relief. He wasn't used to suffering such feelings, and didn't know if he liked it.

Not that anyone was asking him. This was Life, and things were happening to him in the arbitrary way he had always associated with other people's messy little lives.

And he had another thought, which he didn't like any better. Thank God, was the thought that came to him. Thank God yesterday had been Thursday, not Friday. He couldn't have borne it, waiting till Monday.

A suit had already occupied the other end of the bench, pretending to survey the crowd in a lordly and inquisitive manner, but sneaking surreptitious glances at his seat mate. Instead of squeezing in between them, Ged squatted down at the end of the bench by Elie.

He slid the back of his hand up the outside of her leg, from ankle to knee, brushing nylon. Even nylon was electrifying, on her flesh.

She looked at him with one of those ghostly smiles. Maybe she thought a real smile would splinter her make-up. She moved her hand down to meet his, a brush of fingertips that made something lurch violently inside him, as if an immovable object had yielded to some irresistible force.

'Why don't you meet me by those heroes over there?' He nodded in the direction of a statue looming in the distance, and rose and walked away.

He walked in a big circle, watching her. When she got up, he started to make his roundabout way towards the sculpture.

It was a war memorial, he saw as he approached: a group of men equipped with flat-brimmed helmets and fixed bayonets, preparing to charge some invisible enemy. A monument to its era, as much as to the courage of the men it commended. No-one put up war memorials any more, and not because there weren't any more wars. War had become a shameful thing, to be forgotten as quickly as possible rather than immortalized. Physical courage was in bad taste, smacking as it did of macho values. As for the endurance of suffering, if a world war were to take place now, the country would go bust from paying compensation for all the trauma.

He waited for her in the shade of the eastern side. The benches along the path to the west were crowded with old ladies, all hatted and coated, as if confidently expecting a dramatic change in the weather.

He leaned against the granite plinth, watching her come across the lawn. With every step her high heels sank into the turf and had to be yanked out, until she was obliged to walk on her toes, in shoes that were almost all toe anyway. He watched her teeter and trot, persevering until she finally, literally, tripped into his arms.

At that point he was no longer a dispassionate observer.

'Did you get back in time last night?'

'Not quite.' She was breathless, maybe from the run across the grass, or maybe not. He caught a whiff of fear again. 'He said he'd already rung twice. He wasn't very happy.'

'Did you manage to cheer him up?'

'I hope so.' She giggled. 'I told him I'd been in the bath and lost track of the time.'

She turned her face upwards, expecting him to kiss her. He saw no reason to disappoint her.

After some stirring minutes devoted to relatively innocent physical expressions of desire, he drew her into the shadow of the soldiers. With shrubbery shielding them from the other compass points, they might have been alone in darkness, like the night before, with the statue standing in for the fence, and the chatter of the old cold-blooded women making up for the noise of Knightsbridge traffic.

He undid the top two buttons of her blouse, then reached inside to lift one breast from its nesting place. He took a moment to admire it, with eye and hand. He enjoyed the idea of exposing her beautiful breasts to view in a public place. Not that anyone was in a position to enjoy the sight with him, except the immortal young men up top.

He put his other hand up her skirt and down inside her tights and knickers. This time, instead of pretending that her body belonged to someone else, she turned herself in towards the secrecy of the statue with a sigh and a sensuous wiggle, like a child who has just learned a new and enjoyable game and wants to play it at every opportunity.

As he stroked her, she set her hands flat against the face of the stone. She laid her own face against the back of her hands, while her breasts, hot in the cool shadow, were pressed to the granite below. Her thighs strained against the unyielding surface, her hips jerked back and forward again as if between two lovers, one of mortal clay and one of eternal stone. She was whimpering when she came, biting her wrist to stifle the sound, slamming her belly and his hand into the rock.

'What have you done to me?' she whispered. She had collapsed against him, too drained and dizzy to be properly indignant. 'We can't carry on like that in broad daylight.'

'We just did,' he pointed out. He meant to sound cool and in command of things, but his voice shook. He was soothing her, straightening her, hauling up her knickers and rebuttoning her blouse, before anyone happened to notice them there in the pool of darkness. It was hard to do, because his hands were shaking as badly as his voice. 'Don't you like it?'

Of course she did. That was why she had come here, to let him frig her into a frenzy. His hand was bruised from the force with which she had driven it against the stone. He hadn't noticed at the time, any more than she had noticed that her teeth had drawn blood from the back of her wrist.

She was still hiding behind her eyelashes when she said, 'That's never happened to me with a man before.'

'Only with women, you mean?'

'No!' She sounded faintly shocked, then shy. 'I mean . . . myself.'

He approved the note of shyness. An old-fashioned girl. 'What's the matter with your boyfriend?'

'He just wants me to do things to him.'

'The selfish swine. I'd drop him if I were you. He obviously doesn't appreciate you.'

'And you do?'

'What do you think?'

She gave a small shudder, possibly a response to the movement of his thumb across her clothed nipple. She brushed his hand away. 'I've got to go now.'

'You've always got to go. You're a bloody Cinderella. What about tonight?' Friday night, last chance before an endless weekend.

'The same pub?'

'I haven't got time for the pub tonight. I'll meet you by the gate at ten.'

She hesitated. 'But I've got to be back by eleven. My boyfriend—'

'Yes, I know, he's going to ring you then. But we won't need long, will we?'

She ducked her head and looked away as if she hadn't heard him. Not the last bit, at least. Perhaps she couldn't handle that much frankness.

She was waiting by the gatepost, standing just out of the light, scanning the road with a faintly anxious expression. Because eleven o'clock was approaching, he supposed.

He had come through the park, which she had evidently not anticipated. He stood to one side and watched her a while, enjoying the sight of her when she thought herself unobserved. There was a subtle difference in her stance; maybe she held herself more carefully in public. And her face – out of school, so to speak – looked young and vulnerable, as if the make-up had become invisible.

But he didn't bother to look too long. He had other enjoyments on his mind. It was, say, sixty hours, two and a half days, since he first encountered her, and he still hadn't had the pleasure of her cunt around his cock. He was glad he hadn't rushed it, after what she had said about her boyfriend, but he wasn't going to go home unsatisfied for a third time. Christ, if he couldn't get her outside of him within the next few minutes, he would deserve whatever happened instead.

He stepped up behind her. As her head began to turn, he caught her wrist and swung it up behind her back in a playful arm lock.

By that time she had caught sight of his face. 'Oh, it's you! You scared the life out of me. My heart must be halfway to the moon by now.'

'So it should be, when I'm around.'

He let go of her wrist, put his arm around her, turned her and drew her through the gate, into relative darkness. They sat down on a bench in one of the unlit side paths. Or rather, he sat down and pulled her down on to his lap so that she was facing him, straddling his thighs, her knees resting on the bench on either side of him.

She put her hands on his shoulders, waiting for whatever he wanted to do. Too compliant for his taste. He wanted her to want him too much to wait.

She was wearing a dark sleeveless dress with a scooped neckline and a short flared skirt. Maybe she had dressed up for him. He pushed the straps of the dress down off her shoulders. He ran one finger around inside the neckline, in a single movement sliding the dress down and lifting her breasts out into the freedom of the night.

'Someone might see,' she whispered.

'What a thrill for them.'

It was a thrill for him. The dress, bunched beneath her bosom, performed as a primitive corset, pushing the breasts up and together. In the darkness they looked like shadowy glimmers of Platonic perfection. But when he touched them, they felt breathtakingly real.

After waiting sixty hours, he decided he could stand to wait at least another sixty seconds for fulfilment. He took a moment to enjoy those wonderful breasts.

That set her to squirming, pressing her crotch against his prick as if by accident, as if she was unaware of what she was doing to him. He reminded her, by sliding his hand up her skirt, in through the high wide leg of her knickers, and stroking her bottom, as firm and smooth and inviting as her breasts.

He ran his finger down the valley between those buttocks. He could feel her anus, pulsing and puckering against the joint of his finger like the mouth of some exotic sea creature, bound to the rock, compelled by the tides.

He brought his hand around to the front, to push the crotch of her knickers aside. He parted her neat little pubic mane, one finger on either side, teasing her with the middle fingertip. She was breathing more quickly now, her body jerking erratically as if subject to small strokes of lightning. She pulled herself up against him, whimpering in his ear, bouncing that beautiful bum around on his thighs.

By now his hand was as wet as if she had pissed on it. He slid his finger along the cleft of her cunt, right back to the cleft of her arse. It was open now, gaping with hunger, begging for him. He slipped his fingertip inside and felt it clench around him. Warm, wet, and tight, everything a man could want in a woman. What was a little shit between lovers?

She grabbed his head in her hands and bit his earlobe. She was virtually sobbing with the two-edged pleasure of delight deferred.

He had to take his hand out of her to unzip his jeans and haul out his cock, which by now felt like a case for the Guinness Book of Records. He took hold of her hips, two-handed, and jammed her down on him, jammed himself up into her. Halfway to her tits, by the feel of it. She nearly chewed his earlobe off.

She began bobbing up and down on his cock like a frenzied pony on a carousel pole, fucking herself on him as if her life depended on it. Her whimpers turned to yelps. He was coming to his own climax, and barely had the wits to press her face against his shoulder, to stifle her telltale cries.

Instead of the usual aftermath endearments, 'You make too much noise,' he told her.

'Sorry.' She was still breathless, apparently with astonishment as much as anything. 'I wasn't expecting . . . I mean, I've never . . . not like that.'

'Your boyfriend has a lot to answer for.'

He caught the approaching sound of shoe on gravel. It only took a second to push the straps on her dress back into place, but he tucked those exquisite breasts out of sight with extreme regret.

She lifted her head in alarm. He drew her back down to his shoulder again. 'Don't panic, it's OK. If we stay like this, we're all right.'

They almost weren't all right. The shoes belonged to a man walking his dog. The dog, perhaps attracted by the smell of sex, showed an alarming inclination to stick its nose under Elie's skirt.

She started up again, eyes wide, unsure of what was happening, since the dog and man were behind her. Ged held her close with one arm and discouraged the dog with the other hand. He managed to fend it off until its owner hauled it away, muttering alternate curses (at the dog) and apologies (to Ged and Elie).

Elie put her arms around Ged and giggled against his neck. 'Do you think he guessed?'

'The dog certainly did.' He stroked her hair, feeling protective of her for the first time. Thinking in the primeval *us* and *them* mode, instead of the even more atavistic and atomistic *me* and *her* which had started this crazy adventure. 'I've messed up your make-up again, haven't I?'

'You like doing that, don't you?'

'Don't you like me doing it?'

'Mm.' She nuzzled his ear, the one she had savaged in her passion. It still hurt, but he didn't care. 'Do you do that to your wife?'

'She doesn't wear much make-up.'

'No, I mean . . . You know what I mean.'

She might have meant several things. Do you fuck her in the park? Do you stick your finger up her arse? Do you screw her till she screams? He answered to the one meaning that she almost certainly had not had in mind. 'I still have sex with her, if that's what you mean.'

Sex with Polly was nothing like sex with Elie, and it never had been. Polly in bed was like Polly in the kitchen, a competent cook, a competent lover. She did all the right things, when she felt like doing them. Of course he still had sex with her; he couldn't live without sex, no more than he could live without food, and she was the provider of both. But it wasn't what he would call exciting, and hadn't been for a very long time. Polly had orgasms because she was entitled to have them, not because she couldn't help herself.

'I have to go.' Elie crawled off him, reluctantly. 'I told you, my boyfriend's ringing me again tonight.' She smoothed down her skirt and adjusted her shoulder straps. 'I should get changed before he calls. He wouldn't like me wearing this sort of dress when he's not about.'

Ged was amused – and gratified to hear that she had indeed dressed up for him. 'He's not going to know what you're wearing, is he?'

'Sometimes he asks.'

'You could lie.'

He caught a little flicker of fear, thrown off with the toss of her head. 'Why should I lie? I don't like lying.' She looked down at him, still on the bench. 'Do you lie to your wife?'

'Not if I don't have to.'

'Will you lie about where you've been tonight?'

'I've only been for a walk. I go for a walk almost every night. I got into the habit when we had a dog.'

'What happened to your dog?'

'He died.' He was silent a moment, remembering the dog; a uniquely sober-minded red setter, with a rare sense of his own due and dignity. 'They all do that, eventually.'

He stood up and took her hand. He turned it over in his and tilted the palm towards the nearest lamp, conning the lines he couldn't see, searching for clues to her life. If he were his mother, he would have asked to read her Tarot.

She said with touching timidity, 'What about tomorrow night? It's Saturday.'

'I'm – we're going out to dinner.' We, meaning he and Polly. He found himself wishing *we* were he and Elie. Now that it came to the point, he didn't see how he could last the weekend without touching her. But the park would be crowded, full of children and everyone else, if the weather was fine. 'Can I come and see you? Sunday some time?'

She pulled her hand free. The jerky movement suggested . . . irritation? Alarm? 'You can't come to my flat.'

'You said your boyfriend is away.'

'Yes, but he . . . His friend lives downstairs. He might see you. He watches me come and go.'

'He spies on you for your boyfriend? You mean the bastard doesn't trust you?' He spoke with some anger, an illogical rage in view of what she had just been doing with him.

She didn't seem to share his indignation. 'Well, he's away a lot. Anyway, it's his flat, not mine. I only live there. And I've got to go. He'll get suspicious if I'm late again.'

By Monday, despite having persuaded Polly into sex on Sunday morning as well as Saturday night, Ged felt as if he had just spent a year in a monastery. And when he saw Elie sitting on her usual bench, it felt more like a decade. But he sat down on the far end of the bench as casually as if his cock hadn't suddenly turned itself into a truncheon stuffed down the front of his trousers.

She turned her head to look at him. Her nostrils quivered, her eyelashes flickered, her lips trembled as if not quite daring to smile. He had an impression that something had happened, something had changed things.

'Everything OK?'

'Yes.' She closed her mouth and opened it again. Gorgeous mouth, he thought. He would have to get her to put it around his cock sometime, lipstick and all. 'My boyfriend's coming tomorrow.'

'You don't sound pleased.'

'You're the one who won't be pleased. I can't see you while he's around.'

'Why not? You don't spend your lunch hours with him, do you?'

'He's very jealous. Sometimes he comes to see me in the store, just to . . . just to make sure I'm there.'

'But he can't expect you to be there if you're having your lunch,' Ged said in what he thought was a remarkably reasonable voice, considering how much he suddenly wanted to do something unpleasant to this unknown person.

Her fingers were fidgeting with the chain around her neck. She was staring at the path in front of her. 'I can't. I daren't take the risk.'

'What does this git have going for him? He's lousy in bed,

and he makes a nuisance of himself. Is he rich, or what?'

'Yes.'

'Yes, what?'

'Yes, he's rich. Stinking rich, in fact. So what? Is it a crime to be rich?'

He stared at her, a shop girl wearing the latest in designer clothes. 'So he buys you things, does he? Buys your clothes, for instance?'

'Why shouldn't he?' She sat up, stiff and defensive. 'If he wants to be generous, what's wrong with that?'

'Nothing, nothing. I might even admire a man who knows what he wants and goes out and gets it. Nothing but the best for him: high-class clothes on a high-class tart.'

Elie jumped up and ran.

She couldn't run very fast, in her high-heeled sandals on the gravel path. Ged got up and went after her, caught her and held her in spite of her struggles.

'Let me go. I'm not staying here to be insulted.'

Some prehistoric stratum of his mind wondered whether it was worse for a woman to let a rich man buy her sexual favours, or to let a stranger fuck her for free. But he didn't say anything about that. He found he liked the sensation of holding her against her will, even if she wasn't struggling very hard.

'Let me go,' she repeated. She was still putting up a formal resistance, wrenching herself against his grip like a bluebottle fly ritually thumping against the windowpane. 'I have to get back to work.'

'Will you meet me tonight?'

She stopped her struggle. 'What for?' she wondered, making a rather touching stab at sarcasm. 'I mean, why would an upstanding citizen like you want to hang around with a tart?'

'What do you think? I want to buy you.'

'Isn't he phoning you tonight?'

'Not tonight. He's already on the plane. It's a long way from Beirut.'

They were drinking champagne in a hotel room. Vintage champagne, four-star hotel. He couldn't begin to afford it, but what the hell. Polly thought he was playing cards with Rufus and his mates. He would just have to make bloody sure he got to his credit card statement before she did.

'Why Beirut? What's in Beirut?'

'That's where he lives. He's Lebanese.'

'You mean he doesn't live in London?'

Elie swallowed champagne, looking suddenly flustered. 'Well, he comes here quite a lot. That's why he keeps the flat.'

'And why he keeps you.'

She set her glass down, with a certain emphasis. 'I didn't come here to listen to snide remarks.'

'No, I know. You came here to get fucked.'

She stood up and slapped him. He liked that. Such a delightfully old-fashioned way to behave. As old-fashioned as the concept of a kept woman. Maybe she had learned these things from the romantic rubbish she read.

He stood up too. She backed away. He caught her by the wrist.

It was a game, he understood that. A game to get them where they both wanted to go. She liked games; he liked that in her, too. So many things he liked about her. He would have to find out what sort of games she liked best.

'Not a good idea, hitting me,' he said quite softly. 'I can hit you back. Harder.'

He watched her swallow. She must have had trouble swallowing, because she put up her free hand to stroke her throat. To stroke that god-damned golden chain.

'Did he put that collar on you?'

'What collar?'

She looked genuinely puzzled. He put a fingertip to her throat, ran it under the offending chain. 'This. You always wear it.'

She went to touch it, and touched his finger instead. He couldn't tell how much of an accident that was. 'He made me promise to wear it. To remind me of him.'

He twisted the chain around his finger, maybe making it a little too tight for her comfort. She put up her hands instinctively, to protect herself. 'Ged, what are you doing?'

'Reminding you of him.' He looped his finger under the chain again, pulling it tighter still. Playing games.

Elie astonished him by falling to her knees, grabbing his wrist with both hands as she went down. 'Please don't. Please don't hurt me.'

She seemed to be in genuine fear. He was appalled and ashamed, as if he had casually threatened to punish a dog and then discovered that its previous master used to thrash it.

He squatted down beside her and disentangled his hand from the chain. 'Is that what he does? He hurts you?'

She shook her head dumbly. Her eyes were still frightened, still fighting to hide it.

He wasn't sure if he believed her. It didn't matter, he would find out. He was going to find out everything about her. He took hold of the chain with both hands and jerked in opposite directions.

It snapped quite easily; it was twenty-two carat gold, soft and nearly pure. Nothing but the best from that bastard.

If he had thought she was afraid before, that was nothing to her response now. 'What have you done?' She grabbed at his hands, at the ends of the chain dangling from his fist. Under her make-up, she was white with fear. 'You've broken it! What have you done? He'll kill me!'

He stood up and drew back, keeping possession of the chain. 'Tell him it was an accident. Accidents happen all the time.'

'Give it back to me. It's mine. He gave it to me.' Her light voice slipped easily into a soft childish mode. 'Please, please, please, give it back to me.'

He turned his back on her terror. God, what a callous shit she was turning him into. Allowing him to turn

himself into. He stretched himself out on the bed, tucking
the hand with the chain under his head. He hadn't bothered to take off his shoes. He was paying a bloody fortune
for the privilege of putting his shoes on the bed. 'Persuade
me.'

She recovered at least a little of her composure, enough
to get her off her knees. Enough to let her realize that he
was only playing games. 'How?'

'Take your clothes off. Do it nicely.'

Elie turned her back to him, as if out of modesty. Her
dress was a skimpy, stretchy little black number, the kind
that took about a yard of material and cost several
hundred pounds. Undoubtedly bought for her by her
Lebanese owner, who wouldn't like her wearing it when
he wasn't around. She took hold of the hem with both
hands and pulled it up, peeling the dress off over her head
like some exotic insect shedding its skin to metamorphose
into a sexual stage. She did this slowly, almost dreamily,
with unselfconscious sensuality: the changeling creature
uncovering and discovering its new self.

She had her arms crossed over her head, the skirt of the
dress a veil before her face, a crescent of bare back
showing between the black fabric of the dress and the
waistband of her sheer black tights. Under the tights, her
knickers were visible only as a black triangle across the
lower back, a V with the point disappearing into the cleft
of her bottom. The skin of black nylon made her pale flesh
dusky, as if the metamorphosis had included a change of
race into something more southern. It also made her legs
the same colour from heel to hip, two long stems of female
flesh swelling upwards into buttocks like the fruit of
fantasy. The black seam of the tights divided one perfect
ripe roundness from another.

To Ged it was a glimpse of sexual paradise, a fleeting
image of essential femaleness, and all the more powerful
for appearing almost accidentally. As if he had been
loitering invisibly in her bedroom, had caught her

unawares as she went about her private female rituals, mundane and mysterious.

The dress went on upwards and over her head. She draped it neatly over the back of a chair. The prim gesture with which she smoothed the skirt inflamed him even further. He would have thought that an impossibility, since every ounce of blood in his body already seemed to be devoted to the physical expression of a state of extreme sexual excitement.

Bending towards the mirror, her eyes lowered to avoid meeting his in the glass, she unhooked her bra. She sat down on the corner of the bed to remove the tights, then stood up again with her back to him while she took her knickers off. This time it was not a private act; she was shedding the last of her defences, leaving herself entirely vulnerable to him.

As foreplay, it was a dynamite performance.

He swung his feet over the side of the bed and stood up. With a gesture he invited – commanded – her to take his place. When she lay down, he knotted the broken chain around her ankle. Now she had her precious collar back. And this time, he had put it on her.

She touched the chain, to acknowledge that it was there. Then she curled up on her left side, away from him, wrapping her arms around herself, leaving nothing visible but her limbs and back.

Even her modesty aroused him. Something more to strip off her, now that she was naked. 'Why don't you show me what you've got?'

She looked up at him, oddly shy and curious as a kitten. 'What do you mean?'

'You know what they do in those magazines. They hold their pussy open.'

He thought she was going to claim that she'd never read any of those magazines. No bloody romance in them, after all. But she surprised him. She raised one knee, keeping her feet together, making a wide angle between her thighs.

She used one hand to do what he had asked, not moving her gaze from his face.

He paused with his shirt half off, leaned over to touch her: a light, almost gentle touch, exploratory rather than invasive. It wasn't just his wishful thinking; her performance had turned her on as well as him.

He came down naked to the bed, pulled her feet apart, put his head between her legs.

The secret smell of a woman filled his mouth and nostrils, choking him with pleasure. He began to eat her out, licking, sucking, nipping, nibbling, flicking his tongue like a seductive snake into every crevice and crack, intoxicating himself with the heady, earthy taste and odour of her arousal. He had to hold her by the hips to stop her thrashing about. To keep his snout in her trough, so to speak.

She locked her legs around his neck and climaxed, shrieking like a siren (the mermaid kind), all but drowning him in her.

When he came up for air, she was splayed across the bed, still heaving and gulping for breath like a landed fish. Surrender, of sorts.

He took her body captive inch by inch, again using his mouth and teeth and tongue. He worked his way up her, leaving her belly and breasts damp with the odour of her own orgasm, a gamy and unladylike spoor to mask the delicate, *respectable* scent of her perfume.

At last he kissed her mouth, putting his tongue in.

She opened her eyes. The look in them was a little dazed, even a little scared. She knew he had won. She belonged to him now. The chain on her ankle proved that.

But she spoke up bravely enough, deliberately insolent. 'You're a bloody caveman.'

'You're a fucking tart.'

'So fuck me.'

She wrapped her arms and legs around him, sliding her body into its proper place beneath him, like a lock presenting itself for the turning of the key.

96

He had meant to make her take him in her mouth, meant to come in her face, to show her who was her real master, not that god-damned Arab. But before he could pull himself up, his cock had homed in to her cunt, or maybe her pussy had kissed his prick. However it happened, they were hopelessly deep in sexual congress before he could do what he had intended.

Whatever that was. He couldn't quite remember any more. He couldn't recall any world before her, any time prior to this moment.

The elemental pleasure of holding her and having her was moving him now: moving to increase her pleasure and postpone his own, moving them both together towards climax. She came again, in a spastic flurry of arms and legs, squealing as if he had tied her up and tortured her.

He hardly heard. He was coming too. Spilling himself, irretrievably deep, into the unknown heart of her.

There was an after, of course. And a before.

In the after he was lying on his back, a cigarette in one hand. The other hand was stroking Elie's arm that lay across his chest, running his thumb along the inner edge between shoulder and elbow. Getting to know the shape and feel of her.

'What's this?'

Her face was pressed into the crook where his shoulder met his neck. He could feel her lips move, feel the warm explosion of breath when she spoke. 'What?'

'These little . . . scars, are they?' Small silver lines, criss-crossing the inner curve of the arm. He turned it to get a better look at them. Random marks, no pattern to them. He couldn't imagine what kind of accident could have produced wounds like that, and in such an unlikely place. 'How did you get them?'

She had gone rigid as he spoke. She pulled her arm away. 'They're old.'

As an answer, it might have been calculated to arouse

his interest. Her left arm was behind his head; he raised himself on one elbow and caught her by the wrist before she could withdraw it. It bore the same markings, but more densely. There were none on the lower arm, none on the outer side of the arm. If you wanted to keep some damage secret, the inner skin of the upper arm was probably as good a place as any: a surface that would almost always be held facing the torso.

She stared at him, daring him to ask again. He was holding her by the wrist; he ran the fingers of his free hand up her arm, from wrist to breast. They were very small scars, only visible because there were so many, and he was so close.

'Who did it?'

She looked away. 'I did.'

'You cut yourself?' He turned her head to face him. He wanted to see what was in her eyes. 'Why did you do that?'

'I suppose I wasn't very happy at the time.' She put her hand over his, where it was holding her jaw, making her look at him. She didn't try to pull his hand away. She stroked it. 'No-one else ever noticed.'

'Because you did it where it wouldn't show.'

'It wasn't meant to be a ploy for attention.'

'What else was it? Self-mutilation, that's seriously mad behaviour.'

'Then I must have been mad.' Since she couldn't turn away from him, she closed her eyes. 'I was ashamed of myself for doing it. But I was ashamed of myself for all sorts of reasons then.'

Then? When was then? 'Such as?'

'I'll tell you some time. Not now.' She ran her hand up his arm, the way he had done to her. Pale female hand upon swarthy male skin, like an old Egyptian painting. 'Right now we're supposed to be enjoying ourselves.'

He went back to the bench the next day, even though she had said she wouldn't be there. He didn't quite believe her, not after the night before. He didn't really believe she could keep away from him, no more than he could keep away from her.

But she was true to her word. The only person there was a fat woman feeding pigeons.

He stayed away himself after that, at least until Friday. The longest four days of his life, hoping and fearing that her bloody boyfriend had gone home sooner than expected, and that she herself had been waiting in vain. But even on Friday the bench was without her.

Monday he had a lunch date to go to. He felt absurdly virtuous about avoiding the park. But then he disgraced himself by walking through later in the evening. Like a dog sniffing for some lingering scent of a bitch, he told himself scornfully.

Tuesday he saw her. He made himself walk past without looking, and keep going without looking back. When he heard the irregular crunch of high heels punching through gravel, he walked even faster.

'Mr Hawke!'

He was so surprised that he stopped. She caught him up, touching her hand to his arm with a breathless, nervous, tentative shyness, as if he were a stranger. As he was, of course.

Except that she had called him by his name, which he had never revealed to her.

'Mr Hawke, I wonder if you could autograph your book for me?'

She was holding out a copy of *Old Adam*. He stared at the book, then at her. She waited, unsmiling, still with that curious shyness.

'Is this a joke?'

'Isn't it – isn't it yours?'

'Yes, but how on earth—?'

'Not my sort of book, you mean?'

That was her dig at him, not the other way round. He had the grace to regret, though not quite to acknowledge, his unthinking intellectual snobbery.

But she was offering an explanation anyway. 'I was in a

book shop yesterday and they had a big stack of these, on a table right in front of the door. I don't know why I picked one up, but I did, and then I saw your picture on the back flap, so I bought it.' She spoke breathlessly, from the run perhaps, and diffidently now. 'Will you sign it for me?'

He had waited a week to see her again, and had wanted her so much, every minute of those seven days and nights, that he had thought when he met her next he would need to throw her down wherever they happened to be and screw her on the spot. But now, seeing her standing almost humbly before him, her lovely face flushed with some strong feeling that overrode the tyranny of her make-up . . .

Now he discovered in himself quite other, and more dismaying, responses. Emotions, not desires. The caveman she had accused him of being stood abashed, struggling to invent lyric poetry out of the stunted, savage vocabulary of rape and pillage.

He said gently, 'I'll sign it when you've read it.'

She looked down at the book, assessing its contents. 'How will you know I've actually read it? I could just read the blurb and try to bluff.'

'I'll be sure to interrogate you thoroughly. What makes you imagine reading it will be a chore?'

'Oh, I'm sure it won't be.' She gathered the book to her bosom and held it there with both arms. He envied his own creation. 'I browsed a bit and it actually looked quite good.'

'So glad you approve,' he said sardonically, and then repented of this unwarranted brutality in the face of her apparently honest enthusiasm. 'Has the Beast of Beirut gone home, then?'

'Don't call him that. He's quite nice really. But no, he's gone to New York. He'll be back on Friday.'

'Does he keep a girl in New York as well?'

'I don't know.' The idea appeared to take her by surprise. 'He's never said.'

'Well, he wouldn't, would he? But would you care if he did?'

'I don't know.' Again the novelty of the question was made clear by her tone. She added pointedly, 'But it's nothing to do with you, is it, whatever he does?'

Just as long as he's not doing whatever-it-is to you, he thought.

But that thought itself was improper, and alarming. It really was nothing to do with him. She was nothing to do with him. Having sex with a woman didn't automatically invest that woman with any significance in his life. And this one was a whore, just as much as the ones who stood on the street corner. Calling her someone's mistress didn't alter the basis of the oldest transaction in the world, money for sex.

But he hadn't bought her. He had had her for free.

And he wanted her again, free or for sale.

'How are you getting on with the book?'

'I'm only on page ninety-two. I can't read it as fast as usual,' Elie explained apologetically. 'Sometimes I have to reread bits to make sure I've understood them.'

'It's harder when you don't know what's going to happen, is it?'

'But more exciting.' She looked more nervous than excited, as she sipped wine and glanced around the tiny restaurant. 'I've got to be back by eleven again. Ben said he'd ring me before he got on the plane.'

Ged glanced at his watch. 'It's only nine-thirty. You've plenty of time.'

He was surprised himself by the earliness of the hour. Before coming here, he had spent the briefest eternity of his existence in a hotel room with her, alternating between frantic fucking and leisurely lovemaking. For the previous two days they had only managed to squeeze a couple of couplings into hasty late-night meetings in the park, brief animal encounters of a sort that merely fuelled his desire for her.

And hers for him, to judge by her behaviour in the hotel room. She had had the gold chain repaired, she said, but she no longer wore it when she was with him. Along with the collar, she had shed that odd air of submission which must have become a habit in her dealings with the man who paid her rent. For Ged she was free now, in more ways than one: showing preference in her pleasures, allowing herself the indulgence of his attentions, and responding to him with the intensity of long self-denial.

He looked at her now, recalled her as she was an hour ago. Her composure had been restored along with her make-up, but he chose to detect a dusky flush still glowing under the artifice. If only it could have been visible tomorrow, when she met her master again.

'Ben? That's his name? What's the rest of it?'

'It's a really long name. Ben is just the middle bit. He tells everyone here in London to call him that, because English people have such trouble saying his real name.'

'Including you.' She raises artlessness to an art form, he thought in sour admiration. Impossible to press her on any matter, when she simply yielded at every point. She left him feeling like a brute of unparalleled insensitivity, without anything even gained by brute force. This time he persisted, trying another angle. 'How did you meet him?'

'He was buying perfume.' She paused fractionally. 'For his wife.'

That was meant to put him in his place, and almost succeeded. 'Is she Lebanese too?'

'No, French.'

'He tells you all about her, does he?'

She took no notice of the sarcasm. 'Why shouldn't he? It's not as if I wanted to marry him.'

'Why don't you want to marry him?'

It was so easy to take her by surprise, and so pointless. She struggled to articulate the obvious. 'Well, I wouldn't want him around all the time. Not for the rest of my life. I'm not in love with him, or anything like that.'

What was like love? Pity or passion, maybe. Or even

comfort. Enough like love for a while, at least. Enough to pass muster and cause marriage. Enough to ruin a life.

He had a thought – no, not so well formed as a thought, only an inkling of an idea – that his own life was ruined. The only life he would ever have, half over, and ruined. He was married to a good woman, with two healthy, handsome children. Married to a woman who did not move him, with children who had turned into secretive strangers. And he had no hope of immortality through his indifferent writings, wrung so painfully from a Beta-minus talent. He had long ago, he imagined, reconciled himself to the notion of dying without hope, but living without hope was a much harder thing.

What had happened to that innate expectation of the unexpected, that wishful promise of excitement still to be experienced, which had for so long duped him into dealing with existence? When, where, had it gone?

Damned if he knew. But at any rate it had come back. Reappeared a couple of weeks ago.

His life was still ruined, of course. The only thing more disastrous than being married to a boring woman, et cetera, was having all that and this too. Married to a worthy woman and besotted by a whore.

He would have hailed her a taxi, but Elie said she would walk. It was only a short way from here, she said.

He didn't know how she could even walk across the street in the sort of shoes she liked to wear, vampish things with four-inch heels and often not much else to them. Dead sexy, of course. 'I'll walk you home.'

'It's all right. I'll be all right on my own.'

'Are you worried about your friend's friend spotting me? I don't have to go right up to your front door.'

Seeing that he wasn't going to go away, and eleven o'clock was coming closer, she eventually agreed to be accompanied, at least to the corner of her street. On the way he entertained a fantasy about following her into her flat and making love to her there, of doing things to her body to drive her to distraction while she was talking to her keeper on the telephone.

Why only a fantasy? There was nothing impossible about it.

'Let me come up with you.'

'No. Go away. I shouldn't have let you come this far.'

He caught her arm. 'What if I don't let you go?' He made a show of consulting his watch. 'You've only got five minutes to get up there. What will he do if you're not there to answer the phone?'

'Ged, let me go. I have to go.'

She was speaking softly, so as not to attract the attention of passers-by, but she was pleading in earnest. When he didn't answer, didn't release her, he felt her go rigid. Her fingernails, elegantly manicured and painted, scratched at his hand. Like a dog scratching at the door to be let out, he thought.

She was whimpering rather like a dog, too. At least like a child. 'Please, Ged. Please.'

'Only three minutes now.'

Alarm turned to panic. For a moment he thought she might attack him in earnest. One-handed. 'Please.'

'Why? What will he do to you?'

She pulled herself up and together, apparently seeing for herself the futility of physical resistance. 'If you don't let me go right now, I'll never see you again.'

By her choice, did she mean, or by his doing, this Levantine godling who made her shake with terror? No time to ask, no point in asking. Ged let her go.

With only one thought in her head, the need to reach the flat and the telephone, she didn't even look back to see him watching her. Watching which door she fled to.

He noted the number. Committed it to memory.

We should spare some pity for our ancestor Adam, so unjustly cursed by so many for so long; and for Eve his wife, branded temptress in the vain hope of saving us from our own sins. For everyone before they're done will have tasted the bitter fruit of knowledge. And always of their own free will, that two-edged gift of God.

In this case too, banishment followed. Ged was forbidden to see her or speak to her, as long as her master was in town. And she did this, not out of faithfulness but from fear. Fear of what, exactly, she never said. She wouldn't even admit to her terror. But he could smell it in her. Taste it even, when he kissed her goodbye at the corner of the street.

He knew the first few letters of her first name. He knew the house where she lived, but not which floor she lived on. He knew every painted nuance of her countenance, the depths and curves of her body, the smell of her perfume and of her desire. Nothing, and everything. A stranger and a haunting.

This time he only endured his exile for a day and a night before taking action. He began a systematic search of the perfume sellers of Knightsbridge.

When he found her, he was surprised by his own sense of relief. Not that he had tracked her down, but that she hadn't lied to him. She was caged within an artificial island festooned with bottles and boxes in co-ordinating colours and bearing the name of a well-known couturier.

Elie seemed startled to see him. 'What are you doing here?'

'Isn't this a perfume counter?'

'Yes, of course it is.'

'Then I suppose I must have come to buy perfume.'

That startled her even more. 'Really? Do you know which scent?'

'No, not really. I came to see you.'

She put on a primly scandalized face, as if he had made an obscene proposal. 'You're not allowed. I told you.'

'That's absurd. Why can't I talk to you?'

She looked around at the aisles full of potential customers, negotiating the reefs and shallows of her department in order to get to wherever they really wanted to go. Whether because it was considered a glamorous attraction, or because no-one would ever buy cosmetics or perfume if they didn't have to navigate these siren-haunted straits to get into the store, it was a curious fact that every department store in the country set up its most frivolous stall right in front of the main entrance.

'It's dangerous. He might see us.'

'Don't be silly. A big-shot wheeler-dealer millionaire must have better things to do here in London than spend all day spying on you.'

'I told you, he stops by to see me when he's in the store. But he doesn't like me working here. He says it's common.'

'Where does he think you should work?'

'He doesn't want me to work. He wants me to travel around with him. Last night he offered me lots of money to be his personal assistant.'

'And you don't want lots of money?'

'Of course I do. Everyone does.'

Elie turned away then, moving over to tend to a real customer, enquiring in a soft little singsong if she could help them. Another one came up and lurked while she dealt with the first person.

Ged gave up, temporarily. He hung around a neighbouring counter with a rival's name plastered all over its products, trying to look like a man waiting for his wife. It was a quarter of an hour by the clock, half a year by his own reckoning, before he managed to have a word with her again.

'Don't you get a tea break or something?'

'Yes, of course. They have to give us breaks, it's the law.'

'Good for the law. When is it?'

She consulted her watch – a very expensive one, no doubt a gift from Lebanon – and made a small but fetching moue as she reflected on the results of the consultation. 'In about half an hour.'

'Then I'll be back in half an hour.'

'No, don't,' she said, flustered. 'Just wait outside that door over there. I'll come out and talk to you.'

He went away and came back in twenty minutes, just to be on the safe side. He stayed as near to the door as he could, while still keeping an eye on her. It wasn't that he didn't trust her not to disappear in a different direction, he told himself.

He told himself all sorts of things, but none of them could disguise the humiliation of his position. One thing he couldn't manage to tell himself was that he was in the grip of some grand passion, or that she was a woman of rare capabilities. Rare beauty, yes, but that was no excuse for him to be behaving like this, hanging around the fucking cosmetics department, grinding his teeth with jealousy and rage, waiting for some other bugger's floozy to condescend to speak to him.

Putting it like that finally drove him out of the door, if only to leave himself some nether level to which he could still sink. To which, at least for a while, he could congratulate himself on not yet having reached.

When at last she came out, she insisted on walking while they talked. They walked in a big circle around the block, their conversation being interrupted from time to time by strangers passing between them, or momentarily overwhelmed by the turmoil of traffic.

'So what are you going to do?'

'What do you mean?'

'I mean, are you going to take up this job offer?'

He had done his best to put inverted commas of sarcasm around the last two words, but she didn't notice, or chose not to. 'I don't know. I told him I'd think about it.'

'What's there to think about? Money's money, isn't it?'

He was icy with fury by now, but again she responded to the literal sense rather than the tone of what he said. 'Yes, but I don't know if I could stand to be around him all the time. He's very . . . demanding.'

'I can just imagine.' And he could. It was horrible, imagining what her master might demand of her. All the things he wanted from her himself.

They were coming up to the door again. She uttered her usual refrain. 'I've got to go now.'

'When—' He couldn't make himself say it. 'When . . .'

She leaned towards him, touched her fingertips to his arms. Just enough to make him an object, an obstacle to be passed around rather than a goal to be passed through. 'He's going to Amsterdam tomorrow. But he'll be back again the day after that.'

'You're not supposed to be here. Ben wouldn't like it.'

Elie waved a flurry of frosty pink nails at the contents of the flat. An elegant flat, a suitable backdrop for her. Whatever else one might denounce him for, her master had either excellent taste or the sense to hire the services of someone who did. The latter, more likely; the flavour of the place was generic rather than individual.

She giggled and covered her mouth, looking over her pink-tipped hand with huge amused eyes. 'He wouldn't like it at all.'

'What would he do if he knew?'

For once she didn't seem much concerned. Perhaps it was the soothing effect of the brandy they were now enjoying. Brandy often had that effect, especially when taken after champagne and claret. Also, it was only ten-thirty, and she was sitting right next to the telephone. 'Throw me out, I guess.'

'Is that all?'

'Isn't that enough? Where would I go? I couldn't afford a place of my own.'

'You could flat-share with friends. That's what most people do.'

'I don't know anyone I'd want to live with. Anyway, this place is so nice, I really wouldn't want to give it up.'

She was curled up on the small settee, managing to look appealingly childish and immensely feminine at the same time. Ged had made himself comfortable in a chair opposite, a position which gave him the best opportunity to admire her. Admire her appearance, at least. He wondered if she knew what she was saying. He decided to translate for her. 'So you're perfectly happy to sell your body to this bastard in exchange for somewhere to live, is that it?'

'That's what everyone does, isn't it? Every woman, I mean.'

'I think there's usually a certain amount of sentimental attachment in the equation.'

'Hypocrisy, you mean.'

This cold-blooded cynicism unnerved him, coming from her, spoken in her soft girlish voice. 'If you're talking about traditional marriage, it was meant to be an arrangement for raising children. Children were the point of it, not flats in Mayfair and designer clothing. Anyway, you told me he already has a wife and a family back in Beirut. You're not married to him, and you're not really even living with him. You're just making yourself sexually available whenever he wants you.'

'What's wrong with that? So it's a business arrangement, OK, so what? I can walk out whenever I want to.'

'It's prostitution, that's what's wrong with it. What's the difference between you and the tarts at King's Cross?'

'I live here, that's the difference. This is my home. My mother lived with my father and he paid the mortgage and bought her clothes and everybody thought that was OK. Are you saying it's a marriage certificate that makes the difference? Nobody believes that nowadays.'

'And does your mother approve of your relationship with this guy?'

'She doesn't know about it.'

'Why not? Why don't you take him home for Sunday lunch? "This is Ben, I can't remember his last name, he pays my rent and screws me whenever he's in town."'

Elie looked appalled, but not for the obvious reasons. 'I couldn't do that. He'd think I was crazy. And he'd think she was . . . I think he'd laugh at her.'

'What's so funny about your mother?'

'Nothing. She's not funny at all. She's terrible. She nearly ruined my life.'

'Everybody's mother does that.' But he was intrigued. Another little piece of knowledge. 'How did she ruin your life?'

'She tried to turn me into a model.'

A cigarette was necessary before this dreadful story could be told. She lit one with her usual grace, and smoked it with the air of an angel addicted to the devil's pleasures. 'She signed me up with an agency when I was fifteen. I got quite a lot of work, enough to mess up my exams. I left school without anything to show for it. But I was making good money at modelling, so it didn't seem to matter.'

She stopped speaking but went on smoking, staring into space.

He prompted her gently. 'And then?'

'Well, it— I was— Well, it's a crazy way to live. They make you starve and they treat you like cattle. On about your weight all the time, sizing you up like a piece of horse-flesh, till you feel guilty for even looking at food. Everybody's on drugs. You have to be, you couldn't stand it otherwise. And there are lots of guys who . . . well, I suppose you could call it a bribe. Not even a business arrangement.'

'And that's all your mother's fault?'

'She wouldn't let me quit. She was thrilled that I was famous for being beautiful. If I'd been brain-dead it wouldn't have mattered to her, just as long as I looked good. She'd always dressed me up in frilly clothes and kept my hair long, bows and curls and all that sort of thing. That's what men really care about, she told me. Brains won't do you any good, she used to say, it's a pretty face that comes out on top every time. I told her I hated modelling, but I couldn't tell her about all the rest of it. I couldn't, could I? How could I tell her I was going around like a zombie all the time, and having sex with people I didn't even want to know?'

She ground out her half-smoked cigarette, pressing her thumb down on the still-glowing tip without even noticing. Her face had changed, gone almost gaunt with tension, giving her a new and alarming sort of beauty.

He recalled the little scars. 'Is that when you started to cut yourself?'

'Yeah.' She wouldn't look at him. Afraid of what he might see, maybe. 'It sounds crazy, and probably it was. The first time, I had a razor blade. I was thinking about cutting my wrists. Only thinking about it. And it sounds silly, but I thought I couldn't stand the pain. So I . . . sort of tested. Higher up, where it wouldn't show.'

'Where it wouldn't hurt so much?'

She shook her head, ignoring his sarcasm. Her dark hair swung with artful naturalness. 'I told you it sounds crazy. But it made me feel better, I don't know why. Even the pain was a kind of release. Drawing blood made me feel real, somehow. And scars are anti-beauty, aren't they? It was like giving the whole rotten circus one in the eye. And then when no-one noticed, I realized I could do it any time I wanted. It gave me a weird sensation of power. Like smoking dope in Scotland Yard.'

Still she didn't look at him. She looked at her hands, which were holding each other. 'Finally I had— I went— Well, they called it a nervous breakdown. My mother called it a nervous breakdown. It makes me sound like a delicate little flower who couldn't cope with the cruel hard world. What happened was, I tried to kill myself. Alcohol and pills, very original. They put me into one of those places for a while, the private ones where they keep you doped and tell you not to worry, and smother you with flowers. You can't really go crazy in a place like that. It wouldn't seem like appropriate behaviour.'

'How did you get from there to here?'

'When I came out, someone from the agency found me this job. Selling perfume. No serious stress, no certificates of education required, just a pretty face and a proper accent. Maybe my mother was right after all. But I was living at home again, and I couldn't stand that. My mother was really disappointed in me for messing up my big chance, and she just couldn't stop telling me about it.

'Then Ben came along and made me an offer. A proposal, he called it' – she gave a little laugh – 'but not the usual kind. And I thought . . . well, I thought I could handle that.' She stirred, as if breathing for the first time in a long time, and lit herself another cigarette. 'It's been OK.'

Ged held out the brandy bottle – Ben's bottle, finest French cognac, a couple of centuries old, astronomically expensive, all of which added immensely to his enjoyment of it – and she held up her glass for refilling. 'But not so OK that you don't feel the need to pick up strangers in the park.'

'As OK as your marriage, I should think,' she said sharply. 'And you're the only stranger I've ever picked up.'

'Why did you do that? I've often wondered.'

'I just liked the look of you.' She rubbed her glass with the palm of her hand. 'No, that's not true. I chose you because I wanted to find out what was behind that impenetrable face.'

She had chosen *him*? Well, she had, of course. It was only that he'd never thought of it like that.

She gave him a guileless glance, with one of those infinitesimal smiles that he found so alluring. 'Do you have children?'

'Yes.'

'Little ones?'

'Big ones. I've been living in a household hell of adolescent angst for years. Don't let me tell you about it.'

'That's all right, I don't want to know. I have enough to feel bad about.' She looked at her wrist. 'He'll be ringing in a quarter of an hour.' The thought made her visibly uneasy.

'Was your mother afraid of your father?'

'What? What do you mean?'

'You were comparing this' – he waved the bottle around the room – 'to your parents' marriage. I was wondering how well it compared.'

'You think I'm afraid of Ben?'

'You think you're not?'

'Well, he doesn't beat me, if that's what you're thinking.'

'Bully for him. So what does he do, to make you afraid of him?'

'I'm not. I wouldn't be here if I was.'

'Maybe you're here because you're even more afraid of leaving him. What would he do if you left him?'

She got up and walked towards the window, away from him. 'I told you, it's a business arrangement. I can change my mind any time I like.'

'But what if you left him for someone else? You said he's the jealous type.' Unlike me, he thought sardonically. 'What if he thought you'd been taking his money and putting out for someone else? He might think he'd been swindled.'

She swung around to face him, her voice high with anger but low in volume. She was, as in the cliché, even more beautiful when she was angry. 'What do you want me to say? That he'd send someone round to beat you up or kill you? He's not a gangster, or anything like that.'

'Would you know if he was?'

'I think I would. He takes me out with his business associates, you know. That's partly what he wants me for, to socialize with him and let him show me off to his clients.'

'So it's not all blow jobs and buggery.'

Elie looked surprised and faintly embarrassed, which amused him. He had only been guessing, and aiming to annoy. In her own unlikely – and to him endearing – manner, she was as prudish as any maiden aunt, if such creatures still existed. She said primly, 'He's much more interested in business than in sex.'

'Then he must have a very interesting business. What does he do for his clients?'

'What does he do for them? What do you mean?'

'If they're his clients, he must be selling them something. What's his line? How does he make his money?'

'I'm not sure. I've asked him about it, but he's always quite vague. He says he runs a general trading company, and he has to keep an eye out all the time for a good deal. But that's not a crime, is it?'

'Profitable commodities aren't always legal.'

'If you mean drugs,' she said huffily, 'I'm sure he wouldn't be involved in anything like that.' Again she eyed her watch. 'He'll be ringing any minute now.'

'Then there's not a minute to lose.'

He crossed the room to sit down in the corner of the settee where she had been sitting, next to the telephone. He caught her hand to pull her down to him.

To his surprise and gratification, she came down willingly. She let him kiss her, even let him unbutton her high-necked dress to caress her breasts. But very soon she felt obliged to remind him that she had only let him come up on condition that they didn't make love. 'It wouldn't be right, not in his flat,' she repeated.

'Honour among whores,' he murmured. It was confided to her left breast, and she either didn't hear or decided not to hear.

She jumped when the phone rang. Literally jumped, right out of his arms. But he caught the sensation of her heart leaping violently with instant tension and terror.

She was standing to attention, speaking to the man in Amsterdam. Ged heard her saying she had been out for dinner with an old school friend, explaining away her breathlessness because she had only just come in.

While she murmured lies to her master, her lover unbuttoned her dress all the way, and stripped her of her knickers. He pushed down his trousers, pulled her down on to his cock.

She couldn't say no, couldn't make a fuss, couldn't do

anything that would even hint that she was not alone. She had to let him fuck her while she was obliged to murmur inanities to another man.

The situation clearly aroused her, enough to overcome her fear. She began to move her body with some abandon, and to hide her mouth in his hair in order to muffle her grunts of pleasure. She told Ben, in even more breathless tones, that she had to go and pee.

She dropped the phone, and slammed herself down upon Ged with frantic deliberateness, uttering sounds of sheer animal sensuality and sexual extremity that would normally never have got anywhere near her lips. Her hair flew into wild disorder, her face contorted into agonies of delight.

It was enough to bring any man to orgasm. And so it did: the only man around, at least. The only one on hand to enjoy her display of violent physical pleasure, along with the sensations it provoked in him.

'You weren't supposed to do that. You promised.'

She must have hoped to sound indignant, or at least reproachful, but the lineaments of desire satisfied betrayed themselves in her face, giving the lie to her complaint. She was clinging to him, damp and limp.

'I couldn't help it. You're irresistible.'

'Don't you try to make it my fault. What if he heard?'

'Heard what? I didn't say a word.'

'You know what I mean.' It still embarrassed her, the idea of making noise while making love. In contemporary culture, the whole of the Western world was desperate to display itself as sensual to the point of idiocy, but Elie would have preferred to pretend that she didn't know the meaning of the word.

'Tell him you were turned on by the sound of his voice,' Ged suggested dryly.

She sat up, still astride him, absent-mindedly running a hand up the back of her neck and into her hair. Everything she did was so graceful, so pleasing to the eye, that he reckoned she could have made a living by charging people to watch her go about her ordinary affairs. And maybe that was what she did; it was one way of describing her relationship with Ben.

She was describing it now, in another way. 'He wouldn't believe me. It's not . . . not like that between us.'

'So you said. A business arrangement, you said. What's jealousy got to do with business?'

'He wouldn't be jealous, exactly. But he always says he's bought the exclusive rights to me.'

'Then he's cheating you. You're worth more than he's giving you.'

She ran her hand up the back of his neck, into his hair, just the way she had done it to herself. Only this way round it was a million times more sensual, and not remotely absent-minded. 'Why don't you make me a better offer?'

Since her mouth was so close, he kissed it. 'I haven't got any money.'

'Money isn't everything.'

And there it was, the incredible, dreaded thing. The miracle that his subterranean self had prayed for, that his conscious mind had feared all along. This marvellous creature, sexy as sin and puritanically prim, wanted him to marry her. Or something like that.

You couldn't trust anybody these days, not even a whore picked up in the park.

He disentangled her arms from around him. 'I'm not sure what you have in mind, but I can't even afford to keep you in a bedsit in Clapham. I have a mortgage to pay and a family to support, remember? And my books are un-fortunately not number one international bestsellers.'

She stared at him for a measured moment. The lambent clarity of her eyes was . . . not clouded, not darkened . . . veiled, perhaps. She had withdrawn her soul from his observation.

And now she withdrew her body. She stood up and buttoned up. 'You'd better go. Sometimes he rings back later.'

*   *   *

When he got back to domesticity, Polly had gone to bed. Louise was watching television at the back of the house, with the cat in her lap. Either she had been out earlier in the evening, or she had taken to wearing mascara and eyeliner to school. Thirteen going on eighteen was how she looked. Perhaps an understudy to Cleopatra.

She might have been going about like that for months, he realized, and he only noticing now because he had been sensitized to such things by Elie's artifices. But upon reflection he decided that the embellished eyes had appeared quite recently, as a result of her acquisition of contact lenses. She had only had them about a month, and already managed to lose one. Luckily you could get insurance for such calamities.

Calum wasn't home yet, according to Louise.

'What's he doing out so late on a week night?' Ged demanded, as if Louise were her brother's keeper.

'Same as you, I expect.'

He had to struggle to stop his face from jumping around.

At least it felt like a struggle, though he knew from other people's reactions to him that his features were not inclined to be expressive of his feelings. Come to that, his feelings were not inclined to be expressive of whatever it was went on inside his head. Now he wasn't sure which was worse, the idea of his adolescent son having sex with some foolish young female, or the notion that his own adultery was somehow visible to his daughter. A spiritual Scarlet Letter, maybe, screaming out to the psychically gifted.

He made himself ask. 'Which is?'

'Getting pissed.'

She hadn't taken her eyes off the TV screen, he realized, so it couldn't be anything in his appearance. The smell, might it be? A bouquet of champagne and claret and cognac. Disguising, it only now occurred to him, the smell of sex and the scent of all the elements that made

117

up Elie's elaborate cosmetic façade. He wanted to defend himself, but had an idea it might be safer to allow the lesser accusation.

Or better still, not to answer to it at all. After all, he was the parent, supposedly the one in charge around here. He didn't have to excuse himself to a child.

He said evenly (he thought), 'Surely a man can enjoy a few drinks without being denounced as an alcoholic.'

'Don't try to defend yourself, Daddy. It only makes you sound guiltier. Anyway, *I* don't care if you want to make a pathetic attempt to relive your youth by carousing with Rufie.'

'Well, if *you* don't care, why mention it?'

'I only mention it because Mummy did. Just before she went upstairs.'

'And did she by any chance tell you to go to bed, just before she went upstairs?'

That put the shoe smartly on the other foot. Louise looked sulky. She scrunched herself down further into the depths of the sofa. 'I just want to finish watching this programme.'

'What programme?' Ged sat down beside her and stared at the screen. Three bodies of indeterminate sex were doing something obscure to each other in a large bed. 'What's this about?'

'The guy in the middle thinks he might be gay. But he's not sure. So these two friends have offered to help him find out, by letting him have sex with each of them. One's a man and one's a woman,' she added helpfully.

'How very public-spirited of them.'

Louise giggled. 'You're shocked, aren't you, Daddy?'

'Why on earth would I be shocked?'

'Because your idea of sin is smoking a spliff.'

If only it were. 'What's your idea of sin?'

'Well, it's nothing to do with sex or drugs, like most people seem to think.'

'Why not?'

'Because those are things that people enjoy, and they

don't hurt anybody else, so yeah, why not?'

'Well, if those activities are certified sin-free zones, what do the hardened sinners get up to nowadays?'

She took a while to think about this. It turned out that the delay in response was caused by having to wrestle with the concept of sin, once sex and drugs had been subtracted. 'You mean, what kind of things are wrong?'

'I think that's the usual definition.'

'Well, OK, racism, I suppose. Pollution. Killing endangered species. Things like that.'

'Are you often tempted to kick a Paki or harpoon a whale?'

'Don't be silly, Daddy,' she said sharply. 'Are things only wrong if you want to do them?'

'On the contrary. I have an idea that contemporary sins only involve things that other people want to do.'

Louise was getting bored with moral philosophy. 'Well, what I want to do right now is watch this film. Is that a sin?'

She didn't wait for an answer before returning her attention to the screen. Since there was nothing else to do, he did the same.

The entirely sinless activities of the people in the bed had become slightly more explicit. To judge by their relative positions, one of the men appeared to be buggering the other; the bottom one (so to speak) seemed to have his face in the woman's crotch. Perhaps they had overheard Louise's absolution.

The odd thing was that Ged couldn't decide whether he ought to be shocked. Certainly he was at least vaguely shocked by the idea of his pubescent daughter watching people getting up to things that he hadn't even known were possible until he was almost old enough to vote. Though at the time, such discoveries had intrigued rather than scandalized him. Had opened up a whole new world of fantasy and potential experience.

What if they had the same effect on Louise?

He decided, quite suddenly. 'You shouldn't be watching this crap.'

'It's not crap. It's had terrific previews.'

'Those cretins will hype any bloody thing they think is fashionable. No, make that anything they think will make money for somebody. They live in their own decadent little world, which doesn't involve boring old-fashioned activities like bringing up children.'

Louise stretched and sighed. 'Daddy, if you want me to go to bed, just tell me to go to bed. Don't make a moral issue out of it.'

'Well, then, go to bed.'

'I will, when this programme is over.'

Short of flinging her over his shoulder and hauling her upstairs kicking and screaming, there didn't seem to be a lot he could do to change her mind. He felt faintly ridiculous, not knowing how to exercise effective parental authority, supposedly the most natural and necessary authority in the world.

His mother had never worried about that sort of thing. If he didn't bother her, she didn't bother him: that had been the arrangement. Like two adults living together. Only it hadn't been two adults, it had been a mother and her child. And all that had taught him was how not to bother your mother.

He had another stab at this situation. 'When is it over, then?'

'Twelve-thirty.'

'That's three-quarters of an hour from now, for Christ's sake. What time do you get up for school?'

She gave him a look of infinite scorn. 'Same time as usual.'

'What time is that?'

'If you got up with the rest of us, you'd know.'

'Since the rest of you are the ones who need to be somewhere at a particular time every day, I let you have first crack at the bathroom, that's all. It's generosity, not laziness.' He did a quick calculation, based on general principles. 'Look, you're supposed to be at school by nine o'clock, and you can't get there by that time if you get up at eight-thirty, which is when you'd be getting up if you were enjoying the eight hours of sleep, minimum, that a growing girl needs. So push off to bed right now, and no more argument.'

She went, sulking elaborately. But she went.

He found himself frustrated by the fact that there wasn't any way to go out of his way to avoid seeing Elie. With her master in town, she wouldn't be available for him anyway; so not seeing her was an inevitable state of affairs, rather than a deliberate act on his part. He had no way of letting her know that she had done something unacceptable, in trying to breach the boundary between fantasy and life.

If he were as rich as bloody Ben, he might have managed both. Installed her in a Parisian *pied-à-terre*, perhaps, where she would come into existence only as he chose, to do whatever he demanded of her. No cheeky children, no grocery shopping, no dry-cleaning to be deposited and retrieved, no car repairs, no daydayday foreverness of mundanity, watching your future unravel. Like sitting in a stalled commuter train while the world drove by.

If he could have afforded Elie, then at least that corner of his life, call it the Parisian corner, would have been different. More like . . . like . . .

Like living in a bloody cognac ad, he supposed.

The admission shamed and enraged him. Advertising had a lot to answer for, messing about with a man's daydreams like that. Infusing every ambition with the subtly stale odour of banality, the slime of pseudo-sophistication.

Was Elie herself banal? Not as long as she belonged to another man. And she belonged to that man in a peculiarly primitive way, bound by money and fear rather than morality and social pressure. The oldest profession, they called it, and so it seemed it was. Even apes behaved that way.

Now she had invited Ged to make an offer of his own

for her. Money, it appeared, was not the only marketable currency.

But he couldn't afford the other, either. Couldn't afford to jump off the stalled train and abandon the domestic equivalent of a steady job. Dammit, he didn't want his life turned upside down, he just didn't want it to stop.

There was nothing to be done over the weekend, anyway. He couldn't even not walk through the park at lunch-time. He spent it shopping with Polly, taking the car through a car wash, mowing the small, sparse back lawn, having a row with Calum about bringing a girl home for the night . . .

That one turned into a row with Polly as well, when she decided to take Calum's side. 'In tribal societies, it's considered perfectly normal for adolescents to have sex with lots of different partners before they settle down to marriage.'

'I don't give a damn how many people he sleeps with, I just don't want him doing it in my house. This is not a brothel.'

'Don't be absurd. It's his home too. Why on earth shouldn't he be able to bring his girlfriends home?'

'She's not his girlfriend, she's just some tramp he picked up at the pub.'

'Don't be so absurdly sexist. Women have a right to exercise their sexuality without being sneered at.'

'OK, OK, but she can bloody well exercise it elsewhere. I don't want to meet strangers coming out of the bathroom on Sunday morning.'

'Well, you've met her now, so she's not a stranger any more. Anyway, it's better that he brings them home, isn't it? Then at least we know what he's getting up to.'

'I think I could probably guess, in any case. And I can't imagine why you think we ought to concern ourselves with Calum's sex life. I don't even want to know whether he has one.'

'It's no use putting your head in the sand, Ged.' Polly looked stern and reproving, in her best social-work manner. 'Ducking your parental responsibilities doesn't help anything. Look, he's your son, and I haven't even been able to get you to talk to him about AIDS and contraception.'

'If he doesn't know all about that, he must be blind, deaf and dumb. Anyway, you don't want him to get the idea that authority figures approve of condoms. If they really wanted kids to use them, they'd have banned the sale of them to anyone under eighteen and started a rumour that condoms cause cancer.'

'You've missed a brilliant career as a child psychologist, I can see,' Polly said acidly. 'Are you going to be quite so cavalier about that sort of thing when Louise starts getting involved with boys?'

'Louise can do what she likes, as far as I'm concerned. Don't forget, in tribal societies it's considered perfectly normal for adolescents to have sex with lots of different partners.'

Whereas, in more advanced societies, the adults carried on like that too.

Elie hadn't said how long Ben was going to be around this time.

Ged went through the park on Monday. He hoped she would be there, simply so that he could ignore her. But she wasn't.

Tuesday, Wednesday, she still wasn't in the park. He sat down for a smoke on the usual bench, but it wasn't the same thing at all. He craved her, the way he craved a cigarette when he was in a situation – at home with Polly, for instance – where he couldn't have one.

No, that wasn't quite it, he told himself, pushing down a vague sense of panic at the thought that he might be addicted to Elie. He didn't want a cigarette, he wanted to smoke a cigarette. He didn't want Elie, he wanted to screw Elie.

Either way, he was frustrated in his desire.

On Thursday, after he had passed the park bench

without a glimpse of her, he found himself heading for Knightsbridge. But she wasn't behind her counter. Having lunch with that god-damn Arab, he supposed. He went back later and she still was nowhere to be seen. There was another woman in the booth, peddling Elie's line of goods.

She was nowhere on Friday, either. He finally persuaded himself that asking the new woman about Elie would not arouse instant suspicion in anyone.

'She's on holiday,' the girl said brightly. 'She won't be back till Monday week.'

Two weeks. It was unendurable. Why hadn't she said something? Warned him somehow.

Warned him how? He had deliberately avoided giving her any access to his life. He at least knew where she lived, but she knew nothing about him except his name and occupation.

Besides, it didn't matter whether she was in London or on the other side of the world. While she was with Ben, she was forbidden.

What was even less endurable than her absence, was the idea that he should find a fortnight without her unendurable. He was truly addicted. To a brainless trollop.

Time to give her up, surely. Her and the smoking.

'Why don't we try something different for a change?'

This suggestion was addressed to Polly. He stood behind her as she faced the mirror, bare-bosomed, brushing her short fair hair by lamplight. Calum was out, presumably pursuing his adolescent sex life, while Louise was sleeping over at a friend's house, no doubt trying out various styles of eye make-up. Calum's and Louise's parents were alone, for once.

'Different? Like how?'

He had given some thought to this question. But obviously not enough: when confronted with down-to-earth Polly, even half-naked Polly, most of his thoughts seemed to belong to another universe.

'Like, for instance, I could tie you up. Or you could tie me up,' he added, to forestall any accusations of sexism.

'Tie me up how? With what?'

'Well, anything. Red ribbon, if you want. A pair of tights, or a couple of my ties. Shoelaces, even. What bloody difference does it make what I tie you up with?'

'I just wondered, that's all. I was trying to envisage the whole thing. What do you want to do after you've tied me up?'

'Well, screw you, what else? That's the point of it, isn't it?'

'I don't know, I've never done it. Isn't it kind of uncomfortable?'

'Look, if it's comfort you're worried about, you can do it to me. I don't mind a little discomfort in the cause of a good screw.'

'I didn't mean that. I just meant, you know, something minor can really mess it up. Like a pebble between your shoulder blades when you're making passionate love out of doors. You know the sort of thing.'

'Yes,' he said. 'Yes, I know exactly the sort of thing. Now do you want to do this or not?'

'Of course I'll do it, if you want to. What exactly do you want me to do?'

'Do anything you please. There wouldn't be much point your tying me up, if you're expecting me to give you orders about it.'

'Well, it was your idea in the first place. I thought maybe you had something particular in mind.'

Like spontaneity and enthusiasm, he thought, watching her dig around in her lingerie drawer.

'Here,' she announced triumphantly, 'we can use these tights. They've got a hole in one toe, so it doesn't matter much what happens to them.'

'How much did they cost in the first place, for Christ's sake?'

'Ninety-nine p. Why on earth would you want to know that?'

'No reason. I was just wondering about relative values.' Still standing behind her, he unbuttoned her jeans, pulled them down her thighs, watched himself do it in the mirror. 'Suppose you had to pay for sex, how much would you be willing to pay? Ninety-nine p? Five quid? A hundred pounds, a thousand?'

'Depends on the quality of the sex, I suppose.'

'What would a thousand-pound screw be like for you?'

'Mm, let me think.' She kicked off her jeans and knickers and lay back naked on the bed, still clutching the holed tights in one hand. She closed her eyes to help herself think. 'I'd be floating in a pool of warm water, and people would come up and caress me. I wouldn't even look at them, I'd be like Tiberius in his pool in Capri, letting slaves pleasure me. I'd just close my eyes and enjoy the sensations all over my body.'

'That sounds more like a massage than a screw.'

'So what? I can spend my money any way I like, can't I? A thousand-pound sexual massage sounds perfect to me.' She opened her eyes and saw him watching her. He didn't know what she could see in his face. 'What about you? What would you buy for a thousand pounds?'

'A lot of things. I don't suppose there's much you can't buy for that kind of money. Sex isn't a scarce commodity.'

'But what do you want most?'

The thought of what he wanted most, the thing that was finally free and yet more than he could afford, the thought of that gave him back his erection. He didn't answer her, he just lay down on her and entered her without preamble. His head was elsewhere, of course, in another woman's body.

Maybe she took what he did for his answer. At any rate, she didn't object to the absence of ritual foreplay as she would normally have done. She was even ready enough to take him.

But not entirely without protest. 'Hey, I thought you wanted to tie me up or something.'

*   *   *

After two weeks of absence, the sight of Elie was like a thunderstorm in the desert.

She wasn't reading. She was just sitting there, alone on the bench, her hands interlaced in her lap like an old-fashioned schoolgirl. She was staring at her hands. They were summer-brown, the same as her face and arms and legs. A holiday tan.

He sat down beside her, waiting to see what she would do.

'I didn't know if you'd come,' she said to her hands, speaking softly, as if she didn't necessarily want him to overhear. 'I thought you might have given up on me.'

'Why?'

'When I was gone so long.'

He shrugged, even though she wasn't looking. 'Were you away with Ben?'

'Yes.'

'And was it good?'

'It was dreadful.'

She jumped up and crossed the path, heading across a lawn towards the duck pond. He went after her. She clutched at the rail around the pond, swaying forward as if she was contemplating death by drowning.

He came to stand beside her, near but not touching. They both stared out at the ducks. At one mallard in particular, swimming round and round in pointless circles.

'He heard us. On the phone.'

'Heard what?'

'Everything. I— I couldn't have rung off properly. Because I was so . . . distracted, I suppose. He heard what we said to each other afterwards.'

'How do you know?'

'He told me. He asked who you were.'

'Did you tell him?'

'How could I?' She turned to look at him, a cool, painful glance. 'I don't know who you are. You've been careful to let me know nothing.'

'But you do know my name.'

'I said I didn't. Only your first name.'

'And did he believe you?'

'I don't know.' She rubbed one brown hand over the other in some agitation of the spirit. 'He pretended to believe me. But that made it worse. Only a whore would go to bed with a man whose name she didn't know. That's what he said. He kept calling me a whore. I can't tell you what he said. What he did.'

He came closer, watching her. 'What did he do?'

'He did lots of things. He kept me in tears the whole time. But the very worst thing he did . . .' She hesitated, steeling herself to describe it. 'He came back to our hotel room on the last night, with two men. He said they were his friends. They were all drunk. We had another drink in the hotel room, a glass of brandy. I had one too. He insisted I should.'

She was pressing her hands flat to her waist now, literally holding herself in. 'Then he said . . . he said those men had come up to have sex with me. He said he had invited them up. He said he'd told them he had a whore in his room, and they could all share her. Me.'

'What did you do?' Everything that Ben did to her was an unforgivable brutality in Ged's view. This latest outrage was only the worst of many. So for him right now the most important thing was, what had *she* done?

'Well, I said . . . I said no. And he said he wasn't asking me, he was telling me. He said he paid me to do what he wanted me to do, and if I wasn't going to do what I was paid for, I'd have to get out of his room. So I did.'

She rubbed the heel of her hand across her cheek, much as she might have scrubbed away tears, though no tears were visible and her mascara remained unsmudged.

Ged found himself wondering, shamefaced, how much of the truth was in this tale. Most of it, maybe? All of it?

And if not quite all, where was the lie?

'When did this happen?'

'Last week. Last Friday.'

'And where were you?'

'In Mauritius.'

'So how did you get back here?'

'Oh, he gave me my return ticket and my passport, and gave me two minutes – exactly two minutes, he timed it – to pack my bag and get out. I couldn't fly home till morning, of course, so I spent the night on the beach. And when I got back to London and went to the flat to get the rest of my things, I discovered he'd had someone change the locks. So all I've got are the clothes in my suitcase. Good for a holiday, but not much use for my job.' She indicated the creamy cotton dress she was wearing. 'For work I've got this, and a blouse and skirt, and that's all.'

'Where've you been living since you came back? Not on the beach, presumably.'

'I've been sleeping on the sofa in a friend's flat. Cherie. She works with me. I just told her we'd had a row.'

She turned for the first time to face him. He closed his hand around her wrist, the one still pressed to her body. 'Is that true?'

'About Cherie? Of course. Why shouldn't it be true?'

There were reasons why it shouldn't have been true – because, for instance, what Ben had said about her was true, wasn't it? – but that wasn't what he had been asking after. 'Not Cherie. The rest of it. What he did, what you did.'

'What do you mean? Why would I make up such a terrible thing?'

He tightened his grip on her. He wanted to shake the truth out of her, but he had no way of doing that. Shaking her, yes, but the truth was another, harder matter. 'Maybe you didn't say no. Or maybe he didn't let you go like that.'

'I did. He did. It was just like I said.' She started to cry at last, improbably large tears rolling down her cheeks, leaving trails in her make-up. 'Ged, don't be mad, please don't. It was your fault anyway, I told you not to do that, when I let you come up to the flat. And now I've got no money and nowhere to live, and I don't know what to do.'

He still wanted to shake her, out of fury now because he knew that she was about to bring his tediously comfortable life crashing down around his ears. But she was right; it was his own fault, all the things that had happened and were going to happen. A form of suicide.

And proof that there's no such thing as a free lunch.

So instead he took her in his arms and let her get on with her sobbing against his shirt, while he threw away his whole elaborately constructed edifice of 'normal' life. Maybe he had never deserved that. Maybe he simply wasn't normal. Maybe his crazy parents had somehow doomed him.

'It's OK.' While he held her and stroked her hair, he thought of the scars on her arms. He couldn't leave her now, could he?

He told himself that, because it was such a rotten thing to do; to leave his wife and kids to go and live with his mistress. He told himself that behaving honourably towards Polly would mean behaving like a cad towards Elie.

Somebody – not him, one of them – was going to have to suffer for his sins. Wasn't that the very definition of a shit?

Concentrate on Elie. It was Elie who needed him now. Elie whom he wanted, but he chose not to think about that. 'Elie, don't cry. It's going to be OK. I'll find somewhere for us to live together.'

That part was fatally simple. Telling Polly was harder.

Theoretically, he could have put it off until he had found a flat in which to live his new life. But even in theory, the notion of pretending to Polly that nothing had happened or was about to happen sounded improbable, if not intolerable. The idea of hanging around after he had told her was unthinkable. He had to confess and go, even if it meant camping on Rufus's sofa for the next few weeks.

Polly didn't believe him at first. At least she professed

not to believe, even when she was in the bedroom watching him pack a suitcase. 'I can't believe this,' she said.

'What exactly can't you believe?'

'That you'd do a thing like this. Grand passion isn't your style. It's not *ironic*.'

'Maybe real life gets in the way of irony sometimes.'

'You call this reality? I call it bloody fantasy.'

She went on watching him, standing before the door as if to bar his exit. There were as yet no tears, thank Christ, he thought, and then thought what a selfish bastard he was to even think like that. But of course if he weren't a selfish bastard he wouldn't be doing this in the first place.

But he had a right to his life, didn't he? He would only ever get one life, and it belonged to him, not to Polly.

As for his children, he wondered if they would even miss him, seeing they were so seldom at home, and took so little notice of him when they were there. After all, he didn't do the cooking, or iron the clothes, or find the missing schoolbooks, or do the other mothering sorts of things. What sorts of things were fathers supposed to do, anyway? Pay the mortgage, tell them to go to bed, try to discourage them from bringing their girlfriends home for sex. What was there to miss in all that?

'Who is she?'

'I told you, you don't know her.'

'But she must have a name.'

'She's called Elie.'

'Elie Who?'

He didn't know. He'd never asked and she'd never volunteered. He was leaping into chaos and disaster for the sake of a girl whose name he didn't know. 'I don't know.'

'I can't believe you don't know her name.'

He shrugged. He couldn't believe it either. Not that it mattered. What difference did her name make to anything?

'What's she like?'

'What do you want me to say? She's young and pretty.'

'Naturally.'

'Would you rather I left you for some middle-aged hag?'

'Actually, I might. At least it would make a change. Something to laugh about.'

She brooded, a long way from laughter. 'What does she do?' When he didn't answer, she added nastily, 'For a living, I mean.'

'She's a shop assistant. She sells perfumes and cosmetics.'

'Oh, Ged. You *have* gone mad.'

'I know.'

Her mood was mysteriously lightened after that. He understood much later that she had decided then he would be back soon enough, that this was only a temporary humiliation. Perhaps he thought the same himself, at the time. What's done can be undone, surely?

Life wouldn't be fair, otherwise.

8

By morning the fog had vanished, to reveal the face of yesterday's alternative universe: sand and rocks and a wide grey ocean, several hundred feet straight down.

Calum was fascinated. He roamed the rim of the plateau, leaning over tree trunks and peering down into danger. If he had been ten years younger, Ged would have told him to keep away from the edge of the cliff. He still wanted to say it, nineteen or not.

Angelina said it for him, when she came out on deck with fresh coffee. 'Watch yourself there, Calum, or you'll start a landslide and we'll all end up in the ocean. More toast?'

'Yes, please.'

Now there was a word that had never featured much in Calum's vocabulary. A sign of maturity, or best behaviour for Angelina's benefit?

She would have put any man on best behaviour. She was a very attractive girl, and all the more attractive for not even trying. This morning, instead of the navy dress, she was wearing jeans, with a striped blue and white cotton shirt. Her sun-streaked brown hair was piled up on top of her head in a fetchingly casual manner, as if she had pinned it there simply in order to get it out of the way, with no thought of style or glamour.

Her figure was far from ideal in the high-fashion sense. In one dimension there was not enough of it, because she was quite short, and in another dimension there was definitely too much of it, heavy breasts and curving hips and buttocks well in evidence. Nothing wrong with any of that, though, from a masculine point of view.

She wasn't trying to be sexy; the jeans were not noticeably tight, the shirt was buttoned to just below the collar. Ged had observed an infinite number of times that for every woman who dressed and conducted herself in a manner obviously calculated to attract the attentions of men, there were a dozen others who went about apparently oblivious to their own advertisement of sexual delights.

Maybe the Muslims were right. Locking up women, or shrouding them in tents and veils, was the only way for them to avoid presenting their bodies to strangers. Tits were tits, there was no getting around it. Every glimpse or hint of cleavage, every silhouette of bosom, every buttock in motion, every evidence of waist or thigh . . . to their owners, they were just a normal and unremarkable part of life and the universe and everything. But seen from outside, from the other side, they were something quite different: a constant reminder of, an invitation to, the very ground and bass motif of human existence. A reminder of past and potential pleasure.

So Angelina had a world of pleasure, pleasure to be given and received, inside her shirt and jeans. But she appeared to think it was there mainly for things like cooking breakfast and helping her grandmother with the gardening.

She interrupted his speculations on the contents of her head and clothing by brandishing the coffee pot at him in a meaningful way.

He held up his empty mug and took it away full. 'What's that noise?'

'Trucks on the highway, I guess. It runs right along the base of this cliff. Malachy was forever complaining about the encroachment of civilization.'

The sound grew louder. If that noise was the highway,

then it was on its way up the mountain and needed work on its muffler.

'Jesus,' muttered Angelina.

He hadn't heard her swear before, and wondered what could have reduced her to profanity. 'What is it?'

'Jesus,' she repeated, this time without any sign of annoyance. 'He claims it isn't supposed to be pronounced like that, but I can't say it the way he does. Anyway, most people call him by his other name.'

'Christ?'

She giggled. 'George. Only he spells it different, with a J. And it's supposed to be pronounced in a funny way too, but nobody ever does. Not even him, most of the time. I guess he's given up.'

So the poor bugger had a name that people were either embarrassed to say, or couldn't spell and couldn't pronounce. So much for the great multicultural experiment.

The racket grew to a crescendo that implied imminent catastrophe, then sputtered out altogether. Charles bounded off to investigate, and reappeared escorting a slight figure in full biker's regalia.

The biker clambered up on to the deck before removing his helmet. He did this cautiously, as if he might inadvertently remove his head as well. But the head stayed firmly screwed on; a head with flattened black curls, a curving nose that went on just a shade too long, a dense moustache, and a slightly succulent mouth. The mouth was chewing gum.

'Hi, Angie. Who are these guys?'

'They're not guys, they're—'

'No, don't tell me, let me guess.' He stared at Ged for the space of three chews. 'It's the long-lost heir.'

'Not lost,' Ged amended. 'Just mislaid.'

'He's Ged Hawke.' Angelina pointed. 'He's Calum Hawke. And he's Jesus George Bravo.'

'*Jesús*, my dear. Jesús Jorge.' The biker unbuckled and unzipped his jacket to reveal a black T-shirt which said

'JESUS SAVES' in large red letters. 'How do you like my personalized T-shirt?'

Angelina gave it a disapproving glance. 'I'm surprised you haven't been struck down by lightning.'

Jorge peered down at his chest. 'What's wrong with this? It's a perfectly respectable religious slogan.'

'Not the way you mean it, it isn't. And don't think God won't know the difference.' To Ged she explained, 'George did his doctorate on Malachy, see, and now he teaches art history at the university over in Eugene. Only he got in the habit of coming around here, and he can't seem to break it.'

'It's the book, my angel, the book. *Malachy Hawke: His Life and Art*, by J. J. Bravo, Ph.D. The definitive work, complete with lavish colour reproductions and extensive interviews, because you know he was famous for refusing to be interviewed. And now the son of a bitch has gone and died on me before I'd finished it.'

Recollecting the rest of his audience, he made a flourish with his helmet in Ged's direction. 'Sorry, I didn't mean to sound disrespectful about your father. You must be still suffering from grief and shock. Those are the first stages of bereavement, aren't they?'

'I think your bereavement might be greater than mine,' Ged said dryly. 'You knew him and I didn't. You were writing his biography?'

'Yeah, but he wasn't supposed to know that. He might not have approved.' Jesús Jorge sat down on the bench in front of the picture window and set his helmet beside him. His hair, suppressed by the helmet, was already beginning to reassert itself, to take up its rightful space in the world. 'Angie sure didn't approve, when I confided my intentions to her. She hasn't let me set foot in the studio since Mal died, have you, my angel?'

'That's nothing to do with me approving your schemes or not.' Angelina handed him a mug of black coffee without asking if he wanted it. 'I just didn't want you messing around with things before Ged got here. It's his house now, after all.'

'Is that so?' He gave Ged a curious glance over the coffee mug. 'You've agreed to clean up after Mal, have you?'

'I haven't agreed to anything yet. I'm still thinking about it.'

'You're still thinking about whether or not you want to inherit a fortune?'

'Is it really a fortune? That's what his agent said, but that's the sort of thing agents are paid to say.'

Jorge looked knowing, or tried to. His face was too round, his eyes too wide-set for cynicism. Even with the improbable moustache, he looked about fifteen, though he must have been a good deal older than that to have acquired a doctorate. 'You're not an artist yourself, are you?'

'No, a writer.'

'Ah.' He nodded, as one scholar to another. 'What sort of stuff do you write?'

'I'm a novelist.'

'Ah,' Jorge repeated, this time in a different, more distant tone. 'I don't read much fiction. Haven't got the time.'

'As it happens, I don't have much time for art history, so we're even. But I'd be interested in hearing what you have to say about those paintings.'

Jorge chose not to notice the dig. 'Well, when it comes to art, I wouldn't trust anyone from New York as far as I could throw them, but it is true that Mal's work is hot right now. That's pretty ironic, considering he hated the whole art establishment. He did everything he could think of to undermine the concept of a market in art.'

'But that was what made him rich.'

'I don't think he gave a damn about being rich. He just liked painting pictures.'

'Isn't that what every artist says?'

'Sure, sure, there's Duchamp's toilet, and performance art, and so forth, but in Mal's case it might actually have been true. What do you think, Angie?'

Angelina considered. 'He didn't care about being rich,' she allowed. 'What he wanted most was to control his own life. But I don't see how he could have done that without being rich.' She gestured, a flourish that took in the whole mountain. 'This place, for instance. It gave him privacy, and peace and quiet, and everything else he wanted. But he couldn't have gotten a mountain all to himself if he wasn't rich.'

'OK, he was lucky,' Jorge conceded. 'But it wasn't because he was commercially minded. You have to admit, he was not a commercially minded man.'

'He was no good at paying his bills, if that's what you mean.'

'God, Angie, you're such a tough babe. I reckon that's why Mal kept you around. You were the only one who had the nerve to tell him off when he needed it. But don't give me any guff about not liking him, because I won't believe you.'

'Of course I liked him. I wouldn't have worked for him if I didn't like him.'

'Why'd you like him, then, if he was just a rich skinflint?'

''Cause he was a *funny* rich skinflint.'

She flounced back into the house with the empty coffee pot, do-se-do-ing in the doorway past Calum on his way out.

Calum squatted down to thump Charles in a friendly way. He spoke to Jesús – Jorge – without looking up. 'What was all that about Malachy trying to undermine the establishment?'

'The art market,' Jorge corrected. 'He thought the visual arts should be a visual experience. Names and pedigrees shouldn't matter.'

'What have pedigrees got to do with art? I thought they were for the likes of Charles here.' Calum's hand came down on the dog's ribs, harder than ever for emphasis. Charles rolled on to its side and twitched its enormous paws in a high degree of pleasure.

'That brute has nothing whatsoever to do with pedigrees. Never mind interbreeding, he looks like an interspecies cross to me.' Jorge wrinkled his nose in disapproval. 'Somewhere between a dinosaur and a moose.'

'Lucky for you he didn't hear that.' Calum switched his attention from ribs to ears, energetically tugging and rumpling them. Charles sank deeper into bliss. 'What about these pedigrees?'

'Well, pedigree in an animal means being able to trace its ancestors. With a painting it means being able to track its previous owners, maybe right back to the artist who painted it. That's how you know it's the real thing. But Mal insisted pedigrees were shit. Snobbery, he called it.

'He was fanatical about the whole business of buying and selling art. He said they'd turned him into a goddamn brand name, and he aimed to screw them for it.' Jorge paused. 'I heard a story about that. I don't know if it's true or not. Probably is.'

'A story about what?'

'Screwing them for it. Literally. Some journalist wanted to interview him and he said no dice, unless she let him f—' Jorge caught the disapproving eye of Angelina and hastily changed his phrasing. 'Unless she agreed to go to bed with him.'

'And did she?'

'Well, yeah. Sure. Naturally. He was a good-looking guy, and a famous artist to boot. Something to tell your grandchildren, you know? I mean, *I* would have gone to bed with him, if he'd asked me to. Matter of fact, I even dropped a few hints, but he didn't pick up on it. Too damn straight, I guess. Some people are so fussy. What I always say is, it's all the same in the dark.'

'George,' said Angelina, 'these people don't want to hear about your appalling sex life.'

Jorge grinned, not at all put out by her rebuke. 'Speak

for yourself, Angie. Anyway, that's the thing that made me wonder about the story. I mean, normally they might have had a chat and a few drinks, and then felt friendly enough to continue the conversation in bed. But he made it, like, the price: first we f— sorry, engage in sexual intercourse, then we talk. He didn't need to do that, did he, if he just wanted sex with her?' He sounded genuinely mystified.

'Then we must assume that wasn't his primary aim,' Ged suggested dryly.

'Yeah?' Jorge's head swung up to stare at him. 'So what do you think he was up to?'

'Perhaps he wanted to put the transaction on a proper commercial basis.' Ged set his coffee mug down and stood up. 'Angie, is there a telephone in this place?'

'There's a cell phone. I'll bring it out here, the reception's better.' She returned almost immediately with the telephone, a large, clumsy, old-fashioned type. 'That Bradford guy bought it for him so they could keep in touch. No way was Malachy going to pay to run telephone wires up this mountain. But it costs a fortune to use, so he never did.'

'You mean he really was a skinflint?'

'No, not really. But he had too much respect for money to throw it away. Just like my grandma. Poverty does that to people.'

'Was he poor before he got rich?'

'Dirt poor, so he said. It wouldn't surprise me. Indians mostly are.'

The word, spoken so casually, hit Ged like a physical blow.

It had never crossed his mind, not even when he had met Malachy in New York. He had looked his father in the face and never made the connection. Because it was his father, all he had seen there was himself. Individual resemblances, not racial ones.

And his mother had never told him. Maybe she hadn't known. Or maybe she thought it an irrelevant detail, the word that made sense of his own face.

Black hair, swarthy skin, high broad-bladed cheek-bones. Even the impassive countenance that so seldom betrayed his state of mind. The 'gypsy' face that his schoolmates used to torment him for. His father's face, as Rene Deforte and Angelina had both observed.

He clamped his teeth down on his astonishment.

Calum was less guarded, with less reason to be. After all, he had Polly's Anglo-Saxon looks. 'You mean he was a real Red Indian?'

'Cheyenne. Didn't you know?' Angelina glanced from fair son to dark father. 'It wasn't any secret. He just never made a big thing of it, the way some people do. He was really only one-quarter Cheyenne. His grandfather was full blood. He used to say that if his grandpa had been black instead of Cheyenne, he'd be a quadroon, and his kids would be octoroons. That word always cracked me up.' Evidently it amused her even now, since she was laughing as she spoke. 'How'd you like being an octoroon, Ged? I don't know the word for an octoroon's kid, if there is one. What about *macaroon*, Calum? Or maybe *doubloon*? Malachy said that octoroons are literally pieces of eight.'

She leaned against the door frame, covering her laughter with her hand, as if she had an idea it might not be quite polite to joke about such things, about words that once had tragic and shameful significance.

'Even one-sixteenth counts as blood, doesn't it?' Jorge remarked. 'I think that's enough to give you rights, to live on the reserve and share in all the tribal rights.'

'You're kidding.' By now Calum was bolt upright with amazement. 'What kind of rights?'

'Depends on which tribe. Hunting rights and things like that. Or a share in the casino.'

'Where do casinos come into it?'

'Gambling restrictions don't apply on the reserves. They can do what they like. Apparently it's like minting money. And it's nice to see the Indians playing whitey for suckers, just for a change.'

By now Angelina was looking as surprised as anyone. 'You mean these guys,' she waved at the two Hawkes, 'count as real Indians?'

Jorge nodded. 'I believe they do.'

'But that's crazy. Ged, OK, maybe. He really does look like Malachy, except for the blue eyes. But Calum's *blond*.'

'It ain't a beauty contest, Angie. Look, the thing is, you can't change who you are, who your parents were, and so forth. For instance, Germany counts people as German even if their great-great-great-grandfather went off to live in Kazakhstan and they can't speak a syllable of the language. Same with Israel and the Jews. Doesn't matter what you look like on the outside, it's what's in your blood that counts.'

Angelina sniffed disapprovingly. 'I thought we were all just plain ordinary Americans in this country. And I was always taught it's purely the state of your soul that matters.'

'Well, maybe they reckon there's such a thing as a Cheyenne soul.'

9

'Cheyenne? Sure he was.'

Rene Deforte was happy to confirm the truth of Angelina's remarks. 'The Northern Cheyenne Reserve is over in Montana, where Mal came from. So did I, for that matter. But my dad's ranch was up by the Canadian border, and Mal's folks lived down south of Billings.'

'Is that why you became friendly?'

'No, not really. But I won't say it made no difference, us coming from the same part of the country.' Deforte was smoking a smaller cigar this time, hardly more than a portly brown cigarette. He squinted through the smoke, peering at Ged across his desk. 'Roots are funny things.'

Funny things. Ged could vouch for that. He was feeling distinctly queasy, in a spiritual sense.

His father had been a stranger. His mother had spent her life wandering, in search of some anarchic utopia. Maybe he himself had married Polly for the sake of her roots; she knew her parents and her grandparents, and where they all had come from and gone to. Polly had Family, where he only had relations.

Now he had roots in some alien culture. Distant, tentative ones, but they showed in his face. Impossible to deny them.

Deforte was still watching him with that air of shrewd naïveté. 'It's fashionable nowadays, being Indian. Native Americans, they call them. Or maybe it's First Nations now, I can't keep track of these fads. But Mal was born way back when being Indian was only a tad less unfashionable than being Negro.

'It was Mal's grandfather who was full blood, so technically Mal was only one-quarter Cheyenne. Funny how they reckon up these things, isn't it? You'd think that when you got to be more than half white, they'd round things up and reckon you're white instead of whatever. But it don't seem to work that way. One little drop of other blood in you, and you're labelled one of them.'

Ged supposed that if that was how they reckoned things here, then he too was 'one of them'. An octoroon.

Deforte was still explaining whatever it was he wanted to explain. 'I can tell you, Jed, way back then in Montana, Indians were seen as drunken bums. And maybe they *were* drunken bums. Take away a man's livelihood and religion and self-respect, and don't be surprised if that's what you end up with.

'Not so long before that, these same drunken bums were considered brutal savages. Not so long before. Mal told me his grandfather had been in the village that Custer was attacking when he got himself massacred. The old man was only a kid at the time, but he was still around to tell Mal all about it, sixty years on. All about how his own father had taken the scalp of one of Custer's men.

'Think about that, Jed. From warrior brave to drunken bum in one man's lifetime. I don't know what that does to the way a fellow feels about his origins. All I know is that Mal left home at sixteen, and he never went back to Montana.' The lawyer gave an eloquent shrug. 'He claimed he was allergic to the cottonwood trees. Lots of folks are. Can't get away from cottonwoods in Montana.'

Ged decided he was allergic to hayseed sermonizing. 'I think you misunderstand me, Rene.' He made himself pronounce it in that absurd American way. 'I don't have all that baggage. Where I come from, the Cheyenne are called Red Indians. People think they go about wearing war paint, with feathers in their hair. They're viewed in a romantic light.' He paused, a brief silence that said, Think about that, Rene. 'I suppose I was only asking because it took me by surprise.'

'OK, fair enough. And I just thought you might want to know about your dad, that's all.' Deforte puffed on his baby cigar, smoke-signalling a truce. 'How're you getting on with Angie? She looking after you all right?'

'She's fine. She seems a remarkable girl.'

'She's a good kid,' Deforte agreed cheerfully. 'And it's all her grandparents' doing. Her ma disappeared when Angie was five, went off to find herself or some such thing. Then her dad found himself a woman in Seattle, and left Angie with his folks.

'The old man, he's dead now, he ran a stud farm. I bought my kids' horses off him. They landed here after the war, with nothing but the clothes on their back, and managed to get themselves a little place the other side of the valley, up in the mountains beyond Sweetwater.'

Ged was already learning how to interpret these remarks. 'The valley' was invariably the Willamette Valley, the heart and soul of Oregonian civilization. 'The mountains' were not the green coastal hills near Corvallis, but the much grander and more glamorous Cascades. It had been a Cascade peak they had caught sight of in the sky, that very first evening.

'Angie started out to be a nun,' Deforte went on chattily, 'but that didn't work out. Knowing her, I'd guess it was something to do with those vows they have to swear. She would have coped all right with the poverty and chastity, but obedience was maybe a little too hard for her.'

'A nun?' Ged had to light another cigarette to cope with that news. His father shacked up with a teenage nun. Christ Almighty. 'That seems rather . . . old-fashioned.' Just what he had thought about Angelina herself, he recalled.

'It was her own idea, seemingly. One of these tomfool notions girls of that age get hold of. Then she came back home and this job with Mal turned up, so I put her on to it.'

'What did her grandmother think about her working for Malachy?'

'She wasn't too keen at first. She didn't know about Mal's reputation as a womanizer, of course. It was just a general suspicion of rich guys. Seems like the nobles back in Poland didn't use to behave real well towards the peasant girls. She insisted on meeting Mal. She wanted to interview him – like *she* was proposing to give *him* a job.'

'How did that go?'

'Well, the woman was never born that Mal couldn't charm the pants off, when he had a mind to. Course, there was no need for him to go that far with Grandma Rudniki. She asked her questions and Mal answered them. Angie had to interpret for her. The old girl won't admit to much English, makes Angie speak Polish at home. But the fact is, Angie was more than a match for Mal if anyone was.'

That was his way, Ged supposed, of shrugging off responsibility for having put a fox in the hen coop. No, the other way round: shoving a hen into the fox's den. 'Why did the previous, er, housekeeper leave?'

'Well, it seems she'd gotten it into her head that Mal should marry her. Some people have no common sense, do they? She had just about as much chance of marrying the Prince of Wales. These days, sharing a bed don't signify a blamed thing, and she must have known that when she let him into hers. But there's no reckoning the female mind. So they had an almighty row, and she packed up and left.'

Another puff of cigar smoke, another abrupt change of subject. 'Well now, Jed, you've had a chance to look around, and a chance to sleep on things. What do you think about your old man's will?'

'I think he had his nerve,' Ged said bluntly. 'You've admitted that he knew how to find me. He could have tracked me down beforehand. He could have *asked*.'

'Maybe he was scared you'd turn him down.'

'So he tried to force my hand? I don't like blackmail and bribery.'

'Harsh words, them. One way, you get a fortune. The other way, you don't get some money you didn't even know existed.' Deforte examined the tip of his cigar. 'Are you a rich man yourself, Jed?'

'No.'

That was putting it mildly. He was barely scratching a living from backlist royalties, book reviews and the odd piece of journalism. He hadn't realized, before he left her, how much his economic security had depended on Polly's steady income. Or, until she left him, how much Elie's earnings had meant. If he didn't finish his next book soon . . .

Finish it? He'd barely started. For the third time.

Maybe the creative well in him had finally run dry. A suicidal thought. Without a book fermenting inside him, without an interior world evolving, he might as well be dead.

'Novelists are hardly ever rich,' he pointed out.

'Artists neither, from what I can tell. Mal more or less got rich by accident. All he cared about was painting. And all the money really did for him was let him go on painting.' Another calculated study of the burning tip. 'It's like that with writers too, isn't it?'

'Something like that, I suppose,' Ged admitted. He had to, since he had just been thinking it himself.

'Money is nice, though. Especially for a man with a family.'

'I'm divorced. My children are fairly well grown up.'

Some treacherous corner of his brain raised the spectre of Elie. Elie who had wanted a baby so badly. Elie who wasn't there any more. 'I have no serious family commitments,' he went on resolutely. 'I also have no time to hang around here. That studio would take weeks to sort out.'

'Well, it's up to you, of course.' Deforte was suspiciously soothing. 'You said you were curious about your dad. Well, that's his life in there. It's a mess, but I guess you could say his life was a mess too.'

That seemed to be hereditary. Oh, shit. Why did he

147

have to think about Elie now? Thoughts of Elie were addictive. And painful. 'Let me give it a little more consideration.' He stood up to go. 'By the way, do you know a man named Bravo? Some sort of friend of my father's?'

'Jesus?' Deforte must have known perfectly well how Jesús was meant to be pronounced. Still, since he couldn't even pronounce his own name properly, it could hardly be held against him. 'Sure I know him. Funny little guy, but sharp as a tack. He's always getting asked for his ID in bars, on account of only looking half his age. I think that's the reason Mal took a shine to him, the fact that he comes across as a crazy kid instead of some mouthy art expert.'

'So he really is a reputable scholar?'

'Sure. He's the big authority on Mal's work. He knows more about it than anyone alive. You can trust him that way, if that's what you're asking.'

It hadn't been because of money that he had refused to let Elie have a baby. It hadn't been the money at all. He wasn't that sort of mercenary monster, to deny her what she desperately wanted because it would have meant him buying a cheaper brand of whisky and drinking less of it. There were all sorts of other reasons.

He just couldn't seem to think of any of them right now.

Instead, he found himself thinking about Rufus Spencer.

Rufus was the reason he had never followed his father's advice to take a bus ride around America. He had met him the day after the meeting with Malachy. Unlike Ged, Rufus had had plans – even if those plans were only to drift around the world for a year or two, doing drugs and touring the low spots. He was on his way to San Francisco, and he persuaded Ged to go with him. And then to carry on to India, or wherever. He was very persuasive. Which was doubtless how he had ended up rich.

Ged had gone along with Rufus's ideas about aimlessness because it seemed to be the thing to do. Everybody was doing it. Even bad drug trips, semi-starvation and venereal disease counted as romantic adventure. It wasn't until he discovered his mother had gone off to Tangier, till he realized that 'everybody' included her, that the glamour wore off. At that point he had given it up, and gone back to London to write the novel that had been germinating inside him throughout his travels.

Rufus had given up the hippy life at the same time, but hardly for the same reasons. For Rufus the whole episode had been part of his career plan, establishing his counter-cultural credentials before setting out to get seriously rich.

Rufus was the sort of wide boy who prided himself on being on the in, knowing everything it was necessary to know. Conversely, what Rufus didn't know wasn't worth knowing. Ged wondered how Rufus would have reacted to a revelation that his father – Rufus's father, not Ged's – had been . . . what was Malachy? A Red Indian? A Cheyenne? Not a white man? A member of an alien race? 'One of them'?

And which would disturb Rufus more: the gist of the revelation, or his own ignorance?

There were no surprises in Rufus's ancestry, of course. Like Polly he had well documented roots, though not quite the same sort. His family had spread out in the course of helping to run the Empire, but they kept close track of each other. Rufus had cousins all over the world. Ged had met Rufus's parents, in the days when they were still married to each other. He had even met a couple of Rufus's grandparents. You knew where you were with Rufus.

Elie came back into his head. Came back into his body, which was where he knew her best. Her absence imploded inside him, his craving for her, his missing her nearness. He almost drove off the road, into the side of the mountain.

Did he love her? He didn't know. Not unless love was

like toothache, or maybe cancer. A persistent, pervasive, and possibly incurable torment.

Rather like not being able to write. Only he hadn't minded that so much, while Elie was around.

Rufus thought he knew everything. Ged didn't even know what was inside his own head.

10

It was Rufus's fault that Elie had left him.

They had been out for dinner with Rufus and his current concubine. Dinner in a trendy restaurant where the food was notoriously of uneven quality. Where the chef waited for customers to complain about the bad bits, so that he could have a public row and throw them out of the restaurant and get his name into the papers yet again. As a marketing device, it was much more effective than merely serving reliably good food.

Rufus was paying. He did something scammy in the City, and made vast sums of money out of it. He claimed he was only helping other people to get rich, and therefore deserved every penny he made, but Ged was always suspicious of this story. The money had to come from somewhere, didn't it? So somebody somewhere had to have lost it, in order to make Rufus and his spivvy clients rich. After all, it wasn't as if he was selling books.

Rufus's girl said something about babies. A friend of hers had just had one, and this girl – Lucy was her name – couldn't see what the big attraction was. They were smelly and fractious and had to be minded every minute, which Lucy reckoned would blow a big hole right through her social life.

'I mean, I *enjoy* going to parties,' she explained earnestly, glaring at Ged as if expecting him to challenge her on this point. 'Why should I have to give up something I enjoy, all because of a baby?'

'No-one's suggesting you should, darling,' Rufus soothed. 'Me least of all.' He reached over to give her something between a pat on the hand and a slap on the wrist.

Ged wondered if she knew she was only a nine days' wonder. She happened to be tall and blonde, but it wouldn't have been her size or colouring that made Rufus select her as a suitable ornament on his arm and in his bed. The one thing that all his women had in common was an overriding concern with their appearance, and a corresponding obsession with fashion. Not just fashion in clothes, but in behaviour, in speech, in lifestyle. They were always the cutting edge of cool.

So having babies was definitely passé.

Elie spoke up – to everyone's surprise, since she seldom took part in dinner-party debates. 'What happens if you get tired of parties?'

Lucy gave her a look of scornful incredulity, like an adolescent unable to envisage reaching the wrinkled side of forty. 'If I ever do, then *maybe* I might start thinking about babies.'

'Maybe you'll be too old by then.'

Lucy shrugged. Old was something that happened to other people. 'That's no reason for ruining my life right now.'

'But having a baby is the most important thing a person can do,' Elie persisted. 'That's what we're here for. Our children are all that's left of us when we die.'

The other woman rolled her eyes, while rolling the tip of her cigarette in the ash tray. Cigarettes must be in. Possibly instead of babies. 'We've got beyond all that, haven't we? Modern society offers so many different forms of immortality, we hardly need the primitive biological version.'

Elie had been firmly put in her place, but she didn't seem to notice. 'Suppose you were madly in love with

Rufus, wouldn't you want to have a baby by him?'

Lucy shot Rufus a glance from under her eyelashes, managing to be sultry and silky and ironic all at once. 'The thing I love most of all about Rufie is his complete lack of interest in babies.'

Elie said afterwards, 'I don't like that Lucy.'

Her vehemence took Ged by surprise. She was seldom vehement about anything, and usually expressed opinions in a timid, almost apologetic tone. 'Why not?'

'She tries to pretend she's just like a man.'

This seemed an improbable accusation, given the obvious time and trouble and expense Lucy had gone to, in order to exaggerate her female attributes. 'How does she do that?'

'Claiming she just wants to have fun. Going on about parties and babies like that.'

'Why would she lie to us?' Ged wondered dryly.

'She was trying to impress Rufus.'

'Did she succeed?'

'I don't suppose he noticed. He never takes the slightest notice of anything his girlfriends say, does he? Because he knows they won't be around for long. Either he gives them the push before they can do it to him, or he drops them when they start to get serious.'

'You sound as if you disapprove.'

'Well, he just goes round in circles, doesn't he? He keeps going out with those tremendously glamorous women, just to prove he can do it. But in the end he doesn't really want them. They bore him. It's all for show, isn't it? His whole life.'

She gave him a nervous, sidelong glance, as if she might have revealed too much – about Rufus, or about herself? – and added more diffidently, 'It's no wonder he doesn't want to hear about babies. I don't think he could cope with something *real* like that.'

Ged didn't want to hear about babies, either. But it was soon after that dinner party that Elie started talking about them. Talking about babies after they had made love.

After three years of it, sex with Elie was still incredibly exciting. Sometimes it happened unexpectedly, or in unseemly places. He would look at her and want her, and miraculously have her. Want her in a particular way, and have her like that. His own desire seemed to strike sparks off her, igniting a mutual sense of urgency.

Even in bed, at the mundane end of a mundane day, her response to his touch came shyly, sweetly, and ultimately very sexily. She could make as much noise as she wanted in the privacy of the bedroom, and by God she did. Knowing that he could please her so hugely made him want to do it as often as possible.

Or in the middle night, waking to find himself suddenly insomniac with lust, he could roll over on to and into the heat of her body, finding there comfort and relief, and sleep again. Sometimes she scarcely wakened, but she never pushed him away. She said she liked the unexpected reminder that he was there, and that he wanted her.

Polly had never gone in for the unexpected, and had forbidden him to disturb her precious sleep 'just because you happen to have a hard-on'. He wondered now how he could ever have imagined that Polly could give him, or would even want to give him, what he needed. But in those days he hadn't understood the importance of being sexually obsessed with the woman who shared his life.

After three years of happy obsession with Elie, it seemed to him more than ever a miracle.

Now she started to say things. Always the same sort of thing. For instance, when he had just fucked her in the farthest, emptiest corner of the supermarket car park on a Friday night, on account of having happened to look down the front of her blouse when she bent over to take the groceries out of the trolley at the checkout, she said afterwards in her charming, breathless way, 'Wouldn't it be thrilling if you'd just made me pregnant?'

'I thought you were on the pill.'

'I can't stay on the pill for ever. It's not good for my health.'

'There are other ways of accomplishing the same thing.' His heart sank, recalling the endless god-damn condoms he had endured in his streetstalking days.

'What if I want you to make me pregnant?' She looked at him with those incomparable eyes, full of liquid light. 'Don't you want to make a baby in me?'

In theory, removed entirely from reality, he would have loved to do just that. Making babies, as his father had evidently understood too well, was not only a biological imperative but also a way of establishing your ownership of a woman. And he wanted to own Elie, in a way that bastard Ben never had.

But in real life babies were not so much evidence of their father's machismo as unhelpful people with their own demands. The needs of children took precedence over the needs of their parents. That was how it had to be, and very right and proper from a social or biological perspective. But from a personal perspective, he didn't see any reason why he should have to go through all that again. It was scarcely worth turning his life upside down just to make a very basic physical point about his relationship with Elie.

Besides, children cost money, and he didn't have any.

'We can't afford a baby.'

'Why not? You won't have to carry on paying for Louise much longer. Why can't we use that money for a child of our own?'

'That's not enough to bring up a child.'

'Then how does Polly manage?'

'Because she makes more money than you do,' he said brutally. 'And you wouldn't be able to spend your salary on clothes any more.'

'I wouldn't mind.' Catching his sceptical glance, she repeated, 'No, really, I wouldn't. Children are the most important thing in the world. Much more important than clothes.'

But not more important than sex.

At least, that was how he felt. Everything with Elie right

then was pretty much the way he wanted it to be. He didn't even mind that she couldn't cook. If worst came to worst, he could survive on cheese sandwiches and frozen pizzas, but he couldn't live without fucking Elie. Sex was definitely more important than food.

He didn't want babies disturbing the happy hedonism of his present life. Not that he was addicted to partying, as Lucy had claimed to be; just that babies were fatal to their parents' sexual activities. As he knew far better than he wanted to.

He couldn't say that. It would sound too selfish. Was it really selfish to put your own considerations above those of children who didn't even exist? And it wasn't as if he hadn't already made his contribution to posterity.

'Look, Elie, even if children really are so almighty important, I already have two of them. I've done my duty, I don't want any more.'

'But you never see the ones you have.'

'That's not my fault. They don't want to see me.'

'Don't you miss them?'

'Of course.'

He had to say that, whether or not it was true. He didn't know if it was true. He deliberately chose not to think about his children, who refused to see or speak to him. If he were to let himself think about it, the thoughts might be unbearable.

He couldn't afford to take that chance. Couldn't afford to feel . . . what? Grief and loss? Or the truth about what he had done, in leaving them for Elie? Ruining people's lives, as Polly put it. Were lives so readily ruined as that? He didn't know.

In the face of his silence, Elie had tactfully changed course. 'Your mother had no money, but she managed to bring you up.'

Neither half of that sentence was exactly true. His mother had a small allowance, bequeathed by her grandfather, a dour Midlands industrialist who had luckily died when she was too young to have engaged in any serious misbehaviour of the sort that would almost certainly have had her disinherited. The allowance was just enough to let her thumb her nose at conventional society without starving in consequence, which an unluckier rebel might well have done in those far-off Fifties, before single motherhood became first a political and then a fashion statement.

The other part, about managing to bring him up, misleadingly suggested a programme of deliberate, or even instinctive, maternal activity. Keeping someone else, especially a small child, fed and clothed alongside yourself was the most basic form of social behaviour. Even animals did it, even for young creatures of another species. In Ged's view it hardly counted as 'upbringing'. But dragging a child from one commune or squat to another, from one group of strangers to another, the environments getting more and more bizarre as more and more people took to this sub-social lifestyle and more and more drugs were designed – and all the time treating him as baggage that could be ignored whenever it wasn't actually demanding something – that sort of behaviour definitely counted as something else.

He had never held it against his mother, because she obviously meant well. She meant well by everybody. Not a mean bone in her body.

Becoming old enough to earn his own living, to leave home, to order his own existence, had been for him a liberation as great as for any fugitive from an oppressively strict parental regime. When he married Polly he was marrying Croydon, safe and predictable, a haven of convention and uneventful peace.

Polly, of course, thought she was marrying Bohemia, natural man, excitement and spontaneity, a penniless writer with a gypsy face, a hippy mother, and a famous, faraway father.

Her parents had not approved. The divorce would have demonstrated their superior wisdom. He hoped they were getting some pleasure from that, since they seemed to have such a limited amount of pleasure in their lives.

Marrying Polly was all so long ago, nearly twenty years. Christ, he had been a kid then. His own children were nearly grown up now.

And now Elie wanted him to start all over again.

He couldn't stop her going off the pill, if that was what her doctor had told her to do. It meant messing about with condoms and diaphragms. Rubber sex, as he thought of it. Christ, what the human race had had to endure before the pill.

It also put a damper on spontaneous sex in places like car parks, unless he happened to have one of those bloody bits of rubber on him.

Elie took to tempting him. 'Let's just do it. Just do it now. It'll be OK,' she said, writhing like a succubus against him. And from her point of view, of course, it would indeed be OK, whatever the result. He punished her by making her go down on him, and refusing to do the same for her.

She begged him in bed, at the point and in the tone with which she might otherwise have been begging him to perform some erotic service. 'Please give me a baby,' she would whisper, getting more and more desperate and breathless as he moved her towards climax. 'I want your baby. Make a baby in me.'

In those circumstances he found her pleas enormously exciting, a sexual come-on that increased his own pleasure. After all, *baby* was a four-letter word. And making a baby was just what they would have been doing, if it hadn't been for modern medical progress.

But none of that meant he actually wanted one.

She went from pleading to tears and accusations. If he loved her as much as he'd loved Polly, he ought to want to have a baby with her too. People who were truly in love usually wanted to have a baby together; that was how *normal* people behaved. Was she supposed to go to her grave childless, just because he happened to have been married before? Or was there something wrong with her, that he didn't want her to have his baby? Maybe her genes weren't clever enough for him.

And then to hints of a *fait accompli*. Supposing she accidentally found herself pregnant, what would he do?

He was reading a newspaper when she said this, so he didn't have to look at her when he answered. 'I'd suspect it wasn't an accident.'

A long pause. 'But what would you do?'

'Accidents can be amended nowadays, can't they?'

Her voice went very small. 'What do you mean?'

He did look at her then. He set the paper down and looked at her very deliberately. 'You know what I mean.'

It stuck in his mind, afterwards, too late, the way she had looked back at him. A strangely stricken look, pale and wide-eyed, mouth a little open, stare a little dazed. As if he had threatened to hit her, and she had believed the threat.

11

Grocery shopping was the bane of mankind.

In the good old days, when it meant hunting down a mammoth, with the risk of being trampled by your prey, or of ending up as someone else's dinner, or of abject failure and starvation, these considerations must at least have taken most of the boredom out of the process. Deciding which pizza topping to buy didn't get the adrenalin flowing in the same way. Not even blowing the budget on steaks and champagne could offer that old primeval thrill. And there was no way out of it: if you wanted to eat, you had to shop.

Even in the wilds of Oregon, it was impossible to escape this tragic aspect of the human condition. When Ged had set off on his unspecified errand – actually just to see Rene Deforte, but going out without explanation is the last bastion of masculine privilege – Angelina had thrust a shopping list through the open car window, as he was starting up the motor.

And *she* was supposed to be working for *him*.

The nearest town was at the mouth of the river that ran alongside the road through the mountains. Its name declared it to be a port, and boats of various sizes and styles pottered there, busy beyond the shoreline or at rest in the estuary. The weatherboarded buildings lining the streets had rectangular false fronts and open wooden verandas, lending the port the look of a Western frontier town.

But of course this had been the final frontier. The goal of all those mythic covered-wagon trains, crammed with pioneers, their hopes and household goods. This was the edge of the western world. One could go no further in the search for whatever-it-was, the want of which prevented true fulfilment.

The supermarket at the world's edge was doing its best to provide fulfilment. Here as everywhere, that meant crisps and sweets, pop and booze, to judge by the amount of shelf space devoted to these items.

Angelina's shopping list ignored their existence. Things in tins and boxes were not needed either. Fruit and vegetables, meat and milk, that was all she wanted. Pretty much the converse of any list Ged might have put together, if he had been the sort of person who composes shopping lists.

He could cope pretty well without sweets and snacks, but not without alcohol. He made his own addenda to the list: beer, whisky, cigarettes. A former nun, even one who had been shacked up with the likes of Malachy for a couple of years, was unlikely to place the proper importance on those items.

Mentally he debated the merits of Scotch versus bourbon, standing with a bottle of each in hand. If he was going to be stuck here for any length of time, he would probably need both. And if he decided to tell Deforte to stuff the will up his arse, and head back to London, he'd still probably need both.

'Angie didn't put that on her list, did she?'

That had to be a telepathic stranger, since he didn't know anyone here. Well, yes, come to think of it, he did. And that was who it was: Malachy's biographer.

Jorge – or Jesús, as he must prefer to be, since he was still wearing the self-advertising T-shirt – must have drawn up his shopping list along the lines of Ged's hypothetical one. His basket was stuffed with tins and bottles and packets, and not a sniff of a vegetable. Perhaps there were male and female shopping lists.

Ged dropped both bottles into his own trolley. 'I thought Angie said you lived in Eugene,' wherever that was. Back in the Willamette Valley, presumably. Most places were.

'I've set myself up at a campground,' Jorge explained vaguely. 'Is this luck or is this luck? I've been wondering how to fix up a chat without Angie around, and bingo, here you are. What do you say we take this here beer and go sit on the rocks down there?'

Ged asked cautiously, 'What did you want to talk about?'

'That's for me to know and you to find out,' Jorge retorted, steering for the checkout. 'What do you want, a formal agenda?'

The sea fog had disappeared, or not yet appeared, or decided to skip its appearance altogether for today. The ocean, deprived of its veil of mystery, was in an irritable mood, smacking the rocks at random and flinging its fishy spume about. Sun and sea breeze contended for mastery of the micro climate, taking it in turns to bring up sweat or shivers on any flesh within reach of their powers.

The beer was the same as ever: cool and simple, full of fizz and devoid of taste. A natural metaphor, maybe, for the culture that produced it.

Jorge pulled his boots off – serious leather, black and buckled, presumably designed for kicking the motorbike into submission when it refused to start – and dangled his bare feet down the steep seaward side of the rock, bait to tempt the sulky waves. 'You been to see Rene?'

Ged grunted noncommittally. He had just discovered that if he lay belly down on the slab of rock, which tilted slightly landwards, he could get the benefit of the sun's warmth with very little interference from the wind. He folded his arms along the rim of the rock, rested his chin on his arms. The effect, with the breeze in his face and the sea spray growling just out of reach, was something like virtual surfing.

Jorge took no notice of this response, or lack of it. 'Are you going to do it? What Mal wanted you to do?'

'I don't know.'

'What do you mean, you don't know? You don't know if you want to be rich?'

'I don't know if I want to let him get away with it.'

'Get away with what?'

'Doing whatever the hell he pleased for his whole bloody life. Having kids and walking away from them. And then expecting me to pick up the pieces, just because he was my father.'

'Also because he's arranged to make you rich if you do it.'

'Then why me? Why not arrange to make someone else rich – his lawyer, for instance, or his agent, or even you – in return for sorting out the mess?'

Jorge had to reflect before replying. Maybe it hadn't occurred to him that he could just as easily have featured in the will. 'It's not the same. You're his son.'

'I know. That's what I just said. That's why he wanted me to do it.' Ged pushed himself up and back, on to his knees, fumbling for his cigarettes. He rocked back on his heels, breathing smoky carbon monoxide instead of fish-fragrant ozone. 'What about Angelina?'

'What do you mean, what about Angie?'

'You said you wanted to talk to me without her around.'

'Oh, that was just because she might not approve of what I want to do.'

'Which is?'

'Well, it's this book I'm writing.'

'The Definitive Life and Work?'

'No, no, that's not really a problem.' Jorge sounded vague, probably because half his attention was focused on opening a new tin of beer. 'I got enough out of Mal to be able to waffle up a doctorate, and I've picked up a lot more from him and other people since then. But when he died,

I thought, hey, there's bound to be a lot of interest in him. People are always interested in artists' lives, especially the freakier ones, and Mal was pretty freaky all right.'

'Because he turned himself into a hermit?'

'Hermit, my ass. I should have even half the action he was getting when he was supposed to be old and sick. And in his prime . . . well, I've heard some amazing stories. Not from him, I might add.'

'Discreet, was he?'

'Only in the sense that he kept his mouth shut about what he got up to. Otherwise . . . Well, just for instance, he met some woman at a party in a penthouse, and when they left, she got into the elevator with him on the thirty-third floor, and by the time they got out at the ground floor, she was pregnant.'

'One of my twelve brothers, I presume.'

'No, I think she got it fixed. Anyway, you see what I mean.'

Ged saw, all right. 'But out here he seems to have settled down to monogamous fornication with his house-keepers.'

'The hell he did. A guy like Mal, he could no more give up women than he could give up painting. I don't think he could've done it even if he'd wanted to. The women wouldn't leave him alone. He had one here in Oldport, and another one down in Florence, and some professor at the university in Corvallis, and then there was one that used to turn up every summer in a cabin up the coast. Those were just the ones I happened to find out about. Plus, of course, as you say, the ones that actually lived with him.'

'According to Rene,' Ged recalled, 'he blamed his profession for his promiscuity.'

'Well, he did have a thing about being an artist. I got the impression he felt it justified his existence somehow. I don't know what he thought the rest of us did to deserve being alive.' Jorge paused, then harked back to his original topic. 'Anyway, you can understand that when I spoke to a couple of publishers about Mal, they were interested all right. There is definitely an interest in a biography of him.'

'And Angelina doesn't approve of this?'

'She did at first. When she thought it would be based on my thesis, which is all about his art, of course. There are several books out about his work already, but nothing based on conversations with the artist. And you couldn't do anything definitive before he'd actually died, if you follow me. I've already negotiated a contract for a book along those lines, a proper scholarly work, y'know? That's no problem. I'll just touch up my thesis here and there, and flesh it out a bit.'

'Then what is the problem?'

'Well, a book like that will be great for my career as an art historian, but it's not likely to be a bestseller, is it? I mean, think of the price, with all those colour reproductions. Mal's paintings are incomprehensible without the colour. And the reading public isn't seriously interested in art, anyway. But a popular biography, now that's a different matter. Biographies are big news. People are surprisingly keen on reading about what famous people got up to. And Mal was famous for being anti-fame. He refused to be interviewed, he never went to night-clubs, he didn't hang around with celebrity friends. All he did was paint and fuck. It was a brilliant career move.'

'And now that he's dead, you want to make money out of him.'

'Well, why not? He's not around to care. And somebody's sure as hell going to do it, so why not me? I mean, at least I knew him.'

Jorge jammed his beer between his thighs to keep the wind from knocking it over. He leaned back on his hands, tilted his face up to the sun, closed his eyes. His nostrils heaved with the effort of inhaling the ocean. 'I love this coast. It's so god-damned inhospitable. Rocky and foggy, too cold for a swim, no amenities, no easy route inland, and the beaches stink of rotting fish. But it's beautiful as hell. The geographical equivalent of Mal.'

Ged recalled his father, the one time he had seen him; remembered the glamour his presence had cast over ordinary things, in the enchanted eyes of his nineteen-year-old son. 'Was he beautiful?'

Jorge opened his eyes. He stared out to sea. 'You could have cut off his head and stuck it on Mount Rushmore, he had that kind of physical presence. Hell, he must have been sixty when I first met him, and yet I couldn't get his face out of my mind. It went with the sort of person he was. Impassive, quiet-spoken, real reserved, you know? But deep and different, underneath. Made you want to know him better, no matter how well you thought you knew him already.' He turned his head to glance at Ged. 'You could do it too, you know.'

'Do what?'

'Write a book about him. You're a writer, aren't you? And he was your father.'

'But I didn't know him. I only met him once.'

'So what? That's what the book could be about. The Famous Father I Never Knew.'

Ged shrugged. It sounded as likely as any other idea he had entertained for the last three years, and about as likely ever to get written. 'Angelina wouldn't approve.'

'She might not mind. I mean, you have a right to your father's life, don't you? Besides, the real reason she doesn't approve of what I'm doing is because she doesn't like my approach.'

'What sort of approach is that?'

'Well, I told her it was all the publishers' idea. I mean, it's the publishers' job to know this kind of thing, isn't it? What will sell and what won't. So when they say, look, what is needed here is real human-interest stuff, dishing the dirt and so forth . . . well, who am I to argue?'

'That means sex, does it?'

'Not just sex,' Jorge amended loftily. 'Relationships.'

'Non-relationships, you mean. My Famous Father With Whom I Had No Relationship Whatsoever.'

'You and twelve other guys, according to Rene. Not to mention any daughters. And every one of those kids by a different woman. Christ, Mal had relationships coming out his ears.' Jorge closed his eyes again, the better to envisage these. 'That's what I wanted to ask you about.'

'What? My mother?'

'Not her in particular. I'd just like to talk to all the people on that list of his heirs. Talk to their mothers. See what's happened to them all. I might even get a third book out of that.'

Ged tossed the tail end of his cigarette into the water and stood up. The waves hissed and spat at him in protest. They were closer now, striking higher up the side of the rock; the tide must be coming in. He moved away from the edge. 'I shouldn't think solicitors are allowed to give away information like that.'

'You're not a solicitor.'

'And I don't have the information.'

'You would if you were the executor. Hey!'

The shout came too late. A rogue wave shattered against the slanting rock, a kamikaze breaker that reached its target, spattering them both, Jorge all over, Ged to his knees.

Jorge clambered to his feet, cursing. 'God damn it, my beer's got sea water in it.'

Ged thought of pointing out that this might improve the taste. Instead, as he watched the remains of the wave climbing over and into Jorge's boots, he simply observed, 'Looks like you've got sea water in everything.'

Jorge shrugged and shook himself, throwing off fat salty drops. 'Well, what the hell, I'll dry out on the motorcycle.' He picked up his boots and turned them upside down to drain, banging the heels together to encourage the water to leave. 'In fact I think I'll do that right now. I should be getting my groceries back to the campground and doing rugged primeval things like impaling wieners on sticks and roasting them alive. Think about it, will you? The book, I mean, not the wieners.'

12

'Yeah, I know about the book. George confessed.'

Angelina was standing at the kitchen table, stuffing a
chicken – a disgusting process which would result in a
delicious dinner. The cats were hanging about in ostentatiously casual poses, eyeing the bird with expressions
that said she needn't waste her time roasting it.

Ged was watching Angelina, not the chicken. She had
an air of innocent assurance, a naïve, childlike confidence
in herself and in the world, that he found peculiarly attractive. Perhaps the attraction was a poignant one; like all
forms of innocence, it was fragile and doomed.

She explained about the book, or the confession. 'First
he said he was turning his thesis into one of those big,
classy art books with lots of colour pictures. I didn't see
anything wrong with that, and I don't guess Malachy
would have either. An artist naturally wants people to look
at his pictures, doesn't he?

'But then he started asking me about all sorts of other
things. Mostly women. And any stories to do with
Montana.' She glanced at Ged, a look of curious delicacy.
'You know that's where Malachy was from?'

'I know. Rene Deforte told me.' And the newspapers.

'Good. So I finally said to him, Look, George, I don't
see what women and Montana have to do with a book
about painting. And then he said, well, it wasn't just

about Malachy's paintings, it was about his whole life. A biography.'

From her scandalized tone, she might have been accusing Jorge of pornography rather than biography. 'What's wrong with that?'

'Malachy would be turning in his grave, if he had one. He thought artists should be anonymous. He said the painting should be famous, not the painter. And George knows all that perfectly well.' Evidently Malachy's views were gospel in her eyes.

'But he might not agree with that thinking,' Ged pointed out. 'Most people wouldn't. And there's no way my father could impose his will on the rest of the world. Maybe Jorge feels it's better for any biography to be written by him, rather than someone who didn't know Malachy so well.'

'What's worse, to be betrayed by a friend or by a stranger?' She stooped to stow the chicken in the oven, then straightened again. 'Calum's taken Charles for a walk around the mountain.'

'More likely Charles is taking Calum for a walk,' he suggested, mindful of the dog's size. 'There's no chance of them getting lost, is there?'

'Charles knows his way home. Worst that can happen is they meet up with a bear.'

He thought she must be joking. 'You have bears around here?'

'Just black bears, this side of the valley. They don't usually eat people. And there aren't a lot of them left now. The more people, the fewer bears, and more's the pity. That's what Malachy used to say.'

'He was fond of bears?'

'Not specially, but he preferred them to people. He claimed to prefer almost anything to people, but I don't know if I believed him. He had this romantic image of himself as a natural-born hermit. Now it's true he wasn't the partying type, but he'd never really lived on his own.

He always had some woman to look after him. Not like the real hermits, who used to live in caves and wouldn't let any woman within a mile of them.'

'What about you? You've been living on your own here since Malachy died, and it must have been lonely even when he was alive. And you're only twenty, not sixty-six.'

Angelina glanced at her surroundings in vague surprise, as if this idea had never occurred to her. 'I don't mind,' she said simply and truthfully. 'I'm not the partying type either.'

He was going to have to make up his mind quickly.

Did he want the money? Silly question.

Did he want to let his father bribe him into behaving as if they had been a normal family? To let him get away with treating his women and children like shit, and then having his son turn up, all is forgiven, to take charge of his affairs? That was a tougher one.

If Malachy hadn't been rich and famous, no-one would give a damn what happened to his effects when he died. A crazy old bastard dying in a filthy hovel? Easiest just to burn the place down.

And people who died without children, even these days, were regarded as failures in some important sense. Not just the Darwinian sense of having failed to pass their genes along to the future, but the cultural sense of one's life losing meaning at the moment of death, if there was no-one else for whom it had unique and irreducible significance. My father, my grandfather, my son. The people who made me of their own mortal fabric. The man to whom I can never be irrelevant.

So society had not yet decayed down to atomized individuals. Not if even a man like Malachy, who had made a career out of thumbing his nose at convention, could be so desperate to ensure that he was not regarded by history as a sad old man who had chosen liberty and found death, rather than opting for fatherhood and immortality.

So OK, good for society. Good for Malachy. But was

Ged going to let himself be used like this, to allow his father a cultural dignity and regard he didn't deserve?

The studio was flooded with sun, as it had been when he first saw it. Once more he was struck dumb at the spectacle of a wallful of his father's paintings.

Seeing them all together like this, a universe made from Malachy's mind, the effect was astonishing, compelling, alarmingly unsettling. There was the sheer intensity of repetition, each canvas squarely confronting the same concerns. There was the contradiction between the deliberately obvious flat surface of the canvas, and the startling sculptural effects created on it. There was the insistent simplicity of primary colours, denied and defied by the subtle gradations of shade and shadow. They exerted a primitive emotional power, but were unmistakably an intellectual exercise. The shapes within the squares were distinct and yet illusory. Like painted ghosts.

It would have been an unimaginable luxury to have the walls of his own sitting room paved with those paintings. The colours were so rich, he could all but taste and smell them. The shades of each colour were so infinitely varied from square to square, so evocative of so many contradictory things, that the emotional impact was as great as the aesthetic one. He felt as if he could have sunk his hand into any one of them and entered another world: a world made entirely of lemon rind, or rose petals, or lapis lazuli.

Malachy himself was here, Angelina had said. There were several terracotta pots scattered around the room, and one of them held his father's ashes. The one nearest the door, he guessed. Correctly.

He had never seen the results of cremation before. Bodies burned well, he discovered. No cinders, only bone-white ash. And not much of that: he could have contained the mortal remains of his father in his own two hands. They were big hands, true, but his father had been a big man.

More of a myth than a man, he thought, where he

himself had been concerned. The handful of ashes was like the dregs of a dream.

He straightened and turned away, to survey the other remains of his father's life.

Amid all the clutter, one thing struck him as especially incongruous: the filing cabinet. In anyone else's house it would have been an ordinary, almost essential fixture, but in the middle of this unbelievable chaos, it seemed more like an ironic reflection on its surroundings.

He manoeuvred his way over to the cabinet. It stood out from the surrounding rubble like a skyscraper in some ambitious prairie town. But unlike your average skyscraper, the cabinet had been Malachized, draped with fern and ivy like an ancient garden ornament.

He tried to open the top drawer. It resisted. And no wonder: it turned out to be jam-packed with apparently unpaid bills and unopened bank statements and dead cheque-books and suchlike.

He tried the next one. The same sort of rubble, only dustier.

The third drawer was also a jumble, but mostly of photographs.

In the bottom drawer, among other things, he found a hardback copy of *Old Adam*.

He took it out and opened it. There was nothing written on the fly leaf. Something had been stuck between the pages. A flimsy little notebook with wide-ruled lines, the kind that young children use at school.

He took the notebook out of the novel. It had numbers written on the front. He picked it up and flipped through it. The handwriting was in a round, painstaking, American style. It didn't look like the writing of someone who wrote a lot.

When he closed the book again, he realized that the numbers on the front were the year he had been born.

He reopened the previous drawer, the one full of photographs. The topmost photo was a black and white shot of Angelina, with a cat in her lap.

Another photo, this one of his father. Maybe Angelina had taken it, because Malachy was in the same chair, with the same cat sitting on the floor in front of the chair. He was looking at the cat, and the cat was looking at him, both in a friendly fashion.

More photos, picked up at random. An unknown girl in a bikini, perched on a rock in the sea. Then the same girl on the same rock, wearing only the bottom half of her bikini. Next she was lying belly down on the rock, wearing nothing at all.

Here was Malachy in this studio, scowling at something on an easel. An older photo of a younger Malachy, standing in a city street. New York, maybe.

Ged studied these for several minutes. He took a moment to wonder about the girl. Angelina's predecessor? He compared his father's several faces, noting in what ways he had aged since that meeting in New York, in what ways the image was like his own. Looking, now, for signs of Cheyenne blood.

At that moment he realized what he was doing. Understood what his father had been doing. Grasped what inheritance was all about. Why there was no escaping it.

Other people, as it happened, because Malachy Hawke was a famous artist, would probably be interested in these photographs. Jesús Jorge Bravo would certainly be interested. Also Bradford Welles the Twenty-Third. But only Ged – or Calum and Louise, or those twelve other sons and their sons, or the unnumbered and unknown daughters and granddaughters – only they would be interested for the right, the essential reasons. Only they could give a real human meaning and value and purpose to these pictures.

If Malachy had been Joe Bloggs, if he had died without descendants, if Ged had been his executor only, no relation – then all those photographs, maybe a lifetime of memories and events, would have been thrown out, destroyed. And why not? The only person for whom they had significance was dead. There was no room in the world for mementoes of unknown dead people caught in pointless trivial acts. That was the opposite of history, the past as rubbish.

Still holding a handful of photos, he closed the drawer. He closed and locked the studio door, and went across the deck to the house. He had some half-formed idea of showing the photographs to Calum, seeing what sort of interest his son might take in his father's life.

He had just gone through the sliding door into the living room, when Charles came in after him with a crash and clatter. It bounded up to him and skidded to a stop on its backside, looking expectant. It was actually quite a handsome dog . . . horse . . . whatever it was. Its canine ancestors had been of the pointy-nose, pointy-ear variety, with a coarse, dense, upright coat and a bushy tail. Its vigilant ears and canny eyes implied an active rather than a contemplative spirit. Right now it was obviously waiting for some action from Ged.

'What have you done with Calum?'

He looked at the open door as he spoke. The dog turned to look too. Then its great head swung back towards Ged, and on around to point in the direction of the kitchen. Whatever it was waiting for must have something to do with food. Most things did, where dogs were concerned.

'Where's Calum?'

This time he didn't look at the patio doors. But the dog did. A moment later, Calum appeared on the deck.

That didn't mean the dog had understood the question, of course, or even that it had the slightest idea who Calum was. It might have turned to look because it could hear someone coming. Now it turned again to Ged, staring at him earnestly with its eager eyes. He had an idea that if he moved away it would follow him.

'What do you think it wants?' he asked Calum.

Calum sniffed at the hint of roasting chicken. 'Supper, I should think, same as me.'

'But why pick on me? I've never given it anything to eat.'

'Most likely it knows you've taken over from the old man.'

'Is that what I've done?'

Ged looked down at Malachy's face in his hands. He looked at the chaos around him. 'House and contents' included the dog, presumably. Though he didn't see how the dog could possibly know that. Or know that he had only minutes ago decided to agree to the terms of his father's will.

Had understood, that was, that he could never have refused his father's legacy. Not when his father had left him the ashes of his life.

13

'What have you done with Calum?'

It was Polly asking, this time. And Ged, not Charles, being held responsible for Calum's whereabouts. Ged was back in London and Calum was still in Oregon. An attempt to convey this information had resulted in the encounter with Polly.

Ged was not sure why he had gone round to the house to deliver his message. He had rung up, but the answering machine wasn't on. So he drove over with some vague idea of leaving a note, and by the time he got to Notting Hill, she had come home.

He had always said he lived in Notting Hill, because that had street cred and even a touch of raffish respectability. The kind of place a writer might live if he was not, on the one hand, composing cutting-edge post-modern conundrums, nor on the other hand writing with a hypodermic needle. The house was actually on the cusp between Notting Hill and Bayswater, but Bayswater gave off a whiff of cheap hotels, cheap tourists, cheap whores.

Polly let him into the sitting room with an air of grudging suspicion, as if he might have come round on some unwelcome or illegitimate errand. Doorstepping for Jehovah's Witnesses, for instance, or checking for cock-roach infestation. Her reaction wasn't all that surprising; this was the first time he had been in the house since shortly after he left her, three years ago.

During his last few weeks of living in this house, he had spent his days – when he wasn't wandering around Hyde Park, keeping an eye out for Elie – pacing the garden, smoking. He couldn't smoke in the house, even when Polly wasn't there, because if Polly came home and smelled smoke, she would also smell a rat. He wasn't supposed to be smoking.

Well, at least now he didn't have to stand in the rain, an umbrella in one hand and a cigarette in the other.

He sat down on the sofa – still the same sofa, and even more, ah, domesticated. Polly perched on the edge of an armchair, looking as if she didn't expect this to take long. Warning him not to take long. Making him feel more than ever like a double-glazing salesman.

She hadn't changed. It wasn't that she was ageing well, more that she hadn't really aged at all. If she had suffered as much as she claimed, it certainly didn't show. She was trim rather than slim, a neatly parcelled female body. Her fair hair was still in the same style, short and fluffy, showing no sign of grey. He even recognized the jumper she had on. It made him feel vaguely nostalgic for her.

He hauled out a packet of cigarettes and held it up. 'Do you mind?'

She couldn't really say no. He was a guest in her house, not her husband any more. He had to ask, and she had to say OK. She looked surprised at first, then the opposite, as if it was just what she should have expected. 'I thought you gave that up years ago.'

'For about six months.'

She did some mental calculations. She had always been good at that sort of thing, numbers, dates, anniversaries and so forth. 'Does that mean you'd started smoking again while you were still living in this house?'

Her tone suggested this might well have been an even bigger betrayal than screwing Elie. My ex-husband, the rat, he was actually *smoking* behind my back.

Ged shrugged and lit up. He was a rat, there was no getting around it. She didn't know the half of it and please

God never would. To divert her he asked, 'Where's Lulu?'

When had he last seen Louise? That last day, the last time he had come home to this house.

He had come to remove his worldly goods. Meaning, mostly, the word processor that he needed to write, and the books that he needed to read. A writer without books was like a bird without the sky. But was he still a writer now, after three years of silence? Since Elie left, he couldn't even concentrate enough to read.

He had sneaked back in the middle of the day, to avoid a pointless confrontation with Polly. From the pub down the road he had checked that no car was parked in the tiny square of pavement between the steps and the wall. But Louise had been parked in front of the television, in the family room at the back of the house.

And that was the last time he had seen her. He remembered exactly how she had looked. She was wearing faded jeans, a top that ended well above her navel, and no make-up. She had piled her long hair up on top of her head in a fashionably haphazard way, dark strands spilling down to frame her face. That scrubbed and rather spotty thirteen-year-old face looked babyish by contrast with the casually sophisticated hairstyle, with the young woman's body filling out the young girl's clothing.

Ged had been startled to find her there. He had presumed she would be in school, till he recalled that the summer holidays had begun. A fortnight after having moved into a world where schools and children did not figure, he had already forgotten these familiar patterns.

Louise too had been startled, even when she saw who it was. 'Daddy, have you come back?'

The look on her face, surprised delight, made him feel far worse than any accusations from Polly. Not just because he was hurting his daughter, but because she had given him the power to hurt her.

He shut his mind to that. He kept it focused on Elie, the reason for all this emotional brutality. 'I only came to get some things.'

Brief delight, already vanished. 'You mean you're not coming home?'

'What made you think I might be?'

'Something Mummy said.'

He hadn't a clue what Polly had told her: what excuses had been made, what reputations blackened. He hadn't spoken to his children since making the decision to leave. Obviously a complete shit, and a coward to boot. Perhaps that was what Polly had told them. 'What did she say?'

'She said you were having a mid-life crisis and you'd run off with some trollop, but she didn't expect it to last.'

Ged didn't either, when he thought about it in those terms. Squatting in Rufus's flat – by good fortune, Rufus had just been heading abroad on holiday with his latest sexual accessory – he and Elie had opted to eat out or take away rather than cope with Rufus's minimally equipped kitchen. But what if eating out was Elie's idea of normal life? What if she really couldn't cook? Just for instance. Though at that point in their relationship, the prospect of living on endless take-aways and frozen dinners seemed almost a fair exchange for the privilege of fucking her.

No point trying to explain that kind of adult logic to a thirteen-year-old.

He sat down on the dilapidated sofa alongside Louise, not knowing what else to do by way of showing sociability. He noticed she was wearing her glasses. After she had pestered him into forking out a fortune for contact lenses, because glasses were totally out for anyone who was in. 'I thought you hated wearing glasses.'

'I do. But I've got an eye infection and I can't wear the contacts for three weeks. I take these off when I go out anywhere.'

'How do you see?'

'I can see everything I need to, Daddy. I just can't see the TV without them.'

They both stared at the television. Some sort of quiz game, apparently, in which penalties were awarded as well as prizes. Anyone giving three wrong answers had to sit in the corner with a dunce's cap. Two minutes' viewing made it clear that even giving the right answers didn't prevent the contestants from making complete fools of themselves.

Ged had never watched daytime television, on the same principle as a man who never touches liquor for fear of becoming alcoholic. This example of the genre suggested he need not have worried. 'Lulu, why are you watching this?'

'Why not? What else is there to do?'

'You could be reading, for instance.' He added, in churlish below-the-belt fashion, 'You wouldn't need to wear glasses to do that, would you?'

She gave him a quellingly sardonic look, which said perfectly clearly that if he wanted to try telling her what to do, he would at least have to live in the house. 'I read all the time, Daddy. In bed, or at the weekend. But when there's nobody around here during the day, it's too quiet. When I'm all on my own, I like a little noise to keep me company.'

She turned her attention, or at least her gaze, back to the television screen. She was holding herself rigidly, as if undergoing a formal and unpleasant interview. 'You told Calum he couldn't bring his girlfriends home to sleep overnight. This house is not a brothel, you said.'

'Calum has a different girl every week. I thought he ought to take the trouble to introduce them to his family, assuming he even knows their names.'

'Well, at least he didn't run away with one of them, did he?'

Ged said gently, dryly, 'Are you suggesting I should have brought Elie back here?'

'No!' She jumped up, suddenly vehement. 'You're my father! You're not supposed to have girlfriends! You're not supposed to run away from home! All that stuff is for kids like me and Calum, not for people's parents!'

He didn't have to answer that, because she ran out of the room.

Three years ago. The last time he had seen her. Sitting on the sofa, right next to him.

The subject of Louise appeared to make Polly nervous too. She clasped her hands in her lap. 'She's out some-where, I suppose. Out with her friends. I haven't seen a lot of her lately, to tell you the truth.'

She lifted her gaze from her hands, which were holding each other quite tightly, he saw, as if she were praying with especial earnestness. She glanced at him, a skittish, uneasy look. He thought she was going to say something serious, tell him something that was troubling her. But then her eyes slid away, and she said something else. He didn't know what she had been about to say, he only knew it wasn't what she did say.

'Kids don't hang about the house much these days, do they? When they do come home, they bring their friends with them. And when they're really on their own, they put on those headphones and go into another world. They're like ants, they just can't cope with solitude.' She jumped up, unclasped her hands. 'Do you want some coffee?'

The coffee came in on a tray, along with cups and saucers, a sugar bowl, a pair of spoons, and a jug of milk. Polly always did things like that. The way they were done in Croydon, he supposed; the way her mother did it, as if the vicar had come to call. Even when the caller was your ex-husband, and you knew perfectly well how much milk he liked in his sugarless coffee.

She had also brought an ashtray.

'Where's Calum?' she asked again.

'He's still back in America.'

'Doing what?'

'Sorting something out for me.' He took a mouthful of coffee, then a lungful of smoke. 'My father left me his house and everything in it, in return for being his executor. It's a god-awful mess. Calum is going through it for me, throwing out rubbish, making an inventory, looking for any evidence of investments or bank accounts, all that kind of thing.'

Polly looked incredulous, as well she might. But it wasn't his father's will that was exercising her astonishment. 'You're expecting Calum to sort out a mess for you?'

'Why not? I'm paying him for it.'

When Ged had offered him the job, Calum asked how much. You tell me, said Ged. And Calum, to his father's surprise, looked around the studio and said, How about that painting over there? The red one, top right.

'How very generous of you,' Polly observed tartly. 'But Calum's much better at making a mess than sorting one out.'

'He's got to grow up some time.'

'Why? Nobody does any more. Everybody just does what they like. Though I can't see that they're any happier for it. Are you sure it's a good idea, leaving him on his own?'

'He's not quite on his own. There's a housekeeper to look after him, and help keep his nose to the grindstone. Anyway, I think he got the message that this is important, because it's not just me involved.'

Polly's response, when she had heard the terms of the will, was predictable. 'What about his daughters?'

'Girls don't count, it seems.'

'How unbelievably Victorian.' By now Polly had settled herself properly into her armchair, holding her coffee cup in her lap, looking thoughtful. 'The whole scenario is Victorian, though, isn't it? An old man and his housekeeper and a house full of rubbish.'

'Valuable rubbish. Each of his paintings is worth a small fortune in itself, according to his agent. And the housekeeper was obviously his mistress.'

'That sounds quite Victorian too. I'd forgotten your father was an artist. Forgotten all about him, in fact. I didn't even know he knew you existed. Or that he cared. Funny what old age and impending death does for people's value systems. Almost as if we still, in our hearts, believe in hellfire.'

'Maybe just the opposite. Maybe it's because we don't believe any more in our own immortal souls. So other people are all the immortality we have left.' Ged stubbed out his cigarette and set his empty cup and saucer back on the tray. 'It's going to take Calum a while to do the job. I've written down the address and phone number for you, if you want to give him a ring.'

She followed him to the door. Having been reluctant to let him in, she now seemed reluctant to let him go. 'I haven't asked how you are. Aside from being rich, I mean.'

'I'm not rich yet. I haven't seen a penny of it so far.'

'But it's just a matter of time, isn't it? How's the book going?'

She meant his latest book, whatever it was. As soon as he finished a book, there was always another one waiting in the wings, demanding to be written down. Until now. Until Elie, he thought unjustly. 'It's not. Not going, I mean. Robin's been nagging me about it.'

'You're rich now,' she pointed out. 'You can afford to tell him to go to hell. You don't need to write books any more.'

'What would I do instead?'

What would I do with my life, he meant. She misunderstood him. 'Don't tell me you've been infected with the puritan work ethic, you of all people! You've never really done the nine to five, you don't know what it's like. If I could afford to chuck in my job, I wouldn't have any trouble whatsoever finding other things to do.'

A frivolous Polly was a new one on him. 'What would you do?'

'Go to Paris and kit myself out for a new life, for starters. Then I'd find a toyboy and take a trip around the world.'

She paused, smiling, looking up at him. She had gone from tension to ease, and now to sudden nervousness. She touched his arm. 'How much?'

'What?'

'How much would you charge, if you were a toyboy?'

'I think they get paid in gifts. Sports cars and Rolex watches and suchlike. Anyway, I'm too old to be a toyboy. Even thirty would be pushing it, unless you were over eighty.'

'I'm not ageist about these things.'

She was serious, he realized, or serious enough. She was propositioning him. His ex-wife, inviting him to screw her.

There wasn't any way she could have known about Elie's disappearance, not if Calum hadn't known. And Ged wasn't going to tell her, just in case she started getting the wrong idea.

On the other hand, three months without Elie was a hell of a long time. A hell, literally. He couldn't remember when he'd been without sex for so long. Not since he was a kid, surely. And there was nothing complicated about this. Polly was just offering him a fuck. It wasn't as if it was the first time they'd ever done it.

Calum had said she hadn't got a man. Maybe she was desperate too. Evidently it had taken her three years to really start missing it. Something in there about the basic incompatibility of the sexes.

She was stroking his arm, her smile growing tremulous. He had to make up his mind. Right now, before things got sticky.

Well, why not? He could simply shut the door and screw her on the spot, and then leave. Didn't even have to take off her clothes, or his. Just do it standing up, against the door. He'd done that before, but never to Polly.

That was quite an exciting idea. A little bit like . . .

STREETWALKING

Alone, aloud in the raptured ear of men
We pour our dark nocturnal secret . . .

Saturday night had always been sex night, while he and Polly were married.

A habit, not a rule. The arrival of Saturday night was a necessary but not sufficient condition for sexual intercourse to take place. Other events might intervene to prevent it. Any number of other events, in spite of Ged's best efforts.

Saturday was good because no-one had to get up the next morning, because Polly often got into a pleasantly tipsy and therefore readily arousable state, because the children were more likely to be out or away from home. The rest of the week was bad because Polly was exhausted, because the children were underfoot, because (Polly maintained) the sight of all those foolish little girls she had to deal with, and their hapless babies, was enough to put her off procreative activities for ever.

Not quite for ever, fortunately. Just till Saturday night.

Decorous little grunts, mm-mm-mmm, were the nearest Polly ever came to abandon. Something to do with a Croydon childhood, Ged supposed. Being a social worker probably didn't help either.

She regarded sex not as a passion or even a pleasure, but as something necessary for mental and physical health, like muesli or jogging. She had explained the facts of life with clinical detail and dispassion to a bewildered Louise and a squirming Calum. Ged suggested to her that such a frank approach might be enough to destroy their interest in sex for some time to come, thus saving her a great deal of worry. But that was not, it appeared, her intention.

'It's best they should get the facts, rather than hearing rumours and rubbish from their friends, isn't it? The more they know, the less they're likely to get into trouble. And I want them to feel they can talk to me about anything that's bothering them.'

Ged tried to imagine his adolescent self asking his mother about anything to do with sex. No chance. Not because she would have refused or become embarrassed, but because she would inevitably have illustrated any advice with practical examples from her own personal experience. Occasional unsolicited tips from her lovers had been no more helpful, since each man invariably took a view of sexual relations completely contrary to his predecessor's.

Polly's idea of a healthy sex life was of course a tasteful one. Clinical terms were preferred to crudities, and anything remotely vulgar did not feature at all. Sexy underwear was sexist. Ditto pictures of naked women. X-rated videos were right out.

In the beginning Ged had taken her straightforward approach as evidence of freedom from hang-ups. It took a few years for him to realize his error, and a few years more to understand what the problem was.

The problem was that sexual intercourse is not necessarily sexy. And the other side of the coin, that the essence of sexiness lurks in nuance and evocation, not merely in the physical act. And even that orgasm is not precisely the same thing as sexual satisfaction.

What Polly wanted to do was to take the vast twilit universe of sex, the immemorial underpinnings of human existence and high civilization, wanted to drag it by the ears from under the bed, wash its mouth out with soap, and hang it up to air in the sunshine.

That was her hang-up.

Not that it might have been much different, he thought then, if he had married some other woman, or none at all. Rufus changed his women almost as often as his underwear, but despite his lurid descriptions of erotic adventure, none of the women who were reportedly such hot stuff in bed had held his attention for long.

That might have been something to do with Rufus, or the women who were attracted to him, or an instance of a wider problem, some flaw intrinsic to the human condition. Ged couldn't make up his mind about that. All he knew was that the healthy exercise he took with Polly every Saturday night failed to reach undefined but important parts of him.

Not that he knew what would.

Or could have, if the question of adultery had not stood in the way. He had been faithful for sixteen years. He didn't want to throw away all that virtue for the sake of . . . what? Excitement? The forty-year-old equivalent of joy-riding?

The night before his thirty-ninth birthday, he watched a man pick up a girl, just off Bayswater.

There was a gaggle of girls – women – impossible to tell their ages, since they were all dressed like oversexed eighteen-year-olds and wearing enough make-up to disguise the Phantom of the Opera. The man in the car in front of him pulled up to the kerb, and one of the women came over. In less than thirty seconds she had climbed in and been taken away.

It looked so neat, so polished, so uncomplicated. The man beckoned, the woman went. All for a tenner or so.

He wasted a great deal of time, over the next few weeks, trying to construct in his mind what happened after that. The images, the possibilities, obsessed him.

He told himself it wasn't like having an affair. There wouldn't be an 'other woman', just a random female body. Men always said things like *it didn't mean anything*, and women never believed them. But it would have to be true, if you were talking about sex with scrubbers.

He imagined explaining that to Polly.

Aside from the implication that he was the kind of loser who needed to pay for adultery, the idea of 'any old body' as a rival might strike her as insulting. And she would have principled feminist objections. Possibly the sexist implications would be even worse than the adulterous ones.

Well, she didn't need to know, did she?

And suppose . . . just suppose he wanted to put such a scene into a novel.

He needed to know, didn't he?

In practice it wasn't quite so neat. The other guy must have been lucky, or a regular, or maybe he hadn't cared which woman he got. Ged discovered how much he cared when the wrong one came over.

She was too big, that was the trouble. A whore for the 1890s, not the 1990s. Her cleavage started just below her chin, and showed no sign of stopping short of her waist. It would have been like having sex with some Palaeolithic fertility goddess, all breasts and buttocks.

He considered pretending that he had made a mistake, or that she had misunderstood his intentions, or even simply keeping his eyes shut throughout the process. But he was the customer, damn it. He didn't have to settle for green when he wanted blue.

He didn't even have to be polite about his preferences. 'Not you. Your little red-headed friend.'

'You want Ginger?' She looked miffed, insofar as any expression could struggle through the ritual layers of make-up. Maybe they took it in turns, maybe it was her turn for a trick. But she beckoned the other woman over without a word, and yielded her place at the car window.

Ginger had frizzy hair, too bright to be unnatural. Her throat and arms, the only skin in sight uncontaminated by cosmetics, were so white as to imply strictly nocturnal habits. Her bosom was about a quarter the volume of her colleague's.

He asked how much. Not that he cared.

She recited a menu, like a waiter announcing tonight's *specialités du chef*. So much for straight sex, so much for oral sex, so much for manual sex, other requests negotiable, condoms obligatory. All in a strong northern accent.

He ordered a blow job, because it seemed less adulterous. It surprised him that oral sex was cheaper than the vanilla variety. He would have guessed the opposite, to judge from Polly's reluctance to oblige in that regard. She had given him one for his birthday: that was how rare an event it was in their bedroom.

The redhead got in.

He drove away, a little faster than he had intended, feeling like a schoolboy on his first date. He had seen somebody else do this much, but what happened next was still a mystery. 'What do you—'

She gave him a sharp look. Perhaps he wasn't supposed to speak until he was spoken to. She had a peaky little face underneath her mane of permed red hair. Not unattractive, he thought, though it was hard to tell what she really looked like, especially in the dark. 'You turn left up here, then you turn left again, and then you go into any little road along there. They'll not be bothering us along there.'

He made the first turn as instructed. Shame saddled him with diffidence. It wasn't true that no-one would know, he realized now, too late, no matter what happened next. This girl would know. She would know he was the kind of man who paid strangers to have sex with him. Whatever kind of man that was.

He made an attempt to normalize the situation, to summon the first-date illusion. 'Where are you from?'

Again she glanced sharply sideways, this time assessing him. Maybe wondering whether to bother with an answer. After all, he wasn't paying her enough to pretend that either of them cared. 'Leeds.'

'Don't they have street corners in Leeds?'

'It's too cold up there. I don't fancy freezing my arse.'
With the skirt she was wearing, that might well have been
an occupational hazard. 'Turn right here, and pull over
anywhere you can.'

'Don't the neighbours mind?'

'Bugger them. I'm only trying to make a living.'

'Why this way?'

'Because we won't get no trouble here.'

He paused to angle the car back into an unoccupied and
unlit stretch of kerbside. When they were safely parked,
he turned off the engine.

This wasn't going to work, he realized. To be precise,
the appropriate part of his anatomy wasn't going to work.
He discovered that there was nothing intrinsically exciting
about sex with a stranger. Not, at least, with this particular stranger. Something about her brisk, matter-of-fact
attitude, as if she were taking orders in a café. A sort of
prostitute version of Polly.

Or maybe it was only a case of first-night nerves. To
give himself time to relax, he pursued the conversation. 'I
meant, why make a living this way?'

She turned to face him with an air of impatience. 'Did
you want to talk, or did you want to screw?'

'I was just curious.'

An ambiguous answer, he realized as soon as it was out
of him, and therefore truer than he had intended.

However she took his words, she was offended. Her
tone showed it by sharpening. 'If you want to take up my
time with chitchat, I'll have to charge for that too. I could
be making money with some other bugger, you know,
instead of passing the time of night with you.'

A surge of anger took him by surprise. He heard himself
say flatly, 'How much to hit you?'

She stared, silenced. Wondering how crazy he was,
maybe.

He was wondering about that himself. He realized that
for a moment he had genuinely frightened her. For a

moment her waitress persona had vanished, leaving only a small woman at the mercy of a big man.

Just for a moment, of course. 'I don't do that kinky stuff,' she told him coldly. 'Now are you going to get on with this or not?'

A minute ago he would have told her to forget it. But that sudden revelation of her essential vulnerability, and his own potential power, had given him the physical response he needed.

Prostitutes always claimed they were in total control of the situation, but funnily enough their clients always seemed to think that *they* were in control. And it wasn't the men who were apt to be found dead in a lay-by.

Maybe the hookers' insistence on routine was there to disguise, from the punters and from themselves, how much their façade of control relied on the kindness of strangers.

She handed him a packet reeking of strawberries. That solved one small mystery of life. He had occasionally wondered who on earth bought those flavoured condoms. Though upon consideration, sucking rubber (or whatever they were actually made of) would almost certainly be better than taking a stranger's smelly and possibly diseased genitals into your mouth. It was astonishingly intimate, oral sex.

Well, if she didn't mind, why should he?

For the first time in his entire sex life, he had nothing to concern himself about, except what he was feeling and what this woman was doing to him. He owed her nothing, except ten pounds.

As orgasms go, it wasn't bad. Nothing special. He suffered some obscure disappointment, obscure because he wasn't quite sure what he had been expecting. That sex with a stranger would be sexier, maybe.

He offered her a cigarette afterwards, ignoring a bizarre impulse to apologize for treating her like a sex object. Damn it, she *was* a sex object. That was how she made her living. And surely the one enormous advantage of buying sex was never having to say you're sorry.

'Shall I take you back now?'

She nodded. She was dragging on the cigarette as if smoke was the purest form of air.

'Why do you do this?'

'For the money, what do you think?' She gave him one of her sharp sidewise looks. 'How about you?'

'I told you. Curiosity.'

Next time he wouldn't bother with what she had called chitchat. He didn't want to know these women, he just wanted them to do things for him. Next time . . .

It took him a month to decide there was going to be a next time.

Aside from the danger of getting caught (though like all danger, that was a pro as well as a con), he wasn't sure the result was worth the risk. Physical sensation was only a part of sexual reward. And if the woman was going to behave like a dental hygienist, there wasn't much else in it for him. He wasn't going to load himself down with guilt and shame, or risk public humiliation and the break-up of his marriage, for the sake of sex with some old pro. He wanted a whore, for Christ's sake, not a bloody worker in the sex industry.

He remembered the moment when he had broken through the crust of custom that protected her. When he had threatened to hit her. The memory of her swiftly suppressed fear was arousing even now. And shaming in equal measure.

He wasn't the sort of guy who went around hitting people, or even threatening to hit them. Maybe, after the initial shock, she had picked up on that herself. But just for a moment she had believed him capable of violence. Just for a moment he had unwittingly tricked her into stepping outside her carapace of routine, and so he had glimpsed other possibilities in this game.

Maybe what he wanted was a different sort of woman. One who hadn't hardened yet.

He drove around for a while, keeping an eye out for the right sort of girl. He finally found her, slim and young, standing by herself. She had a face, not a mask. When she came up to the car window she seemed almost shy. And when she opened her mouth she was clearly a Londoner.

'How much?'

'For what?'

'Just a fuck.'

'Ten pounds.'

That had been the price for oral sex, last time. Straight sex had been quoted at twice as much. He wondered if this girl had reversed the order of preference, or if she was simply cheaper. 'You're on.'

She got in. Into a stranger's car, but that was part of her job. She gave him directions.

While he was driving where she had told him to go, he considered how to take this encounter outside the rigid structure of streetwalking orthodoxy. 'What do you charge just for riding around for a while?'

'What do you mean?'

She was looking at him as if he was a pervert. Anything out of the ordinary must be suspect to these women. Tempting them to break their routine was threatening behaviour in itself. 'I was just wondering how much your time is worth.'

'Oh.' She considered this with a frown. 'Well, I don't much mind what I do, as long as you pay me. Nothing kinky, mind.'

'Then we'll make it up as we go along, shall we? Nothing kinky, of course. Are you wearing knickers?'

'What? No.' She added almost wistfully, 'Not much point, is there?'

'I'll pay you a pound to prove it.'

'To prove what?'

'That you're not wearing knickers.'

Another suspicious look. 'You want me to pull up my skirt?'

'I should think one more inch would be enough to make the point,' he said dryly.

'Well, OK.' She looked down at her lap, an oddly modest glance. She had short dark hair and big gold earrings. An ordinary sort of girl. She took the hem of her skirt in both hands, hiked it hip-high, and then carefully smoothed it down, allowing him in between a glimpse of pale belly and dark pubic hair, courtesy of a passing street lamp. 'Now you owe me a pound.'

'I'll give you another pound to pull your skirt up and keep it up.'

'Two pounds,' she retorted, getting into the spirit of the bargaining.

'OK, two pounds.' He waited till she had exposed herself again, then added, 'Five pounds for touching.'

'Touching?'

'There.'

He was making her nervous again. She looked at him and then out at the houses on her side of the car. 'That's eight pounds already, not counting the fuck.'

'Trust me, I can afford it.' He slid his left hand across her thigh. 'Open your legs.'

'One pound.' But she opened them without waiting for his agreement.

He drove one-handed for a little way, exploring her with the other hand.

She giggled.

'What's so funny?'

'Nothing.' Another giggle, alongside a wiggle to imply she was not actually made of plastic.

'What?'

'I was just thinking about a guy named Bernie.'

'I'm not paying you to think about other men.'

'No, no, it's not like that.' Distracted, she forgot to pretend to be aroused. 'He lived with my mum for a while, when I was a kid. He used to give me sweets if I'd let him do that to me.'

Ged took his hand away. To pull off the road. 'Is that all he did to you?'

'All *he* did to me, yeah.'

He turned the ignition off. They sat a moment in silence and darkness.

'Let's get into the back,' she said at last, there being no money in memories. 'But first you owe me twenty quid.'

'I make it nineteen.'

'Twenty.'

Something sly in her look told him that she knew very well what the true total was, and had been hoping that he didn't. It was only a pound, but he saw no reason to let her cheat him. 'You know very well it's nineteen.'

'I was counting as we went along. It's twenty.'

He dug into his pocket and hauled out a crumpled five pound note and four pound coins. She counted it, and gave him a puzzled look.

'This is only nine pounds.'

He was already starting the motor. 'Forget the fuck.'

'OK, OK, you only owe me nineteen. Have it your way.'

He glanced over at her. She had pulled up her skirt again, to tempt him into forgetting his temper.

But it wasn't quite so simple. Not irritation but rage. And loathing and disgust, for her and for himself. What would make him want to screw a sleazy little tart who couldn't resist trying to con him out of a pound? A pound, for Christ's sake. When she was a kid she used to do it for sweets.

And that was the other thing, the other reason why he wasn't going to screw her now. He wouldn't want her to confuse him with some child-abusing bastard named Bernie.

He hadn't got this right yet, he realized. On the one hand, he wanted a woman, not a professional sex machine. On the other hand, he only wanted a woman, not a human being. He hadn't worked out how to get exactly what he wanted, no more and no less.

He went hunting again. That was how he thought of it now. Hunting what? Women, on the face of it. Sex. Excitement. Variety. On the face of it.

He was starting to get really fussy now. Any old slag would definitely not do. He wanted something with an edge.

Tonight's edge was a waif with short spiky silver-bleached hair. And thirteen rings: five on her fingers, one on her thumb, three in the lobe of one ear, two in the upper curl of the other ear, one in her left nostril, and one in her navel, artistically displayed between a hip-hugging skirt and a rib-skirting top. And that wasn't all, as he was to discover.

'Do you sleep with those things on?'

'Why not? Then they don't get nicked.'

He assumed this concern was born of experience. 'Who nicks them?'

'My boyfriend. He can get pretty scummy when he needs a fix.' She gave him a shrewd look. 'You like that kind of thing?'

'Drugs, you mean?'

'No, these.' She gave the navel ring a tug. 'I've got more of them.'

'Where?'

Again the assessing glance, like a rug-seller eyeing up tourists in the kasbah. 'It'll cost you.'

'How much?'

'Ten quid on top.'

'On top?'

'Of whatever else you want.'

They settled on twenty-five pounds all in, for a guided tour of her body jewellery and a standard screw.

She pulled up her top to reveal her nipple rings. Her breasts were not large, and the jewellery installations tended to overwhelm the visible flesh. One of the rings had several fine gold chains suspended like a tassel. The other one had the chains arranged in a series of loops, on either side of the nipple.

She twitched her torso to make them move, and watched the results with satisfaction. 'Classy, eh? That's my own design.'

'Very nice,' he agreed, since it was the only possible response.

'Now I'll show you my anti-rape device. That's what I call it. My boyfriend calls it my chastity belt.' This was, predictably, a tiny padlock joining two rings, one in each of her outer labia. 'There's only one key, see? He keeps it when I'm not working, and when I go out on the street he gives it to me, and then I give it back to him when I come home. Usually I take it off myself before I turn a trick, but since you've paid extra, you can unlock it.'

Ged stared at the minute scrap of metal she placed in the palm of his hand, along with a condom packet. She had already arranged herself in a suitable pose, and was waiting with some impatience for him to unlock the goods he had paid for.

'What if I lose the key?'

'I can always get a locksmith, can't I? But then I'd have to charge you for the cost of replacement, so you want to be careful. Just get on with it, would you? I haven't got all night.'

He looked from the key to the girl. Her pale painted face and thin naked body were looped and studded everywhere with gold, like a bride in some primitive culture delivering dowry to her groom, along with proof of her enforced chastity. Her posture – on her back, legs apart – was submissive enough, though hardly chaste. But then the whole point of chastity was the undoing of it. Post-modern prostitution.

He never let a whore have everything her own way. Maybe he wanted to let them know that the transaction could have gone quite differently, if he had had other things in mind. Or maybe he was only reminding himself of other possibilities. Before using the key, he pushed one finger between the rings and into her, knowing she wouldn't like that.

She didn't. She brought her thighs together – point-lessly, since that only froze his hand in the act of invasion. 'What the bloody hell are you doing?'

'I'm just curious.'

'Curiosity's extra.'

'But I've already paid for the use of your cunt, haven't I?'

She must have seen the justice of this assertion, since she didn't press her complaint. In return he removed his finger, unfastened the padlock, and gave it to her, along with the key.

He was vaguely disappointed that when it came down to it, the vaginal rings didn't affect the quality of the sex. He speculated that if they had reversed positions, the trailing breast-chains might have offered an interesting sensation. The thought occurred to him too late, when he was already riding up the wave of intensity that would spill into orgasm.

One difference the body jewellery did make was to the subject of post-coital conversation. For once he didn't need a cigarette to distract him from the inevitable moral and emotional hangover.

'Didn't it hurt, getting those rings put in?'

'No more than getting your ears pierced. The ear lobes are one of the most sensitive parts of the body, did you know? Anyway, it's like those initiation rites they have in African tribes. And once they're in, they stay there. I didn't take them out even to have my baby.'

He found the idea of her being a mother far more shocking than any of her exotic decorations. 'Who looks after your baby, while you're – ah – working?'

'My boyfriend does.'

'The scummy one?'

'He's OK most of the time. Just when he can't get the cash to score, that's when the trouble starts.'

'What does he do?'

'Well, he nicked my mum's bag, once.'

'No, I mean what does he work at?'

'Well, nothing. He's on the social, isn't he, same as me. They got me the flat, on account of the baby, so it works out OK.'

'Then why do you . . . work?'

She shrugged. 'It pays for things.'

Like drugs, he presumed. 'Your boyfriend doesn't mind?'

'It was his idea. He likes the money.' She gave him another one of those bargaining looks, glancing off his wedding ring. 'What about you? You've got a wife. What do you do this for?'

He shrugged in turn, and didn't respond. The answer, whatever it was, lay locked up deeper than he cared to dig.

At street level, on foot, they came right up to you. He didn't like that idea, them picking him rather than the other way round. Did they try every man, or was there some special look about him? They came up like shadows, calling to him from the shadows, shadowing him for a while as they whispered their promises of pleasure. Selling lies.

One of them took a different tack. She tried pleading.

'Please, mister.'

It sounded like the beggar girl, the one he had introduced to the game. He turned to look.

It wasn't the beggar, of course. It was a different girl, a mousy blonde. Whey-faced, except for the purple bruising around her eye, and the red swelling at the corner of her mouth. She had made some perfunctory and unsuccessful attempts to disguise her injuries with make-up.

'Please, mister. I'll give you a good time, mister.'

There was an odd note of terror in her appeal that caught his curiosity. Something to do with the beating she had been given, he suspected. He slowed up, keeping half an eye on her, over his shoulder. 'What did you have in mind?'

She moved closer, whispering, though no-one else was near enough to overhear. 'Full sex, no condoms. Only twenty quid.'

Now he understood her diffidence, if not the tone of terror. Unprotected sex was the black market of the sex trade, unadvertised, unofficial. Condoms were a bloody nuisance, of course, but they were used to protect the man as much as the woman. Sometimes the man would offer the woman extra money to forget the sheath. Sometimes the woman would accept, if she was desperate for the money. But he had never yet heard of the woman offering to forget it. And this one wasn't even asking for more money.

He yielded to curiosity.

He followed her down an alleyway between two buildings, down into the darkness, edging past dust bins, down to a padlocked gate. She turned there, leaning back against the gate, and pulled up her skirt in a businesslike way. Well, it was business, wasn't it? Cock in cunt, no frills, no personalities, no consequences.

That was the theory.

With some other woman he might have taken a risk, but not with a prostitute. 'Have you got a condom?'

She seemed bewildered by the suggestion. 'Yeah, but I thought . . . I mean . . . Well, OK. Whatever you say.' She dug into her bag and produced a familiar foil packet. Banana flavour. Maybe the condom makers' idea of a joke.

'Why don't we do it the other way?'

'The other way?'

'You turn around and bend over.'

She opened her mouth to object, then closed it again. 'No buggery, mind. Buggery's extra. I don't do that sort of thing.' After a moment she added, 'Normally.'

Curiosity again. Polly had always refused anal sex, not for puritanical or (more characteristically) hygienic reasons, but for physical ones. Sodomy was only practicable with little pricks, she said. He had asked her how she knew, but she refused to tell. 'How much?'

The woman licked her swollen lip. 'Fifty pounds.'

'Forty.'

'Forty-five.'

'Forty.'

She glanced from blank wall to blank wall, as if expecting a counterbidder to come out of nowhere and rescue her. 'Forty, OK. I wouldn't do it normally, you know. Only I got to take some money home to him, or else.'

Or else another black eye, at a minimum, he guessed. He felt no guilt about taking advantage of another man's brutality. He hadn't yet got round to thinking about it like that.

He watched her turn and bend, setting her outspread hands against the wooden gate. He pushed her skirt up to her waist. Looked down at her white arse, glimmering in the anonymous light of London.

He ran his hands over that naked bit of body, temporarily in his ownership. He was surprised, then not surprised, to feel what could only be raised welts on the soft skin. They went with the black eye and fat lip, he supposed.

It was more exciting like this, he discovered: aping the anonymity of beasts, without even the humanizing element of a stranger's face. And buggery added an extra edge to any encounter. He wondered if she would have been desperate enough to let him do even this without a condom.

Afterwards he offered her a cigarette. It was a way of dissociating himself from what he had done, a way of pretending this was an ordinary acquaintance.

She took it, of course. He had never met a prostitute who didn't smoke. There were probably no teetotallers among them, either, not to mention less conventional substances. They stood and smoked, facing each other across the narrow space between the two brick walls.

She peered at him through the mutually generated smog of tobacco. 'Why'd you take the offer and then change your mind? You weren't interested till I said no condoms, but then you used one in the end.'

'I suppose I was curious.'

*   *   *

He grew choosier each time. Some nights he went home with his money still in his pocket, if he didn't spot anyone he fancied.

They had to be young and reasonably attractive, not too much make-up, neither fat nor skinny. He preferred the young ones, not just for the obvious physical benefits of youth, but because they were less likely to have developed that shield of jobsworth indifference that made him want to hit the stupid cows who flaunted it too brazenly. A hint of vulnerability, of uncertainty, even of unwillingness – that was, to his own shame, what gave him most pleasure about the business. There was no point wallowing in moral degradation if the people you were wallowing with refused even to acknowledge the nature of what it was you were both doing.

He liked the idea of picking and choosing. He liked to drive past, looking them over, letting them know what he was doing, so he could come back and point and beckon. That one. You. You're for sale, I'm going to buy you. Get in, shut up, lie down, open your legs. Sometimes he thought he might even be willing to settle for shoving the money up their cunt in lieu of his prick. Not the young and nervous ones, of course; they were still only too well aware of what the bargain actually involved.

And he did feel sorry for them. Some of them, at least. All of them, maybe. But never sorry enough to stop buying them, much less to forgo the privilege he had paid for.

The prettiest girl was standing off by herself. He wasn't even sure at first if she was for sale. She was still there when he returned, which made him more confident. And she came over to the car when he pulled up.

'Can I take you for a ride?'

She smiled and got in. He liked that. They often stopped smiling as soon as they'd struck their bargain. She was slim and dark, with long glossy hair, wearing a short, but not outrageously short, denim skirt, and a jumper that at least allowed her to breathe. Her make-up was restricted to her eyes and mouth. She didn't look like a whore at all.

He wondered for a moment if he'd made a mistake, until she smiled again and spoke. 'How far do you want me to go?'

A middle-class girl. He'd never encountered one before. There must have been plenty of middle-class hookers about, but presumably they could afford to keep themselves off the streets.

He decided to drop the euphemisms, the menu language. 'How much would you want to let me put my prick into your pussy?'

She cast her gaze downwards and smoothed her skirt over her legs. Had he shocked her? He hoped so, improbable as it seemed. 'The going rate is twenty pounds these days. But I think I'm worth at least thirty.'

He gave her the money right then. He usually waited, made them ask for it. In return, without a word, she handed him a condom. The most basic of bargains.

He drove her to one of the usual places. As soon as he had parked, he reached over to touch the swell of her breast under the jumper.

No bra. They usually rigged themselves up in Madonna-style undergirdings.

When she didn't push his hand away, he slid it under the sweater to stroke her bare breasts. He saw her shut her eyes.

He got out and went round to her side of the car. He opened the door to invite her outside. When she reached for the back door handle, he stopped her.

'We'll do it right here. In the street.'

Her eyes flickered – with surprise? alarm? He didn't care which or what. And she didn't protest.

He pulled up her skirt so that her bare bottom touched the car door. She kept her hands against the car, leaning on the window, submitting to him the way they all did, had to do, if they wanted his money. She closed her eyes again.

He sheathed himself, first with the rubber and then in her. He fucked her the way he did them all, without compassion, without consideration, as if she were one of those obscene inflatable dolls instead of a living woman. That was the only way he could bring himself to do it. It was also the main thing that made it worth doing.

She kept her eyes firmly shut and her face entirely impassive, as if nothing at all was happening to her, as if she wasn't being consensually raped by a complete stranger in public view on a London street.

He peeled off the condom and dropped it under the car. He hated those things, especially afterwards. He hated everything about this. Afterwards.

All the pleasure came beforehand. The anticipation, the stalking, the choosing, the bargain, the cool and brutal business of fucking a woman you'd bought and paid for: the sum of all that made up the enjoyment that he got from doing this. Made him feel that he was still alive.

Was this living, what he was doing with these women?

It was maybe like torturing small animals. Or smearing yourself with shit. And finding it the most exciting and pleasurable thing you had ever done.

The girl had opened her eyes again.

'I thought whores were supposed to at least pretend to be enjoying themselves,' he told her.

'You want acting? Acting will cost you more.'

'Would you fake it for twice the price?'

She thought about it and shook her head. 'No. Not for any money.'

He opened the door to let her climb back in. It was the first time he had offered a whore such courtesies, had been able to offer them. Usually the women didn't wait.

He slid behind the wheel again. 'Tell me, why would a nice respectable girl like you want to sell the use of her private parts?'

She pushed her hair away from her face and leaned back into the seat as he started the motor. 'I'm a student. I got tired of being poor.'

'What kind of student?'

'An art student.' She added defensively, 'I don't see much difference between doing this and posing nude for life classes.'

'Maybe there isn't much difference for you,' he said dryly, 'but there sure is for me.'

'What about you?' she asked sharply. 'Why would a nice respectable married man like you waste his time and money screwing streetwalkers.'

He did her the honour of thinking about that for a minute. 'I suppose I must enjoy it. Can't see why else I'd bother.'

'You're the Professor, aren't you?'

He thought for a moment that she must have mistaken him for one of the lecturers at her art college. 'What?'

'One of the others mentioned you. I talk to them sometimes. It's safer that way, we can keep an eye on each other. Just in case anyone has a problem customer.'

'Just the sort of problem you might run into in a life class, you mean.'

She shook her head in annoyance or embarrassment. Her hair fell down around her face. 'This woman said you had sex with her and then asked her all sorts of questions about herself. I thought maybe you're doing some kind of sociological study, going native or undercover in order to get the real low-down.'

'That's a great idea. Using government money to screw whores, that's really brilliant. You could say you were doing grass-roots research and alleviating poverty, all in one project.'

'Well, if you're not doing that, what are you doing?'

'Nothing. I'm not a sociologist or a psychologist or anything like that. I'm just – well – curious.'

'About what? Streetwalkers?'

'I suppose so.'

About himself, more likely. An abstract curiosity, watching from intellectually dispassionate heights while his unhinged libido or subconscious or death-wish or whatever it was floundered around in the mire of the lowest intersection between power and sex.

'And you? You just decided one day that you'd stand on a street corner and see what offered?'

'No. No, actually, it offered itself. Any woman who walks around here has men creeping up in cars and asking how much. And one day when I was absolutely flat broke and wondering how on earth I was going to pay my rent at the end of the month, some guy came along and asked me how much. And I – I just did it.' She stopped and covered her face in her hands. 'Twenty pounds he gave me. He was old and fat. I was disgusted – with him, with myself, with the whole idea.'

She lowered her hands without raising her head. 'But twenty pounds . . . well, it wasn't enough to pay the rent, but it only took a few minutes to earn it. If I turn ten tricks a week, that's ten thousand pounds a year. More than enough to pay the rent. I don't have to be a starving student. I won't even have to be a starving artist when I graduate.'

He looked at her. It dawned on him that they hadn't gone anywhere; he had turned off the engine some time ago. 'You're not like them,' he said, nodding his head in the direction of Bayswater and the poor painted women back there. 'Twenty pounds for them. Not for you. Not even thirty pounds.'

'You think I don't know that?' Her head came up again, with a scornful flash of the eyes. 'If I wanted to do this seriously, I'd go in for Discipline. It's completely safe. There's no danger whatsoever of being raped or anything, because they're there in order to be meek as mice and take orders from you. In fact it mostly doesn't even involve having sex. They get off on being humiliated or thrashed or whatever, and they don't really want a woman's body at all.'

'How do you know all that?'

'I talked to a woman back there' – she too nodded towards Bayswater – 'who used to do that kind of thing.

She said the only real problem was trying to keep a straight face, because these guys were so pathetic. And profitable – hey, she was raking it in, she said.'

'So how did she end up on the street?'

'Her boyfriend talked her into trying to blackmail one of her clients. The whole thing backfired badly and they both ended up in jail. Then when she came out, none of her former customers would have anything to do with her, for fear of being blackmailed themselves. So she was stuck.'

'She couldn't think of any other line of work she might profitably pursue?'

'Evidently not. Anyway, she said she couldn't stand having to get up in the morning. And speaking of getting up in the morning, aren't you going to take me back?'

'Oh. Yes. Of course.' He restarted the engine. 'You know, you could always write a book about your adventures. It wouldn't matter if you couldn't write, you'd get a huge amount of free publicity for it. They'd fall over themselves to interview you. You'd make a fortune.'

He glanced at her. She stared at him. 'And be known for ever as a whore?'

'So it's not quite like life classes.'

She turned to stone before his eyes. Her tongue tripped up over simple words. 'How can you say – I mean, you're in the same – what you've been doing . . .'

He thought of a lot of things right then. He thought of suggesting that she drop the street corner routine and let him buy her on a regular basis. He thought of proposing that they both forget this incident and meet again next week as if they were strangers; start things over from scratch, without the money. He even thought of introducing her to his agent.

But what he actually said, to his own surprise and shame, was something very different. 'You're the seller, I'm the buyer. You're the woman, I'm the man. Not the same thing at all.'

He thought she might jump ship right there, even

though he had started to move the car down the street. Instead she leaned back and closed her eyes, the way she had when he was screwing her.

When they were near the corner where he had picked her up, he pulled over to the kerb. 'You can get out now.'

She opened her eyes. Black as blazes, they were. He had to bite his tongue to keep from apologizing. Poor people, the scum of the earth, people like him, they couldn't afford apologies.

'Tell me one thing,' she said, surprisingly quietly. 'Why are men always the buyers, women the sellers? Is it because men always have more money than women?'

'No, I don't think so.' He thought about that honestly, to do her question justice. 'I think it's because men want more than women.'

'What do you mean?' She looked at him, stony-faced again. 'What more do they want?'

'I don't know.' He reached across her, pushed the door open for her. 'Maybe that's the problem.'

Well, he had given all that up long since, all the dubious, degraded pleasures of streetstalking.

An addictive pleasure, with an addict's inevitable escalation of the dose. For him the drug was not sex but something stronger, a search for ultimate experience, a defining moment that would strip off the skin of thought and leave him naked to sensation. Perhaps he had assumed he could only find it in a context where mutual habit had had no chance to form, where no obligation would encroach.

Elie had cured him of that delusion. If he had wanted something more, she had given him more than he could have imagined. She had turned his formless desire into longing.

Whether or not she ever came back to him, he knew something now for certain. He knew that he could never go back to Polly. Just in case he had ever seriously entertained any other idea.

For one thing, the quickie in the doorway had been a disaster.

Polly didn't want to do it like that. She wanted to go upstairs with a bottle of wine and make an evening of it. Make a ritual of it. Make it like it was before.

Ged didn't want a ritual, he wanted a screw.

She had her reasons, he knew, apart from sentimental ones. She took a long time coming, and anything that lasted less than half an hour was unlikely to end in her satisfaction. He had a theory about women – every man has dozens of theories about women, and this one was no more likely to be correct than any of the others – a theory that the women who liked sex least were the ones most likely to insist on achieving orgasm every bloody time a man so much as touched them. Not surprising, perhaps, if that was the only enjoyment they got out of it all.

If he wanted five minutes maximum and she wanted thirty minutes minimum, disaster was inevitable. She had let him have her the way he wanted, thinking it was only the overture. When she realized he meant it for the whole performance, she burst into tears and accused him of brutality.

'Polly, that's ridiculous. You asked for it.'

'Not like that, I didn't. Not to be thrown against the door, and – and – raped! You didn't even kiss me.'

She was using the door as a wailing wall, turning away as if she couldn't bear the sight of him. Preventing him from walking out. 'So what? You don't have to do it the same way every time. There's no book of rules.'

'It wouldn't matter if there was. You never take any notice of rules. You just do what you want.'

After what seemed like a lifetime of doing what other people wanted, especially what Polly wanted, Ged thought that was a bit rich. But he didn't have to do what she wanted now; he wasn't married to her any more.

He didn't even have to hang around and let her make scenes at him.

He picked her up and put her down, well out of his way.

She was too stunned by this physical high-handedness to make a proper protest. And then he walked out.

Pretty much what Elie had done to him, except that she did it when he wasn't there, and entertained no accusations of bad sex. No accusations at all. She had just packed up and disappeared.

14

Angelina came out on to the deck, and looked at Calum lying in the hammock. A disgusted look, if only he had been awake to see it.

At least, she hoped it would have been disgusted. There were complicating factors, feelings that were far from disgust, floating around in her head when she looked at him.

Normally guys with hair like his, dreadlocks or elf locks or whatever they were, made her feel nervous, and doubly nervous when they had rings in weird places. They were cool and she was not. As far as she could make out, the whole concept of cool was to know everything and desire nothing, which sounded pretty boring and pointless. But that didn't prevent her from being intimidated by the physical embodiment of such an ethos.

She found Calum especially intimidating, but not because of what he said or did. Because of what he made her feel.

Maybe that was only because he was English. Maybe that was why she found him so different from all the other boys she had ever known. The guys back in Sweetwater were a bunch of jerks anyway. Giving them up had been the least of her concerns when she went into the convent.

But she wasn't getting paid to swoon over some foreigner. And Calum's dad wasn't paying him to lie around in a hammock like a bum. 'Calum, if you're not going to work, you might as well pick yourself up and go home.'

Calum stretched and yawned and rearranged himself. Charles, sprawled under the hammock, or as much of himself as would fit under it, did the same thing at almost exactly the same time. The cats, who had tucked themselves into the nooks and crannies of Calum, didn't stir at all, not even when Charles bumped the hammock and set it swinging. The colours of the jumbled animal bodies, including Calum's nearly-naked one, made a pleasing harmony of browns and buffs and bronzes, with a stronger note from the marmalade cat and a brighter one from the sun-coloured streaks in Calum's hair. The textures were different too: stiff or soft, long or short, straight or curly. It reminded her of a story in her old fairy-tale book, a story called *The Many-furred Creature*.

'I'm relaxing,' Calum replied without opening his eyes. 'It's a natural part of our biorhythms to relax after lunch, my gran says so.'

'Then I think I'll do a little relaxing too. You can make your own supper and wash your own dishes, from now on. I'm going on strike.'

'God, Angie, you're such a tough babe.' This time he did open his eyes, and grinned. 'Isn't that what Jesus said? Have I quoted him right?'

She steeled herself to ignore the effect his grin had on her. He probably practised in front of a mirror. 'Don't call him Jesus, it's not respectful. To the real Jesus, I mean, not George. And it's not right for you to tell your dad you'd do something, and then not do it.' Promises were important. She didn't want Calum to be the sort of person who didn't keep them.

He stretched again. It gave her a funny feeling when he did that, watching the contours of his body change as this or that muscle came into play, while he unfurled his arms and then refolded them across his chest.

'I'll get up if you bring me a cold beer.'

'I'll bring you a cola.'

'You really are a tough babe.'

But he sat up and swung his legs over the side of the hammock, shifting his bare feet to find a spot on the deck that was not already occupied by some part of Charles. The cats slid down the canvas to the lowest part, where Calum was weighing it down. They slid without resistance, like inanimate objects.

When he stood right up, the hammock bounced. The cats shook themselves and gave him dirty looks, but almost at once they resettled into one big knot of many-coloured fur.

Angelina brought him the promised cola. He emptied the can in a few long pulls. And handed it back to her, of course, which was at least better than leaving it to roll around on the deck.

'Je— George, I mean, says you used to be a nun. Is that true?'

'I was a novice,' she agreed carefully. She had found that people reacted very strangely to this information. As if they had found out that she used to be retarded, or used to be a fascist. 'I never made it to the fully-fledged stage.'

He didn't show any sign of more than curiosity. 'Did you leave, or did they throw you out?'

'They chucked me out.'

'What for? Sneaking a man into your room at night?'

She guessed he thought this was funny. 'If I'd wanted a man in my room, I wouldn't have become a nun, would I? It was for arguing with the Mother Superior. She said it showed a lack of humility and an inclination to disobedience.'

'I'll bet it did.' He was grinning again. 'What were you arguing about?'

'I'll tell you some other time. Right now you've got to get to work.'

'I'm surprised they didn't offer to make you the Mother Superior,' he grumbled, following her over to the studio. 'What exactly am I supposed to be doing?'

'Sorting all this out, of course.' Angelina surveyed the

enormous room, the enormous task ahead. 'If you ask me nicely, I might give you a hand.'

Secretly, she was not dismayed but delighted at the prospect of cleaning up this mess. She had been itching to do it since the day she arrived here.

That was the day she had proposed a clean-up to her new employer, thinking this appalling state of affairs must be due to his previous housekeeper's laziness.

But Malachy had looked down at her out of the corner of his left eye, the one with the drooping eyelid. He did that, as she was to discover, when he was angry or offended. Over my dead body, he had growled.

And so it was.

Calum was staring at the shambles with something less than delight. 'I'll ask as nicely as you like. Where the hell do we start?'

Angelina had already given this question some consideration. 'Why don't we kick off in this corner, right here by the door? We can work along this wall till we reach the back wall, and then kind of roll it all up towards the far wall. If something is garbage, we throw it out. If it's important, we put it in a notebook.' That had been one of the items on the shopping list she had given to Ged. 'We have to make an inventory for your dad.'

Progress was slow at first, because Calum wanted a consultation about every little thing.

'What do I do with this?' He was holding up a red clay flower pot.

Angelina had found a coffee tin full of marbles. They were vintage marbles: clear as ice, revealing a frozen trail of bubbles; milky white, with swirls and streaks of colour like storms in a small moon; the kind you can't buy any more. Valuable, probably. She was trying to count them, to make sure none got lost.

'Mark it in the book and set it out on the deck for now, until we've cleared some space in here.'

'What, a flower pot? My father isn't going to be interested in flower pots, for Christ's sake.'

'How do you know what he'll be interested in? We'd better leave everything up to him. It might be antique.'

'Oh, all right.' Grumbling to himself, he scribbled in the notebook and went out to deposit the pot on the deck. He came back inside, dived into the debris again and emerged with another flower pot, this one in two pieces. 'What about this? This one has got to be rubbish.'

'Twenty-two, twenty-three . . . Yeah, but don't throw it away. I can use the shards for drainage in other pots.'

He brandished the two halves impatiently. 'So what do I do with it?'

'Put it on the deck, but don't mark it in the book. No, wait a minute, we'd better keep a separate list of everything that goes into the garbage bags, and show it to your dad before they get thrown out. Twenty-nine, thirty, thirty-one . . .'

'Angie, what do you want me to do with this mirror?'

'Make a note in the book and take it outside, Calum. Twenty-seven, twenty-eight . . . Oh, heck, I'd better start over again.'

'What's the use of dumping everything outside? We'll end up with a clean studio and a tip of a deck.'

'But at least we'll know what we've got. Anyway, we're only doing that for now, because there's no room in here yet. Now zip your lip and use your common sense, or I'll never finish counting these things.'

'What things? Hey, those are cool. Let me have a look.'

She gave him a push instead, to head him back to the front line. 'Calum, for the Lord's sake, get on with it. You can admire these allies later.'

Some time later, she became aware that things had gone a little too quiet. Calum had been trekking in and out with the flotsam and jetsam of Malachy's life, but she hadn't heard him for a while.

She found him on his knees, between an unhinged,

paint-daubed door and a stuffed Canada goose. He was leafing through a tattered notebook.

'What's that?'

'I think it's something my father asked me to look out for.'

'What kind of thing?'

'I'm not sure. He said something about diaries.' He closed the book and held it up. The only thing written on the front was *1967*. 'Does that look like a diary to you?'

The idea of Malachy keeping a diary was a new one to Angelina. He hadn't seemed the type; for one thing, it suggested a certain amount of personal organization. Her curiosity was stirred. What kind of things would he have written about? What clues would they give to the soul behind that dark, impassive face?

But famous people's diaries were valuable and important, no matter what was in them. 'Why don't you take it over to the house? We can look at it later.'

By supper-time they had already cleared a space halfway down the length of the western wall. The deck in front of the studio was littered with rescued objects of varying value and interest. They had filled two plastic sacks with what they reckoned to be garbage, and carried them off the deck to prop them against the far side of the studio, by the stable. Angelina warned Calum once more that they were not to throw anything away without asking Ged.

'In that case, is it a good idea to leave these rubbish sacks outside?' he wondered. 'The stuff inside might get wet.'

Angelina dismissed this possibility. 'We've tied up the tops, and we have to put them somewhere. Anyway, it never rains here, this time of year.'

'What, never?'

'Not that I can recall. It rains all winter, but never in the summer. That's why forest fires are such a problem.'

Each sack was equipped with an itemized list of its contents: clean rags, painty rags, newspapers, old shoes, bald paint brushes, dead mice, etc. Calum discovered that when Angelina said not to throw anything away, she had a very literal view of what 'anything' meant.

'How do we know but what Malachy might have meant those mice to be art? I read in the paper about somebody exhibiting a dead cow.'

'They're not art, they're just something the cats dragged in,' Calum argued. 'One is completely mummified and the other one's infested with maggots.'

'That might be the point.'

'What point?'

'Something to do with death. All flesh is grass, that kind of thing. Artists are obsessed with death, aren't they?'

'I wouldn't know. I don't know any artists.'

'Sure you do. Your dad's a writer, isn't he?'

'Not the same thing at all. Anybody can read a book and say what they think about it, but when ordinary joes criticize art, they're called philistines. Besides, I thought it was sex artists are supposed to be obsessed with.'

'I expect they are. But that doesn't make them any different from every other man on earth.'

After supper, when Calum was settled in front of the living-room fire, with his bare feet resting on the hearth and a happy cat in his lap, Angelina assessed their progress. Pretty good for an afternoon, pretty rotten for a whole week. Something would have to be done, or they'd be here till Christmas.

'Calum, why don't you set yourself regular working hours, like a normal job? Eight o'clock to twelve noon, then—'

'Eight!' he interrupted indignantly. 'Eight o'clock in the morning? Are you kidding?'

'Well, all right, nine,' she conceded. 'That'll give you time to eat a proper breakfast.'

She always enjoyed this time of day most. Partly because her work was done, and partly because after supper they sat and talked. Once she had talked with Malachy, now she talked with Calum.

217

He had different routines back in London, seemingly. On the first night, he had asked, 'Where's your telly? Buried in the rubbish, I suppose.'

'Telly?'

'TV. Television.'

'There isn't one.'

He had given her an incredulous glare.

'No, honest. Malachy didn't hold with TV.'

'What's that mean? It was against his religion?'

'He didn't have any religion that I knew of. No, he just didn't like it. He said television programmed people. He said the idea of the whole country sitting around staring at the same stupid thing was a real scary idea.'

Calum's expression had changed from disbelief to astonishment. 'But I never heard of anyone not having a TV. It's like not having a telephone.'

'Well, I've never had a TV either,' Angelina admitted. She knew from experience that this was like saying she had never worn shoes, or had always been made to sleep on the floor. 'My grandma doesn't have it, and we weren't allowed to watch it in the convent, and then I came to live with Malachy. So I've never had a chance to miss it.'

'God, that's just so weird. That's the weirdest thing I've ever heard.'

But he seemed to be over his withdrawal symptoms by now, after a TV-free week. 'Do you want to have a look at the diary now?'

She had almost forgotten about the diary. Now, reminded, a scruple smote her. 'Maybe we shouldn't. I wouldn't have read his diary while Malachy was alive. And now it belongs to your dad.'

'But he asked me to look out for it. He would have said if we weren't supposed to read it, wouldn't he?'

'Well, OK.' His argument might have been sophistry, but she went along with it because she was as curious as he was. No, more curious; she had known Malachy, he had not. 'But you'd better be the one to read it. Malachy was your grandfather. I only worked for him.'

'How come you call him Malachy, when everyone else calls him Mal?'

'Well, he was my boss, and he was an old man. It didn't seem respectful.'

That amused him, for some reason. 'Were you respectful in bed?'

'In bed?' She repeated the words before his meaning hit her. Then she turned red.

She couldn't have Calum going around with ideas like that about her, and she guessed where he had gotten them from. 'Rene was only joking. You heard him say so. I know Malachy had all those girlfriends, but it wasn't like that. I just looked after him. He was old and sick, and I'm—'

She had been going to say, I'm a virgin, which was the truth. But then she thought she wouldn't say that, after all. It was no business of his. 'I'm not into old men.'

'OK, OK, I believe you. Thousands wouldn't, but I do.' He was still amused, but this time maybe by the way she had reacted. Overreacted. After all, who cared, nowadays, who went to bed with whom?

He opened the notebook and studied the first page. A look of bafflement crept over his face. 'I can't read this writing.'

'I can. I'm used to it.'

He thrust the journal at her. 'Read it to me, then.'

It was strange to see Malachy's familiar handwriting all over the page, like a voice from the grave. If she hadn't known better, she would have thought it a child's script, the letters large and uneven, the hand of someone relatively unused to writing. 'The first entry says January the twenty-third. I guess he didn't write in it every day. It says "Untitled Red Number 35".'

'Fantastic. What the hell does that mean?'

'It's a painting. He always named them like that. The colour, and then the number. The number is the next one of that colour. Here, I'll show you.'

She rummaged around in a stack of books and found

one about Malachy's paintings. 'Here, look here.' She held it over so that Calum could see for himself. '"Untitled Blue Number 4". "Untitled Yellow Number 22". They're all like that. I asked him why he did that, and he said, A painter shouldn't try to be a poet.'

'Can I have a look at that?' Calum took the book out of her hands and propped it on his knees, taking care not to disturb the cats who were curled up on his lap. 'What else does that notebook say?'

'The next entry is for January the twenty-ninth. "Untitled Woman Number 69".'

'Another painting? This is going to be really riveting stuff, I can tell already.'

'I guess it must be a painting, but I've never seen one with a title like that. There was never anything but the colour and the number.'

Calum was browsing through the book of paintings. 'No Untitled Women in here that I can see. None in the index, anyway.'

'For February the fifteenth, it says, "Model Number 29".'

'No Models mentioned in the index, either. Do go on, I can hardly wait.'

'The next line says, "Untitled Red Number 36".'

'Now we're making progress. The first one was Red Number 35, wasn't it? Must have been his Red Period.'

She ignored this flippancy. 'Here's a longer entry. It doesn't have a date. It starts, "Model Number 29"—'

'We've already had that one.'

Angelina ploughed on dutifully.

'She must be a virgin, she's so shy. I have to leave the room while she undresses. She lies face down on the mattress and covers herself head to toe with the big red cloth. I come back in and rearrange her and the cloth to my satisfaction. I paint the contours of her thighs under the cloth. I leave the room again while she gets dressed. Then we have coffee.'

After three days of this, she consents to drink her coffee with the cloth wrapped around her, naked underneath. The next day she starts to talk. She talks every day, while I paint her. After seven days, I am allowed to pat her [ahem] her ass, when I finish the draping. By ten days, the pat is a stroke.'

She was beginning to wish she could put her hands over her ears, so she didn't have to hear what she was reading.

'Before two weeks are up, the routine has changed. For one thing, I don't have to leave the room. She strips and lies down. I cover her with the sheet. I paint her. She talks to me. I uncover her – that always seems to silence her. I strip and cover her.'

'Gosh,' she interjected rather breathlessly, 'does that mean what I think it means?'

'I don't know.' Calum was looking down at the open book of paintings, so she couldn't see his expression. 'What do you think it means?'

'You know.'

If he did, he wasn't admitting to anything. So she had to add, 'Like a stallion covering a mare.'

He looked up at her now, with another one of those grins. 'Is that what they call it, what horses get up to? Fancy you knowing a thing like that.'

'My grandpa used to breed horses,' she said with as much dignity as she could muster in the circumstances. 'And I don't think I'm going to read any more of this.'

'Oh, come on, you can't stop now.' After his initial show of boredom, Calum was now looking much too interested to suit her. 'You said you'd read it to me.'

'Well, all right, but you can't watch me while I'm reading.'

'What do you want me to do, leave the room?'

That nearly made her blush. He was quite good at making her blush. 'Close your eyes and cover them with your hands,' she said firmly. 'And no peeking.'

'Cross my heart and hope to die.'

She checked carefully all the same, just to make sure. Then she turned her back to him, cleared her throat, and went on.

'"We dress and drink coffee. We talk. I am not allowed to mention the fact that I" – I'm not going to say that word – "that I you-know-what her."'

'That's what it says? "You-know-what"?'

Calum's voice was muffled, which meant he must be keeping his promise, and his hands over his eyes. 'No, it doesn't say that. That's what I put in.'

'Hey, now, no censorship. The man was an artist, he's entitled to his artistic freedom.'

'Well, he was free to write what he liked, and I'm free not to read it to you. I'll read it to myself.'

'Can I watch while you read it to yourself?'

'I guess you're free to do what you like, too.'

She scanned the next few pages. There didn't seem to be any more passages like that one. There were a couple more Untitled Reds (Numbers 37 and 38), two more Untitled Women (70 and 71), and a note about the sale of some Untitled Reds, but no more Models.

The entry for 19 June was 'Untitled Child Number ?' It had a line drawn through it, in ink of a different colour. Not to obliterate what had been written, just to cancel it out.

'Gosh,' said Angelina.

'Gosh what?'

'I just had an absolutely awful idea.'

'Well?'

'I'm not going to tell you. It might not be true.'

In November the entry read 'Model Number 30'. Not long after that was another undated entry, a long one. She stopped reading it when she realized what the entry was about – or rather, how it was bound to end. It had to end like that because that's what it was in there for. She suspected that any episode which hadn't ended that way didn't get into the diary.

A few months further on, another entry said 'Untitled Child Number ?', just like the first one. But this one had not been crossed out.

She put the notebook down. She couldn't read any more. If it was true, it was terrible. If it all meant what she thought it must.

Calum was looking at the book again, not at her. 'Angie, what was the name of that Red painting in the diary?'

'Which one? There were lots.'

'The first one. No, I mean the second one. After the entry about Model Number Such-and-such.'

She picked up the notebook and found the entry. ' "Number 36".'

'That's what I thought. It's right here. Look at this.'

She went over to see what he was pointing at. It was an absolutely typical Malachy Hawke painting, red all over, but some bits made darker than others to suggest a shape, another dimension. In this case the darker bits formed two V shapes, one tucked inside the other, the space between them gradually narrowing as they came to a point. Or rather, they didn't come to a point, because they reached the bottom of the painting before the lines could come together. If you looked at it in another way, the two dark Vs and the brighter V between them formed two rounded lengths converging.

The title was 'Untitled Red Number 36'.

'That must be the one,' Angelina agreed. 'Well, well. And the date there is 1967. What about it?'

'Look,' Calum turned the book upside down. The bottomless Vs became topless As, without the crossbar.

'So what?' Angie repeated.

'Don't you see? It's just what he said he was doing. He was painting her legs, under a cloth.'

So he had been. She saw it now. The point of intersection would have been the woman's crotch, but he had run out of space before he got that far up.

'Well, then, that must be Model Number 29, in "Untitled Red Number 36". That solves one mystery,' she said briskly. 'Now what do you think this means?'

She showed him the 'Untitled Child' entry that had been crossed out.

'I suppose that means he put her in the club. Pregnant,' he explained, when she looked puzzled. 'Not surprising, is it? Since we know what he was doing.'

'Why is it crossed out?'

'Maybe she got herself out of the club.'

'An abortion, you mean?'

'Or a miscarriage. At any rate it must mean the child was never born.'

'Then look at this.' She showed him the long entry that followed the entry for Model Number 30, let him read a few lines and then pulled it away.

He tried to grab it back. 'Hey, I haven't finished.'

'You don't need to finish. You know what it's about.'

'That doesn't mean I don't want to finish reading it.'

'Just because you want to, doesn't mean you should. Now just look at this.'

'Untitled Child Number Question Mark? That's the same as the other one.'

'No, it's not. It isn't crossed out.'

Angelina sat down on the hearth, next to Calum's feet. She looked at him. He looked at her.

'What an old bastard,' he said. 'Thirteen sons, no wonder. I'm surprised it wasn't ninety-nine.'

'A lot of them probably got crossed out.'

She got up and walked away from him. She couldn't go far because she kept stumbling into things. There were so many things to stumble over, and she couldn't seem to see them.

'Angie?'

She couldn't seem to speak, either. She had an idea that if she uttered a single word, something terrible would happen. She would start to cry. It was only the words stuck in her throat that were stopping her from crying.

'Are you OK, Angie?'

She shook her head. She couldn't stumble around

224

blind, so she came back and sat down on the hearthstone again. She put her hands over her face.

Calum put something furry on her lap. It was Miss Fudge, the fluffy tabby cat, still cosy and purring from Calum's own lap. 'You need her more than I do.'

That made her laugh, and laughing made her cry. She stroked Miss Fudge to console herself.

'Why are you crying?' Calum wanted to know. 'Tough babes don't cry.'

'I guess I'm not so tough after all.' She wiped her tears away with the heel of one hand, stroking Miss Fudge with the other. 'I can't believe he did all that. All those women! Model Number 29 means there were twenty-eight of them before her. And him going about it so cold-bloodedly.'

Calum said dryly, 'How did you think he managed to have so many kids?'

'Anyone can make a mistake. Even thirteen mistakes, I guess.'

Angelina sniffed into a handkerchief. It was a big plaid one that had belonged to Malachy. He used to go through them by the dozen, because he kept using them as paint rags when he couldn't find a proper rag. Sometimes he'd stuff the hanky back in his pocket and forget what he'd done with it, then later on use it to mop his brow or blow his nose, and end up with paint on his face.

Must be war paint, he had said, when she pointed it out.

The recollection made her feel like laughing now, and crying all over again. She thought she'd known Malachy, known him in the intuitive way she called 'seeing souls' – though it didn't really make use of her physical senses. It was more a form of understanding. She had thought she *comprehended* Malachy.

'He was careful not to make the same mistake twice,' Calum observed. 'Rene said every one of his sons had a different mother.'

'That's what I meant. It's like he was doing it deliberately.'

'He probably was. So what? Look, Angie, he wasn't raping them, was he? If they decided to take their knickers off for him, they must have known what the consequences would be. If he managed to get them up the duff so quickly, it had to be because they didn't do anything to stop it happening. What are you laughing about?'

'Knickers.' She stuffed the hanky into her mouth to keep from giggling, because it wasn't polite to laugh at the way other people talked. 'It's such a funny word, that's all. Is that what you call panties in England?'

'Panties is a pretty funny word too, I'll have you know.' Calum was smiling broadly, showing no sign of taking offence. 'Listen, about this diary. What do we think an Untitled Woman might be? There were three of them in there, from 69 to 71.'

'Same thing as a Model, I suppose, only not a model.'

'Just a bit on the side, you mean? Maybe so.' He was flipping through the diary, pausing now and again to read some things in more detail. She didn't have to guess which bits those were. 'You think I should phone my dad, to tell him we found this diary? I don't even know why he wanted it.'

'Phone him in the morning. He'll be in bed by now, won't he?'

Angie set Miss Fudge on the hearth and stretched herself. She felt stiff and cramped and utterly exhausted. Crying really knocked the stuffing out of you.

15

She could feel it now, the familiar sense of weightlessness. The relief of freedom.

If she reached up, she could touch the ceiling. If she rolled over, she would see herself lying in bed.

She didn't roll over. It still scared her to see her own body like that. As if she were another person altogether. She had this fear that the body on the bed would open its eyes, and someone else would look out at her. Alice had told her that couldn't happen: if her body opened its eyes, she would be back inside it. But she was not quite convinced.

She hadn't done this since Malachy died. She had been waiting for him to come to her in dreams, to let her know that he was OK. Like her grandfather had done.

Two months after his death, she had dreamt of a knock on the door of her grandmother's house, and when she went to open the door, her grandfather was standing there, smiling. She wondered why he was knocking on the door of his own house. And then she remembered that he didn't live there any more. While she was wondering and remembering, he came up to her and took her in his arms, and hugged her without a word until she felt warm through and through, and comforted entirely. Then he was gone, and she shut the door. But she woke up knowing he was all right.

Malachy hadn't come back yet.

He had asked her, a few days before he died, if she believed in life after death. He hadn't put it like that, of course. What he said was, 'What do you reckon, Angie? You think when we go, that's it?'

She didn't need to ask what he was talking about. On bad mornings, he could hardly get his body out of bed. She said truthfully, 'It isn't what I think, it's what I know. I know there's more than that to it.'

He looked at her with that slow smile unfurling across his face, making creases of the lines in it. She would have said it ambled across, but that would imply aimlessness, and Malachy never did anything without some purpose in mind. 'Now, Angie, how could you possibly know a thing like that?'

She could have told him about coming out of her body, or about the body of the resurrection that lives within our mortal flesh and bone. But she didn't think he would believe any of that. Instead, she told him about her grandfather dream.

Malachy took her hand and opened it up inside his own, because his was so much bigger. His hand was the colour of old leather, the back rough and deeply furrowed, the palm frayed and callused. He had paint stains on his fingers. He was dying, but painting was his life. He would die with paint on his hands.

He ran the ball of his thumb down the curved crease that followed the base of her thumb. The lifeline. 'Tell you what, honey. If I find myself still around afterwards, I'll come back and knock on the door of this house, and you can let me in.'

He hadn't come back yet.

Maybe that was just as well. She would have a few things to say to him about the way he had treated those women. How on earth could he explain himself, she wondered. And what difference would it make to his fate, now that he was dead? What difference would it make that he had done wrong to so many people, his lovers and his sons? Not to mention his disinherited daughters.

If she had come across the diary while she was here on her own, she would have found its contents unbearable; a posthumous betrayal of her friendship, her love for someone she had thought a good man. But Calum was with her to soften the blow. Not only by what he said, but by the fact that he was himself the eventual consequence of one of those callous seductions.

To think of Calum was to wish for Calum. And in her state of fleshlessness, to wish was to act. She found herself in Calum's room, floating over Calum's bed.

The eyes in this body never minded the darkness. She could see the curve of his back as he lay on his side, the blanket crumpled around his waist, his face half hidden by an upflung arm. Sleeping bodies were a mystery in themselves, she thought, left so unregarded while the spirit went wandering. She felt vaguely ashamed of herself. It was too much like spying, overlooking him when he wasn't even there to defend himself.

She was drawn down to him none the less, like a dust mote on the indrawn breath of an angel. She reached out to touch his hair. She knew he would never feel it. No harm done, she thought.

At that moment he rolled over on to his back, and with the same motion pushed the blanket away. The hand that had thrust the blanket aside brushed right past her nose, startling her.

But not nearly as startling as her view of him now, sprawled naked on the bed.

She had never seen a naked man before. Naked boys, yes, because a gang of them used to go skinny-dipping in the river that ran behind her grandmother's house. But she discovered now that there was as much difference between a boy and a man as between a girl and a woman. And it was the same sort of difference. Not just a change in size and shape, but a transformation into a sexual creature. Her own response to the sight of him made that clear.

She hadn't known it was possible to have sexual feelings in this disembodied state. She had assumed that those were physical reactions, brought about by the body itself. No-one had ever told her that the largest human sex organ is the mind. The flood of desire took her by surprise, and panicked her back into her own body in her own bed.

And there she lay, wide awake, staring into the darkness. She wasn't seeing darkness, she was seeing Calum. Calum as she had just left him, brazenly bare and unaware. Calum relaxed by the hearth, in shorts and T-shirt, firelight gleaming off every golden hair on his arms and legs. Calum leaning on the rail to look down at the sea. Calum smiling at her . . .

Calum not knowing that he made her feel like this.

Like this. Her heart crashing in her ears, pounding against her ribs, as if she had the sea inside her, the sea in storm. Her flesh hot as a fever, too tender to bear the weight of blanket or gown. Her body restless, hankering, stirring her inarticulately and with blind intent.

She pushed away the covers, pulled off her night-gown. She lay back on the bed, as naked as Calum had been when she saw him. As he was now, in the room across the hall. She spread her legs to make a wide V, like the hidden girl in Malachy's painting. She ran her hands down from her breasts to her thighs, feeling the fire in her skin. She wondered how different Calum's touch would be.

She wished he would come in and . . . cover her.

16

'Calum?'

Angelina gave a rap on the door, and a long, listening pause. Not a sound. No, a faint sound, the creak of the bed as a body rolled over. A sigh, as of a sleeper disturbed.

She rapped again. 'Calum, you have to get up. It's eight-thirty. You said you'd start work at nine.'

Another pause. More creaks and sighs. Mumbling, even.

'Calum, I've made you coffee. But you'll have to come out to get it.'

She wasn't going in there, not knowing what she knew, not even if his golden-brown limbs were all safely tucked under the blanket. She used to go into Malachy's room every morning, to give him his wake-up coffee in bed. But that wasn't the same thing, not the same at all.

After about five minutes of knocking and pleading, she managed to get a promise from behind the door that somebody or something would be emerging in the not-too-distant future.

He finally appeared just after nine o'clock, yawning and jamming his fingers into the tawny tangle of his hair. Angelina had seen no evidence, in the state of his hair or anywhere else, that he even possessed a brush or comb. Maybe that was the point of having hair like that; it allowed you to travel light. And anyway, his hair, like everything else about him, was absolutely perfect just the way it was.

A girl at school had told her once that when you dreamt of someone, it meant your souls were meeting. From what Alice had told her and taught her, she knew that that was maybe more true than her school friend could have guessed.

And last night hadn't been a dream. She had been perfectly well awake. Had even been able to notice, in the midst of her turmoil, that he had a small blue butterfly tattooed in the hollow of his right flank. Not that she would ever get the chance to check her recollection against the reality.

She could only hope that Calum had been as deep asleep as he had looked to be. Though she also knew, from previous experience, that even if he had been awake and looking straight at her, he would never have seen her.

All the same, she had to fight down a tendency to blush when she pushed Calum's coffee mug over to him and he smiled at her. She couldn't return the smile. She couldn't even look at him. She had to turn her back to him and busy herself at the stove, breaking his eggs into the frying pan.

'Sorry I'm late,' he said to her back, mistaking her evasive action for disapproval. 'I thought I'd catch another couple of minutes' kip, and next thing I knew it was nine o'clock.'

'That's not too bad for the first morning.' It was actually the ninth morning, but she didn't bother bringing that up. She was surprised he was even apologizing. To her. As if she had some sort of authority over him. 'You don't need to say sorry to me. I'm not your boss.'

'No, you're my manager, aren't you?'

She shoved a plateful of bacon and eggs at him, catching his grin right in her midriff. Did he know? He couldn't know. He couldn't know any of it. Least of all her wishes.

She ducked her head to avoid his eyes, then ducked out of the room, mumbling about feeding the fish.

It was better when they were at work in the studio. As long as she didn't have to look at him, she could respond quite normally to his questions or comments. All three cats watched uneasily from the door. Perhaps they suspected that their carefully hidden trophy mice were about to be thrown out.

Calum raised his head at the sound of a distant growl. The cats raised their heads along with him. 'That sounds like your friend Jesus.'

'He was Malachy's friend, not mine. And don't call him Jesus.'

'Give the guy a break. Nobody named Jorge ever got famous.'

'Jesus isn't famous. He's God.'

'Well? You can't get much more famous than that.'

They had to stop the argument when Jorge walked in, leather-clad and helmeted, with Charles right behind him. He made a show of peeling off his gauntlets and flinging them on to the floor. 'Despite appearances, this is not a challenge,' he assured Calum.

Appearances were all that mattered to Charles. The dog seized the nearest glove and ran out on to the deck with it. He dived under the hammock and set to work on his booty, growling happily over it like a cat with a particularly juicy mouse.

'Hey!' Jorge ran out after him. 'You give that back, you flea-bitten son of a bitch!'

Charles went on gnawing. Jorge put out a tentative hand towards the nearest end of the gauntlet. Without lifting his head or letting on in any way that he even knew what Jorge was up to, Charles rumbled deep down in his throat.

Jorge snatched his hand back. 'Angie, come and rescue my glove. The T. Rex has mugged it.'

'Fight your own battles,' Angelina retorted. 'You're bigger than he is.'

'Only while he's on all fours. And when it comes down to teeth, it's no contest.'

'Well, my teeth aren't any bigger than yours.'

'Have you any idea what those gauntlets cost?'

'More than you could afford, I expect. That'll teach you to be extravagant.'

'God, you're heartless, Angie.' He came back inside the studio, leaving the gauntlet to its fate. He picked up the other glove and impaled it on the upthrust handlebar of one of the dead bicycles, so that the bicycle appeared to be waving a greeting or calling for help. 'Hey, Cal, did Angie tell you she's a Pre-Adamite?'

'What?' Calum had his personal stereo on, and was not paying much attention to events outside his head. He unplugged one ear. 'What's a Free Adamite?'

'No, no, a *Pre*-Adamite. The Church of the Sainted Alice Day.'

Calum did pause at that, at least long enough to glance at Angelina. 'I thought you were Catholic.'

Angelina glared at Jorge. He was just making mischief, she could tell. 'Not since they threw me out of the convent.'

'What did you expect? They threw you out because you weren't a proper Catholic. Convents aren't supposed to harbour heretics,' Jorge explained to Calum. 'Angie had a number of doctrinal bones to pick with the Pope.'

Calum was looking at Angelina again, more puzzled than curious this time. 'You mean you took all that sh— that stuff seriously?'

'Well, of course. Why else would I have wanted to take orders?'

'Seems to me that was your problem,' Jorge remarked. 'You didn't want to take orders.'

'That was their problem, not mine. You can't just hand your conscience over to somebody else.' She appealed to Calum. 'You can't, can you?'

'I haven't a clue what you're on about,' Calum confessed. He added hastily, 'But don't bother to enlighten me.'

'You're right, we're supposed to be working, not

arguing about religion.' She swiped her forehead with the back of her wrist and surveyed the shambles around her. 'This is going to take us till the end of the month, even if we go at it every day.'

'My services are at your disposal.' Jorge made a little bow, rather neatly for a man who had never actually seen anyone do it in real life. 'I could make myself useful by photographing the paintings. It's important to keep a visual record, just in case.'

Angelina surveyed him with the same weary speculation she had just given to the room. 'If we take you up on that, George, you are plain forbidden to remove anything from the premises. Not even in the cause of art or science or truth or beauty or any such foolishness. What do you think, Calum?'

Calum did his own survey of the room. He stuck both hands into his elaborately matted hair, lifting it and letting it fall without any concern for how it rearranged itself. No vanity, thought Angelina, or else absolute conceit. 'We could do with another pair of hands. And somebody who knows what they're doing, because I haven't got a clue. What do *you* think?'

'Well, I guess it'll be OK. All right, George, if you have nothing better to do than root around in Malachy's garbage and take pictures of his pictures, you're welcome to do it. Matter of fact, I think you owe him, since you're getting two or three books out of him. But you're not pumping us for dirt to put in that biography of yours. OK?'

Jorge spread his leather arms melodramatically. 'You're a hard woman, Angie. But yeah, you're right, I owe Mal.'

'You owe him a heck of a lot,' Angelina said sternly. 'You'd be zero without him. The world's foremost expert on nothing. He was real good to you. He never talked to anyone else the way he talked to you. And he let you hang around here and all.'

'I know.' He said it simply. He was looking around the studio with an odd expression on his face, wistful or forlorn. As if he had lost something important, but wasn't quite sure what.

She was so used to him deliberately playing the fool that when she saw real feeling in him, she didn't know how to take it. There was no reason why he couldn't have been as fond of Malachy as she herself was. She had no monopoly on love.

She tried to make some amends for her harsh words. 'Actually, George, Calum is right. We really should have an expert like yourself around while we're sorting this out. We wouldn't want to damage anything valuable.'

'Right.' The lost look vanished, as Jorge straightened to attention. 'Happy to be of service. Just let me slip into something more comfortable.'

He stripped off the biking costume to reveal his black and red JESUS SAVES T-shirt, like a butterfly coming out of chrysalis, or Superman making a timely exit from a telephone booth. 'Where do I start? Instruct me.'

'Well, you won't be able to start taking pictures until we've cleared some space to do it in. So for starters, why don't you sit down over there by the door with this here notebook, and write down what we find? And don't write down anything we haven't told you to,' she added, just to be on the safe side.

Calum was showing more enthusiasm for his job today, though he tended to get side-tracked by fiddling with the things he dredged up. Angelina couldn't complain about that, because she realized it was the 'lucky dip' aspect of the work that mainly motivated him. It was not until he struck a vein of elderly cameras, and both he and Jorge became absorbed in admiring their features and guessing their antiquity, that she felt obliged to recall them to their duties.

'These cameras are pretty cool,' Calum remarked approvingly. 'But I don't see what was the point of keeping them, when they were just going to get buried in this shambles.'

'Malachy claimed he could find whatever he wanted,'

Angelina told him. 'I used to tell him I didn't know how the heck he could find a thing in this place. He said when he wanted something, it gave off some kind of vibrations to help him track it down.'

Calum gave her a funny look. 'You believe that, do you?'

'Why not? Why would he tell me lies?'

'Maybe it was supposed to be a joke.'

She considered and rejected this hypothesis. 'I don't think so. He said these vibrations were a sort of scent, like tracking an animal.'

Calum looked amused, in his straight-faced English way. 'Maybe he had a Cheyenne nose, to go with his Cheyenne soul.'

They were accompanied in their labours by the tinny, intermittent leakage from Calum's personal stereo. His incredulity when he learned of the absence of television was nothing compared to his reaction to the discovery that there was no radio in the house. *Not even in the pick-up truck.*

'How can you work without a radio?' he had demanded, in a tone that implied, How come you haven't died of boredom?

'I told you, Malachy didn't like noise. He wanted peace and quiet.'

'So, OK, he was crazy. What's your excuse?'

'I like to think. All that racket stops me thinking.'

'You get used to it. After a while you don't pay much attention to it.'

'Then why bother with it in the first place?'

He had given her a long and not very friendly look. 'You don't mind if I plug into my Walkman, do you, while we get on with this? I mean, I wouldn't want you claiming that I'd interrupted your thoughts and prevented you from inventing the wheel.'

From time to time she glanced at him, wrapped up in his own world of sound. A world she was cut out of, not just because she couldn't hear what he was hearing, but

237

because she wouldn't have felt whatever he did if she heard it. She could put a ring in her nose, but it wouldn't make her cool.

It was well after lunch when Calum straightened and pulled out the earphones with a practised gesture, like a doctor unpeeling a stethoscope. 'I've found another one of those diaries. 1982.'

'Just stick it in that filing cabinet.' Angelina cast a sideways glance at Jorge. 'We can look at it tonight.'

Jorge's ears were already flapping. 'What diaries?'

'Nothing,' she said firmly. 'There are no diaries, as far as you're concerned.'

'Angie, you can't torture me like this. You know Mal refused to talk about his work.'

'Maybe there was a good reason for that.' Angelina straightened herself to look up at the paintings on the walls. Primary colours, uncomplicated lines: the sophistication of perfect simplicity. 'Abstract art doesn't really lend itself to chatter. It's kind of like maths. Either you get it or you don't.'

'So what was he writing about in these diaries?'

'Nothing,' she lied, with only a tiny twinge of conscience. 'He was only keeping a record of each painting he'd completed, and each painting he sold.'

'If that's all that's in them, why can't I read them?'

'Because they're private. It's rude to read other folks' diaries.'

'But you've read them, haven't you? Enough to tell me what's in them, at least.'

'We only took a look at them because Calum's dad asked him to look out for them.' Her eyes widened with sudden recollection. 'Gosh, Calum, you were going to call him today. What time is it?'

Calum consulted his watch, a luminous lime green Minnie Mouse device with a pink plastic strap. 'Ten past four. That's – let me see – about midnight back home.'

'Heck. I guess it's too late to call now.'

Calum shrugged. 'It's not like he has to get up to go to

work in the morning. And he seemed to think it was important.'

'Well, it's up to you. He's your dad, not mine.'

'He might as well be yours, for all I have to do with him.' Calum brooded, then brightened. 'Come to think of it, I bloody well hope he's fast asleep. I'm going to ring him right now.'

'The phone's in the kitchen. Take it outside, you'll get better reception. George, you stay right here,' she added sharply, noticing Jorge edging towards the patio door. 'Charles will bite you if you set foot across that threshold. No, wait a minute, I take that back. We've taken up enough of your valuable expert time today. Thanks heaps for your help.'

Jorge looked slightly stunned at this abrupt dismissal. 'I don't mind staying for a while.'

'I don't guess you do, but I wouldn't dream of asking you to.'

'Shall I come back tomorrow?'

He sounded almost shy, not at all his usual brash and bouncy self. She wondered if she might have hurt his feelings. 'That would be great. I'll even cook you breakfast, if you turn up before nine.'

She escorted him off the premises. As politely as possible, of course. He took for ever to gird himself up in his biking gear. Then he clanked out on to the deck and glared at Charles, now upside down and fast asleep. The dog's deep breastbone clove the breeze, the way the keel of a ship would slice the waves. His enormous paws were half raised for potential paddling.

'What about my gauntlet?'

She could see the remains of the vandalized glove, lying in a sodden heap under the hammock. 'I'd say your gauntlet has had it. Better send the bill to Calum's dad. I guess Charles is his dog now, whether he wants a dog or not.'

When she came back up on deck after sending Jorge on his way, Calum was leaning against the rail, talking into the phone. His flat tone made it clear he was talking to an answering machine.

'Hi, Dad, it's Calum here. I just wanted to let you know we found a couple of those diaries you asked me to look out for. I didn't know if there was anything special you wanted to know about them.'

Angelina went over and leaned against the rail next to him, staring down at the sea. Listening to Calum leave a message for his father on the other side of the world. She couldn't imagine what that other side was like. She had never been farther east than Bend, the other side of the mountains from her grandmother's farm. The ocean down below marked the westernmost edge of her life. The north and south boundaries were Seattle and Eureka.

'Everything's cool here,' Calum confided to the tape. 'Angie's been really helpful. I mean,' he turned to smile at Angelina, 'I wouldn't have had a clue what to do without her. She deserves a pay rise.'

Angelina poked him with her elbow, but that only widened his grin. He pressed the END button and handed her the phone. 'Now you owe me one.'

'He'll think I asked you to say that,' she protested.

'Who cares what he thinks, as long as he does it?' He reached down to rub the keel of Charles's chest. The dog's hind leg twitched in response. 'Since you sent Jesus home, does that mean work is over for the day?'

'No, I was just getting rid of him. I don't want him knowing anything about those notebooks.'

'Why not?'

'Because he'll tell the world about them in that biography he's writing.'

'So what?'

'Well, for one thing, Malachy wouldn't have wanted him to do that.'

'How do you know?'

'Stands to reason, doesn't it? If you'd been getting up to awful things like that, would you want everybody to know about it?'

Calum came back to lean one arm on the rail. 'Maybe he didn't think they were all that awful. And he must have wanted somebody to know, or he wouldn't have written it all down.'

'It's a diary! People can write all sorts of things in a diary, because it's supposed to be private.' But she had an unwelcome intuition that there might be something in what Calum had just said, so she came up with a counter-argument. 'Maybe he just wanted to sort of get it off his chest.'

'Maybe he just wanted to remind himself about it.'

That was an even more uncomfortable thought, and Calum's grin made it worse. Men were so . . . crude? Physical? Dirty-minded? Probably they would say that women were too prissy. All she knew was that if any of Malachy's models had written about their adventures with him, they would never have put down anything like those passages in the diary.

Calum began to entertain himself by pulling needles off a fir twig and chucking them down the mountain. He didn't look very well entertained. The grin had been replaced by an expression of surly boredom.

She should have been put off by that. Normally she didn't take to bad-tempered people, or those who chronically find life tedious. But on Calum that look simply made him more exotic, more intriguing. It reminded her that he lived in another world, an alien, dangerous, inexplicably exciting place. The world of men.

Remembrance of him naked flooded through her again. She wanted to turn away, in case he looked at her and saw what was in her mind. She wanted to touch him. To make him naked again.

Those thoughts seemed to set her on fire. She could feel herself burning and shaking. She moved away from him, for fear that he would feel the heat in her. She had heard those phrases so often, *on heat*, *have the hots*, but never till now had she felt the physical sensations that must have given rise to them.

Calum was still dismembering and dispatching bits of tree, taking no notice of her. Which was lucky, but disappointing. 'Let's do something tonight. I've had it up to here with this healthy country living.'

'Like what?'

'Dunno. Whatever. Aren't there any discos around here, or pubs with live entertainment?'

'I guess there must be, but I don't know where they are. There'll be lots in Portland, but that's about two hundred miles from here.'

Calum grunted. 'I wouldn't trust that heap of rust to get us there and back. If Malachy was as rich as Rene says, what the hell was he doing driving around in an utter wreck?'

This slander surprised Angelina. Malachy's old pick-up truck wasn't a whole lot worse than the one her grandfather used to drive. 'As long as it runs, why not run it? It got him wherever he wanted to go. He didn't need to get around much, you know. And he didn't believe in buying new vehicles. Once when it just plain dug in its heels and refused to start, I asked him why he didn't buy a brand-new model and save himself all that hassle, and he said new cars were a big rip-off. He said you lose about half the value just driving them home from the dealer's.'

She reflected a little further on Malachy's motoring habits. 'Also I think he kind of liked the challenge. Of keeping it running, I mean. He was always fooling around with it. Kind of a hobby.'

'Funny hobbies he had. Putting people in the club, and driving a refugee from the breaker's yard.' Calum tossed away his last denuded twig and turned to her. 'Think hard, Angie. Isn't there anywhere we can go, just to get away from here? What do you usually do for excitement?'

'Well, nothing.' She shrugged. 'I don't need much excitement, seemingly.' Simply looking at Calum was about as much excitement as she could stand. She backed off to look at him from a safer distance. 'What do you do for excitement, back in London?'

He shrugged too. Even in London, life could be tedious. 'Go to the pub, usually. Maybe a club or disco or a party, that kind of thing. And I like a rave, if there's one going.'

That sounded pretty tedious to her. She had always hated dances and parties, always felt as if everyone else was speaking a different language at such events. And the music was invariably so loud it was like physical blows, hammering at her head and thumping on her chest, making her heart beat to someone else's rhythm. Like being possessed.

'Is that exciting?'

'Depends.'

'On what?'

He gave her a different sort of glance. His mouth looked amused now, not bored. 'I don't think I ought to tell you, seeing how seriously you disapproved of old Malachy.'

He didn't need to tell her, not after that. No wonder he'd said those models were to blame as much as Malachy.

For a moment she experienced the terrible yawning emptiness that opened up inside her whenever she was in a situation that made her feel stupid. She knew why she felt it right now. Because if Calum had met her at a party, he wouldn't have bothered to pick her up. He wouldn't have even noticed her. She'd have been hiding in a corner, sipping at a Coke, dressed inappropriately, ill at ease, bored, dying to go home.

If she'd been a different kind of girl, maybe the kind that enjoys parties, she might have taken advantage of his teasing remark to flirt with him. But she didn't know how to flirt, and she didn't know how to respond when men flirted with her. So she walked away from him, heading back for the safety of the house. 'Sounds like it's just as well I don't know of any of those kind of places around here. But if you really want some excitement, you can come with me on Sunday, to visit my grandma.'

Now why in the world had she said that? Calum

wouldn't want to do any such corny thing, no matter how desperate he was for a change of scenery. Sweetwater didn't count as excitement anyway, not in anybody's view. And if her grandmother caught sight of Calum's dreadlocks . . . earrings . . . nose ring . . . Not to mention finding out that they were sleeping in the same house, with nobody else to chaperone. If her grandmother heard about that, she'd make her give up the job and come home.

Luckily, Calum would only think she'd been joking.

She had reached the door to the living room when she heard him say, 'Only if I get to drive the pick-up.'

1957

The trouble with living is that it gets in the way of your life.

If I don't look out, I'll end up too busy to do anything real. It seems like most people do nothing but make the bed every morning and mess it up every night.

17

'Cheyenne?'

Ged's mother repeated it in a tone of disinterested interest, as she might have said *cretonne*? or *Chianti*? if he had happened to ask about them instead. 'I don't recall. I've never heard of any such people. Not that I recall. What difference does it make?'

'No difference.' Ged didn't know if he was lying or not. He amended that, to make sure he wasn't lying. 'I mean, it doesn't matter whether he was Cheyenne or Sioux or Apache or whatever. Did you know he was an American Indian? That's what I'm asking.'

'I don't know. I don't remember.' This was very likely true. Melissa floated through life in another dimension, aided by soft drugs and constitutional inattention. 'He didn't talk about himself much. He didn't talk much at all. Scorpios don't, you know. Of course you know, you're a Scorpio yourself. Actually, he was quite magnetically moody, in a deep sort of way. It was frightfully attractive.'

She watched her son light a cigarette, registering delicate and not-quite-non-judgemental disapproval. 'I wish you wouldn't smoke, darling. You know it's so bad for your health.'

He waved away the smoke, along with the stink of incense that pervaded his mother's tiny flat. The house was owned by an old friend of hers, an ex-traveller who had inherited it from his grandmother, and most of the tenants were people with firm but unusual ideas about how society ought to be organized. 'It's self-defence against your bloody joss sticks. I'll bet they're not good for your health either.'

'They're good for my spiritual equilibrium. Besides, the air in London is appalling,' she added, as if that was any excuse for making it still worse. 'Would you like more tea?'

He shook his head. It was green tea, probably long past its best-before date, and it made even American beer seem flavourful by comparison. She had offered him a glass of one of her home-made wines ('cherry, plum, carrot, beet, parsnip, you name it, I've got it') but he knew from experience that those would be even less drinkable than the tea. Though not for want of flavour.

'Didn't he say anything about his childhood at all?'

'Darling, that was forty years ago. How could you possibly expect me to remember?'

Ged could remember forty years ago. He could remember his whole life, even the bits he would rather have forgotten.

He remembered longing for a 'normal' life. His ideas of normality grew from glimpses of the lives of other people, other children at school, other families on television. 'Normal' life meant living in the same place for more than a year, attending the same school with the same friends for more than one school year. It meant being sent to bed in time to get a proper sleep, and being roused and readied for school in the morning. It meant living with your father, instead of a succession of your mother's friends, many of whom she didn't seem to know too well, and some of whom were very odd indeed. It even meant calling your mother Mum, instead of having to call her by her name, as if he was no different from anybody else where she was concerned.

Not that she drank or mistreated him or anything like that. On the contrary, she claimed to love him, and almost certainly did. She held her son in the same stream of haphazard benevolence and erratic enthusiasm that characterized her relationship to the whole of the world. People were naturally good, she held. It was only The Rules that caused problems.

She was a pioneer, a hippy before hippies, an earth-mother to the movement when it finally came along. In a city as large and cosmopolitan as London it had always been possible to live a nomadic, anarchic, low-budget life among like-minded people, but as soon as communes were invented, she moved into one, taking Ged with her. That didn't last long, but it didn't matter. There was always somewhere else to go, to look for a place where there were no Rules and everybody could be naturally good.

When she discovered astrology and the Tarot, there was no turning back. She had found her métier.

Schooling became more erratic, more irrelevant, as he grew older. His mother didn't make him go. The teachers didn't notice if he wasn't there. That was unsurprising, since at any given time he hadn't been there not long before, and soon enough wouldn't be there any more.

But he could read, and he did. He read everything he could. Some of his mother's friends had some very strange books. It was more rewarding to pursue his own interests than to sit in a classroom full of strangers, learning nothing much.

Friendships were temporary. And there were other limits to intimacy, internal ones. Forever living among strangers had built up an all but insurmountable reserve within him, an armour not very far below the surface of sociability.

Among children any oddness is ruthlessly punished. He was good at sports, which helped, and also good at sarcasm, which did not. Some days he had to fight his way home. Because he was tall, and tough from a brief lifetime of fending for himself, he usually won. Small consolation.

They called him Gypsy Ged, on account of his mother's unconventional costume and lifestyle, and his own dark skin. But gypsies could at least live among their own kind. What was his kind?

He didn't know, even now. Being one-eighth blood kin to a tribe of total strangers didn't really provide you with a handy spiritual home.

Melissa's mind was running along different channels, as usual. 'They're very ecological, those native people. Kitty says you can do spiritual holidays with them. She knows somebody who went on one. They put you out on the prairie all by yourself with no tepee or anything, and you've got to stay there for three days and nights with nothing to eat and only water to drink.'

Ged didn't expect to make much sense of anything his mother said, but even by her standards this sounded incomprehensible. 'Why?'

'Apparently fasting purges the soul. You see visions and talk to the spirits.'

'A spiritual health spa.' As package holidays went, this one sounded like a real money-spinner: charge the punters for room and board, then send them outside to sleep and refuse to feed them. And after all that, they go home thrilled, to brag to their friends about the experience. 'Are you going to try it?'

'Oh, a holiday like that would be much too expensive for me. I did once try fasting for a whole day, but my stomach was growling so much I couldn't concentrate on my mantra.' She chewed thoughtfully on what she had described as an organic wholemeal rice cake. 'Now that I think of it, I must have sensed that aspect of Malachy. It was probably what attracted me to him. He was a very deep person, very spiritual.'

Very spiritual people were unlikely to devote a substantial part of their energies to promiscuous fornication, Ged suspected, but he didn't bother to contradict her. 'In what way?'

'He seemed very self-contained, very focused. The kind of person who accomplishes great things. I felt a tragic past in him. Perhaps the tragic history of his people.'

'What people? He was three-quarters white.'

'Yes, that's right. I remember now.' Melissa brought her hands together in triumph. 'His father was named O'Hara. I remember because he used to joke about being part cowboy and part Indian. I'd forgotten about that. How could I forget a thing like that?'

'Beats me,' Ged agreed. 'If his father's name was O'Hara, why was he called Hawke?'

'How would I know? Maybe it was his mother's name. It sounds sort of Red Indian, doesn't it? I think they're supposed to get their name from the first thing their mother sees after they're born. Or maybe it's the father.'

'Do you remember anything else?'

'He was lovely.'

She rested her chin on her hand, staring dreamily into space. Great veins stood out on the back of her hands. The joints of her fingers, above the assortment of rings she wore, had started to swell with arthritis. Her face, which looked surprisingly smooth at a distance, had cobweb lines creeping across it. Her eyelids drooped at the corners, though admittedly to exotic effect. Her hair, which she still wore long and loose, was more white than blonde. Yet she sounded like a young girl when she spoke of her long-ago lover.

'He had a lovely body, hard and smooth. I've never fancied hairy-chested men. I remember wishing I could paint him, the way he painted me. I used to watch him work while I was posing for him. I watched his hands and his face. I could sit for hours watching him, enthralled by him. I'd never met anyone like him. I never have since, for that matter.'

'What happened?'

'What do you mean, what happened?'

'Why did you break up?'

'Well, he couldn't really concentrate on his painting with a baby around. And then he decided to go back to America. So that was that.'

'He walked out on you, you mean. Didn't you resent that?'

'I was devastated, darling. Naturally. But I realized that these things almost never work out.'

'What things? Having babies? Loving artists?'

'Long-term relationships. Look at you and Polly, for instance.'

Ged had no interest in doing any such thing. He changed the subject. 'Do you recall him keeping a diary?'

This required a serious effort of thought. She put her hands to her head, fingers outspread like psychic spiders. 'Not particularly,' she announced at last. 'He used to make notes in a book. Notes about his work, he said. I don't remember him writing anything else. Why?'

'I found a notebook in his studio, with the year of my birth written on it. I thought it might be a diary.'

'You shouldn't read other people's diaries. They're meant to be personal and private, like the thoughts in your head.'

'But he's dead now, he can't possibly care. And it belongs to me. It was part of the contents of the house. Part of my inheritance.' He asked out of curiosity, 'What would you do with it?'

'Burn it,' Melissa said firmly. 'There's no way you can inherit the thoughts in your father's head.'

She stood up and took away the tea cups. 'Sorry to rush you, darling, but I've got to get ready. Kitty will be here any minute. We're going out to save some trees. I don't mind being chained to them, but I do hope I won't have to climb them. I'm not terribly good at climbing trees. I never was, even as a girl. It looks like rain, doesn't it? Remind me to take my umbrella. Do you want your Tarot read before you go?'

'No, thanks.' She always asked him that, and he always declined. Obviously she still lived in hope. He moved over to the door, then stopped to ask another question. 'Did he ever send you any money?'

'Good heavens, no. He didn't have any to send. He was just a poor starving artist.'

'He was rich when he died.'

'Fancy that,' she said calmly, just as if Ged had said, He was bald. 'I can't imagine him rich. But it was nice of him to leave some of his money to you, wasn't it?'

'Was it?' *Nice* was an odd way to describe his father's motives. 'What I meant was, you can have some of the money. When I get it.'

'That's very sweet of you, darling, but what would I do with it? I'm not starving or anything.'

She was rattling things around in the sink, rinsing out the cups and saucers. Old age and settled living must have brought out some vestigial domestic instincts in her. She glanced up at him, her face alight with a happy thought. 'Oh, Ged, I know what I'd like to do, if I had a bit of money. Kitty told me about these spiritual holidays they do in America. You go and live with one of the tribes, and they put you through a ritual fast.'

'I know. You already told me about them.'

'Did I?' She looked genuinely surprised. 'When did I do that?'

'Just now. We were talking about Malachy being part Cheyenne.'

She went back to rattling the dishes. 'They're a Red Indian tribe, aren't they?'

He stared at her with faint alarm. She had always been vague and absent-minded to an infuriating degree. But losing all recollection of a conversation that had taken place only minutes before suggested something more serious than distraction. How old was she now? Sixty-six, the same age as Malachy. Too young to start losing your memory, surely?

Just like Malachy had been too young to die.

'Melly, are you feeling all right?'

'I'm feeling fine. Why shouldn't I be?'

'No reason.' He couldn't say, I think you might be losing your marbles. 'I just wondered if it's a good idea for you to be out chaining yourself to trees. The weather isn't as warm as it was. And you're not as young as you were.'

Now she was staring at him. The shock of sudden role reversal, perhaps. He had never worried about her before; it was for mothers to fret about their children, not the other way round. Until . . .

'None of us are, darling,' she observed, with a rare edge to her voice. 'I think you must be feeling a little bit ancient yourself, to start nannying me. The day I'm too old to do what I want, that's the day I'll lie down and die.'

To his surprise, he could hear the same edge in his reply. 'You've always done what you wanted, haven't you?'

'Life's too short to do anything else.'

'I thought you believed in reincarnation.'

She looked bewildered. 'What's that got to do with it?'

Nothing, obviously. So much for religion. The distance of death makes *de facto* atheists of us all, he supposed. He had yet to discover what death's nearness would do for the soul.

Back in the flat, love nest turned torture chamber, he was confronted yet again with a different identity crisis. Was he or was he not a writer?

If yes, why wasn't he writing?

He printed out all that existed of his new book, three years' work for fifty-two pages. He settled himself to concentrate, to read it with a punter's eye.

Three years, three fresh starts, and it still didn't work. It read like something someone might write with their mind on other things and their pen on auto-pilot. All the characteristic traits of his style were exaggerated beyond indulgence: cool appeared indifferent, spare became skeletal, dry was flat, irony invisible. After fifty-two pages it was still going nowhere.

Another dead end.

He distracted himself from potential panic by ripping the fifty-two pages to shreds, and then deleting the whole thing from his computer. What he needed was a new idea, and the confidence to summon some enthusiasm for it. But as far as literary invention was concerned, he appeared to be brain-dead.

It wasn't just his writing but his life that had reached a dead end. Since Elie left, the only thing that had tempted him out of bed in the morning was an abstract curiosity about what might happen next. If he lost even that limited taste for the future, there would be no point getting up. And nobody who would notice if he didn't bother. Literally as well as literarily, he might as well be dead.

At that existential nadir, his glance fell on his father's notebook. *1952*.

It put Melissa rather than Malachy into his mind. He wondered, in an impersonal way, if his mother really was losing her memory. They said it worked backwards: recent events first to go, childhood lost last. That was only fair, since it kept the oldest, most distant things alive longest, crystallized in the mythic distortions of a child's understanding. How long, after the average man's death, before the living memory of him had died too?

His mother had all but forgotten his father. His father, when Ged met him, had all but forgotten his mother. So much for love.

But his father must have written it all down in the diary. Must have put his experience of Melissa, and of Ged himself, down in ink on paper. That wasn't living memory, but it was immortality of a sort. And surely his father would have appreciated the irony of having his death finally bring him alive in his son's mind.

He opened the book.

1952

L'art, c'est le vice.

I'm looking for Miss Right.

She could be anywhere, couldn't she? The colour of her eyes, the size of her tits, the size of her eyes and the colour of her tits, none of that matters. The kind of thing that will make her Miss Right, it's not that kind of thing. I'll know her when I see her.

Everybody wants to be Miss Right. They come up to me on the sidewalk. They follow me down the road. They whisper their clichéd come-ons at me: *Fancy a bit of it, darling? I'll give you a good time, love. Hey, handsome, I've got something special for you.*

They don't say it the way it sounds. They slur it, like they're ashamed of what they have to say. They rub themselves against me, cats begging for scraps, making a purr of their pleas.

They don't want me. They want my money.

Miss Right will be looking for something more. She'll be wanting to make something meaningful of her pointless little life.

That's where I come in.

I'm an artist. I make things meaningful.

*　　*　　*

This one can do without my money. She says she'll settle for cigarettes.

She leads me into an alley. An alley cat.

She says she's seventeen. She looks like a skinny fourteen-year-old.

She shows me her tits when I ask her. She has small ones, fourteen-year-old ones. Two fried eggs, as they say back home.

The wind blows down the alley. She shivers. No wonder, with her bare boobs hanging out. Her ribs are showing too.

I ask her how long she's been doing this. Two years, she says. Two months, I reckon. She still seems a little shy about her work.

I fuck her in a doorway, standing up. She's tight and dry. She doesn't really want me, I can tell.

She doesn't really want me. She's not the one.

Another one who doesn't want money.

This one's just too drunk to care. But not too drunk to squeeze into the toilet with me. It reeks of piss in here, but I'm used to suffering for art.

Love, she calls me. They all call me that. They call everyone that. Love is the common currency of whores in this city.

The top half of her blouse is unbuttoned. She does that whenever she goes down the pub, she says. It puts her in a party mood, she says. She giggles when she says that.

I undo the rest of the buttons. Her tits are bigger than the last one's, but then she's more than fourteen. Closer to forty.

I feel her up. She giggles. Not like the last one. Maybe fried eggs don't have the right nerve endings.

She holds her skirt up, inviting me to fuck her against the door. That's the only way to stop other people from barging in, because the lock on the door is broken. If it weren't for the stink of piss, you might think screwing is the only thing anybody uses this toilet for. That, and writing important public messages on the wall.

JUDY AND SAM.

Trevor Curtis is a cunt.

I shagged Susie on this spot.

MY PRICK IS BIGGER THAN YOURS (with illustrations).

FOR A GOOD TIME RING . . .

But you can't call my girl. You have to pick her up in the pub.

Her cunt is big and wet, like her kisses. She wants a man, all right, but not necessarily me in particular.

Somebody tries the door while we're fucking. Just a minute, she hollers. My whore is hollering to another guy while I'm fucking her. He's the next customer, maybe. Well, that's the nature of whores, I guess.

But not the nature of Miss Right.

Miss Right does not live in a cat house. That I know, absolutely.

So when this one says she's got a room, I think, No.

I say I've changed my mind. She looks disappointed. Too much money, I say.

She looks me up and down, and says she'll do a blow job for a bob. Meaning she likes the look of me, I guess.

A bob is a shilling. A shilling, what's that worth? I work it out that she's a two-bit whore. A joke she wouldn't get.

I'll have it right here, I say.

She looks insulted. Just because I said a bob, you don't need to treat me like that, she says.

I meant I can't wait, I say. Meaning I don't have time to waste. She wants to think I mean something else, something a little bit kinder to her. I let her think what she likes.

We step into an alleyway. This city has alleys everywhere, and alley cats. She goes down on her knees and takes my cock in her mouth.

The result is disappointment. She has no imagination. She's not an artist, even in her own profession.

When I come, she turns her head to one side and spits it out. Spits me out of her mouth.

Miss Right would never do that.

Are there no aspiring artists around? Not even a touch of taste and discretion? Nobody hankering for immortality?

Miss Right will be a natural. She'll know what to do without being told.

This one catches my eye behind the bar in the pub. A pretty girl, dark hair, dressed in a sleazy sort of way. They all do that, here. I guess that's what these folks like.

The beer tastes like boiled piss, but it gets you plastered just the same. I polish off my pint double quick, just in case. In case I'm in luck.

She gives me the eye as she goes by me, on her way to the washroom. Confident. I like that. Showing a little style.

Come closing time, I go outside and hang around. Nothing wrong with that. Folks don't have to go home just because the law wants them to.

After a while she comes out. She saunters past me, giving me the eye again.

I catch up with her. That's not hard to do, she's not going anywhere in particular. Waiting for me to catch up, maybe.

Can I walk you home? I ask.

That's very kind, she says.

I take her by the hand. She moves in closer to me, snuggling up as we walk.

We agree that it's a fine night. A little foggy, maybe, but at least it's not raining. It's almost always raining here. And even when it's not, there are no stars to be seen. What's a sky without stars? Hell's idea of heaven, I guess.

She asks where I come from.

Montana.

Is that in America?

Yeah. The site of Custer's Last Stand.

She doesn't understand, of course. No reason why she

should. Every nation fights its own battles, and no others.

She walks a little slower, dragging at me. She puts her other hand around my bicep, leaning against me. Her breasts are pressed on either side of my arm. The back of my hand that's holding her hand is pressed against her crotch.

We stop in the street. We kiss. I cup her pussy with my hand, right through her skirt.

She likes that. She enjoys it for a while.

Then she says, I live right around the corner.

In one of those rundown row houses. A basement apartment, it turns out. All these places stink of cabbage and onions. The stench of a thousand years of boiled cabbage, that's the historical legacy of the poor.

I ask who lives with her.

No-one, she says, no-one.

At this point I don't suspect her of lying.

We go inside. No-one sees us go in. She's careful about that, because the neighbours would gossip.

I'm careful too. For different reasons.

Now what does she like, this young lady? Are we compatible? Miss Right has to be compatible with me. She has to want what I want, right up to the very last thing.

I try one thing, I try another thing. Now this is nice: she likes it all. She likes to be spanked, she likes to be buggered.

Do you think she'd fake it for me? Would she do a thing like that? She has no need to lie to a one-night stand. Truth in strangers as well as in wine. And she makes all the right moves. Right moves from Miss Right.

Oh, Miss Right, is it really you?

Jesus, she says. She's whispering. Jesus, if only my husband could do it like you.

Can Miss Right be Mrs Right?

I don't think so.

By the time dawn is getting up, I've stuck my dick into just about every place it'd fit. But this isn't art any more. I gallantly hide my disappointment, and sneak

away before the neighbours are up and around to disapprove.

Doesn't anybody want to be immortalized?

All these fools stumbling through life, no idea where
they're headed, no idea what it's for. Suffering for
nothing, like a beaten dog. Dying none the wiser. I can
save them from all this.

It's a question of intention. It's a question of awareness.
It's a question of art.

Art isn't a stone with a shape. Art isn't paint on canvas,
you bet it's not. Art is the mind making sense out of chaos.
Art is some scrap of the universe touched with intent by
an artist. Artists are the real priests. They're the only ones
who can offer salvation.

If I paint your portrait, you might think I've immortalized you. But I haven't: it's not you that's been given
significance, it's the image I've made of you. That's not
you. You still die like a dog, knowing nothing. But the
image, the art, that little piece of meaning in a meaningless world, that's indestructible. That's all that's left of
civilizations when they're dead and gone.

Death is the most meaningless thing of all. Birth is pregnant with possibilities, almost none of them to be realized,
but at the time of birth they're there, waiting their chance.
Death contradicts possibility. It's the end of the world, the
end of meaning. The end of asking.

Immortality means turning the end of the world into art.

Miss Right, I'm coming to save you from yourself.

I pay my models. At the beginning, anyway, before I start
fucking them. After that they do it all for free, the sitting
and the screwing, and even the cooking and cleaning. I
don't ask, they just do.

So why shouldn't I pay Miss Right?

You can buy anything, Christ knows. You can buy
death: gangsters and governments do it all the time. You
can buy life: my father bought mine. And you can buy sex:

men have been doing it since men were men.

And why not? What's wrong with that?

Every buyer means a seller. People are willing to sell life, sell death, sell sex. Selling their soul, but the buyer isn't buying souls. Buying life or death or sex, but not souls. So who's buying the soul that's up for sale?

Christ knows.

Women selling the use of their cunts, that's the oldest and lowest profession. Selling the most vital thing a human being can do, as if procreation was a sack of potatoes. Fucking should always be free. When money comes in the door, freedom flies out the window.

When money comes in the door, art goes down the toilet.

Just before sunset she comes up to me in the road, the one that runs north of Hyde Park. She wants the usual thing. I'd like to think she wants my body, but she only wants me to want hers. My money is what she wants.

An ordinary girl, not fat or thin, not too old, not too young, her hair a middling mousy shade, her eyes the colour of mud. Funny how it doesn't seem to matter what they look like. Being female is enough. Any old whore can be a whore.

Maybe it's the way she speaks that catches my attention. I can't tell one English accent from another, but I know a yokel when I hear one. I was a backwoods boy myself, once upon a time.

It's a warm evening, after the first really warm day I've known in this country. Never really cold, never really hot: that's what it's like over here. Couldn't be more different from the place where I was born.

And the sky is never blue. The sun is shining, the sky should be blue. Maybe it's like the coal dust that gets into a miner's skin: the everlasting fog and smoke that hang around this city have gotten into the grain of the sky. The weather can't get that grey right out, no matter how hard the sun shines.

Well, it's shining now, just before it goes down. I lure my girl into the park with promises. I want to make sure she's the Right one.

The park is full of everything, men, women, children, dogs, horses, pigeons, ducks, ice-cream sellers. I tell her it's too hot to do it right now. We'll do it in a while, I say. I offer to buy her an ice-cream cone. She is so surprised, she says yes.

The ice cream tastes like sawdust. But at least it's cold, not like the beer they sell in the pubs. We lick as we walk, and she tells me about herself. She's a country girl, come up to London to make her fortune. Fortune means luck as well as money, but there's not much luck to be had.

Or maybe there is. Things might be worse, back on the farm.

She got herself a job as a waitress. Her story was, they paid her so badly she had to steal from them to make a living wage, and then she got sacked for it. By that time she didn't really care, because one of her customers had offered to pay her for more than his meal. Now she makes more money from whoring than she'd ever done from waitressing.

She tells me all this without a blush. Well, why not, since she thinks I'm just another customer. I ask anyway. 'Why are you telling me this?'

'You asked, didn't you? Besides, I like your accent. Where do you come from?'

Since she won't have heard of Montana, I just tell her I'm American.

Her eyes light up, as much as mud can be said to shine. 'Oh, American! I like Americans.'

'Why?'

'They're all rich.'

'Not me. I'm a poor starving artist.'

That doesn't put her off. Either she figures I'm lying, or artists have celebrity value. 'I've never met an artist before.'

'There's a first time for everything, they say.' I look down at her dumb, pasty, pointless little face, and I tell her something true. 'I don't have any money, but I can make you famous.'

'I've never had my picture painted.' She glows and giggles and leans against me, looking coy. 'Would I have to, you know, take my clothes off?'

'Would you mind?'

That sends her into a storm of giggles. 'It's not like I'd never done it before.'

The sun has gone by now. Also the people, including the ice-cream sellers. They've taken their horses and dogs away with them, and the pigeons and ducks have gone wherever they go to sleep. 'Why not do it right now?'

'Do what?'

'Take your clothes off.'

More giggling. 'You're not going to paint me right now, are you? You haven't got any paints or brushes or anything.'

'I wasn't meaning to paint you right now. I had something else in mind.'

She looks around at the absent people, at the wide dark lawns and gravelled avenues. 'We can't do it here in the middle of the park.'

'We could go into those trees over there.'

She looks at the trees, and then she looks at me. 'Promise you'll paint me later?'

'I promise I'll make you famous.'

It's surprisingly dark among those trees. Surprising in the middle of a city.

I see no reason to be brutal about this. It isn't every day a man creates the ultimate work of art, and it'll be the last day this woman becomes one. So we might as well enjoy ourselves before we get down to business.

I tell her to pull up her skirt. When I put my hand on her crotch, she looks surprised at first, then pleased. It seems her previous lovers – customers – have been clumsy and careless. But they were paying for their own pleasure, not hers. This time she'll be paying for both her own and mine.

We crouch down together in the darkness, like hunted animals hiding out. But this is the lamb lying down with the lion, hunter and prey consorting. I've looked long and hard for this girl, and now at last I'm going to have her.

Because this is Miss Right.

I stroke her into submission. She makes small squeaks and sighs, a mouse under the hawk's talons, already resigned to her fate. To her immortality.

She goes down on all fours, reduced to an animal absurdity. The crumpled skirt around her waist, and the high-heeled shoes she won't take off, represent the last shreds of a pseudo-civilized skin, mocking her pretensions to anything higher.

Well, we're all animals, of course. But artists are something else as well.

I make her wait like that, like a horse saddled and bridled, awaiting its rider, while I take off my clothes. I wouldn't normally do that – it's for whores to go naked in public – but this time is different. This time is serious.

I take her from behind, using my hand to keep her happy. The ground is grassy, damp from the incessant English rain. When she starts to come I push her down. She collapses under me, slipping on the wet grass, the wet earth, still straining against my hand to squeeze out the last little fit of pleasure.

The last of her pleasures, except the final one.

I take my hand from her crotch and use it to cover her face. It's a big hand, it fills up her whole face, eyes to chin. Her nose and mouth fit into the palm of my hand, still slick from her cunt. The last thing she smells and tastes will be her own pleasure, stopping up her breath.

She bucks under me, tries to bite me, but I don't give her the space to do it. I'm pressing quite gently, my hand across her face, her head against my shoulder. I wouldn't want to hurt her. There's a difference between dying and being hurt.

I'm still in her, still fucking her. It's a funny thing that her struggle against death feels no different to me than the seizures of her climax.

'It's OK,' I tell her. 'It's OK. Tomorrow you'll be famous. Your picture in all the papers. Famous for ever.'

She's still fighting. Not against me: against death.

I come.

By the time my body stops moving, hers has too.

Did I lie?

I did not.

I went home and painted her. From memory. Her peaky little face, her muddy little eyes. She would have been thrilled to see it.

They found her in the morning, not quite in the way she died. She didn't deserve to be found in that state. I'd rolled her over on to her back, pulled her skirt down, brushed the earth off her face, closed her eyes to the darkness. She looked perfectly peaceful, from what I could see. A perfect work of art, made from a flawed creature.

She was in all the papers, too, just like I told her. An old photo, taken on some seaside holiday.

The police asked if anyone had seen her that evening. No-one had. We'd walked together through the park, and no-one had noticed her. She was that sort of girl, ordinary, insignificant. She'd have gone to her grave unnoticed, if it wasn't for the manner of her death.

Plenty of people must have noticed me. A tall swarthy foreigner with a beak of a nose wouldn't go unremarked. Some of them might even have recalled the girl who was with me. But the police were asking their question the wrong way round.

A perfect work of art, I said. But not as it turned out.

Maybe we're not meant to make a masterpiece out of

death's unmeaning. Maybe perfection is just not native to this world. Because in the papers it said she'd been three months pregnant.

Two deaths instead of one.

Not Miss Right after all.

18

'What I'd like to know is, what did he need all those models for?'

Calum was standing in the middle of the living room, frowning down at the books spread out on the floor. Books about Malachy's paintings.

Angelina was watching Calum. The firelight had turned him to gold; not sharp bright yellow gold, but dusty hazy tawny gold. His hair and skin had almost merged into one colour, the sun having lightened the first and darkened the second.

'All artists need models, don't they?'

'Not if they're not painting people, they don't.' He waved at the pictures on the floor. 'These are all abstract. If he painted from anything, it was just simple objects. That one over there might be a box under a blanket. This one's maybe a snake in bed. Most of the others don't look like anything in particular. They're just colours and shapes.'

'But you found that one in the big book, the one that we know was definitely a woman's legs.'

Calum came back to the fire. He sat down, stretched out his bare legs to the hearth. Every hair on those legs made a gleam and a shadow. Angelina could have counted them. Would have counted them, in her obsessive desire to know more of him. We are told that in the mind of God, the very hairs of our head are numbered. It was that sort of knowledge that Angelina wished to have of Calum.

1971 was on her lap. A glass of wine was in her hand, her fourth glass of wine. To cater to Calum's hankering for excitement, she had opened a bottle of wine for dinner. By the time that had gone down, along with the dinner, it had seemed like a good idea to open another one. And by this time, an hour later, almost anything seemed like a good idea.

'That one, OK,' Calum allowed. 'But most of them are nothing like that. He was interested in colour and shape, not women's legs. Well, he was, but not for that purpose,' he amended with a grin. To call it a grin made it sound superficial, but there was no other way to describe the wide flashes of amusement which split and lit his face without warning. They transfigured him, swinging him from moody discontent to sunny delight. 'Anything exciting in that notebook?'

'The usual, I'm sorry to say. We're up to Model Number 47 by now.'

Calum picked up his wine glass, leaned back and settled one bare ankle over the other. 'What's his technique this time?'

Angelina glanced at the passage below the entry for Model Number 47. 'Let's see. He gets her to . . . No, I'm not going to tell you. I don't believe it. No woman would do that.'

'You'd be surprised what women will do.'

He drank wine, watching her. She didn't know where to look, at the notebook that described such disgusting things, or at the man who made her think even more disgusting things.

He held out his hand. 'If you won't tell me, at least let me read it for myself.'

She couldn't. If he read it, he would know what was in her head. But in her head it wasn't Malachy and the model, it was him and her.

268

Maybe he would know that too. She couldn't let him know that.

She shut the notebook and stood up. 'No. I'm not going to read any more, and neither are you. They belong to your father, these diaries.'

'But they're not *his* diaries. I mean, he didn't write them. And I've a right to know what my grandfather wrote.'

'You know that already. This one's the same as the other one.'

She went over to the desk, stuffed the notebook into the drawer with the other one, and made her way back to her chair by the fire. She found that walking around the outspread books took an awful lot of concentration, especially with her long skirt trying to trip her up at every step.

She sat down with relief, and then discovered that Calum had topped up her glass. 'Oh gosh, I'll never get through all that.' She put up her hands to her cheeks, feeling the heat there. 'I've already had too much.'

'You look just fine to me.' He was watching her again, with a speculative air. 'Did you ever sit for him?'

'Not like that! But he did use to say to me, Come and talk to me while I work.' That was a small euphemism. What Malachy actually use to say was more like, Stop fooling around with those god-damned dishes, Angie, and come and keep me company. Sometimes he would add, What d'you think I'm paying you for? A remark which, under the circumstances, still puzzled her.

'What did you talk about?'

'Oh, everything under the sun. God, for instance.'

Calum gave her a funny look. 'What is there to say about God?'

'Well, we talked about what God is like. Malachy didn't believe in God. He said He was just an old man with a big stick. Something from a fairy tale.'

'That sounds kind of old-fashioned to me,' Calum said dryly. 'My view of God is more like something between Father Christmas and a social worker. Bigger on reward than punishment, you know? And deeply caring. But still, like you said, something from a fairy tale. No wonder nobody believes in Him.'

'No wonder, if that's what they think.'

This time his look, though still amused, was curious. 'You think different?'

'Yes. And so should you.'

'Why? Will I be sorry when I die?'

He was only teasing, but she was in earnest. 'Yes, you will.'

'Now what have I done, to make you so sure I'm a bad lad doomed to go to hell? Broken all the commandments, have I?'

'It's not like that. It's like . . .' She fumbled to explain what it was like. 'At school, when we were studying a poem or a book, the teacher would say something about a character in the book, or a line of the poem, and everybody would write down what he said and try to memorize it for tests. But I always thought that was crazy. I mean, that was only what the teacher had said, and he was only saying it to help us understand what we were reading. We were supposed to understand the poem or the story, not just repeat what the teacher said.'

Calum frowned, wrestling with this analogy. 'You mean we're supposed to try to understand God, rather than following a load of rules? But what if He doesn't exist?'

'Well, that's what you have to find out. Because if He does, it's the most important thing in the world.'

This idea obviously came as a surprise to him. 'Why?'

'Otherwise you'll have wasted your whole life, won't you? You won't have done whatever you're here for.'

'I thought we were here to have fun.'

She gave him a mildly reproving glance. 'You shouldn't try to be so cynical all the time, Calum. Cynical people are just trying to cover their backside, because they're so scared of being laughed at.'

'I know you're not scared of being laughed at,' he told her, laughing at her. 'You're the least cynical person I ever met. You'll believe just about anything. What about these Pre-Adamites, for instance? Are they some kind of secret sect?'

She'd hoped he had forgotten all that. She wasn't ready to be a prophet yet, no matter what Alice said. 'There's nothing secret about it. It's just hard to explain.'

'What's it got to do with Adam?'

'Nothing, actually. Alice says we should really be called Pre-Eveans, since it was Eve who got Adam into trouble, and that's what started this original sin thing.'

'Who's Alice?'

'Alice Day. A professor at the university in Corvallis. She invented the whole idea of the Pre-Adamites.'

Calum scowled at the hapless marmalade cat, who was draped over his feet. 'There are no such people as Adam and Eve. There never were, I mean.'

'It doesn't matter. Alice says that even if it's just a myth, myths still have meaning and power. But it's the wrong myth, that's the important thing. She's trying to teach people the true myth. I mean, the right one.'

'Which is?'

Angelina decided she needed another mouthful of wine before she could launch into this. 'Well, it seems that Adam had another wife before Eve. A woman named Lilith. The Hebrew scholars said that Adam divorced her because she was too uppity, but Alice says that's just their sexist little minds. The truth is, I mean the right myth is, that Adam had children by Lilith, and we're descended from them, and all that about the apple and the serpent and getting cast out from the Garden of Eden has nothing to do with us. Which means that the doctrine of original sin is all wrong.'

Calum too needed another drink, and took it. 'What's original sin?'

'That's the doctrine that says we're sinful creatures from the moment we're born. We're doomed to do wrong, and doomed to die for it, because the wages of sin is death. That's why babies get baptized, otherwise they'd go to hell if they died. At least that's what the Church says, but Alice says it's all wrong. And wicked.'

'I'll buy that much. Couldn't agree more. Does that make me a Pre-Adamite?'

'No, no, there's a whole lot of other stuff as well.'

Angelina could tell she really was drunk, because at that point she had to put her hand over her mouth to stop herself from telling him the rest of it. About the body of the resurrection, which was never really born and never truly dies. About the reason we're here in the flesh, and the reason we keep getting reborn. About the evolution of the universe, and how time works. About travelling out of the body. About the miraculous moments in which she herself had witnessed the world alive, all shining with the glory of the Lord.

She couldn't tell him any of that.

For one thing, he would think she was completely and utterly off her head. For another thing, even though she believed every bit of it, she didn't understand it all very well herself. Except during those bursts of brief splendour, when the whole mystery of existence informed and infilled her, a mystery no longer.

Some day she was going to have to tell the world. But she just wasn't ready yet.

'Well?'

She blinked at Calum in confusion, having been distracted by the weight of her thoughts. 'Well, what?'

'Aren't you going to try to convert me?'

'Of course not. What you believe is your own business. Everybody is responsible for their own salvation.' She stood up, and nearly fell over. She had to grab the back of the chair to stop herself swaying. 'Gee, Calum, I really have had too much of that wine. I'm going to bed, to sleep it off.'

'I'll escort you. Make sure you get there OK.'

'Don't be silly. I'm only going down the hall.'

But there wasn't any way she could stop him from following her, one step behind her all the way. When she reached her own bedroom door, she leaned on the door-knob to steady herself. It was the closeness of Calum, as much as the wine, that was making her feel light-headed.

'All right, I'm here. I'm OK. You can go away now.'

To her stifled disappointment, he obeyed her.

He was already halfway down the hall when she had an awful thought. She manoeuvred herself around, still clinging to the doorknob. 'Calum?'

He stopped to glance back at her. 'Yeah?'

'Don't you dare read that diary.'

That wide, sudden smile. The sight of it dizzied her dangerously. 'You know what, Angie?'

'What?'

'You're the weirdest girl I've ever met.'

She tottered into the bedroom, all in turmoil. Maybe that was what was wrong with her, the reason why she didn't enjoy parties the way she should. She was a weirdo.

She managed to get herself undressed, but she couldn't find her night-gown. Too late, she recalled that it was hanging on the washing line outside. The house had a drier, of course, but her grandmother had instilled in her the benefits of sunshine and fresh air at work on one's undies.

She couldn't be bothered to get dressed again, find the flashlight, and trek all the way outside to fetch it — assuming she was even physically capable of doing all that. No-one but God would know she was naked in her bed.

To atone for that laziness, she obliged herself to unbind and unbraid and brush out her hair, instead of letting herself forget it for once and rolling into bed as is.

She hoped she wouldn't have any expeditions out of her body tonight. She didn't want to find herself hovering over Calum again. It had been a long time since she had travelled involuntarily, the way she used to do before she learned how to control her trips. The trouble tonight was that she didn't know what difference being drunk would make.

But her only journeys were in dreams.

She dreamt of her mother. She could hardly remember what her mother looked like. It had been so long since she left, and Angelina so small at the time. But in the dream, her mother was not much older than Angelina herself.

She asked her mother about what Malachy had described in his diary. What he had persuaded the model to do.

Why not? said her mother. Some men think we're beautiful down there. Some men.

Angelina was not persuaded, even in her dream. Does that make it all right? she asked.

Anything's all right if it feels all right, said her mother. But don't do anything just for them. They'll say anything to get what they want. You do what you want, and do it for yourself.

The dream-Angelina was suddenly very small, much smaller than her mother, and much younger. Her mother stayed the same, the same young woman. And her mother was saying it again, in a different way. I do what I want, and I do it for myself.

A loud noise interrupted them. It must have scared her mother away. Angelina found herself back in her bed, with someone banging on the door.

Someone? Malachy.

He had come back, as promised.

She threw back the covers, sat up and swung her legs over the edge of the bed. She had to go and let him in. Had to hear him say that he was OK.

A louder noise struck at her, knocked her back into bed. A sound like God knocking on the gate of her soul.

She started up, staring into darkness. The night was suddenly riven by a flash of daylight. No, lightning. And then the rain began to hammer at the windowpanes.

Another sound of knocking. This time her bedroom door flew open. A tall figure swathed in white was standing out there. Standing in here.

For a muddled moment she thought that Malachy had come back to tell her he was definitely not OK, that the

Church was right and he had gone to hell. In her agitation and confusion, she stumbled out of bed again.

'Angie,' said the apparition, 'you told me it never rains this time of year.'

She understood all sorts of things at once, despite her still-drunken state of mind. She understood that a thunderstorm had swept down on the mountain. She realized that the white-shrouded figure was not Malachy in a winding-sheet, but Calum wrapped in his bed-sheet as an emergency means of modesty. And then, as lightning flickered through the darkness, she looked down and saw that she was standing there, right in front of Calum, as bare as the day she was born.

Another crack of thunder boomed, this time so loud it must have been overhead. She winced, expecting lightning to strike, if not the wrath of God.

'Angie, are you all right?'

Calum was right there, the sheet abandoned. Calum was holding her.

'I'm all right.' But she wasn't all right, she was shaking uncontrollably.

She was naked, and Calum was holding her tightly against his naked self. With predictable consequences.

He didn't ask any more silly questions. He kissed her, to stop her shaking. That stopped the physical shaking, but it made her shake harder inside.

They were kissing as if their breath depended on it, instead of just the opposite. He had his hands on her bottom, pulling her in to him, until her stomach was rubbing his erect penis.

She had never had physical contact with a man's genitals before. Even now, she could only feel it as pulse and heat, just the same way she could feel her own private parts. It made her think they must truly belong together, men and women. Opposite, but essentially the same.

Now she was on the bed with Calum, still kissing him. He was beside her, he was on top of her, they were inextricably intertwined. His hand was between her legs, doing impossibly pleasurable things to her.

Very quickly she, or at least her body, understood that he could be doing even more pleasurable things. She didn't know much about sex, but she knew what she liked when she felt it. Like a game of warm-warmer-hot: he stroked her somewhere, and the spot right next to that wanted him even more.

She had her right hand on his shoulder, so she took that for her writing-slate. She moved her middle finger, while she whispered to him. 'Do it like this,' she said, sliding the finger down and around, changing the pressure of her touch as she moved it.

He copied the movement down below, making her body move in unexpected and uncontrollable ways which they both found exciting. She moved him and he moved her.

She whispered. Panted. 'Like this.' And she did to the skin of his shoulder blade what he in turn did to . . . that part of her that some men found beautiful.

Even though she knew different, she told herself she was still dreaming. It made everything OK, to be in a dream.

She could groan and gibber with delight. She could let her body feel whatever it wanted, free of taboo. She could let Calum come into her, let him take her as far up as he could go.

It felt to her like he had reached the innards of her heart.

1961

She wants me to wear a rubber.

I don't use those things. I caught the clap a couple of times, which put me off whores, even when they're for free. But I still won't use a rubber.

It's got to do with consequences. Consequences are the only way you can make a mark on the world. The only way you know you're alive.

If I fuck her and she goes away without some of me inside her, it's like I never did it. I'm not going to be nullified like that. I want to leave my trail behind me, so people will know at least I've been.

That's not a bad epitaph: Malachy Hawke was here.

19

Morning broke, to scenes of shipwreck after the storm. A snapped spar lay heavily across her chest, pinning her to the boards . . . no, the beach . . . no, the bed. And it wasn't a spar, it was Calum's arm.

He was still asleep, drowned in another world. Turning to him, she buried her face in his hair, felt his arm tighten around her even in sleep.

Her head ached a little, as did some other parts of her body. She remembered now what she had forgotten entirely last night, that it was supposed to hurt the first time. She had no recollection of anything but enjoyment. And she had a vague notion that whatever had happened, hadn't happened just once.

For a moment Angelina wanted him to wake up and do it all over again, now that she was awake and sober and ready to remember properly.

Just for a moment, before all sorts of other ideas came into her head. Like, she might be pregnant.

They hadn't done anything to prevent that. Just like all those silly girls with Malachy. She was just as stupid and feckless as them.

But Calum wasn't Malachy, wasn't callous and deliberate about his love-making.

Oh no?

She recalled what he had said he wouldn't tell her. What he had as good as told her, through his joke about

Malachy. All those places he went to, pubs and parties and discos, he went there to find girls. To take them home and seduce them.

Well, if they were anything like her, they wouldn't need seducing. She had literally thrown herself, buck naked, into his arms. She felt like blushing all over.

She made herself do some unwelcome arithmetic. Supposing he only went looking for excitement on Friday and Saturday night. There were fifty-two Friday nights in a year, and the same number of Saturdays. So maybe a hundred times a year he went out to see if he could score. She couldn't imagine that anyone as beautiful as him wouldn't succeed every time. If he had been doing it, say, since he was sixteen, that meant about three hundred girls.

Lord! Even a fifth, even a tenth of that number made Malachy look almost chaste. Though unlike Malachy, that didn't mean he'd actually made any of them pregnant.

Oh yeah?

He hadn't bothered about that problem with her, had he? But of course they had both been drunk, so maybe it didn't count.

Drunk. What other state were people likely to come home from a pub in? He had probably been drunk, or at least not quite sober, every single time, and the girls like-wise. Gosh, when she thought of it like that, it was a wonder the world wasn't filled with bastard babies, seeing it sure was full of horny young men like Calum and dim dumb girls like herself.

She edged out from under his arm and sat up. He didn't stir.

She lifted the sheet. It was some small consolation, after all, to find a blue butterfly tattooed on his backside, exactly where she had seen it in the spirit.

She got herself dressed and into the kitchen, just in time to hear the sound of Jorge's motorcycle buzzing around the mountain like a hell-bent hornet.

Charles and the cats had lined up on the deck, all but holding out their food dishes. She was obliging them when Jorge clattered up the steps. She noticed he was bare-handed today. Presumably he didn't want to offer another hostage to fortune, or to Charles.

'Morning, Angie. Ready to buckle down to work?'

'I am, but Calum isn't up yet.'

'So what? We can start without him, can't we?'

She didn't want to admit that she hadn't had her break-fast yet. That would make him wonder what she had been up to the night before, and well he might wonder. She would never hear the end of it, if he ever found out.

She stalled by offering him coffee, and managed to snatch a slice of bread and peanut butter while she made it. She was pouring a mugful when Calum appeared, looking rumpled. Smiling.

'Morning, Angie. All right?'

He wasn't really asking. This was just his usual greeting, the way other people would say, How's it going? He didn't really care if she was all right or not.

Instead of answering, she fled with Jorge's coffee mug.

Today she was very glad of Jorge's company. Not for its own sake, but because it kept her from being alone with Calum. Eventually she was going to have to be alone with him, but for now Jorge and his chatter – sometimes he was like a one-man radio station, she thought – gave her time to decide how she was going to behave, what she was going to say. And also kept Calum from noticing how quiet she was.

Or so she thought.

After lunch, when she went out the kitchen door to throw the crumbs and crusts down for the birds, Calum came outside after her and shut the door behind him. He looked cold and cloudy.

'What are you doing out here?' she demanded.

'Just what I was going to ask you.'

'I'm feeding the birds. I have to do it out here, so the cats can't take advantage.'

'How thoughtful. How kind.' She could practically hear his teeth grinding in rage, making a kind of thunder to go with the storm in his eyes. He grabbed her arm, taking her by surprise. 'What the hell is the matter with you? You haven't said a single bloody word to me all day.'

'I guess I just don't have a lot to say.' She stared pointedly at the hand on her arm, but he wasn't in the mood for taking hints.

'Some problem with last night, is it?'

'Well, yeah, since you ask, there is.' She moved her stare to his face. 'What if I'm pregnant?'

'Is that all?' He let go of her, the clouds in his countenance already starting to part. 'Don't you know what to do about that? Go to the doctor and get him to give you one of those pills, the morning after or whatever they're called. Why don't you do that right now? Then you won't have to worry.'

And you won't have to worry either, she thought. But she suspected that he never really had, never would, not about a thing like that. Nothing to do with him, was it? He could change a woman's life for ever, and not give it a second's thought.

That was the sort of man she had fallen in love with.

'Listen.' She made herself say the other thing. 'This was just like the others, OK?'

'What? What others?'

'All your other one-night stands. We got drunk and ended up in bed, just like them, didn't we? So pretend you met me at the pub.' She swallowed and had to look away. 'OK?'

'What are you on about?' He seized her arm again. It must have been a habit with him. 'You want us to forget about what happened?'

'I don't guess I could do that, even if I wanted to. Women are inclined to remember how they lost their virginity.'

'You were a virgin?'

She heard the open incredulity in his voice. He was

almost as astonished as when he discovered she had never had a TV set. She forced herself to turn around and look at him. 'Do you have a problem with that?'

He was still holding on to her arm. He seemed to have forgotten about it. 'No I . . . I mean,' he shrugged, 'that's your business. It's just that I never would have thought – well, I mean, you didn't—' He stopped and started again. 'Well, was it OK?'

She knew this was not the moment to giggle, so she bit her lip sternly to remind it of its social obligations. 'It was very nice,' she said as gravely as she could.

The clouds vanished abruptly. The sun came out. He smiled that sudden wide devastating smile. 'Yeah, it was, wasn't it?'

Her mouth refused to take any more notice of instructions to behave itself. It began to smile along with his mouth. To laugh, even. They were both laughing, him and her.

Then he was holding her, and she felt like crying. For her, she knew, he could only ever be a disaster. She loved him, and he wasn't up to anything like that. Not yet, anyway. Maybe not for a long time to come.

He was doomed to do her wrong.

'Listen, Angie, it's too late for you to be a one-night stand.'

'What do you mean? Why?'

'Because it's almost the next night and you're still around and I want to f— make love to you again.'

She lifted her head from his shoulder to look at him. 'Why do you keep changing what you're going to say?'

He was still smiling. Grinning. 'Well, I wouldn't want to shock you. You being so nearly a nun and so recently a virgin.'

She put her head down again, giggling into his shirt. He smelled sunny and sweaty and sexy. 'That's OK. You can shock me all you like.'

'OK, you asked for it. I'll shock the pants off of you tonight.'

After some serious kissing, he amended that. 'Why wait for tonight? Let's tell whatsisname to push off right now, and I'll have your pants off in two seconds flat.'

By his actions he didn't seem willing to wait even until Jorge had gone. She pushed away the hand that had somehow found its way to her breast. 'No, you won't. You'll get me pregnant.'

'Yeah, OK, you're right. Just point me at the nearest chemist's shop and I'll take care of that.'

'Chemist?'

'Where you get medicine, you know?'

'Drug store.'

'Whatever. Let's ditch Jesus and take a trip to town.'

Angelina went back through the house, with Calum behind her. As she crossed the deck and came up to the open studio door, she heard a funny noise. A muffled metallic thump, like the fat ginger cat jumping on to the roof of the truck. Except it was coming from inside the studio.

Calum heard it too. He moved past her very fast, through the door. When she came in a moment later, Jorge and Calum were confronting each other in front of the filing cabinet.

They were only standing there, not moving, not speaking, but it was clearly a confrontation. Calum looked like Charles swaggering up to a stranger, bristles high, legs stiff. Jorge looked more like Miss Fudge standing guard over a moribund mouse.

'You were looking for that diary, weren't you?' Calum spoke quite softly, almost casually, in contrast to his aggressive stance. His hands were hanging loosely at his sides. All the same, he radiated trouble. 'Angie told you you couldn't read it.'

'What?' Jorge's gaze strayed over to Angelina, then back to Calum. 'What are you talking about?'

That must have been the wrong thing to say, because Calum grabbed him by the front of his JESUS SAVES shirt and slammed him back against the wall beside the cabinet.

283

Jorge's shoulder struck the filing cabinet, rocking a bust of Alexander the Great which lived on top of it, among the ferns and ivy. Angelina ran over to catch the bust before it could fall off and break. Then she stood in amazement, clutching Alexander to her bosom, watching what Calum was doing.

He was banging Jorge against the wall. Over and over again. Speaking to him in a way she couldn't believe.

He didn't raise his voice. He didn't even look particularly mad. He just kept slamming Jorge around, telling him not to fucking talk to him like that, and how fucking stupid did Jorge think he (Calum) was, and Angie had told him not to touch the fucking diaries, and if Jorge didn't get the fuck out of here in two seconds flat, he (Calum) was going to throw him down the fucking mountainside, along with his fucking motorbike.

Angelina didn't know how Jorge felt about all this, but she herself was fucking terrified.

Jorge managed to get some kind of answer out in breathless gasps. 'If you'd – let go of me, I'd – do my best to – do whatever you want.'

Calum let him go, with one final shove that sent him flying. He hit one of the bags of rubbish and sent the contents flying as well. Then he scrambled up and ducked past Calum, heading for the door.

At the door he hesitated, looking back over his shoulder. 'Angie, listen . . .'

Calum took one step towards him. Jorge threw up his hands, in horror or surrender, and disappeared.

The motorcycle started almost immediately, and the crunch of tyre on gravel. By the time Calum had gone through the door on to the deck, Jorge was well down the road.

Angelina settled the head of Alexander back into his bed of greenery, on top of the filing cabinet. Her hands were shaking so much, she was afraid she might drop him.

Calum came back inside, and astonished her again. He was laughing.

That scared her even more. Was he crazy or what? The way he had behaved just now . . . It was like something in his head had unleashed another part of him, some vastly more violent and unpredictable part. And now he was laughing about it.

'Come on, Angie, let's go find that drug store.'

She couldn't move. She couldn't stop staring at him. She was terrified.

He was still smiling. 'What's the matter? We decided to get rid of him, didn't we? And it worked a treat.'

'You mean you didn't . . . he didn't . . . Why did you say—? Why did you . . .' She wasn't making any sense, even to herself. She put her hands to her face to steady herself, and tried again. 'Why did you do that?'

'I just told you. To get rid of him.'

'But we could have just told him to go. You didn't have to . . .' She made a gesture with her hand, moving it to and from her chest, still seeing the way he had shoved poor Jorge around. Still hearing the clang and crash of the filing cabinet when Jorge hit it, hearing the thud of his head against the wall.

'Of course I didn't have to. And he didn't have to go snooping for that diary.'

'Are you sure he was?'

'He was standing right in front of that cabinet. I heard him shut the drawer.' He looked at her, no longer smiling. 'What are you so worked up about? I didn't hurt him much. He might even have liked it. Some queers do, don't they?'

That reduced her to speechlessness again. The word, and the suggestion. Nobody could possibly enjoy being hurt and humiliated, could they? And it wasn't Jorge's fault if he was . . . *If* he was. Not that it was any of her business, either way. 'Don't call him a queer,' she mumbled.

'What do you want me to call him? Christ, Angie, you'd make a terrific Sunday-school teacher. Come on, let's go. Where are the keys for the pick-up?'

He was crazy. He had to be.

No sane human being could switch moods instantly like that. For that matter, no sane human being would have beaten up a harmless creature like Jorge, no matter how badly he might have been behaving. She didn't think Jorge had gotten hurt, but he had certainly been scared and shaken, and bruised as well from being slammed against the wall like that.

She drove Calum into town, to the drug store. He came back out in a few minutes, with a plastic bag which he ostentatiously placed on the seat between them. That meant he was going to sleep with her again tonight. It meant he was her lover now.

Her lover, the psychopath.

He was looking at her. Waiting for her to do something. 'What about the doctor? Aren't you going to see a doctor?'

She shivered and shook her head. 'I don't want to do that.'

'You mean you'd rather have a baby than take a pill? You're crazy.'

So they were both crazy. Maybe they deserved each other. 'I might not be pregnant. It doesn't happen every time.'

He shrugged. 'Well, it's up to you. And it's not too late to do something about it, even if you find out you are.'

Have an abortion, he meant. People had them all the time. Also people had babies out of wedlock all the time. It seemed like most people didn't think there was anything wrong with either of those things.

Well, she wasn't like most people in this instance either. But she would rather bear Calum's bastard than kill Calum's baby.

They drove back down the coast. She was still thinking about Jorge, and what had happened to him. 'Calum?'

'Yeah?'

'Do you do that a lot?'

'What?'

286

'Beat people up like that.'

Calum was looking out over the ocean. It was getting on for sunset, and the low-lying sea fog had dispersed, leaving a red path to glory laid out over the waves. 'I didn't beat him up. I just scared the shit out of him.'

'Do you do that a lot?'

He shrugged. He certainly did *that* a lot. 'If somebody's looking for aggro, I don't mind giving it to them.'

'Why? I mean, why do you do it?'

'It's fun, isn't it? You never know how it's going to turn out, which one of you is going to get thumped. That really gets the old adrenalin going. It's way better than all that shit people stick into themselves.'

'Excitement, you mean.' He had been looking for excitement last night, and lo and behold, he had found it in those old standbys, sex and violence.

'Yeah, that's right.' He was watching her, smiling. 'Did it turn you on?'

The suggestion shocked her. She opened her mouth to say, Don't be silly. Then she shut it again.

She had been plain terrified by what Calum had done to Jorge. Terrified while he was doing it, terrified by the thought of it afterwards. But also some dark subterranean part of her had been admiring him. Not for that brutality, but for the coolness with which he was doing it. And also – there was no getting around this – also for the strong smell of danger that surrounded him.

Supposing he had come in from seeing off Jorge, and instead of prudently going to buy condoms, he had decided to finish off what he had started outside the back door. Supposing he had come in, still hot and cool and stinking of violence, and shoved her up against the wall and . . .

She nearly drove off the road. She couldn't stand to think about it. It made her whole body flinch with horror. And excitement.

Calum was still talking to her. He was reading her mind, even the things she couldn't stand to think about. 'Why don't you pull over into this – what does that sign say? – this scenic viewpoint? So we can admire the sunset, or something.'

Or something.

She had come a long way in a very short time. Less than twenty-four hours ago, she had been a virgin. Now she was letting her psychopathic lover lay her down on the front seat of Malachy's old pick-up truck, letting him push up her skirt and pull down her panties and ravish her, right there by the highway. And far from being suitably ashamed, she abandoned herself to sexual delirium.

Afterwards he rescued the bag of condoms from the floor, where it had been knocked in the scuffle. The unopened packets of condoms.

20

'What kind of diary is that?'

Ged answered his own question, though not aloud. The diary of a psychopath.

The diary of his father.

His father was a murderer.

He remembered the man he had met in New York. A normal man. Certainly not ordinary, no, but surely normal. Whatever else murderers were, they couldn't be *normal*. It wasn't normal to kill people. At least, it didn't use to be.

He went over to the window and pulled the curtain aside, to look out on London by night. For all the efforts of the forces of light, it was darkness that had the best of it. Night ruled the world here, if only because every lamp created its own shadows. Terrible crimes were doubtless being committed even now. Committed by terrible men.

His cigarette had disappeared. He lit himself another one. He observed that his hands were shaking.

Killing a whore was a psychopathic act. Everybody could agree on that. What about fucking whores, was that normal? It had to be, if only because so many men did it. You could tell how many, by the amount of whores who made a living off them. It wasn't nice, but it was within the bounds of normality.

Let's move on from there. Being obsessed with whores was a step towards the psychic (psycho?) wilderness.

Spending too much of your time looking for them, picking them up, planning what you were going to do with them, getting off on that before and after, that was definitely sliding into mucky territory. Keeping a journal of your encounters . . .

Well, at least he himself had never done that.

What was it his mother had said? You couldn't inherit what was inside your father's head, that was what she said. But he had apparently done just that. By reading his diary, for one thing. But also because of the whores. Because he had done all that before he read the diary, before he knew what Malachy had done.

What had Malachy done? Murdered a girl to prove some point about art? The motive was even madder than the deed. That sleek specimen Welles had made some comment about Malachy, something about him having moved from the abstract to the actual. Maybe he had done that in more ways than one.

Ged poured himself a large whisky. That was the least he needed, to cope with this new knowledge about his father's past. Then he sat down and read the diary again, beginning to end.

This time, some small particle of doubt lodged itself in his brain.

There was something oddly literary about those encounters. Malachy was clearly not a literary man, but Ged had an idea that if has father had simply gone home and written down a brief account of what he had just been up to, it would not have come out quite so aptly and neatly. Not that it hadn't happened, but that maybe it hadn't happened just exactly like *that*. The chain of events was insufficiently random; each meeting moved the narrative forward to the next one.

It didn't have . . . he groped for the quality it seemed to him now to lack . . . a sense of obsession, sufficient repetition. Surely such a murderer should have been in the grip of some dark necessity, a compulsion to have certain things happen in a certain way each time. It was almost too . . . He paused again, and then he had the clue. Too rational.

The last few sentences gave the hint, maybe. After failing so many times to find a woman who matched his exacting specifications, Malachy finally succeeds. Then he finds that he hasn't succeeded after all. If he were really mad, wouldn't that spur him on again? Whereas, in the diary, he takes this as a sign that he is guilty of hubris, and he gives up. Would a psychopath be so amenable to reason, even reasoning of a faintly superstitious kind?

On the other hand, why had he left the diary right where Ged was sure to find it? The filing cabinet was an obvious place to start browsing, even if he had only been looking for bank statements. Instead he finds a notebook with the year of his birth written on it, inside a copy of his latest novel. His father might as well have put it in an envelope addressed to Gerard Hawke.

So was Malachy trying to confide his deepest, darkest secret to his eldest son? Or had he been doing something altogether different?

Ged took a mouthful of whisky, the last one. He put on his jacket and went out into that criminal darkness, to do some hard thinking against the wind.

The more he considered it, now, the more he was tempted to believe that the dénouement, at least, had been a fantasy. That Malachy should have spent his spare time – whatever time was left over from painting, and screwing Melissa – in wandering around London picking up women: that, Ged found regrettably easy to believe. It was too horribly like what he himself had done before he met Elie. But that his father was doing this by way of a search for the perfect victim, who would also make the perfect work of art: that was a much iffier proposition.

Funny sort of diary, anyway. Even if it were true, it was surprisingly selective about the events in Malachy's life. No hint of the existence of Melissa or the birth of his eldest son. Nothing about his paintings, for that matter.

But of course it made no mention at all of the domestic

life of the author. Nothing in it was strictly incompatible with what he knew about his father's life at that time.

Notes about his work, his mother had said he said. Not notes about his painting, notes about his work. Maybe his work was murder.

Well, there was one easy way to settle the question. The diary referred to a newspaper report. There couldn't have been a huge number of murders at that time. It should be easy to see if any such crime had been reported.

Ged had a friend – more of an acquaintance, really – who wrote for the *Post*, and should be able to get access to their archives. A murder like that, a sex crime in Hyde Park, must have been splashed all over the front pages of the tabloids in those relatively innocent days. Now, no doubt, the victim would have to be a child for it to attract any particular notice.

He hadn't seen Peter, the newspaperman, for a while, so he couldn't just ring him up and explain. He would owe him a drink for the favour.

He could do with some human companionship, anyway. His mother hardly counted as a member of the human race, and rowing with Polly didn't count as companionship. He hadn't yet got round to letting Rufus know he was back in London.

Once upon a time, when he was married to Polly, he had had what passed for a normal social life. Drinks with neighbours, dinner parties with friends, holidays with other couples and their children in some rented cottage in Brittany or the Dordogne. Holidays that Polly would have arranged. Drinks and dinner parties, ditto. He never saw any of those people now.

Some of them had taken Polly's side and dismissed him as a cad. Others he would never have bothered with in the first place, if it hadn't been for Polly and neighbourliness and so forth. And Elie, in Polly's place, didn't go in for entertaining: she was shy, and a hopeless cook, and preferred to see her friends on her own.

It had occurred to him from time to time that if left to

his own devices, he would usually rather have done just that – be left to his own devices. But now, living alone in the Fulham flat, living without Elie, supposedly writing but in reality unable to compose three readable lines together, he was beginning to feel like an urban hermit. If he had been working on a book, he wouldn't have minded solitude; the world in his head would have been all the company he needed.

Maybe he ought to try fasting, like Melissa had described, and see if it brought any inspiration to him. It would at least spare him the trouble of having to feed himself.

Peter the reporter was in fine spirits. He said so himself, and explained, 'I've just signed a contract for my first novel.'

'Wonderful,' Ged congratulated him through gritted teeth. Lately every god-damned second-rate hack was turning into a successful novelist. While he himself appeared to have lost the knack of being any sort of novelist, successful or otherwise. 'What's it like?'

'Well, it's a thriller, of course. No-one reads anything else these days, do they?'

Ged eyed the beaming Peter, who was tubby and balding and drove an elderly Vauxhall, and furthermore had once confessed to being terrified of flying. 'Do tell.'

'It's about one of these American religious cults – you have to set it in America, or at least have Americans in it, otherwise the Americans won't read it – this cult of fanatics who are dedicated to destroying the evil liberal government, and they manage to infiltrate the White House in a way no-one would ever think of, and – well, I don't think I'll say any more, because you're a writer yourself, aren't you? One has to be careful, or people will pinch one's plots.'

'Your secret is safe with me, I don't know the first thing about how the White House works. Do you?'

Peter looked defensive. 'Well, my wife has a friend who

used to be married to some guy who was on the staff there for a couple of months. And there's always books,' he added optimistically. 'How's your new novel going? You must be due for another one to come out, aren't you?'

'I'm working frantically on it,' Ged assured him. 'That's what I wanted to ask you about. I need a bit of research done, and I thought you might be able to dig out what I'm looking for from the *Post* archives.'

'No problem. What do you need?'

'Now that I think of it, maybe I shouldn't tell you. You might steal my plot.'

'OK, OK, I was just kidding about that. You don't write thrillers anyway, do you?'

'No, but maybe I should. If that's the only thing everyone's reading.'

'I take that back too. You know what I meant. It was a general comment, not a personal one. Now for Christ's sake, what is this thing you want me to find?'

21

'MURDER IN HYDE PARK.'

Well, there it was, with all the relevant details. The description of the girl ('a known prostitute'), the holiday snapshot, the shrubbery, the cause of death (suffocation), the pregnancy, a coy reference to what might or might not have been rape. The request for information from the public. The obligatory shock and outrage (on a public holiday! in a London park!).

Everything as reported in the diary.

What did that prove?

Maybe only that Malachy read the papers. Well, he'd obviously read the papers, however you wanted to take the diary. He could have picked up the clues and written what amounted to a short story around them. It was an odd way to write the story, starting from the other end, as it were, but that didn't signify.

Maybe he had known the girl. Maybe he had even screwed her. Given his later behaviour, maybe the baby was his.

The only details that might give the game away were ones that hadn't been included in the newspaper report. Reports. It would have been in all the papers. How was he going to check them all, to see what they had said and they hadn't? And how, more than forty years later, would there be any way of discovering details that hadn't been mentioned in the papers? If those details contradicted the diary, then the story was fiction. But if they corroborated it . . .

He started his train of logic all over again. Supposing his father really had committed a murder, what difference did it make to anything? The old man was dead, beyond justice. It wasn't as if he had ever known his father, had any illusions to be destroyed, any cherished relationship to rethink. Not as if anyone else had ever been convicted of the murder. Why would he want people to know his father had killed someone? Come to that, why would he want to know it himself? What difference would it make to him?

He didn't know what he thought about that. So he went back to the beginning, and started from a different angle.

He had never heard any reference to Malachy's literary ambitions. That didn't mean he hadn't had any, of course. Almost everybody did – and nowadays almost everybody seemed to be trying to realize them. Perhaps, when his painting career took off, he had decided to stick with that and forget about being a writer.

Calum had left that message about finding more diaries. Their contents would surely give a clue to the nature of this one. If they were full of such stuff, then he could safely assume it was fantasy. Not even Malachy would have had the time and energy to engage in serial murder whilst turning himself into a world-famous painter and seducing women by the dozen.

Seducing women. That bit rang true. Whether or not the murder in the diary was for real, Ged was confident that the sexual encounters surely were.

They had a curious consistency about them, with odd features recurring. The girl had to be a prostitute, or at least an easy lay; they were apparently all lumped together as whores, in Malachy's Montanese (Montanic? Montanian?) morality. She had to agree to have sex with him for nothing. Not because he had no money, but because of his stated belief that buying and selling sex was a truly terrible thing. On the evidence, worse than murder.

What on earth could he have meant about his father having 'bought' his life?

There were other oddities. Married women were not eligible for seduction. Pregnant women were out of bounds too. Perhaps it was the idea of sexual ownership that held the key here. Perhaps Malachy hadn't held with wronging his fellow man.

Wronging women didn't seem to be a problem. After all, this was the same man who had deliberately disinherited all his daughters. An old-fashioned type, Rene Deforte had said.

On the other hand, there was nothing old-fashioned about his views on art. The stated motive for the murder was the same aesthetic theory that later led people to smash up pianos on video or stand around naked in art galleries. Art lies in what artists do, when they scratch their metaphysical itch. Whatever they bring into being as a result is almost incidental to the act of creation. In this case, the incidental object was a dead body.

Ged rang his mother, hoping she would not be out, chained to or stuck up a tree. Probably not at this time of night, going on for ten o'clock. Being Melissa, however, she wouldn't be in bed yet either.

She wasn't. Distinct sounds of partying came over the line, along with some late-period Beatles music. Not surprisingly, she had some trouble catching the drift of his enquiry.

'What? I can't hear you, darling. We've invited the tree people back here for a cup of tea. We left a boy with a mobile phone on the site, to warn us if the diggers try to sneak back in the middle of the night, but I don't think they will, because the council would have to pay them time and a half. They think of nothing but money, those people.

'What? What do you mean, did he go out at night? I suppose he must have. Why shouldn't he? There was no blackout or curfew then, it was ages after the war. I don't think we even had rationing any more. Not for sugar, anyway. Maybe for meat. That was the last one to go. No, I know you didn't ask about that. I'm just trying to cast my mind back.

'Did he go out a lot? What's a lot? Well, now that you mention it, I wouldn't necessarily have known. I used to go to bed early while I was carrying you, so I wouldn't really know what he was doing at night. What an odd question. What difference does it make?'

The very thing I keep asking myself, Ged thought as he hung up.

He did some mental arithmetic. It must be about two o'clock in the afternoon on the west coast of America. As good a time as any to ring Calum.

The conversation with Calum ran along much the same lines as the one with Melissa, with static interference on the line (or in space, or however mobile phones worked) substituting for a party in the background.

'Calum? Those notebooks you found – have you read either of them? What do you mean, Angie won't let you? That's a joke of some sort, is it? Well, it seemed to amuse you.

'Listen, Calum, I need to know what sort of thing he was writing about. I said, read them and tell me what kind of stuff is in them. No, *I want to know what's in them*. I don't want a blow-by-blow description. Just tell me what type of thing – laundry lists, recipes, or whatever.

'How are you getting on? What? What do you mean, boring? I'm not paying you to be entertained. Well, it's not her job, is it, it's yours. He was your grandfather. Yes, well, I'm sure he would have tidied up if he'd known you were coming. Just think about what that painting you're getting is worth, and get on with it. Of course I'm coming back when you've got it all sorted. That was the idea.'

It might take a while before a report came from that quarter. He had an idea that Calum was not the world's fastest reader, especially with somebody else's hand-writing. Sub-clinical dyslexia, the special-needs teacher had said, which made a change from the previous diagnosis of chronic stupidity. Eventually it turned out that nobody had ever actually taught Calum to read. Polly found a tutor to remedy that, but by then he had developed an allergy to the written word. Now he could read, but he didn't seem to want to. Ged couldn't put himself into the head of someone who didn't want to read.

Ten past ten. There was still time for a quick pint at the pub, if Rufus happened to be home. Their regular was on the King's Road, halfway between Rufus's small but perfectly formed Georgian flat in Chelsea and Ged's tiny, grungy, Victorian flat in Fulham. Halfway between two worlds: between the people who had made it, and the people who were struggling.

Rufus was home. Had just got in, so he claimed, after working late to clinch a deal. A drink, God, he was dying for a drink.

Ged was dying for company. There were too many things in his head that he didn't want to think about. Including some ways of looking for company.

'So what did those American solicitors have to say for themselves?' Rufus wanted to know. 'Did they make it worth your while?'

'I'd say so.' Oregon already seemed years ago. Explaining to Rufus was like rehashing old history. Ged could hardly bring himself to bother. 'My father left me some property.'

Rufus's eyes lit up. Any mention of money acted on him like a trumpet to a cavalry horse. 'What? Where?'

'A house and some of his paintings. I don't know what it's all worth, because the place is a shambles. I left Calum over there to clean things up.'

'Oh, yeah, Calum. I'd forgotten you took him with you. How did that work out?'

Ged shrugged. Things had improved to the point where he had been talking to Calum, a few minutes ago, much as he would have three years ago. Was that an improvement? Surely matters should have matured over three years. Well, at least their conversation had an unmistakable father/son flavour to it, instead of the awkwardness of strangers or the pointed silence of hostility, which was where they had started from a few weeks ago. 'We're speaking to each other.'

'Well, if I think about my old man and me . . .' Rufus paused, before philosophizing, to empty the last of his first pint down his throat and take a mouthful of his second, just to break it in. They had bought a double round, to avoid the rush when the barman called for last orders. 'Things can only get better as the kid gets older. It's not till you start to run into the same problems yourself that you begin to have some sympathy for your father's bad behaviour.'

'Not till you start turning into your father, you mean.'

What did that mean in his own case, Ged wondered. Long before he knew about his father's activities, he himself had started picking up whores. Was he going to end up killing them as well?

That unlikely idea gave him a very odd sensation. Something like drowning, maybe, a nightmare confusion of struggle and suffocation and excitement. Odd enough to make him stop thinking about it.

He wasn't drunk enough to tell Rufus about his twelve unknown half-brothers, or about being a Cheyenne octoroon. Besides, there was something else he wanted to talk about. 'Listen, if you wanted to find out about a murder that had happened, say, forty years ago, how would you go about it?'

'Look in the papers, I suppose. See if it features in any books. There are encyclopaedias of murder, aren't there?'

'I've done the papers. Anyway, I'm looking for information about it that specifically wasn't mentioned in the papers. The sort of thing that wouldn't be likely to get into any books either, unless someone had written one about this particular murder, which they haven't as far as I can tell.'

'Which murder are you talking about? It can't have

been a famous one, if nobody's written it up.'

'No, it wasn't famous. Probably because it was never solved.'

Rufus eyed him curiously over the rim of his pint glass. 'What's this in aid of? Don't tell me you're going to write a book about it.'

Ged was going to say, No, nothing like that, and then explain about the diary. But he didn't say it. Because he had another odd thought, much more welcome than the last one.

Peter had assumed his investigations had to do with writing a book. Now Rufus was suggesting the same thing.

No-one but Ged had ever seen his father's diary. No-one but Ged would know where the inspiration had come from.

He was inspired at last.

Rufus hadn't noticed what he didn't say, of course. 'If you've got the names of the investigating officers from the papers, you could try to track them down, if it wasn't too long ago. Try to find the victim's family, and all that. Journalists do that kind of thing all the time, don't they? So it can't be too difficult.'

'I suppose not. I can only try.'

They were going out of the pub at closing time when Rufus asked if anything else was new. He meant about Elie, of course, but it wouldn't do to put Ged on the spot by asking directly.

'No news.' Ged didn't mention Elie by name either. 'Who knows what goes on in women's heads?'

'I always thought you should have stuck with Polly.'

'I know. You said so.'

A determined bachelor like Rufus should have been pleased, or at least sympathetic, when one of his boringly bonded friends made a break for the freedom he so frequently extolled. But even at the time, three years ago, Rufus's response to the collapse of Ged's marriage had been indignation more than anything.

They had had the nearest thing to a falling-out about it.

'What's your excuse for this shocking act of icono-clasm?' Rufus had demanded. 'I've always regarded you and Polly as a beacon of marital bliss in a naughty world. Don't tell me it was all a fraud.'

'Since we haven't been living our lives for the benefit of their effect on other people, the question of fraud doesn't arise,' Ged had pointed out, in a sharper tone than he intended.

'I wasn't suggesting anything deliberate,' Rufus soothed. 'It's just, you know, you've been married for ever, had the two point four kids, still on speaking terms, even seen in public together. What were we to think but that it was all going swimmingly?' Behind his chronic flip-pancy, he appeared to be genuinely disturbed. 'This destroys my faith in man's better nature.'

Ged said dryly, 'Rufe, you had no right to bribe your conscience with my marriage. I'm not a scapegoat for your lifestyle.'

'How's that?' Rufus looked very slightly puzzled. Looking seriously confused would have been uncool. 'I thought scapegoats were the thingummies that got sent into the wilderness to absolve everyone's sins.'

'That's right. You want me to devote my life to the boring but morally upright option, so that you can screw around all you like without having to worry about the social consequences of that kind of behaviour. You want me to be good for you.'

Rufus ignored this accusation. He had spotted the solu-tion to the mystery. 'So that's what this split-up is all about. You're tired of being good.'

Ged saw no reason to confess that he hadn't been good for quite some time. 'No, it's simpler than that. I'm moving in with someone else.'

'Like that, is it?' Rufus sat up, in surprise or anticipa-tion. 'Anyone I know?'

'No.'

'Well? Age? Colour? Sex? Occupation? Mother's maiden name? Do tell all.'

'You can see for yourself when you meet her.'

Rufus read between the lines of that statement. 'Bit of a babe, is she? You intellectual johnnies are so naïve.'

'Are we?' Ged leaned his head on the heel of his hand and stared at his whisky glass. 'She sells cosmetics.'

'You mean to tell me you're leaving Polly for some slag of a shopgirl? Christ, I didn't think mid-life crises came that bad.'

Well, as it turned out, they came even worse. When the slag of a shopgirl walked out on you.

22

After moving in with Ged, Elie had learned to type – office skills, they called it now, and it didn't involve anything as old-fashioned as a typewriter – and taken up temping. The pay was better, and she had no trouble keeping herself in work. That had little to do with her typing talents, he suspected. Rufus assured him that prestige could be gained from the size of one's secretary's breasts, or her other physical assets, such as being dead gorgeous. Rufus had tried to lure Elie into going to work for him, but Ged vetoed that. He wasn't going to let her become Rufus's trophy. If she was anybody's trophy, she was his.

Whatever the source of Elie's success at temping, it meant that when she left him, he had no idea where to find her. He had discovered immediately that she wasn't where she had been. Maybe she had deliberately changed assignments.

The agency had refused to tell him anything. He wasn't her husband, after all. And even if he had been, she might have been escaping from an abusive relationship. Quite a lot of women were these days, the manager explained, giving him a look that contravened the most basic principle of British justice. The agency would, however, be happy to pass on any message.

Ged didn't fancy explaining his domestic difficulties to someone who had already tried and condemned him, and anyway there was no point leaving a message.

He refrained from thanking her, and left.

He had tried Elie's friends. All professed ignorance, claiming not to have seen or spoken to her for several days. He didn't believe them, but that didn't make any difference.

As a last resort, he had driven up the M1 to her mother's place in Luton. In three years of living with Elie, he had only been there twice. That was twice too often. Luton was a deeply depressing town, and he found dealing with Elie's mother disconcerting.

Something about her hair, maybe. Long hair traditionally implied qualities like informality, even freedom, but this hair was well under the thumb of some internal sergeant-major, every strand an identical length, swaying in glossy unison with the movements of her head. Then there was the vivid lipstick, which literally painted a smile on her face, and the torso which looked and moved as if confined by psychic corsets of a *Vogue*-ish shape and a Calvinist disposition. Altogether it was rather like talking to a middle-aged Barbie doll.

Elie's father had left during the time when Elie herself was enjoying modest fame as a model, i.e., living in a haze of drugs and desperate unhappiness. Like her mother, he had believed that a woman's first duty was to be physically decorative, and strongly approved of his daughter's career as a mannequin. His disappearance, with another woman on his arm, had been deeply resented by his wife: partly for financial reasons, partly as a slur on her womanhood. Or at least her Barbiehood.

Now she lived alone, in an unremarkable flat, in a block from the same clone that had produced half of Luton. She worked for a man who ran a flooring and carpeting firm. Once she had rung up Elie, all excited, because her boss had decided to run an ad at the local cinema and she was going to play the housewife in it.

The carpets in the flat were very new and fairly expensive, Ged observed. Maybe she got big discounts. Or maybe she played the housewife with her boss.

'I haven't seen Elie for ages.' The painted smile was half transmuted into a faintly flirtatious pout. 'She's terrible that way. Never rings, never comes round. I hardly know from one year to the next what she's up to. I don't know what to tell my friends, when they ask about her. She was such a good little girl, so pretty, so well behaved. I think the modelling must have turned her head. Perhaps I shouldn't have encouraged her in it.'

Pushed her into it, more like, according to Elie. Well, he understood physicists to have proved that every event was really several events, depending on where you happened to be watching from.

Elie's mother helped herself to a cigarette and took a moment to enjoy the comfort of tobacco smoke. 'Can I offer you something to drink? Coffee? Whisky?'

He chose whisky. A slight disconnection from his present surroundings could only be a good thing. He took advantage of her absence to light his own cigarette.

She returned with a bottle of whisky and a glass, which she set down at his end of the coffee table. He couldn't help contrasting this business-like hospitality with Polly's genteel vicar-haunted habits. Maybe the vicar hadn't featured much in Elie's childhood.

Elie's mother established herself at the opposite end of the sofa with her cigarette and her own supply of alcohol, a bottle of supermarket Chablis. He got the impression that that was a routine for her.

The impression was reinforced when she raised her glass. 'Cheers.' She took a healthy swig, then held the glass up again, this time to examine the contents. 'I prefer red wine, but if you spill it on the furniture you'll never get the stain out. At least this stuff doesn't show.' She shrugged and took another drink. 'What's happened to Elie, then? Didn't she leave a note?'

'No. But she took her clothes.'

'That's serious. A girl can't survive long without her wardrobe.'

It was the first evidence of a sense of humour that he

had ever noticed in her. He felt obliged to smile. 'The difficulty is, I don't know where she's gone.'

'She can't have gone far, with all those clothes. But she didn't give up her job, did she?'

'No, but it's only a temping job. I don't know where she's working, and the agency won't tell me. Some bizarre rules about confidentiality.'

Elie's mother thought deeply.

He couldn't keep thinking of her as Elie's mother. The woman had a name, and he would have to use it at some point. He did some deep thinking himself. Valerie, that was her name. Valerie Rae.

'They might tell me,' Valerie offered. 'I'm her mum, after all. I could say it's an emergency.' She paused, to give him time to realize the magnitude of the favour she was proposing. 'Shall I have a go?'

'Why not?' He added belatedly, 'I'd be grateful.'

'No problem.' She was perched at the far end of the sofa, an enormous three-seater specimen, the major part of a three-piece suite and an obvious left-over from the days when she had been a housewife rather than a flat-dweller. Her eyes were brightening with plain old-fashioned nosiness. 'What sort of row did you have with her, then?'

He had to say something, and the truth would do as well as anything. 'She wants a baby.'

'Don't you?'

'I've already had two.'

'But she wants her own. That's natural.'

He shrugged.

'Well, maybe you're right.' Elie's mother – Valerie – glanced around the room. The walls were crowded with photographs of Elie. Elie in various catwalk poses, Elie and her mother dressed identically, Elie in an ad for bridal wear. 'You devote yourself to your children for twenty years, and then they disappear. Gone out of your life. Popping in every now and then to say hello, as if you were some distant aunt. What's the point of that?'

She got up, carrying her drink and the cigarette, inviting him to do the same. She pointed to the photo of Elie and herself. 'Everyone kept saying we looked more like sisters than mother and daughter. So I had this done. We do look alike, don't we?'

They did, of course. Which was not the same as saying that one couldn't tell the mother from the daughter. Elie must have been about seventeen, in her physical prime as the unforgiving world reckons such things, whereas Valerie appeared to be an extremely well-preserved thirty-five-year-old. Nothing wrong with that, absolutely nothing, every woman at thirty-five would rather be well preserved than the opposite, but it didn't amount to looking like sisters.

She was still looking expectant, waiting for some suitable compliment. 'It's remarkable,' he allowed diplomatically.

That appeared to satisfy her. She moved on to the next item in her gallery, the full-page advertisement featuring Elie as a bride. 'This one's my favourite. She looks so lovely, all innocent and excited, just the way a bride should look.'

He studied the ad. He never minded looking at pictures of Elie. In this one she did look just the way her mother described her, innocent and excited, and no more than eighteen. In most of the others, the catwalk shots especially, the photographer had done his best to compress her into the cool, jaded image that haunted the pages of women's magazines. How perverse that the fashion industry should be so eager to search out fresh-faced adolescent girls, merely in order to transform them, for the camera and the catwalk, into gaunt, blasé, dead-eyed creatures, fifteen going on forty.

He studied Elie's eyes in the framed photos. Those eyes, as he was too well aware, were the most extraordinary feature of her extraordinarily beautiful face, because they were dark and yet full of light. In the wedding-dress photo, where her face was framed by a lacy froth of veil, the eyes were a match for the brightness surrounding them, glowing with what was meant to be hopes and dreams of happiness.

But in the other pictures, the light had gone out of her. Dulled by drugs, maybe. Or by starvation. She was naturally slim, even now; but in these images she barely had flesh on her bones. The extreme thinness accentuated her cheekbones in a savage, unsubtle manner, turned her into something like a caricature of herself.

'I'd love to have a real one like that,' Valerie remarked, indicating the bridal ad. 'I'd love to see her like that on her wedding day.' She swallowed wine and flashed an accusing glance at Ged. 'When she told me she was living with a married man . . . Well, it was a blow, I can tell you.'

'I'm not married any more.'

'So why haven't you married her, then?'

He shrugged. The subject hadn't really come up. Babies had been the big issue. 'I can't marry her if she's left me.'

Valerie put a hand on his arm. With her other hand, with the glass in that hand, she gestured at the wedding picture. 'Doesn't that inspire you? Wouldn't you like to have a bride who looked like that?'

When he didn't answer, she gave him a sideways, calculating look. 'If she came back to you, would you marry her?'

'I don't know. We've never discussed it. I don't know if that's what she wants.'

'Every girl wants to get married, no matter what she says.' She manoeuvred him back towards the sofa. 'Here, sit down. Pour yourself another drink.'

This time she settled somewhere in the middle of the sofa, noticeably nearer to his end. She took her own advice and poured herself another glass of wine. 'About this business of babies. Wouldn't you like to have children who looked like Elie?'

'In theory, yes. Of course. But children are about as far from theory as you can get, aren't they?'

She needed the rest of her glass of wine before she could answer. 'Well, yes. It's a bit of a shock, really, their physicalness.' She turned to him in a sudden burst of confidential confession. 'Everybody keeps it to themselves, don't they, all the embarrassing bits of life that you can't admit to. But children don't know any better, so they don't bother. They're amazingly frank about it all – burping, farting, pissing, shitting, all that type of thing.'

Ged was astonished by her frank language. And then not so astonished, when he noticed that her wine bottle was nearly empty. She must have started on it before he arrived. He wondered if she had ever actually uttered those words aloud before.

'And then they're so physical in their affection.' She was leaning towards him, touching his sleeve. 'They don't play games. They want to give you a hug and they do it. They want you to hug them and they say so.'

She ran her hand up his arm, gripped his shoulder with a significant intensity of pressure. Her eyes, dark like her daughter's, were glittering with the threat of tears. 'That was so long ago,' she said, making a womanful attempt to swallow the tears. 'She was just like I said, sweet and loving. And now I don't even know where she is.'

Unlike his mother, Ged had never claimed any psychic powers. But now he foresaw quite clearly where this was going to end, if he didn't leave pretty promptly.

He swallowed his disgust, washed it down with whisky. He was thinking of the scars on Elie's arms. This woman, with her plastic persona and naff obsessions, had all but carved them there. The fact that she was drunk didn't excuse coming on to her daughter's . . . her daughter's what? Jilted boyfriend? Even if that was all it amounted to now, common decency ought at least to let the corpse of the relationship cool before making any moves.

Unfortunately he was halfway through his third large whisky, already well over the driving limit. And he needed a favour from her.

He gave the insinuating hand on his shoulder a hearty

pat. Maybe more of a slap. 'Well, that's what I'm trying to do. Find her for you. If you can do your bit with the agency, I'll do my bit with Elie.'

And then he said something quite crazy. 'If I get her back, I'll marry her.'

Was that for her benefit, or his, or just a very clear way of warning her off? Maybe she was right; maybe Elie really did hanker after being Mrs Hawke. Well, if that was what Elie wanted, that was what Elie would get.

Elie's mother took her hands off him. The notion of her girl getting married – in grand, not to say over the top style, of course – was a bribe large enough to let temporary pleasures pass. 'I'll do it tomorrow. First thing tomorrow.'

'Brilliant. And now I really must go.'

And he really did go, despite the whisky. He had driven around the corner and parked, made himself as comfortable as he could in the back seat, and dozed off and on until morning.

When he located the address that Valerie had winkled out of the agency for him, tucked away off Fleet Street, he had not been too surprised to find himself standing in a palace. After all, this was a famous firm of solicitors, and everybody knew that whatever happened, the lawyers won. The marble-paved atrium was about a mile high and a mile across, decked out with palm trees, statuary, a huge fish pond, even a waterfall. All mod cons, as lawyers reckon such things.

The receptionist at the vast semi-circular marble desk agreed to ring Elie. 'Who shall I say is calling?'

He saw no reason not to give his own name. She would have to come down in any case; she couldn't leave him standing in the atrium under the eyes of the receptionist, a taunt and a reproach to her.

He spent the next ten minutes admiring the palm trees and the sculpture, while keeping an eye on the lobby that led to the lifts. When Elie appeared, he intercepted her by stepping out from behind one of the trees.

She recoiled, maybe startled, maybe avoiding contact. 'What do you want?'

Whatever she had been doing since she disappeared, it hadn't been much fun. She looked almost as haggard and distraught as the day when she had told him about being thrown out by Ben. She certainly didn't look like a woman who had left her lover in order to find a better life.

He took her by the elbow to move her out of the receptionist's line of sight, between a tree and a . . . well, a big blob of bronze that looked like an erection running out of steam for want of encouragement. 'Are you all right?'

'Why shouldn't I be all right?'

Because you don't look all right, he wanted to say. But he couldn't say that. Suggesting she looked less than ideal would not only annoy her, but might well strike at the roots of her self-esteem. For all that she insistently declared herself against idealized beauty, she had always gone to a hell of a lot of trouble to subscribe to that ideal in a personal way. If looking good was all you thought you had going for you, then looking not so good must be devastating.

Like not being able to write, when you were supposed to be a writer.

'That's what I wanted to ask you. Why did you bugger off like that?'

Her face went dead. Just like the fashion shots in her mother's flat. He might as well have been talking to one of those photographs.

'I don't want to talk to you. I don't want to *see* you.' She took a deep breath, the only sign she was still alive, not just a zombie with a recorded announcement. 'Don't come here again, because it won't do you any good. If you harass me I'll call the police. I can get a, a – a conjunction? You know, one of those things . . .'

The tape recorder had run out of steam too, or at least out of vocabulary. That touched him in an unexpected way. Anger ran against her grain; she couldn't do it properly. 'An injunction.'

'Yes. That's what I meant.'

'Don't you think you owe me some sort of explanation?'

The zombie in her eyes had gone, driven out by a flash of anguish. 'I can't.'

Couldn't explain, she meant, and he understood. Rationality was not her strong point, but he didn't blame her for that. She was like a kitten which had been petted and mistreated in equal and arbitrary measure; she didn't expect the world to make much sense. Even while opening herself to the pleasure of the moment, she was always half afraid that it would take an ugly turn.

Originally that had been part of her attraction for him, that she was so easy to please, and so easy to frighten. But pleasing her had proved the more rewarding. Besides, he didn't want to turn himself into Ben.

What he wanted right then was to take her in his arms, to – in this den of lawyers, he found himself censoring even his wishes – to *kiss* her. Christ, he even wanted to marry her.

But since he couldn't abduct her under the eyes of the receptionist, he had had to let her go.

He had thought of hanging around outside until she went home, in order to follow her back to wherever she was living. But there wasn't much point. If she didn't want to see him, she didn't want to see him.

He almost said, Let me know if you change your mind. But that amounted to an invitation to trample on him. She was in the wrong, surely? Let her do the suffering.

Only it didn't work like that. Couldn't work like that. Not when he was the one who wanted more.

23

'What's this?'

Angelina looked across the massive workbench, which ran the width of the studio, to see what Calum was holding up. 'It's a mortar and pestle.'

'And I'm none the wiser for that information,' he retorted. 'What does it do? What's it for?'

'You can use the pestle – that's the club thing – to smash things up in the bowl.'

'Smash things up,' Calum repeated, in a tone that evoked images much more violent than the ones Angelina had in mind. 'What sort of things?'

Jorge appeared at Calum's shoulder. Angelina had won at least one struggle against the forces of barbarism, having browbeaten both of them into shaking hands and mumbling an apology for their respective trespasses. Things were more or less back to normal, if you didn't count Jorge's fledgling beard, which made him look like his moustache was trying to colonize his face.

'Pigment,' he announced, peering into the little bowl. He rubbed his finger around the mortar and held it up, the colour of mustard. 'Look, here's the last pigment he used. He must have been working on one of his Yellows.'

'That one there.' Angelina pointed to a stack of paintings along the bottom of the east wall.

The one she meant was obvious, since it matched the smear on Jorge's finger. It was reminiscent of Van Gogh's sunflowers, but brighter and more translucent, especially in the morning light. Maybe something like looking at the layers of heat in the sun.

Jorge stared intently at the painting for a while, then cleared his throat. 'He sure hadn't lost the knack, had he?'

'I don't understand this,' Calum complained. 'What's the stuff in this bowl got to do with that painting?'

Jorge was still lost in the colours of the sun, but he surfaced to offer an explanation. 'He mixed the paint himself.'

Calum looked blank. 'I thought paint came in tubes.'

'The colour in the paint has to come from somewhere, doesn't it? From some animal, vegetable, or mineral. Mal always kept an eye out for natural colours, especially in rocks or soils. He used to experiment with them, see what kind of results he could get on canvas.' Jorge swept an arm along the wall. 'That's how he achieved these amazing colours. You can't buy that kind of subtlety in a tube.'

'He made his own paints?' Calum blinked at the wall of colour. 'I didn't know you could do that.'

'How do you think the cavemen did it? They didn't have an arts and crafts shop at Lascaux.'

While Jorge was educating Calum, Angelina had already gone back to work. She was struggling to move a big blank canvas when she stubbed her toe on something. A stretcher, apparently. But the light wooden frame would simply have been kicked aside. Something behind it was made of more adamant qualities.

'Hey, you guys, there's something back here. Behind these canvases in the corner.'

By the time they had made their way round the bench, she had already exposed what Malachy must have deliberately hidden: a large, rusty, iron-bound trunk. It had an arched top, like a pirate's treasure chest, and a padlock on the hasp.

She stared at it, hands on hips. 'Look at the size of this thing. I can't work out how come I never noticed it before.'

'I don't think he wanted you to notice it. That's why it was where it was.' Jorge gave the trunk a speculative glance. At least he probably thought it was a speculative glance, but to Angelina's eye it had more the air of a hungry hobo watching breakfast being laid for someone else. 'Now what the hell do you suppose he kept in that? He couldn't have fitted any of his usual canvases into a chest this size, even if he rolled them up.'

'It's locked.' Angelina yanked at the padlock to prove it. 'Lord knows where he kept the key.'

'We don't need a key, just a crowbar.'

She disapproved of breaking and entering, not to mention damaging property. But it wasn't up to her to decide.

The three of them stood and stared, without touching, as if it might have been booby-trapped. Maybe it was the presence of the padlock that gave the chest an air of menace and mystery, suggesting the possibility of ill-gotten treasure or human bones, or some other dark secret. After all, what could Malachy have needed to lock up in his own studio?

'A crowbar,' Jorge repeated at last. 'Is there a crowbar in the house?'

Calum recalled having seen a claw hammer on the bench, and was even able to find it again. Equipped with the hammer, he attacked the padlock with alarming enthusiasm. The lock was not particularly robust, designed to discourage triflers rather than determined thieves. It gave without too much of a struggle. He raised the lid . . .

. . . to reveal a paper treasure. The chest was crammed with drawings.

'Fantastic,' Jorge breathed. He was peering over Calum's arm, his dark eyes gleaming with an odd combination of reverence and avidity. 'But why lock them up?'

'Let's have a look at them.' Calum bent down and riffled through the papers on top.

After a few moments he straightened up again, very

316

quickly, as if the trunk really had been booby trapped. 'Cor!'

'What's the matter?'

'See for yourself.'

He lifted the top layer of papers from the chest, and spread them out across the available floor space with a casual toss of his wrist, as if he were dealing cards.

He went on and on, hauling out paper and scattering it around. They had no time to take each one in, only the sheer numbers, and the recurring images. There were dozens of paintings and drawings. The drawings had been done on ordinary drawing paper, the paintings on some sort of heavy coated paper.

'Jesus,' said Jorge.

'Gosh,' said Angelina. 'Gosh, gosh.'

They were all representations of women.

Parts of women. Pieces of women.

Heads without necks, breasts without chests, thighs without knees, bums without backs. An ear with no sign of a jaw. A finger with a ring but no hand. Disconnected heels and toes, elbows, haunches, shoulders. And again and again, a motif that Angelina took a while to make sense of, then nearly blushed when she did. So Malachy really had persuaded that model to let him draw her private parts.

Those were the drawings. The paintings were much worse.

The bodies here were sometimes dismembered, as in the drawings. Sometimes they lacked feet and hands and head. Other times they were intact. Except for the skin.

Here was a complete woman, nothing bizarre about her, except that her eyes were wide with the unalterable stare of the dead, and she was lying on what appeared to be the concrete floor of an abattoir.

A shop window. A butcher's shop. The carcasses hanging in the window for display were all human females, hanging by the heels, hands trussed behind them, like rabbits waiting to be skinned.

Butcher's hooks. Not empty. Haunches with female buttocks, shoulders with female breasts. One of those headless, handless, footless corpses, hanging stiff, flayed like a cow being turned into beef.

No primary colours here. Yet these paintings, like his others, were virtually monochromatic. The basic colour was a dark red, call it oxblood. The flesh – or rather skin, since in this case the two were far from synonymous – was a sickly off-white, the shade of something from a dungeon.

Many of the bodies, or body parts, had been done in a grotesque style, bloated and obese. Their female characteristics were exaggerated in an unflattering manner, supposing flattery could have been of any interest to a corpse.

The draughtsmanship was awkward, even clumsy. Maybe that was deliberate. Or maybe Malachy just couldn't draw.

'Gosh,' Angelina said again.

'Fantastic,' said Jorge. He rubbed his hands, and then his chin. 'Incredible.'

'Untitled women.' Calum turned over one of the paintings and pointed to the number scrawled in pencil on the back. 'That solves one mystery, anyway.'

They stared at each other, still stunned.

Angelina was more than stunned. Even after the evidence of the diaries, she couldn't quite get her mind around this. *Obsession* was one word that kept popping up. *Evil* was another.

But she rejected that one. How could a picture be evil? Evil was what people did. Pictures didn't do anything, they just were. They might portray an evil deed, or the consequences of such a deed, but that didn't justify letting the description transplant itself to the depiction. And it wasn't as if any of this was real. It was only something in Malachy's head.

Had it been evil, when it was in his head?

Calum broke into her thoughts. He had more prosaic

concerns. 'Why did he make them fat? Or did he just pick fat models? In which case, no wonder he got them into bed so easily.'

'No, no.' Jorge was emphatic. 'Mal's idea of a good-looking woman was pretty much like most people's, and a guy like him would have no problem getting real babes. People who knew him in New York told me they just about lined up for him.'

'So he took beautiful girls and made them look fat and ugly. Seems kind of backwards to me. Why would he do that?'

Jorge shrugged. 'Well, he could have been making some kind of point about attitudes towards female body size in our society. Or he might have been exposing our callous treatment of domestic animals, the way we fatten them up in order to kill and eat them. Or it's a comment about human mortality: dead meat is what we all come down to, in the end. Or maybe an ironic reflection on pornography.'

'Or maybe he just didn't like women.' Calum squatted down and began to leaf through the drifted heaps of paper. 'He must have spent an awful lot of time on this stuff. I wonder why he never tried to exhibit any of it.'

'You couldn't show these to people,' Angelina protested. 'They're too grotesque.'

'So what? I thought shock was the name of the game.' Calum glanced up at Jorge. 'Isn't it?'

'Well, yeah, I guess, to some extent,' Jorge agreed. 'But the collectors don't like artists to keep changing their style. They like to know what they're getting. They want to be able to spot their man at fifty paces.'

'So Malachy Hawke means coloured squares, not butchered women.' Calum turned over paper at random, pages of dismembered female parts. 'Does that mean our friend in New York maybe knew about these, and didn't want to show them?'

'Dunno. I'm inclined to think they were Mal's little secret. Why else put a lock on the chest?' Jorge hunkered down beside Calum, studying the bloody images. 'I mean, would you want the world to know you had this kind of thing in your head?'

'Why not? You said yourself he might have been striking a blow against sizism, or for animal liberation, or maybe just waxing philosophical.'

Angelina knelt beside the chest, so that most of the images were facing away from her. Looking at those pictures upside down was just about all she could cope with. 'I think they're pornographic.'

Calum gave her a grin. 'Does this stuff turn you on, Angie?'

'No,' she said seriously. 'But there's something about them . . .' She pondered the problem for a moment, trying to articulate, even to herself, the most disturbing aspect of the paintings. 'I don't mean sexy, that's not the right word. It's too frivolous, and anyway they're not sexy.'

She spoke slowly, searching for a vocabulary to describe things she had never had to confront before. Things she had only lately become aware of. 'It's something deeper down, something to do with sex at the real bottom level. Where you find yourself desperately wanting to do these disgusting physical things with someone who is basically like an alien species. And that scares you. The other person scares you. You scare yourself.'

She had been looking at the picture while she spoke. It wasn't till she lifted her eyes to the other two – the two *men* – and saw them looking at her in a very funny way, that she realized what she had said and how it must sound. 'I mean – I didn't mean that personally,' she floundered. 'I was talking about the human race. Men and women.'

But she hadn't been, not entirely. She had been thinking about Calum. About Calum's body. It had shocked her, maybe more than she was willing to admit, to find how *physical* love was. How intimate you could be with someone who was in so many ways a stranger. Who would be for ever a stranger to her in some ways, just because he was a man.

The flip side of that was physical desire: how much she

320

wanted to do things she quite recently had thought disgusting. It seemed like nothing was disgusting any more, not where Calum was concerned. She even found herself thinking of new things to do or have done to her, a dozen different ways to conjoin his body to hers.

That shocked her in another way, by showing her how much she was still a stranger to herself. Some secret place in her soul was nurturing inexplicable desires and darknesses. The same place, maybe, where Malachy kept his butcher's shop.

The men gave up staring at her and looked at each other instead. Calum said to Jorge, 'I think she means this stuff is *Playboy* without the airbrush.'

The question of whether Bradford Welles knew about the pictures was settled very soon, when Brad himself phoned up that afternoon. Angelina answered, because the phone was in the kitchen (the only place where they could be sure of finding it again), and she was in there, preparing cold drinks, when it rang.

'Angie? How are you? Brad Welles here.'

She knew that already, having recognized his clipped and rapid way of speaking, like a man used to crossing busy streets by dodging moving traffic.

'How's it going?'

'It's going OK. We're working full steam.' She wondered if she should tell him about the dead pictures, but decided that was really up to Calum. Or better still, up to Calum's father. 'We're making a complete list of everything, like Rene said. All the paintings and drawings and everything else. And George is taking photographs of all of them, so nothing can get lost.'

'That's very efficient of you, my dear. Just what I would have expected.' A pause. 'Who is this George? Do I know him?'

'He's Dr Bravo. He's writing a book about Malachy. About his work,' she amended quickly, not wanting to encourage this biography business.

'Bravo,' Brad repeated, not as approvingly as it sounded. 'The name sounds familiar.'

'He comes over all the time. He did his thesis on Malachy, and got friendly with him.'

'Oh, yes, I remember now. I did meet him once. A little guy with a big moustache.'

'That's him. When did you meet him?'

'He was in New York. Doing some background for his book, I guess, or at least his doctoral thesis. He came around to see me. Wanted to talk about Mal. I can't say I was able to be much help to him.'

Because you didn't give him any juicy stories, Angelina guessed. 'Well, he's giving us a hand, as a favour. A favour to Malachy, really.'

'That is very kind of him.' But she could tell that Brad wasn't pleased, for some reason. Just like she could tell that he didn't like Calum, when he added, 'Angie, my dear, it's always a pleasure to talk to you, but do you think I could have a word with young Master Hawke?'

She set the phone down on the counter top, and went out on to the deck to fetch Calum. The phone was entirely portable, of course, but she didn't think that Jorge should be listening in on the conversation. So when she called Calum, she didn't say who it was, just that it was for him.

As soon as he came into the kitchen, he took hold of her and kissed her with the intensity of a man who has had the idea on his mind for quite a while. She was surprised and delighted, but also embarrassed because the phone was right beside them. Eavesdropping, in a way.

'Bradford Welles is on the phone,' she whispered, as soon as she had her mouth to herself again.

'The art shark? OK, give it here.' He took it from her, then bent his head down to the level of her ear. 'You are the most seriously sexy woman in the world.'

After that, she could hardly hear what Calum was saying to Brad. Seriously sexy. Maybe she wasn't just another girl in a pub.

'That's nothing to do with me,' Calum was saying. 'If my father wants you to get involved, he'll let me know, won't he? Personally, I think we're doing fine as it is. We've got the world's foremost expert on Malachy Hawke giving us a hand, if that makes you feel any better about it. Jesus somebody, I can't recall his last name. Well, if that's what Angie told you, I expect she's right. I mean, why would she lie to you?'

'Stupid git.' Calum came up behind her and set the phone down on the counter. 'He's got his knickers in a big fat twist over these paintings. They're *val-u-ble*, he kept saying. As if I didn't know. Just as well he hasn't a clue about the stuff we found today, or he'd really be pissing his pants.'

He lifted her braid out of the way in order to bite her neck, which nearly made her spill the lemonade she was pouring. She could feel his breath on her bare skin as he told her in an undertone what he was going to do to her as soon as Jorge had gone. Something that Malachy had described doing to Model Number 22. He used some shocking language to describe it, too.

She could feel the colour rising in her face as he talked to her, as she thought about what he was saying. Not from modesty or embarrassment, but from the heat of desire.

Just as well she hadn't ended up a nun. She was obviously unsuited to the contemplative life. The first man to come along and show any serious sexual interest in her had her in bed within two weeks, and carrying on like a depraved nymphomaniac very shortly after that.

To cool herself off, she took Jorge's glass of lemonade over to the studio.

As it turned out, Jorge had been in no danger of eavesdropping on Calum's telephone conversation, or his whispered obscenities for that matter, because he was down on his knees in front of the chest, rapt by the dead portfolio.

'This stuff is fantastic,' he announced to Angelina, as she handed him his glass.

'It's a fantasy, all right, if that's what you mean.'

'No, I mean it's brilliant. Really powerful. There's an obsessive aspect to it that kind of grabs you and pulls you right into his mind-frame. Makes you feel what he must have been feeling when he did them.'

Angelina looked down at the painting just beyond her toe. An armless body lying face down, except that there was no head and therefore no face. Buttocks like a Bushwoman's. The Rubenesque thigh had evidently just been severed from the hip; a huge cleaver jutted out at the joint. 'Thanks for warning me, George. I'll be sure to stay away from you when you're in that kind of mood.'

'Now, Angie, don't talk like that. Anybody would think we'd just discovered that Mal was an axe-murderer. Whereas in fact he's a genius. This is what art is all about, Angie. Expanding the limits of the human imagination. Taking us out of the confines of our own little lives, forcing us to think about ourselves and our surroundings in a different way.'

'These are just pictures, you mean. Oh, Sevvie, don't do that.' She bent down to scoop up the ginger cat before he could amble across the painting. 'That's a work of genius, you big juicy orange, so keep your paws off of it.'

Jorge looked pained. He took art, and especially Malachy's art, mortally seriously, and disapproved of her more frivolous attitude. Not to mention the cat's attitude. 'These are just pictures, sure, but they could be anything else. He could have made a play or a film on this theme, or written a poem or a novel, or created a sculpture to replicate what's in this painting.'

'Yuk.'

'Angie, honey, *yuk* is not a word in the critical lexicon. What you mean is that you think you would find that a disturbing experience. But disturbing people is all part of what he had in mind.'

'Looks to me like he mostly had killing women in mind.'

'But this is the aftermath, not the event. There's nothing here to suggest he approves of what he's depicting. If someone painted the bodies on a battlefield, would you say they had killing men in mind? And these bodies are in an abattoir, which puts death into a sanitized, socially approved context. That even puts it into the context of ongoing life, because animals are slaughtered in an abattoir to provide meat for us to eat.'

'OK, George, if you say so.'

She had abandoned the argument, but he was still musing over the gruesome scene. 'Actually, Angie, in spite of what I've just said, I think your original insight is a good one.'

'What insight?'

'That this artistic idiom is a metaphor for sex.'

'Did I say that?' She stroked Seville, to soothe her own agitation at recalling what she had said about the pictures. In front of Calum. 'If I did, I don't think I meant to say it.'

'Now don't be modest, Angie, it was a terrific idea. After all, we talk about men as sexual predators, don't we?'

Still holding Seville as a defence against whatever, she stared at the paintings. 'Why are so many of the women fat and ugly then?'

'What do you want, a rack of supermodels with their heads cut off?' That was Calum, coming up behind her with a full coffee mug. 'Vile bodies, that's the spirit we have here.' He surveyed the acreage of painted paper. 'And this guy was my grandfather? Incredible. He must have been a laugh a minute.'

'He was very funny,' Angelina told him. 'He seemed to me like a real nice, kind man.' Her eyes were inevitably drawn down to what lay at her feet. 'Though I don't know how I'd have felt about him if I'd known he was looking at me and thinking like this.'

'Angie, nobody could look at you and think about this,' Calum assured her. 'If he was thinking any thoughts about you that he shouldn't have, they were more likely to be the kind of thing he put in his diary.'

'That's not a whole lot better.'

She swept out on to the deck, taking Seville off to enjoy a saucer of milk. She wasn't thinking about the paintings now. She was thinking about Calum and what he had whispered to her earlier. About what Malachy put in his diary.

1964

She opens to me.

I like that moment. Like the point when I know a painting's going to work. The moment when a woman becomes my woman, when I can see she wants me. There's a lot more fucking than wanting going on in the world. Contrary to what some people think.

So I don't take her right away. I let her enjoy her wanting. She opens up a little more, getting into the spirit of things, inviting me to drive her crazy. She lets me do it with my tongue. I get to get face to face with pussy.

Tomorrow she'll let me draw her down there.

24

Angelina was so used to Sweetwater, she seldom thought about how it looked. It was something she had been born to: the dusty wide streets, lined with low, scattered, timber buildings; the views of elusive elms that always seemed to be one block over from the street you were on. That was just the way towns were made, as far as she knew. She couldn't see any reason why they should be made any other way.

Calum didn't agree.

When they pulled into the filling station, he leaned out the window and craned his head up and down the wide street, taking it all in. His eyes were unreadable, because he was wearing sunglasses.

'What a dump.'

Angelina felt obliged to defend her home town. 'Well, it ain't London, that's for sure. But hardly any places are.' She licked her dusty lips, working up her nerve to say what she had been thinking all the way across the valley. She wasn't sure which would take more nerve: saying it, or not saying it and taking the consequences. 'Listen, Calum, are you sure you want to come with me to my grandma's? She doesn't even speak English. Not much, anyway.'

'I'm stuck with it now, aren't I? What else would I do?'

'You could stay here in Sweetwater, and get yourself something to eat.'

'And miss your gran's apple pie?'

'I'll bring some back for you. Look, I just don't want you to be bored.'

He turned his head to look at her. He had one hand on the gear-shift knob and the other arm propped on the window-sill. He looked so cool, she could have melted with terror on the spot. 'Angie, I can't imagine any place on earth more boring than this. Your gran's farm can only be an improvement.'

She fluttered her fingers in denial. 'It's not a farm any more. Just a few acres of land, with a market garden and a pasture.'

'Whatever.' He glanced over her head. 'I think that guy wants to talk to you.'

'That guy' was Billy Hobson. He had been in her grade at school, a wall-eyed, round-headed boy. He was wearing a baseball cap with the name of the oil company that owned the filling station. He had been working at the filling station, first part time, then full time, since about the age of fourteen. Right now he was squinting at her, and past her at Calum. The kids at school used to think that because one of his eyes was always focused in the wrong direction, he could see two different things at once.

'Hi, Angie. You want me to fill 'er up?'

'Just ten dollars, Billy. I'm not as rich as all that.'

'Sure thing.' Billy stepped to one side, seized the nozzle and plunged it into the gas tank, before returning to Angelina's window. 'You going out to see your grandma?'

'Yeah, that's right.' She gave him a ten-dollar bill, to get him to go away.

He didn't move. Well, he did, but only to start pushing a squeegee around on the windshield. 'I heard that artist died. The one you were working for.'

'Yeah, he did.'

'So what are you doing now?' He was surveying Calum through the glass as he asked. Scrubbing at a splash that had recently been a grasshopper, and eyeing Calum at the same time.

329

'I'm just looking after the place while they sort out the will.'

She knew he would go away and tell everyone about Calum, starting with Bonnie Brady's mom who worked the cash register inside the filling station.

For sure, he would tell them Calum was her boyfriend. That would be embarrassing. Not because there was anything wrong with the idea, but because it wasn't true.

Calum was her lover, not her boyfriend. Boyfriends had girlfriends, and eventually married them. Lovers had mistresses, and eventually left them.

Billy's story wouldn't be nearly as lurid as it might have been, because Angelina had persuaded Calum to leave off all his jewellery. Almost all, anyway. He was still sporting one earring, to maintain his macho cred and remind her there were limits to his domesticatability. Not that she needed reminding.

It was only a small gold ring. Her grandmother might not even notice it. But she couldn't do anything about the hair, and that was the very first thing her grandmother would notice.

There was one more precaution she had to take. The most necessary, and the most excruciating. She waited until they were free of Billy and the filling station, free of the town.

She wished he would take off those sunglasses, so she could see what he was thinking, 'Calum, listen.'

'I'm listening.'

He wasn't looking at her, he was looking at the road. Which was where the driver ought to be looking, of course. That was one reason she had waited to say it. So he wouldn't be looking at her.

'Don't say anything to my grandma about, um, about the house.'

'What do you mean, about the house? What about the house?'

'I mean, you know, there's nobody else there.'

330

'Just the two of us, you mean?' He still had his eyes on the road, but he was grinning. 'You think your gran has a dirty mind, do you?'

'She'd think it was . . . not proper.' Angelina laced her fingers together in her lap and stared at them. She didn't think it was proper either, now that she thought of it. She found herself rubbing the third finger of her left hand, and made herself stop it at once. 'She'd make a fuss.'

'So what's our story going to be? That my dad's still here? That I'm staying in, what's that place, Oldport?'

It hadn't occurred to her that not telling the truth was going to have to mean telling a lie. She had been thinking that she just wouldn't mention it. But of course her grandmother was sure to ask. She didn't like the idea of lying, particularly to her grandmother. Especially about Calum.

'I'll think of something. Maybe it won't come up. She won't understand most of what you say, anyway. Especially not with your accent.'

'What's wrong with my accent?'

'Nothing. It's lovely.' She bit her tongue before it could betray her any further. 'It's just that she's not used to English accents.'

That worked both ways, she discovered.

Calum didn't understand Polish, so he couldn't hear what her grandmother was saying about his dreadlocks. 'I wouldn't let a horse's tail get into that state,' she told Angelina. 'He'll get lice.'

'No, Babsha, he's perfectly clean. It's the fashion in London.'

'The English have always been crazy,' the old lady declared. 'Why doesn't his father send him to the barber?'

'His father's English too.'

'How is that possible, when Mr Hawke was an Indian? Didn't you say this boy's father is his son?'

'Yes, but . . .' Angelina tried to think of a way to explain, without having to reveal what sort of man

Malachy had been. 'They lost track of each other a long time ago.'

'The war, I expect.' Her grandmother nodded. The war had been an enormous thing in her life. She turned her attention back to Calum, eyeing him in a more benevolent way. 'Ask him if he likes cabbage rolls. I've been cooking all morning.'

By the time Calum had polished off a heap of cabbage rolls and potato dumplings, not to mention half a cherry pie, he had gone up vastly in Mrs Rudniki's estimation. 'I like to see a healthy appetite in a young man,' she confided to Angelina, when they were in the kitchen doing the dishes. 'But tell him he should get his hair cut.'

'I'll tell him,' Angelina promised.

Surreptitiously she examined her grandmother's ankles for evidence of swelling. The old lady was wearing boots; that was a good sign. When her legs were bad, she wore slippers. There was a time when Angelina used to be humiliated by her grandmother's habit of wearing her father's old army boots around the farmyard, but now such footwear had become high chic. Angelina herself had something similar on her own feet, only at much greater expense.

'What do you want me to do for you, while I'm here? Can I feed the chickens, or pick some apples?'

'The chickens I fed before breakfast. The apples, the Boy Scouts come and pick them for me, and take some home for themselves. Don't worry about me, Anjelinka, I manage. You and your young man enjoy yourselves.'

Angelina was more than ever relieved that her grandmother didn't speak much English, and so couldn't say something embarrassing to Calum, something that implied romantic connections between her and him. If she and Calum were having a romance, it wasn't the kind that ended happily. He was sleeping with her because she was the only girl around, that was all. And he hadn't asked her to fall in love with him.

Not really a romance at all, just a dreary tale of folly and stupidity. And sooner or later it was going to hurt.

'He's not my young man, Babsha. I told you, he's Malachy's grandson. He only came over here to clear out the house.'

'What does he do in London? What's his profession?'

Angelina's stomach knotted. She should have known her grandmother would ask. 'I don't know. He never said. Maybe he's a student.'

'What kind of student? A doctor? A lawyer?'

Angelina tried to picture Calum in either of these callings. Not possible. 'I don't think he's going to be a doctor or a lawyer.'

'What, then?'

'I told you, I don't know.' She dared to suggest the awful truth. 'Maybe he doesn't have a job.'

'Sure he has a job, a healthy young man like him. Ask him what he does for his living.'

'I can't ask him now. He's outside. He wanted to see the horses.'

The old lady brightened up again. 'Is he good with horses?'

'He doesn't know anything about them. He lives in London, it's a big city. There aren't any horses in London.'

Her grandmother tched regretfully over the deprived Londoners.

In between fending off her grandmother's persistent curiosity, Angelina was keeping an eye out the kitchen window for Calum. He wandered into view, stopping to stare at his surroundings. Besides the neat little white ranch house, there were the farm buildings, paddock, stable and chicken coop, the orchard, the birches and firs, the icy little river. And the mountains, of course.

Calum was gazing at all this with that half-dazed air of absorption that made him look a little simple. Angelina found it endearing, evidence of some vestigial organ of delight still functioning somewhere inside him. Not yet frozen by the need to be cool.

333

Mrs Rudniki came out to see them off. Calum had climbed up into the driver's seat. Well, it was his father's truck, after all. He leaned down from the window to shake hands with her.

'Tell her thanks for the lunch,' he told Angelina. 'Tell her it was fantastic. Tell her I said she's a brilliant cook, a million times better than you.'

'I'll make you wish you'd never said that,' Angelina retorted. 'When you get fed up with beans on burnt toast, you can apologize.'

She relayed his message to her grandmother, minus the last bit.

The old lady beamed at Calum. Flattery and good looks had never done anyone any harm, Angelina reflected. 'Wait, wait,' her grandmother said to him in English. 'Don't go. Angie, wait.'

She ducked back inside, then returned with a cardboard box in her arms. 'Apples,' she explained, handing the box to Angelina. 'And a couple of pies. There's a chicken wrapped up in the newspaper, I plucked and cleaned it yesterday, and a dozen eggs. Also I put in the rest of the cabbage rolls, since your young Hawke liked them so much.'

Angelina hoped Calum hadn't been simply playing polite on that score. 'OK, Babsha. Thanks a lot.' She handed the box up to Calum, kissed her grandmother, and climbed into the passenger side of the cab.

The old lady was still hovering as Calum stuck the key into the ignition. 'Remember,' she hissed up through the open window, whispering as if Calum couldn't hear, or for that matter as if he could understand Polish. 'Ask him what kind of job he has. And tell him to get his hair cut. It's not healthy like that.'

25

To the west of Sweetwater the mountains opened up, giving a view of the central valley with its flat fields of stubble, dry and exhausted, waiting to be razed by fire, buried by plough, resurrected by rain. A pleasing view for a farmer, but entirely lacking any prospect of anticipation. No wonder Calum was bored.

'Was that exciting enough for you?'

'I expect it would have been a lot more exciting if I'd understood what your gran was saying.'

'Nothing rude about you, if that's what you're wondering. Though she did tell me to tell you to get your hair cut.'

He grinned. 'That means she likes me.'

'Only because you had third helpings of everything. That's the kind of flattery a girl can't resist.'

'Well, it was a brilliant lunch. You really know you've eaten when you have a meal like that.'

'Fattening, you mean,' Angelina muttered, mindful of her grandmother's round contours, and her own deviations from the Hollywood standard.

Calum had caught her surreptitious downward glance. 'Forget fat,' he told her sternly. 'Fretting about fat will drive you round the bend. My mother is really into healthy eating, and it sucks. She's been feeding us nut cutlets for the last five years, trying to starve me to death. I believe God didn't intend men to be vegetarians. My dad moved out after a couple of years of lentils.'

'That seems pretty drastic. Why didn't he just learn to cook himself?'

'Because God didn't intend men to be cooks, I suppose. No, actually he went off to live with some tart half his age. Utterly naff behaviour. Like a dog running away from home to hang around some bitch in heat.'

Angelina had already sensed a stiffness in Calum's relationship to his father, but this news surprised her. 'He didn't strike me as the kind of guy to do a thing like that.'

'That's what I used to think.' Calum scowled at the windshield. 'Basically, I suppose, he's the kind of guy where you never know what he's thinking. I've read a couple of his books, and what they're like, they're like he's God and all the people in the book are suffering from – what was that thing you talked about the other night? Original sin?'

'Might have been. We talked about lots of things.'

'Well, anyway, they're all guilty of something and they all get their come-uppance. But you get this feeling that he's talking about ants or something. Like the characters are a different species from the author, or he's an anthropologist writing up some primitive tribe. It's like, Isn't this interesting? instead of, Isn't this terrible!'

Angelina considered this. Considered Calum's father, what she knew of him. He had a cool, impassive face. Cooler than Malachy's. Maybe it was the blue eyes that gave him that extra touch of ice. He didn't strike her as the sort of man who would want anybody looking into his head.

'That might be just a way to avoid exposing himself. I mean, making any kind of art is really showing what's inside you, isn't it? Because that's all you have to create things from. And that gives people a chance to say, What a jerk, or This guy must be crazy. Maybe leaving your own opinions and emotions out of it is a way of trying to protect yourself.'

'Maybe so.' Calum didn't sound convinced. 'His

writing is kind of like Malachy's paintings, come to think of it. Abstract. Cool. Examining the surfaces, instead of the guts.'

'Well, we know about Malachy and women, don't we?'

'Yeah, but he didn't run off with one of his models. I mean, that would have been getting emotionally involved. And those diary entries, they're cool and clinical too. The anthropologist seducing the women of the tribe.'

Cool, that was the way to be. Everybody thought so, didn't they? 'You're a fine one to talk, Calum. What about all those girls in discos and bars?'

'That's just a game. Something to do. Anyway, that's what they're there for, for Christ's sake.'

Presumably what he meant was that they had gone to those places in the hopes of getting picked up. But the way he said it made it sound like he might have meant that casual sex with the likes of Calum was the whole reason for their existence. Like those houris in Muslim Heaven, who were supposedly created just to provide celestial sexual bliss for the faithful dead (only the men, of course).

Calum was still defending himself. 'What's wrong with f— having sex with a girl who's in the market for sex? It's not like I go about seducing people, not like our Mal. Those babes are out there looking for action. I'm only giving them what they want.'

Was he only giving Angelina what she wanted? Had he looked at her and seen a girl looking for sex? There was nothing in the way she had behaved to tell him any different.

Calum availed himself of her silence to switch to a less contentious topic. 'Speaking of excitement, driving this old pick-up is pretty exciting, I can tell you. She comes up with a different noise every five miles. Do you think we'll make it home?'

'I've taken it on this trip every Sunday for the past two years, and it's behaved itself pretty well every time. I think it knows you're a greenhorn and it's trying to scare you.'

They had crossed the broad valley and were in the midst

337

of mountains once more, on a long upward slope, when he brought the subject up again. 'I think your luck has run out, Angie.'

'Why?'

'Can't you smell it?'

She sniffed obediently. 'The burning smell? Is that us?'

'Nobody else for it to be, is there?'

They were going even more slowly than usual, she noticed. Calum shifted down. The motor hiccuped, before regaining its poise and some of its power. It was making a terrific racket, but she had assumed that was just the low gear. 'What's the problem?'

'Feels like the clutch.'

Angelina clenched her fists and willed the truck up to the crest of the slope.

'We're nearly at the pass. It's mostly downhill from there to Yakuts Mountain.'

'It'd better be.'

They did make it to the top of the pass, at a snail's pace by then. But downhill was not without its hazards either. The ominous burning odour was joined by a whiff of hot metal.

'Is that the brakes? What's the matter with them?'

'I hope to Christ nothing is. They're overheating. I can't use the clutch to control our speed on the down slope, so I'm having to use the brakes.'

'Oh gosh.' Now she noticed that their unusual slowness in going up was being matched by an extra zip to their progress in the downhill sections of the journey. As the road steepened and bent sharply around a rocky outcrop, she had visions of flying right over the thicket of 'Caution 20' signs, to plunge into the river.

She grabbed her grandmother's box of provender to keep it from sliding off the seat. 'Do you want me to drive?'

Calum smiled broadly at the road ahead, a bad omen under the circumstances. 'Are you kidding? This is the most fun I've had since I got here.'

Angelina didn't bother taking offence at that. She knew about boys and cars. Girls just couldn't compete.

They made it around the bend, but only by driving on the wrong side of the road.

On the far side of the curve, a logging truck was inching its way up the slope towards them. If it had been going any faster, she was convinced, they would never have made it back on to their own side of the solid line.

Now they were going up again. Calum was talking to the truck, alternately cursing and encouraging it. Angelina began to talk to God about their problem. Very quietly, so Calum couldn't hear.

Either God or Calum got them nearly through the mountains, to a point where the valley was wider and the road therefore flatter, so they could no longer coast. By now the clutch was refusing to engage even minimally, in whatever gear it was offered. The only thing they could do was to roll the truck off the road, into a picnic area by the river.

'How far are we from town?' Calum wanted to know.

'Only a few miles, I guess. We could walk it, if that's what you're wondering. But Yakuts Mountain is more like twenty miles. It'd be midnight before we got there. And if the fog comes in . . .'

'We're not walking any twenty miles,' Calum announced in a scandalized tone. 'I was just thinking, we could organize a tow back to town, couldn't we? Then we leave this bag of bolts at the garage, and hitch a ride the rest of the way home.'

'But it's Sunday.'

'So what?'

'So it's Bert Baumgarten's dim-witted cousin on duty at the filling station today, and I'm not letting him anywhere near this truck. Not even to tow it.'

'You're very protective of this heap of junk, aren't you?'

'I've gotten fond of it.' Mostly because it had been Malachy's. She sighed, feeling flustered. She was used to dealing with sick horses, but sick cars confounded her. 'I guess it's your dad's truck. You do whatever you want.'

'Why don't we leave it here, and ring up the garage tomorrow morning, when your mate Bert will be about? We should be able to hitch a ride down the coast.' He made a face to show sudden displeasure. 'But we'll still have to hike up that bloody mountain, won't we?'

Angelina had never hitched a ride before. Her grandmother had warned her it was dangerous, and possibly sinful. What she hadn't said was that it wasn't all that easy.

There was not a huge amount of traffic, and none of it wanted to stop. Angelina couldn't really blame them. Even without his face jewellery, Calum's hair-style made him look like something big and thuggish from an urban slum. As the sun sank lower, she was beginning to think their only hope of salvation would be a convoy of Hell's Angels.

In the end, their rescuers arrived in a battered, skewbald, shark-finned Chevy, just about old enough to be Angelina's mother. The driver knew what it was like to break down, she supposed.

She and Calum piled into the back seat, along with her grandmother's provisions. She couldn't leave them behind; the chicken would have gone off by the time she could rescue it tomorrow. Besides, she didn't think anybody driving a car like this would mind the unassuming presence of a dead chicken for a few miles.

The driver was a pleasant-looking man with loose black hair and a brown face and arms. He had on a dark green hat, almost as ancient and battered as his car, its floppy brim pulled low over his forehead to shield his eyes from the early evening sun. His shirt was deep pink, his waistcoat wine-coloured; they had an air of Sunday best.

To call the woman in the passenger seat 'pleasant looking' would have been an impertinence. It quickly became clear that she was the real driver. She certainly did all the talking. Her black and silver hair was immaculately bound into two long braids. She had a bright woven shawl around her shoulders, and a stern cast to her handsome,

340

weatherworn features. Her nose in particular reminded Angelina somewhat of . . .

The woman's voice interrupted Angelina's thoughts. 'Where are you folks heading to?'

'South down the coast a ways,' Angelina said vaguely.

'Maybe you can help us out. We're trying to find someone who lives around here.'

At that moment, Angelina had her first ever premonition. She knew who these people were. She even knew why they were here.

But she had to ask. 'Who would that be?'

'A man named Hawke.'

Angelina glanced at Calum. He wasn't looking at her. He was leaning forward, his hand on the back of the driver's seat, an unbored expression on his face. Don't say it, Calum, she prayed. Please don't say it.

He said, 'My name is Hawke.'

That was what she got for praying to Calum instead of to God.

The people in the front seat were visibly stirred. They unsettled themselves, like a flock of starlings come sundown. The woman screwed her head around to study Calum, his blond dreadlocks and (relatively) pale face. 'What would you be to this man?'

'If you mean Malachy, he was my grandfather.'

She tched, exactly like Angelina's grandmother, to register obscure disapproval. Angelina noticed that she had been careful not to say Malachy's name. Maybe she didn't like Calum using it either. 'Where is he now, your grandfather?'

'He's dead.'

'So we heard.' The woman swivelled her head back straight, and transferred her stare from Calum to the fog that was fingering the windshield. 'He was my grandfather's grandson.'

'You're kidding.'

In view of her grim expression, this seemed highly unlikely. But Calum wasn't taking any notice of that. He was doing some reckoning on his fingers. 'That means you must be his cousin, is that right?'

Another significant silence. 'My grandfather had two wives,' she revealed eventually. 'The first wife had a daughter, who was the mother of your grandfather. The second wife was my father's mother.'

More laborious calculations on Calum's part. 'So that's, let me see, more like a half-cousin. And we must be third cousins, or twice removed, or something like that. This is so cool, bumping into you like this.'

'Not an accident, I think,' the woman said mysteriously. 'It was intended.'

In some ways she reminded Angelina of Alice Day, but much more alarming. She could easily imagine this person scalping somebody, or torturing herself into spirit visions. 'If you knew he was dead, why did you come?'

The Cheyenne woman turned again, to look from Angelina to Calum. She smiled for the first time, a slow, deliberate smile, astonishingly like Malachy's. 'To meet this young man, it seems.'

Calum was plainly intrigued by the idea of these people being his distant cousins. He opened his mouth to say something. Angelina knew what he was going to say. She poked him from behind the cardboard box, where the woman couldn't see, in an attempt to derail his train of thought.

As usual, he didn't notice. Maybe he was mainly thinking of saving himself a steep hike up the mountain. Or else looking for relief from boredom. 'Hey, why don't you come up to my grandfather's house? You can tell me all about yourselves. And about him.'

Angelina sat stiffly, disapprovingly. One corner of her mind deplored this bad behaviour on her part, just because these people were closer to Calum than she was. Another corner said that Calum was about to get into something well over his dreadlocked head. But there wasn't anything she could do about it, not now.

The woman's name was Sheila. At least, she said she

was *called* Sheila. An odd distinction, as if it was only a nickname. Maybe her real name was some long-winded Indian thing, which she didn't waste time trying to get white people to use. Sort of like Jesus George.

The driver was not introduced, and had nothing to say for himself, but Sheila referred to him as Hobie. She didn't actually say so, but it became clear that he was her son.

By the time they got back to Yakuts Mountain, the sun was hovering over the brim of the sea, and the effects of Mrs Rudniki's lavish lunch had worn off. Angelina could see that whatever her misgivings, it wasn't going to be possible to chuck these people out. Not so near to night-fall. Not when they were obviously poor. Not when they had just rescued her and Calum.

Besides, Calum showed no sign of being anxious to get rid of them. Just the opposite.

So she set to making supper for four, putting her grand-mother's chicken to good use, while the others sat around the kitchen table, drinking beer and talking. At least, Calum and Sheila talked. Hobie only shrugged, or smiled shyly when anyone spoke to him. Angelina was just begin-ning to wonder if he was a deaf mute or something, when she heard him say Nope.

The beer, as cold as it was, managed to thaw Sheila. Or maybe it was the chicken that did the trick, stuffed with sage and onion and accompanied by carrots and potatoes, all from the vegetable garden behind the house.

Whatever the cause, Sheila began to talk. She talked about Malachy.

At first she used circumlocutions – your grandfather, my cousin. After a while she forgot, and referred to him as Mal. When she realized what she had said, she looked appalled. But the taboo, or whatever it was, had been broken now, the damage evidently done. After that, she called him by his name like everyone else.

On first entering the house, she had studied the Picasso prints on the living room walls with icy dismay. 'These are not his paintings.'

Calum agreed that they were not Malachy's. 'His stuff is in the studio.'

'Can we see?'

'Why not? Seeing you're family.'

'Not just his family,' she said darkly. 'His people. His history. His blood.'

Calum seemed startled by her intensity, and maybe by her words as well. 'Well, sure, all of that. Just let me get the key and you can have a good look.'

The Untitled Women had been tucked back into the trunk, and a good thing too. Angelina was pretty sure that Sheila would not approve of them at all. She might even be shocked, if only because Malachy had painted them.

Sheila and Hobie entered the studio as if it were a cathedral. The high, light, open construction encouraged the comparison. Sheila stopped in the doorway, raised her head and flared her nostrils. Angelina had the impression of an animal investigating new territory, checking for familiarity and for strangeness.

Hobie's reaction to the paintings surprised her too. Instead of hanging back shyly, as he had done up till now, he wandered from end to end of the canvas-hung walls, staring up at the pictures with a slow and thoughtful gaze.

Sheila must have seen Angelina watching him. 'Hobie is an artist too,' she remarked. 'But in a more traditional style. In our tradition.'

What would a Cheyenne painting be like? Angelina imagined sanitized and sentimental depictions of past glory, famous chiefs resplendent in wampum and war bonnet, and so forth. 'What does he paint?' Meaning, does he paint on tepees or buffalo hides or what?

'Spirit pictures,' Sheila said briskly. 'Like these.'

The notion of Malachy's work as spirit pictures, whatever those might be, was a revelation to Angelina. 'What are spirit pictures?'

'They show the spirit of things, rather than their outward appearance.' Sheila turned to look at her. To size her up, in much the same way as she had taken stock of the paintings. 'You should know. You are a spirit walker.'

Angelina felt like she had just taken a step and found no ground beneath her foot. She understood immediately what Sheila meant by a spirit walker. But how could the woman possibly know about her? And what did ecsomatic experience have to do with Malachy's paintings?

She gestured towards the paintings. 'But he wasn't.'

'No. But he had the sight, though he always denied it. He said it was only superstition. Yet when he came to paint . . .' Sheila used both hands, to include all walls. 'As you see, he painted what he saw.'

And here everybody had always thought Malachy's paintings were abstract. Evidently Sheila knew better.

She stared at Angelina again. 'Your man has the sight, too.'

'Calum?' That startled Angelina even more. So much that she forgot to correct Sheila's assumption about their relationship. 'How can you tell?'

'I can see it in his soul. You can too, if you look. It's Malachy's blood in him. I knew him when I saw him, standing by the road.'

This was scary stuff. Angelina wanted to turn away, but Sheila's stare forbade her.

Sheila came closer, speaking in an undertone, a thick dark voice that might have come from the earth itself. 'When they have the sight, they're blind to the surface of things. They walk right through you. That's what they're like.'

'When I was a child I was very close to him. He was – I thought he was – my uncle.'

They had reached the pie stage by now, and everybody was feeling fairly friendly. Good food did that to you, Angelina had noticed. Not to mention plenty of beer.

And now Sheila was offering confidences.

'Your uncle instead of your cousin, you mean? Now how could a little misunderstanding like that get started?' Calum wondered.

'It was what I was told. No, not told, just given to understand. I thought he was my grandfather's youngest son, my father's youngest brother. He was five years older than me. I worshipped him. I used to say I was going to marry him, the way children do. And I followed him around. I must have made a nuisance of myself, but he was always patient. He showed me how to swim, how to ride. He taught me about necessity. How to be hard.'

She paused to reflect, to recall. 'When he was sixteen, he went away. He never came back.'

Calum was willing to play the straight man in her tale. 'You never saw him again?'

'Luckily, fate was kinder than that . . . I think.'

'So why did he push off? Not to avoid marrying you, I hope.'

'No.' She smiled, for only the second time. 'That was only a childish notion of mine. But after a long while, we heard he was living in New York. And when I heard, I did something crazy. I was only nineteen, everybody's crazy at nineteen. I went to New York to find him.'

'And did you?'

'Yes.' A pause. 'I found him. He was . . . changed.'

'How?'

'Like someone who's suffered some great bitterness, like a spear-point hardened in the fire. Oh, it might just have been that I remembered him as a boy, and now he was a man. But he seemed glad enough to see me. Then I learned that he was living with a woman.

'A white woman, of course.' She hesitated, making the slightest possible grimace. 'You may say, why not? His father was a white man. And his mother's mother, my grandfather's first wife, she was white too, I heard. But I didn't hear any of that until afterwards.'

She wasn't afraid of silences, this woman. Why should she be? The others were all waiting for her to speak again. Even Hobie was listening attentively, in between mouthfuls of ice cream and apple pie, as if he had never heard this story before.

346

She said at last, 'It was afterwards I found out why he'd gone away. Why he stayed away. I went home and asked my father, and he told me what I'd never known. My grandfather had forbidden everybody to speak of it.'

'Some deep dark secret about Malachy?'

Sheila ignored Calum's flippant tone. 'It's plain why they weren't allowed to talk about it, and plain why everyone treated him as my grandfather's son. But when Mal was old enough to be called a man, as we used to reckon it, my grandfather told him the truth, and that was what made him leave the reservation.'

'What was the awful truth?'

'That he wasn't really Malachy Hawke. He was Malachy O'Hara.'

'That white father you mentioned.'

Calum was leaning forward, chin on hand, utterly absorbed. Angelina's attention had to be divided between Sheila's words and Calum's distracting presence. *The sight*: what could that mean? She kept glancing at his face, hoping to divine it, while giving half an ear to Malachy's tale in Sheila's telling.

'He said he was part Irish,' Angelina remarked. 'Malachy is an Irish name, he said.'

'Yes. His father was long dead by then. Dead by the time Mal heard his own story. By the time my father told it to me, my grandfather was dead as well. So I don't suppose it mattered any more. Who cares if a ghost has secrets?'

'But why was it such a big secret in the first place?'

'I guess you could say that my grandfather had stolen him.'

She sketched out the history of Malachy, in pieces and pauses. O'Hara had been a rancher, quite a rich man for those days and those parts. He and his wife had a child who died, and then had no more. The wife had a craving for a baby, as women do, and it grew to dominate her life, as it sometimes does. And the rancher, as he grew older, more and more wanted a son.

How the bargain came about was not a thing that Sheila's father had dwelt on, but in the end O'Hara had given money to her grandfather's daughter by his first, white, wife: paid her to let him impregnate her, and then give the child to him and his wife. He paid for her to go away before she got big, so that no-one would know the truth of it, the true story of his son's conception. Then his wife took the baby for her own, and they called it Malachy after his father's father.

So that might have been all right, and maybe it was all right for a time, but within less than two years two things had happened. The mother of Malachy married a man in town, and had a baby who died, and maybe that turned her brain somehow. And the rancher's wife died.

So there was a child without a mother, and a mother without a child. But of course the child did have a mother, and the mother did have a child. Who could really blame her for taking him back?

She took him to her father, on the reservation, and told him the story. She knew, he knew, that O'Hara would guess who had taken his son, but maybe not what she had done with him. She left him there, with her father's second wife, and went back to her white husband in the town.

When the sheriff came around, she denied what she had done. But O'Hara was not convinced, and he persuaded the sheriff to go out to the reservation with him, to look for his son.

Well, of course everyone said they knew nothing about it. The old chief told them they were welcome to look for the boy anywhere on his lands. Where would you hide a baby in a rocky wilderness? They looked, and found nothing. They looked, and saw nothing. Only little brown Indian children, dirty little Cheyenne babies, playing naked in the dust.

O'Hara saw his son and didn't know him. Maybe he'd always thought of him as a white boy.

★   ★   ★

'But you didn't come all the way here to tell me that,' said Calum. 'I'm glad you told me, but you didn't come here for that.'

'No.'

Sheila had grown grim again, more like herself in the car on the way down from Oldport. Hobie sat up straight, staring intently at Sheila, and then at Calum and Angelina. Hobie knew what his mother was about to say. As for Angelina, she didn't know how she knew it, but she knew too. And then Sheila said it.

'I came to take him home.'

'He's dead,' Calum reminded her. 'You said you'd heard about that.'

'That's why I came. His bones belong to us. They belong on our land. He was one of our people, he should lie with us.'

'But you just told me his father was an Irishman. Real name O'Hara, you said.'

'His name was Hawke. He had a right to that name. That was the name he chose to take, the name he chose to use, his grandfather's name. His grandfather was my grandfather. His blood is my blood. His bones belong with our ancestors.'

'That's ridiculous.' Calum sounded incredulous and indignant, both at the same time. 'He belongs to me as much as to any of you lot, doesn't he? He was my grandfather. Anyway, you can't own a corpse.'

'There isn't any corpse,' Angelina pointed out. 'He's been cremated. It was in the will.'

'Then I'll take his ashes, if that's all that's left to us. We've lost so much, forgotten so much that was ours. We have no history but what we carry in our heads, in our veins. I can't bear to lose any more.' Sheila closed her eyes briefly, then opened them again. 'Where are these ashes?'

Angelina considered this a pointless debate. She didn't care about dead bodies, not even Malachy's dead body. Not when she knew his real, immortal body was somewhere else. Not when he had come back, to knock at the door in the night. But before Calum could say anything, she said to Sheila, 'They belong to Calum's dad now. He inherited everything that was Malachy's. Everything but the money.'

'Your father?' Sheila turned her fierce, black-eyed gaze on Calum again. 'Who is he? Where is he?'

'He's in England.' A vague look of panic crossed Calum's face, probably at the notion of Sheila, with Hobie in tow, banging on his father's door in London to demand possession of Malachy. 'He'll be coming back here soon,' he added hastily. 'If you want to leave your address or something, I'm sure he'll get in touch with you.'

'You know where we live,' Sheila said stonily.

'Oh, yeah. The reservation.'

She went on staring at him. He met her look, reluctantly at first, then more seriously. After all, he wasn't a boy any more. If he had been born in the time of her grandfather's grandfather, he would have been counting coup by now.

He pulled himself up to his full height, a generous six feet, and squared his shoulders. 'Right. I see what you mean. I really do see what you mean. But Angie's absolutely right, it's not for me to decide. My father is the chief where Malachy's estate is concerned. So I'll have to talk to my father about it.'

Hobie dropped them off next morning at Bert's garage. The truck had already been rescued, and was awaiting a decision on its fate. They both waved as the Chevy drove away, but only Hobie responded.

'She doesn't really trust me, does she?' Calum remarked.

Because you have the sight, Angelina thought, whatever that is. A funny sort of sight, that apparently made you blind. She wondered if his father had it too.

'She probably can't get over the idea of a blond Indian. After all, if what George said is true, you're as Cheyenne as she is. There's nothing to stop you from moving in next door to her. What do you think your dad will do about what she wants?'

Calum shrugged. 'If it means more to her than to us, why shouldn't she have the ashes? And maybe she's right, maybe Malachy does belong back there where he came from. It's all terrifically tribal, isn't it? Makes me feel kind of funny, thinking that one day one of them might turn up demanding repatriation of *my* remains. But I suppose it's nice to know somebody cares.'

Angelina felt a flicker of jealousy, and promptly smothered it. Calum and Malachy had a right to have relations, same as anyone else. 'She sure seemed to care about Malachy, didn't she? Considering she supposedly hadn't seen him for forty years.'

'Just what I was thinking,' Calum agreed. 'She tried to make out like this burial business was a tribal thing, but I caught a strong whiff of something a lot more personal. Do you think her manhunting mission to New York was more successful than she let on? I suspect Hobie is one of my twelve lost uncles.'

Angelina had already entertained the same notion. 'I suspect he's your thirteenth uncle. I bet Rene will have to add him to the list of heirs.'

'Well, at least then he'll get something for his trouble in coming here. Hey, how old do you think he is? Maybe he—'

'It's OK, I thought about that too. I asked Sheila. He's only forty-two.'

26

No need to go back to Bayswater this time. Not like the old days, when he was supposed to be out for an evening stroll, or running a quick errand, with Polly at home ready to wonder what had kept him. He was a free man now. He could do what he liked, go where he liked. Shepherd Market, or Streatham Common.

And he had a purpose too, this time. He was doing research for a book. Just in case anybody wanted to know.

Malachy had found women to do it for free. Getting sex for free should have been much easier now than it had been then – Calum had managed to score almost every weekend, Ged recalled, to his annoyance even now – but the rules weren't the same as for a business transaction. To get free sex, he would have to pick up a woman in a bar or some such place. The trouble with women in bars was that they wanted to know your name, and awkward details like that. He didn't want to chat up some tart, he just wanted to fuck her and kill her.

In his head, at least.

When he thought about the practicalities, killing somebody wasn't as simple as that. Killing her in the car meant the danger of leaving evidence in the car, or leaving evidence of the car on her body. Killing a hooker whose colleagues had seen you drive off with her would be dangerous too.

Just as John Lennon had promised, and as Ged had

personally discovered, you could do it in the road and no-one would be watching you. Anyone happening to pass by would ignore you out of embarrassment. But even in today's *laissez-faire* moral culture, most people would probably reckon that embarrassment was no excuse for ignoring a murder.

He had to work out a method, too. Maybe he could try different ways, and see which one felt most satisfactory.

Stabbing meant he would have to be carrying a knife. Well, that wasn't so difficult. Even a jack-knife could do a lot of damage. Even a razor-blade could open a throat.

Blunt instruments must be easy to come by. A brick, a stick, picked up by the wayside. The pavement itself would serve, if he simply brought Mohammed to the mountain, so to speak.

What about a small hammer, concealed in the pocket? The trouble with a smallish thing like that was that he would have to hit her over and over again. He thought about that, putting himself into the mind of a murderer, and decided maybe that wouldn't be a disadvantage at all.

There were various ways of using his bare hands. He could beat her to death. But that sounded like hard work, and uncertain; he might leave her for dead when she wasn't. He could knock her down and kick her head in. Feet weren't precisely bare hands, but the principle was the same, using one's body as the instrument of murder. The notion that, at least theoretically, he was in himself a lethal weapon, gave him a pleasant sense of power.

No, not pleasant at all. Nothing *pleasant* about it. A nasty thrill, that was the sensation. A different, darker flavour, stronger and gamier than the tainted pleasure he used to get from screwing whores, but definitely in the same camp.

Then there were the hands themselves. Traditionally, men used their hands to strangle, but that was not the only way of dealing death with them. Malachy had described his hands by saying they were as big as the girl's face. Saying that when he put his hand over her face, it covered her entirely and left her unable to breathe. Saying he had smothered her like that.

Ged looked at his own hands. They were big, but not clumsy, not ham-fisted. He had always been aware that he had big hands. What he had never known till now was that they were part of his father's legacy.

Love, she called him. Just like the whores that Malachy had described.

Under her make-up she was past her prime, showing the strain of her calling. From experience he reckoned that a streetwalker's prime was no more than seventeen or eighteen, in both the physical and personable sense. After that they shrivelled, or grew blowsy and banal, whichever way drugs and drink and the drifting state of their soul happened to haul them. Being on the game was a young person's game, like Olympic gymnastics or futures trading.

Once he would have ignored a woman like this one, but this time he had a different intention. Maybe it would be easier to kill her if she was well on her way downhill. Maybe she wouldn't mind so much.

Maybe *he* wouldn't mind so much. He'd never killed anyone before, not even in imagination; he couldn't tell how much he might mind.

She took him to a perfect killing ground, a forecourt behind a wall, enclosed on three sides by some abandoned industrial building. Rubble and glass were strewn about. He knew that, even though it was dark, because he almost tripped over the rubble, and he could hear the shards of glass crunching under his shoes. The broken windows gaped around him, darker than the darkness they were standing in, symptoms of some further hell, lower down and blacker still.

He let her give him a blow job, because he didn't fancy fat women. She wasn't really fat, just lumpy and sagging, but it was enough to put him off the idea of entertaining himself with her body. Let her entertain him; that was what he was paying her for.

At first he closed his eyes and imagined she was Elie. But she didn't do it the way Elie had, and anyway thinking about Elie made angry and desolate as much as it aroused him. So he opened his eyes and began to speculate about ways of killing this woman.

There was a brick right beside his foot. His shoe was jammed up against it. He applied pressure and felt it shift. So it would have been easy like that . . .

He imagined grabbing her by her brassy hair, reaching for the brick, bringing it down on her head. Bringing it down again. Again. Harder, harder on her temple, in her face, blinding her, bloodying her, noting her whimpers, noting when they stopped. Noting when she ceased to move, but not stopping till long after that. Just to make sure.

When he ceased to move, he was appalled by what he had done. He had brought himself to orgasm by means of a mental murder.

That had been far from perfect, he decided afterwards. There would have been too much blood, for one thing. Too messy. And then the woman had been hardly worth killing, a blowsy old whore like that. Certainly not worthy to be the centrepiece in a work of art.

It made him uneasy, thinking like that, even if he was only trying to put himself inside his father's head. Had Malachy really thought like that? Had he ever really murdered a woman? Or had he only done what Ged had just done, screwed her in reality and fantasized the killing part?

And what difference did it make to anyone, now that Malachy was dead?

He switched on his computer and stared at the bright blank screen, hoping for inspiration to strike. He had been doing this almost every day for three years now, and nothing useful had happened yet.

But this time he had a way of seeding the rain-clouds, ready words to help him on his way. He entered them on the screen.

I'm looking for Miss Right.
She could be anywhere, couldn't she?
And so on.

He typed a description of the murder of the fat whore, in imitation of his father's style. Colloquial staccato, you might call it. Folksy and obscene, high-minded and deranged. The mind of a homicidal maniac who is also an artist, or an artist who is incidentally a murderer.

It would make quite a change from his own self-consciously literary style of cool irony. Phrases from various reviews of his last book stuck in his mind: 'The style conveys no sense of immediacy'; 'Emotions recollected from the tranquillity of the grave'; 'A sense that life is something that happens to other people, and the more fools they'. The only thing more memorable than your own prose is the prose of people writing about your writing.

Tomorrow night he would go out and find another prostitute to kill. A young one this time, one of the small thin kind. He would put his imaginary hands around her scrawny little neck and strangle her. He had decided that blood was too dangerous.

The phone rang. He started guiltily at the sound, as if he were standing there literally red-handed. He had to wipe his hands on his jeans before he could make himself pick it up.

It was likely to be Rufus. But it might just by some remote possibility be Elie . . .

'Dad?'

Calum's voice crackled at him from the other side of the earth. From the other side of the universe, as far as Ged was concerned. It took him a moment to get his mind into gear for dealing with Calum. 'Yes?'

'Were you asleep?'

What kind of question was that? It had only just gone midnight, and he wasn't a wage slave. Not an old-age pensioner, either. 'No.'

'If you say so,' Calum agreed. 'You just sounded, like,

out of it. You know those diaries you were asking about? Well, we found some more of them, and I read them all, like you wanted me to. What exactly did you want to know?'

Do they describe murders? But he couldn't ask that. 'What sort of thing did he put in them?'

'Well, they're mainly entries about paintings. He put in a note when he'd finished a painting, and then he made a note when he sold one. Also there's some bits about his models. Seems like he was fond of f— taking them to bed, and getting them up the duff. He made a note about that too, when it happened. But that's about all.

'And listen, Dad. We found some other stuff. Different sorts of paintings, really freaky. I won't try to describe them, you can see them when you come over.'

Ged rang off and pondered Calum's news. All of it.

Freaky paintings, what the hell could that mean? There was no telling what Calum would consider freaky, when it came to art. And no point in speculating. As Calum had said, he would see for himself in due course.

As for the diaries, the news was not what he had hoped for. Paintings, models, babies, Christ.

Maybe the diary he had, the first one, had the only murder.

Maybe it was a real one.

1967

Sold: Untitled Red Numbers 23, 25, 26.

I hate being sold. Makes me feel like a whore.

It ain't right, people trying to buy me. All art should be sold nameless. People should be buying the picture, not the painter. They should be looking at the picture, not the price tag. I'm painting pictures, not money.

27

Darkness again. Firelight again. Supper over, dishes washed, feet on hearthstone, cat on lap. Nothing to do now but what she wanted, all the way to bedtime . . . and after.

Angelina had ended up reading the diaries, after all. They at least provided an education, as well as a possible advance warning of what Calum might come up with next. After what he had done to her that day when Brad Welles telephoned, what he had promised to do and then did . . .

Her face was already flushed from the warmth of the fire, but it must have gone pinker still as she recalled what he had done. Right here in this very chair. At least, she had been in the chair, and he had been on his knees.

Remembering made her squirm.

Then she had to calm the cat, who didn't take kindly to earthquakes. Champagne had won the lap lottery tonight. The other two were sharing Calum's unoccupied chair.

Calum himself was exploring Malachy's laptop computer. Looking for computer games, he said. He must have found something of interest, because he was totally absorbed.

'Calum? Did you find a game?'

'I found something better. Listen, what was a technophobe, who didn't have a TV or a stereo or even a radio, doing with a PC?'

'Why not? It doesn't make a noise. And he used to draw on it. He said he liked to fool around with the colours.'

'Well, he wasn't playing Nintendo, I can tell you that much. This is the only game-free computer I've ever come across.'

'So what's the better thing you found? Whatever it is, it sure is keeping you quiet.'

'It's the last diary. *1988*.'

'Anything interesting in it?'

'I'll tell you when I've finished. It's not exactly like the others.'

'What does that mean?'

'Tell you when I've finished, I said. Now shut your gob, girl, and let me get on with it.'

She had never heard the word *gob* used in that context before, but it was clear enough what he meant. Since he was obviously not in a company mood, she decided to go to bed. It was the first time since . . . since the first time . . . that he hadn't come with her.

How long until the last time? Until he went home, or sooner than that? No more than a few weeks of besotted bliss, and then disaster. She was only fooling herself if she tried to pretend that she was really any different than his pick-ups. She was just another form of excitement. When it came down to it, he would leave her and forget her.

That's what she was trying to forget.

She still found it odd to be reminded in the middle of the night that she was not alone in her bed. A cat (or two or three) often slept on the bed, of course, but that wasn't the same thing at all. The cats would waken her with fluttery fairy kisses, brushing their whiskers against her cheek as lightly as a butterfly. Calum had more strenuous and pleasurable ways of waking her when he wanted her.

He did it now, coming to bed after she had drifted off.

She asked afterwards, drowsy again, mumbling into the pectoral muscles which provided her pillow these nights, if he had found anything exciting in the diary.

'Yeah.' He sounded sleepy too. So sleepy that she

didn't take in what he had said, until she recalled it the next morning. 'Those paintings are probably fakes.'

'What do you mean, fakes?'

She was awake now, all right. The sun was streaming into the kitchen, the bacon was spitting in the frying pan, and Calum had just come out of the bathroom, wrapped in an enormous towel.

In spite of the shower he had just taken, his wits didn't seem to be working yet. He stared at her with the slack, open-mouthed expression of the intellectually challenged. Or the half-asleep. 'What?'

'You said those paintings are probably fakes.'

Some dim semblance of intelligence flickered into his eyes and closed his mouth for him. 'Oh, yeah. That's what it looks like, anyway. Wow, that smells good. Let me get dressed and I'll tell you all about it.'

Fakes? What could he possibly mean? That the dead pictures weren't Malachy's? She would have been enormously relieved to think so. But the Untitled Women had been constantly referred to in the diaries. And what would be the point of pretending that someone else's work was yours, if you were never intending to show that work to anyone?

When Calum returned, decently clothed in shorts and T-shirt, she decided to get that sorted out right away. 'You mean the stuff we found yesterday, the Untitled Women?'

'What? No. No, those ones have got to be his, don't they? I mean, they're in the diaries and everything. Besides, nobody knew about them, so he had no reason to fake them.'

No reason to fake them. This made no sense to Angelina. 'If you didn't mean them, what did you mean?'

He waved his hand towards the studio. 'The things on the walls. Other stuff as well, but I can't tell how much. Seems like he started doing it after he built this house. Twenty years ago, didn't Rene say?'

Angelina stood stiff with shock. 'But I saw him paint those pictures.'

'All of them?'

'Well, some of them.' She thought carefully. 'One or two of them for sure, anyway.'

He gave her an odd look. 'Which ones?'

'I'll show you.' She crossed the deck to the glass wall of the studio, and pointed. 'The yellow one, the last one he did. And that one up there. The red one in the top corner.'

He came up behind her and looked where she was pointing. 'The one farthest to the right, by the back wall?'

'That's the one.'

'Angie, how can you be sure? They all look so much alike.'

'They don't look that much alike. The colours are all different, aren't they, like Jorge said? Besides, he painted that red one from a photograph. He had an aerial photograph of a butte. Somewhere in Montana, he said. And you can see how the painted shadows make the canvas look as if it's folding, just the way the land folded in around that butte.' She had a sudden inspired thought. 'The photo is probably somewhere around here. Maybe in that filing cabinet. You can see for yourself.'

'Maybe I will.' But he was looking at her, not the painting. He wasn't smiling, but she felt his amusement. 'Listen, Angie, would you be prepared to stand up in court and swear that you watched Malachy painting that picture?'

'Yes,' she said firmly. 'Why?'

'Because that's the one my father gave me. It's my payment for doing this job.'

He went back into the kitchen to sit down and tackle his breakfast. She followed him, more bewildered than ever. 'You mean, you own a real one and all the rest are fakes?'

'Maybe something like that. I told you, I don't know how many are fakes. Neither will anybody else, even when they've read the diary. He did it like that on purpose, so that no-one could ever be sure.' Calum set his fork down and started to laugh. 'What a bastard. What a brilliant old bastard.'

'Calum, I don't understand any of this. How could he possibly fake his own work? If he did it, then it's genuine, isn't it?'

'That's the thing. He didn't do them. He paid someone else to do them.'

Angelina nibbled at her bacon, hoping food on her stomach would help her brain to work better. Nothing Calum said was making any sense to her. 'Paid someone? Who?'

'He doesn't say. Might even have been more than one person. Anyway, after they'd painted whatever he told them to paint, he painted a copy of it. Both unsigned, of course. He says in the diary that he never signed his paintings, because that would have been part of the process of turning art into property. All he ever did was write a number on the back.

'He arranged for quite a few of those fakes, to judge from what he says. And there was no way, as far as he could see, that anyone would ever be able to know for sure who did which, or even what.'

'Brilliant. I see.' She saw the confusion that Malachy had intended, but not the reason for it. And what reason could there possibly be? 'Why on earth would he do a thing like that?'

'As far as I can make out, it was some kind of revenge on the art market. It seems like he hated the whole idea of a market in art. He thought people should only buy his paintings because they liked to look at them. The notion of somebody investing in them to make money, because he was famous, really got up his nose.'

Angelina brightened. Something she understood at last. 'Oh, yeah, I know. He used to tell me about that. Bloodsuckers and necrophiliacs, he called them. He said they were like the moneychangers in the temple at Jerusalem. The ones that Jesus chased out,' she added, seeing the blank look on Calum's face. 'He, I mean Jesus

363

– the real Jesus, not George – said they'd made it a den of thieves. And Malachy said that was the art market all over, a den of thieves and snobs and vampires. He said the only art they could appreciate was on a dollar bill.'

'Well, that's pretty much the tone of the diary. He seems to have had a thing about it. Funny, that, since that's how he got rich.'

'But he didn't care about being rich.' She caught his frown, and interpreted it. 'Yeah, yeah, I know what I said to George. But the true fact is, Malachy really did not care about money. He only wanted enough to go on painting. After all, the labourer is worthy of his hire.'

She remembered an argument about that. She had been shocked to discover how much Malachy's paintings were worth. 'Doesn't it bother you?' she'd demanded of him. 'People paying huge amounts of money for your paintings, when other people are starving?'

'They are obscene amounts,' he had agreed, 'but if I priced them more sensibly, then the bastards who buy them will make the obscene amounts, instead of me. I'm not working to make someone else's fortune.'

'No, I meant that the people who buy your stuff are throwing away all that money on something completely unnecessary, while other people don't even have the necessities of life.'

Malachy had stopped what he was doing to stare at her, his left eyelid drooping dangerously, the right eyebrow cocked at an aggressive angle. 'You think art is unnecessary?'

On reflection, maybe she hadn't put her case in the most tactful way. Which didn't mean it wasn't true. 'It is, isn't it? We don't need it to live.'

'We do, if we're human. Making art is as much an instinct as eating and screwing. Every culture ever known has had music and poetry and some form of visual art. We're not meant to be animals, living from hand to mouth and day to day. We're supposed to be self-conscious, in the broad sense: to think about ourselves and our situation.'

364

'I know that,' Angelina protested. 'The kingdom of God is not eating and drinking, but justice, peace and joy. That's why I say we can't afford art, not until everybody has justice.'

'Not until Judgement Day, you mean,' he growled. 'We have to get on with our lives, girl. If we're supposedly here to help other people, what are the other people here for?'

He had gone back to work by then, but she persisted. 'I don't mean we should all go off to Africa. I just meant there's something wrong in the way things are organized. If some people have fortunes to spend on frivolity, that's because other people have no money at all. That can't be right.'

'I don't know that the Pope would agree with you, Angie. Popes have always lived in a palace surrounded by beggars, haven't they? And it was some pope or other who paid Michelangelo to paint the Sistine Chapel, for instance. Most of the human race has always been poor as dirt. If we were all equal, we'd all be poor, and nobody would be able to afford art – no time to make it, no money to pay for it. There'd be no such thing as civilization. So, yeah, maybe you're right, civilization is a luxury. Would you rather be without it?'

She knew that if she said yes, he would dismiss her as a barbarian. So she parried with a question of her own. 'Do you mean it's OK for some people's happiness and fulfil-ment to be sacrificed, so that other people can look at paintings and go to the opera?'

He shrugged. 'Truth, Angie, I don't give a damn about folks who admire paintings and dress up for the opera. It's the painting and composing and singing that I'm rooting for. Art is doing, not sitting back and enjoying. Lots of people get a kick out of a walk in the woods, but there's a universe of difference between a forest and a painting. The difference is that some human mind created the painting.

'And not just any mind could have done it. That's important. Why should I throw away my chances of immortality, just to give a mob of strangers an extra meal and a pair of shoes? That way, we'd all have wasted our lives, instead of only some of us.'

'But that's just selfishness, isn't it? Expecting other people to slave away all their lives, so that you can do what you want to do.' She had grown reckless in the heat of argument, forgetting to be polite. Forgetting that he was her boss. 'Who would care if you died without producing a single work of art?'

'*I* would, wouldn't I? That's a big part of what I'm about. Maybe the biggest. Might even be what I'm here for.'

He had looked up then at the canvases on the wall, and then he had looked down at her. He had been speaking with vehemence, but now she saw that his mouth was on the verge of smiling. 'Is all this argy-bargy about justice just a roundabout way of saying you don't like my pictures, Angie?'

So now Angelina was prepared to defend Malachy over accusations of greed. She steered Calum back to the real topic. 'Now are you telling me he deliberately set out to diddle these people who bought his paintings just because he was famous?'

Calum considered, and squared his shoulders for serious battle. 'I think it was a little more comprehensive than that. I think he wanted to subvert the whole system. After all, if the market depends on knowing exactly who painted the picture you're buying or selling, then confusing that issue should undermine the whole business.'

'But if nobody ever found out what he'd done—'

'Then I suppose it would have been just his private little joke. But, Angie, like I said at the very beginning, if he'd really wanted all this stuff, the diaries and the Untitled Women and the fakes, if he'd really wanted to keep it all secret for ever, he wouldn't have written it down.' Calum was looking serious now, just about as serious as she had ever seen him. 'Why do you think he was so keen on leaving this place to my dad? Who else could he really trust to respect his interests and honour his intentions, once he was dead? Anybody else, Rene Deforte or Brad Welles, would have other axes to grind. I think he was trusting my father to do what he wanted him to do.'

'Your dad has his own axe to grind,' Angelina pointed out. 'You said that maybe the only genuine painting over there is the one he gave to you. Why would he want to blab about this faking business, if it means that the paintings he inherited are worth zilch?'

'I never thought of that.' Calum thought about it now, while he mopped up his egg yolk with toast. 'I guess it's my axe too, if it comes to that. I'd probably rather have a rich father than a poor one.'

Angelina was watching him carefully. 'So what would you do, if you were your dad?'

'Well, I can't speak for him. But if it were me, then . . . well, I think I'd think, I hope he'd think, on the one hand, What the hell, I never expected any of this, and I've still got a little piece of paradise left to me. And on the other hand, I think Mal deserves to have his subversion succeed. I can see his point of view. It's not right to betray somebody, if they trusted you. Not even if they're dead. I kind of think we should do what he wanted.'

Angelina couldn't have agreed more, at least about dead people. She knew they weren't really dead, not the way everybody thought they were. She had heard her grandfather knocking on the door. Malachy too, for that matter, though he had gotten himself muddled up with Calum on account of the thunder. And thereby been the cause of her undoing.

'How can you be sure what he wanted?'

'Well, I can't. And it doesn't matter, because it isn't up to me. I'll have to tell my father, and see what he says.'

Calum said that in a funny way, *tell my father*, like a little kid confident that his dad would sort everything out. He didn't usually talk about his father like that. Maybe it was because of his father being responsible for the estate, making all the decisions. Maybe that had impressed him somehow.

Or maybe it was because his father had trusted him with all of this. *Important*, *valuable*, those were impressive words. Maybe Calum had been impressed.

And maybe there was another reason, too. Ged had trusted Calum with his inheritance, just like Malachy had trusted Ged with what was left of his life.

Calum thought a little longer, staring out the window while he thought. 'Listen, Angie, can we take that painting somewhere else? The one that's mine, I mean. I don't want the art shark to get it mixed up with the rest of them, and sell it by mistake. Could we maybe leave it with your gran?'

28

They didn't hear the car until Charles started barking.

Jorge had left early today. He said he had a heavy date. Angelina didn't want to enquire too closely into his social and sexual arrangements, especially since Calum had called him a queer. If Calum thought Jorge was homosexual, then he almost certainly was. Calum had a nose for the seamy side of things, as she had had more than one occasion to notice.

It was that seamy side Calum was interested in now. As soon as Jorge's motorcycle had disappeared down the mountain, he had picked her up and carried her off to bed, ignoring her objections.

'It's too early to stop work.'

'We're only going to take a little break.'

'You won't. You'll fall asleep.'

'I didn't bring you in here to sleep.'

He had dropped her on to the bed by this time. She continued to protest, not because she minded what he was doing, but because it didn't seem right to do it just any old time, whenever you felt like it. Otherwise, judging by her own feelings, people would never do anything else.

'Calum, you can't. Stop it. At least let me get my boots off.'

'No, leave your boots on. That's kind of kinky. I like it.'

So when Charles started barking, Angelina was wearing nothing but her boots, and Calum was completely naked.

If they had been caught out, he would have had less explaining to do.

'There goes Charles.'

'Forget the damned dog. Let him bark.'

'No, it means someone's here.' She tried to wriggle out from under him, almost impossible without his co-operation. 'I have to get the shotgun, just in case.'

'Let me get it.'

'No. You'd miss.' What she meant was that she didn't trust him not to fire it. Shooting people was probably the sort of thing he would call excitement.

'Well, I'd get dressed first, if I were you.'

He let her go, and watched her struggle back into her clothes. She felt like a pervert, having to pull her panties on over those stupid boots. It took ages to get to the point of buttoning up her dress. All Calum had to do was haul on his shorts. He could go outside like that, barefoot, bare-chested, wearing nothing but a ragged pair of shorts (and several earrings and a ring in his nose) and no-one would remark on it. Some things in life were just plain unfair.

She grabbed the shotgun from its hiding place in the broom closet, and stepped out on to the deck to see what was going on.

A man in a straw-coloured suit and hat stood with his back to her, peering through the open door into the studio. Charles was straddling the middle of the deck, barking vigorously, but making no attempt to interfere with the stranger. Some watchdog he was.

'Hey, mister,' she called. 'What the heck do you think you're doing?'

He turned towards her, the low brim of the hat shading his features. 'Angie, this is the second time you've greeted me with a gun. Is it just me, or do you do it to everyone?'

She knew that voice, even if she couldn't see his face. She had heard it only a few days ago. 'Mr Welles? Why didn't you knock?'

'I did. For quite a while. I expect you couldn't hear me,

what with the racket that beast has been making.'

That was a useful explanation, and Angelina let it lie. She lowered the gun. 'Charles, shut up. It's OK.'

Charles had to have the last word, as usual, but after a final insubordinate *wff* he took his proper place alongside her. She could feel Calum behind her. She always knew whereabouts he was. Maybe she could sense his body heat, or smell him. Or gauge his distance from the state of her pulse.

She dragged her attention back to their visitor. 'What did you want? Like I told you, we haven't finished clearing up yet.'

'So I see.' Bradford Welles nodded towards the studio. 'I hope you're not in the habit of leaving the door wide open like that. Anyone could walk in.'

'Not many people around here to walk in,' Angelina pointed out. 'Anyway, we were just having a coffee break.' That was a euphemism, she told herself, rather than a lie. More briskly she added, 'Can we do anything for you?'

'I happened to be out here on business, and I thought I'd stop by. Make sure everything is all right.'

'Of course it's all right,' Calum growled. 'I told you it was all right.'

'You'll have to forgive me, I'm a chronic worrier.' Welles said that smoothly, not at all apologetically. 'These are valuable paintings, in cultural as well as financial terms. I could never forgive myself if anything happened to them, especially since I've known Mal for such a long time. It would be a betrayal of his trust.'

That was the wrong word for him to use. Calum had this thing about Malachy and trust, and Brad Welles didn't figure in those equations. 'I don't see how it's anything to do with you,' Calum muttered.

Brad Welles ignored him and addressed Angelina. 'Is it all right if I go in and have a look?'

She glanced over her shoulder at Calum, who shrugged rather sulkily. 'Can't see why not,' she translated.

They followed him into the studio, Angelina, Calum,

even Charles. Angelina was still clutching the shotgun. They must have looked like a team of bodyguards, or a grandee's retinue.

'This is coming along nicely,' Brad said graciously. 'You're doing a really fine job. Everyone in New York is simply salivating at the thought of these paintings. You said you were keeping an inventory?'

'It's in that exercise book.' Angelina pointed to the work bench. The notebook had a bright orange cover, to make it hard to lose in the chaos that seemed to encompass Malachy and all his works.

'May I . . . ?'

Again she couldn't think of any reason why not. Neither could Calum. When she glanced at him, he grimaced and shrugged again.

Brad followed her over to the work bench. She propped the shotgun against the bench and picked up the book. But when she turned to show it to him, she found him staring past her at something else.

She looked where he was looking.

Jorge had been engaged in the lengthy task of photographing all the paintings and drawings from the trunk, laying a dozen at a time out on the long bench, and photographing each one before returning them to the chest. He had left the last lot on the bench when he went home, meaning to carry on tomorrow from where he had left off. So there they were, in full view: brazen, bloody, cool and cruel.

Angelina glanced back at Brad. He was staring at the paintings on the table with a New York version of open-mouthed astonishment. He managed to keep his mouth closed, but his stone-coloured eyes behind the gold-rimmed glasses grew bigger and bigger, as they took in the whole array. She was reminded of the fairy tale about the dog with eyes as big as millstones.

'Holy shit,' he whispered.

Angelina frowned. Blasphemy was at least a backwards

way of acknowledging the power of God, but scatology was just plain offensive.

Brad wasn't taking any notice of her displeasure. His attention was glued to the dismembered women. 'Where the hell did you find these?'

'They were in that chest over there. There's lots more of them,' she added, and was rewarded by seeing him lose control of his jaw, just for a second. 'We log them into the book when George photographs them.'

'How are you logging them?'

'Malachy numbered them all.' She turned the nearest one over to display the familiar round scrawl. 'They go into the book as UW Number such and such.'

Brad pushed his glasses down his nose to examine the writing. 'UW? What's that?'

'Untitled Woman. That's what he called them.'

'Dr Bravo, you mean?'

'No, Malachy.'

The millstones threatened to fall right out of his head. '*Mal* called them . . . ? You mean you knew about these works?'

'Gosh, no. He had them locked up in that trunk, and then he hid the trunk behind some other stuff. I guess he knew how disgusting they were.'

'They could have been ironic,' Calum pointed out ironically, from the far side of the bench. 'Scathing indictment of American culture, that kind of thing.'

'Ironic?' Bradford placed a perfectly manicured fingertip on the corner of one of the drawings, a depiction of a headless torso resembling the Venus de Milo as she might have looked before joining Weight Watchers. His professional instincts were already overriding his stupefaction. 'Possibly. Possibly. There are certainly elements of irony here. But to be frank, I don't think Mal could have spelled political correctness to save his life.'

He turned on Angelina. 'If you weren't aware of the existence of these works before he died, how do you know about this Untitled Women business?'

'He wrote about them in his diaries.'

'Diaries?' Again he had a visible struggle to compose his features. 'He kept a diary?'

Oops, thought Angelina, I shouldn't have said that. They weren't part of the art, and maybe Calum's father wouldn't want the art shark to know about them. She herself didn't, come to think of it, want him to know. What if he wanted to read them? What if he found out about all the terrible things that Malachy got up to with those models? That was nobody's business but Malachy's. And maybe Calum's dad.

'Just a couple of notebooks, really,' she amended hastily. 'All he did was keep track of what he painted and what he sold. Isn't that right, Calum?'

'Yeah, right.' Calum was studying the pictures on the table, not really listening. He answered without looking up. 'Except for the last one.'

Oh, Calum, she prayed, don't mention that.

But Brad didn't seem to notice what Calum had said. He was too intent on this new revelation. 'Where are these notebooks? I'd like to have a look.'

Calum glanced at him briefly, before returning his attention to the table. 'No.'

Brad looked surprised and offended. He must have thought his request was only a formality. 'Surely it wouldn't do any harm? Those notebooks are valuable documents, if they're authentic. I just want to assure myself that—'

'They're the real thing all right,' Calum interrupted. 'Angie recognized his handwriting. And we managed to identify some of the paintings they refer to.'

'I don't doubt it. But since they constitute part of the estate, it might be as well to make sure.'

Calum's eyes, as Angelina had been able to observe at close quarters on numerous occasions, combined two colours: an inner ring of brown around the pupil, and a wider green band at the outer edges of the iris. Now, as

374

he looked up at Brad Welles, they had gone all green. And cold.

'Angie saw him every day for the last two years of his life. You hadn't seen much of him for nearly ten years, if I understood you right. Are you trying to tell Angie she doesn't know what she's talking about?'

Brad ran his hand over his immaculate haircut, smoothing down his impatience as well as his hair. 'I fully expect to corroborate what Angie says. That's why it's so important that I see them. They belong to your father, and if they're authentic, they're valuable. He might like to know that.'

'I expect he can figure that one out for himself. You're not touching them until he says you can.'

'He's already signed an agreement, mandating us to act as his agents.'

Calum straightened up and folded his arms, looking deliberately thuggish. The face jewellery didn't help – or did, depending on your point of view. 'You're not literary agents, are you?' He jerked his chin in the direction of the chest. 'There's more than enough art over there to keep you busy for a while. Why don't you just get on with browsing through all that?'

'Precisely what I intend to do.' Brad stepped around the bench, towards the chest. Towards Calum, coincidentally. 'I can't understand why you're taking this attitude, Calum. It's my job to help your father realize the best value for his assets. The last thing I'd want is to make trouble for you.'

'Make trouble for me?' Calum stepped to one side. Into Brad's path, as it happened. 'What's that supposed to mean?'

'Nothing.' The agent checked himself, rather than walk into Calum, or be obliged to go around him. 'Nothing whatsoever. What did you think it meant?'

'Not much point saying it if it didn't mean anything, is there?'

Angelina had seen this sort of thing before, usually

when Charles met up with another dog. Circling, bristling, growling, and all over nothing. Men were crazy. She tossed a bone of distraction. 'Mr Welles, would you like some coffee? Or would you rather have lemonade?'

Brad turned to smile at Angelina. He also took the opportunity to sidle around Calum, towards the chest, without loss of face. 'Thank you, Angie. Coffee would be marvellous.'

'Black or white? Sugar?'

'I'll take it straight.'

The way he said that, he might have been intending to mainline the coffee rather than drink it. She felt some small sympathy for him, being bullied by Calum like this.

She knew what Calum's problem was, of course. He didn't like Brad, and he didn't like the way Brad treated him like a kid. Like his father's flunkey. Or even his father's watchdog: a human version of Charles, capable of barking and biting, but not of logical discourse or responsible behaviour. So in response to this insult, Calum was behaving exactly like Charles.

How could she possibly be in love with a man like that?

Love was terrible. She hated it.

She dashed across the deck to make the coffee, terrified that things might have gotten out of hand by the time she got back. But when she returned with a mug of black coffee, she discovered that they were only starting up again where they had left off.

Brad had littered the floor around the chest with the Untitled Women. He was standing in the middle of the bloody mess, turning slowly to survey them all. Absorbing the atmosphere of Malachy's secret world.

'Holy Christ,' he muttered, but not so low that Angelina couldn't hear him. 'Mal, you were a lunatic.'

'Do you really think so?' Angelina leaned across the drifts of painted paper to hand him his coffee.

'Thank you, Angie.' Hot and black as it was, he all but emptied it at one go, and passed the mug back to her. 'And no, not really. If you look at those,' he waved at the walls, 'he was one of the sanest, most logical, most perceptive men who ever lived. But these . . .' He prodded one of the butcher's displays with his elegant shoe. 'It's like Dr Jekyll and Mr Hyde.'

Angelina knew exactly what he meant. She was thinking of the diaries, conflicting with the flesh-and-blood Malachy she had known. But these Untitled Women were unquestionably the worst.

'Don't you think they'll sell?' She was ambivalent on that point, not wanting Calum's father to be cheated, but also not wanting people to admire those terrible pictures.

'Sell? God, yes. Like crazy. There'll be acres of free publicity, and gallons of controversy, and it'll be a status symbol to own one of these. He's a big name, you know, and showing this unexpected side of him will start the ball rolling all over again.'

'How unexpected will it be? George – Dr Bravo,' she corrected hastily, 'says everybody knew he, um, led a pretty funny life, where women were concerned.'

'Artists always screw around,' Brad said bluntly. 'They're fucking rabbits, as bad as movie stars and rock bands. But anybody can behave badly. This,' he indicated the UWs, 'is serious cultural malevolence.'

'But they're only paintings,' Angelina pointed out, obliged against her instincts to be fair. 'People can paint anything, or write about anything, and it's just pictures or words. It's not the same as going out and doing those things.'

Brad glanced at Calum, who had propped himself against the table in order to glower at him. As glances went, it was maybe more like twirling a revolver around your forefinger to intimidate your opponent. 'To tell the truth, that's why I was wondering about those diaries. It did occur to me, when Calum was so reluctant to let me look at them, that they might have some – ahem – some extraordinary revelations in them.'

'Revelations?' Calum stopped glowering and started to

laugh. 'Have I got revelations for you, mate. Did you know you've been selling fakes?'

Fake must have been the biggest insult in the art world, the way Brad responded. He froze. He stared at Calum. His eyes were no longer saucers, only stones. Small hard ones. 'Just what is that supposed to mean?'

'It means Malachy's been sending you fakes.'

'What do you mean, fakes? That doesn't make sense. Are you suggesting he was sending us paintings that weren't his?'

'Well, it seems like that's just what he was doing.'

Brad aimed an outraged finger at Calum. 'Explain yourself.'

'Explain Malachy, you mean? I can't. I can only tell you what he did.'

Angelina felt like sinking down to the floor and holding her head in her hands. Calum shouldn't have done that. He should have told his father first. He should have let his father deal with the problem, instead of using it to taunt his father's agent.

But Calum was ploughing ahead, explaining the solicited fakes, the copies, the deliberate muddying of the trail, all in confusingly intricate detail. He did sum it up neatly, though. 'He wanted to poison the well.'

Brad had listened to all this with a show of patience, but now he turned to Angelina. 'Angie, have you the slightest idea what this lunatic is raving about?'

'Yes.' She put her hands over her mouth, then took them away. She wished she was anywhere else in the world. There was going to be trouble here, she could smell it in the wind. 'It's true, Mr Welles. It really is true.'

'I don't understand. How can you possibly know all this?'

'He put it in his diary.'

'You mean the diary that was simply a series of notes about paintings?'

The sarcasm was patent, and she couldn't blame him. She hadn't been thinking of the business with the fakes when she had said that. 'The last one was different. Calum told you that.'

'Did he?' Brad gave Calum a weary, heavy-lidded glance. 'Where is this f— sorry, confounded diary?'

'It's on the computer. Over in the house.'

Another glance at Calum. 'And can I read it?'

Calum, predictably, shook his head. 'Not without my father's consent.'

'So why should I believe a word you say, if you won't let me see the evidence?'

'You don't have to believe me. Believe Angie.'

Angelina glared at Calum. This mess was all his fault, and now he was shoving her right into the firing line. 'Calum, why don't you just show him?'

'Why should I? I'm not trying to convince him. I don't care if he believes me or not. I'm just warning him.'

'Sounds more like a threat than a warning to me,' Brad observed ominously. 'If some of these paintings are fakes, maybe you'd like to show me which ones.'

'I can't. That's the point. That's the way he planned it. I told you, he wanted to screw the market. He wanted his work to be art, not a commercial commodity.'

Brad flipped a dismissive hand. 'Artist always say things like that. They think it gives them aesthetic credibility. If they've been successful, it implies that the money's immaterial. If they're still struggling, it suggests they've had nobler goals than filthy lucre in mind all along.'

'Well, it looks like Malachy didn't just talk. It looks to me like he put his money where his mouth was.'

'You mean you're putting your father's money where your mouth is,' Brad amended. 'Mal is dead now, isn't he? He can't confirm or deny anything you say, and it doesn't matter to him anyway. But if any of these paintings are considered to be fraudulent, and if that reflects on the authenticity of some of his earlier works, and if the market for his work suffers as a consequence, it'll be your father who loses out.'

He paused, to lend weight to what he was saying. 'Why

don't you think about that for a while, before you start *warning* me with this story about some unbelievable plot that Mal is supposed to have cooked up? For a start, I can't believe he even knew how to turn on a computer, let alone keep a diary in electronic format.'

'I thought it was pretty unlikely myself,' Calum agreed. 'Angie says he liked to play with the colour tricks in the art software. He didn't even have a printer.'

'Then this particular diary isn't in his handwriting, is it? Anyone can type things on a computer.' The agent looked slowly, significantly, from Calum to Angelina. 'Anyone at all.'

Calum was still leaning against the table, his arms folded. His tone had been level enough, so far, but his body language told a different story. He was ready, wary, prepared to get physical. And Brad was pretty well accusing him of . . .

Angelina decided to respond to that before Calum could. 'If you're trying to suggest that Calum or me might have written that diary, Mr Welles, that's just plain crazy. Why ever would we do such a thing?'

'I have no idea.' Bradford paused. He went on staring at them with those stony little eyes. 'Doubtless some motive will appear in due course.'

Calum had made a complete hash of this, Angelina decided. First he told about the fakes – which he never should have done, if only because that was his father's business, not his. Then he got Brad Welles riled up and suspicious. Now it looked like nothing would be done about this whole affair, because Welles had decided it was some kind of crazy plot.

She took a deep breath, and made a stab at sorting out the mess. 'Listen, Mr Welles. Calum shouldn't have said all that, especially not without telling his dad. But you really cannot dismiss the diary. Malachy really did write all that, and I believe he did what he said he did, and you can't ignore it if you're meaning to sell these paintings. I mean, it just wouldn't be right for you to sell paintings that might not be Malachy's. I know he tried to fix it so that no-one could tell which was which, but maybe if we can find out who did the fakes for him . . .'

'Third-party corroboration, you mean.' The eyes were pinpoints now, not even pebbles. 'So the plot thickens.'

'There is no plot,' she said impatiently. 'At least, all the plotting was Malachy's. I know it was wrong of him, even though I see why he did it, but that doesn't change the fact that you'd be selling fakes. And you'd be in trouble, wouldn't you, if word got out about that diary, and other people believed it?'

His whole face turned to stone. 'Are you trying to black-mail me, young lady?'

She took a minute to take his meaning.

Calum got there faster. He unfolded his arms and straightened up and . . . the next thing Angelina knew, Brad was sprawled on the floor, quite a ways from where he had been standing. His glasses had gone flying in a different direction.

Without thought, she threw herself down on her knees in front of Brad. Between him and Calum. 'Mr Welles! Are you all right?'

Brad wasn't looking at her, he was looking at Calum. She had never seen anything like the terror in that grimace, but the fury that went with it was almost as scary. And something else had surfaced in his shocked, wildly rounded eyes. She couldn't have said exactly what it was, but she did know it wasn't what you would expect to see in a man who was looking at another man who had just knocked him down.

By the time those eyes flickered down to her, the expression had changed to plain anger. 'All right? No, I'm fucking furious. Call off your god-damned dog.'

If that was meant to make Calum madder, it succeeded spectacularly. Since Angelina was in the way of his rage, he shoved her aside, towards the bench. Towards the shotgun.

She grabbed the gun. She was shouting, but Calum

wasn't hearing. He was aiming a kick at Bradford Welles's ribs, and Welles was scrabbling on all fours to get out of the way. They were both yelling now, really terrible language. To add to the uproar, Charles started barking.

There was nothing to be done about dog fights but separate the dogs. She aimed the gun at the floor, released the catch, and pulled the trigger.

Everybody stopped everything.

They all stared at her. Even Charles. Then they stared at the hole in the floorboards. Anybody would have thought they'd never seen a shotgun blast before.

Into the silence she said, 'I've still got the other barrel.'

Calum started to laugh. 'OK, Angie, I surrender.' He held up his hands in movie fashion, still laughing.

Angelina took a deep breath. 'Come on over here, Calum. Lie down, Charles. Mr Welles, you're not hurt, are you?'

'Nothing broken, if that's what you mean.' Welles began to pull himself together, smoothing and resettling his hair, his suit, even his moustache, with shaky hands.

She rescued his glasses and gave them to him. He got to his feet, settled the glasses on his nose, and regarded her with a grim stare. 'Try to keep your dog under control, will you?'

She could feel Calum tensing for action. She nudged him gently with the shotgun barrel, to remind him of his manners.

She even found herself apologizing for him, as if her dog had just bitten the mailman. 'Calum didn't mean to do that, Mr Welles. I think he just thought you shouldn't have said what you said to me.'

'He could have used some verbal means of expressing his feelings.' Brad was looking Calum up and down, a coldly supercilious look. To mask the tail end of his fear, Angelina thought, and also that other thing. That odd reaction which she might have recognized if it hadn't been so out of place in the circumstances. 'He is capable of speech, isn't he?'

'Yeah, he is,' said Calum. 'Get the fuck out of here.'

'I can see no point in staying,' Brad said to Angelina, as if Calum hadn't spoken. 'I think maybe I'd better communicate directly with Gerard Hawke about these paintings, since he'll be making all the decisions.'

'That's a good idea.' Calum was looking down at his hands, turning them over, flexing them. 'He can decide what to do about the diary.' He gave Brad a glance that grew into a pointed stare. 'Didn't I tell you to fuck off?'

Angelina fluttered a reproachful hand at him, then went up to Brad and urged him politely towards the door.

'I'm sorry about all this hassle, Mr Welles. Maybe you should have warned us you were coming. You are OK, aren't you? Calum's going to phone his dad, and most likely his dad will be getting in touch with you. Have you got everything you came with? I'll see you out to your car.'

By the time she came back to the studio, Calum was nowhere in sight.

'Calum?'

'Yeah?'

The answer was coming from behind her, from the house. From the depths of the fridge, it sounded like. She tried to gauge his mood from the tone of his voice. He didn't sound mad, at any rate.

There was no point hollering at him about the whole fiasco. From one point of view, he had only been defending her honour, which was quite sweet of him.

'Calum, maybe you better phone your dad. If he'd known about the Untitled Women and the last diary, you could just have told Mr Welles to talk to him, and none of this would have happened.'

'You reckon?' The fridge slammed, and his voice came more distinctly. 'I didn't want to tell him until I'd had a chance to think it all over a little more. But yeah, you're right. Let's tell him now, why don't we? Let's see if he's any better than the rest of us at making sticky decisions.'

He emerged with a can of beer in his hand. He looked

barbaric, decked out like that with gold rings in improbable places. When he stepped within the influence of the westering sun, he turned gold all over. All over his tanned body, his faded khaki shorts, his tawny hair, even his hazel eyes.

When she saw him shining like that, the hair at the back of her neck started to rise.

As he came closer, she could feel that same effect, like a ripple of electric excitement, all the way down her spine. By the time he had reached her, the shock of his presence had reached her tailbone. It shivered itself right through into her belly, heating her up all over down there, starting up a pulse in her private parts.

She made her brain think cooling thoughts.

He's crazy. Crazy and violent.

She remembered him hitting Brad Welles. He had been standing right there, right where he was now, and suddenly just struck out and sent him flying. He was dangerous. Dangerously beautiful, dangerously sexy.

Those aren't cooling thoughts at all, she scolded herself. And then she understood what she had seen in Brad Welles's eyes, when Calum knocked him down.

That revelation surprised her so much, she was shocked. Not at the idea of a man desiring another man; that was what homosexuality was all about, after all. Nor at the knowledge that Brad had been sexually attracted to Calum; if she found Calum sexy and beautiful, why shouldn't other people?

No, it was something else. It was the awareness that Calum had unwittingly aroused Bradford's sexual interest by hitting him. Not by hurting him, it wasn't about that, exactly. It was something about that sudden display of physical violence and physical mastery. Something unutterably primitive.

She understood all of that far too clearly, and her own understanding shocked her still more.

Calum paused to probe the ragged hole in the floor with a bare toe. Not only was he not mad, he was actually laughing. 'Know what, Angie? That was the coolest thing I've ever seen.'

Cool. That struck her dumb. She couldn't do anything but stare.

And he couldn't help but notice. 'What's the matter? Did I leave my flies undone?'

If he had, it would have saved her the trouble of undoing him. She went down on her knees and did something she had never done before. Something she had read in the diaries. She touched her tongue to the tip of his cock.

She didn't have to do any more than that. He reached down and lifted her up, swung her on to the work bench, set her down on top of an Untitled Woman. He didn't take her boots off this time either, simply stripped off her panties and stuffed her with himself.

That was terrifyingly sexy. It made her feel like the drawing underneath her, just a single female body part. No prizes for guessing which one.

29

Half a dozen whores, three chapters and a plot outline later, Ged presented the promise of a novel to his agent.

Who came back to him three days later, always a good sign. People tended to put off giving bad news, so a quick response promised the contrary.

'About this new book. Quite a departure for you, isn't it?'

Was it only his conscience that made him imagine there might be a hidden agenda to that question? It was, after all, the obvious remark. 'Is that a problem?'

'No, no. Quite the contrary. A bid to broaden the readership can't be bad. Serial murderers are hot copy these days. And personally, I think it's brilliant.'

A pause. The *but* pause. 'This guy, he's basically a misogynist, isn't he? Out and out, I mean.'

That seemed a rather genteel way to describe a man who went about murdering women. 'You could say so,' Ged agreed. 'But he does get his come-uppance in the end.'

'So that's all right, then. I just wouldn't want anyone to misunderstand your personal point of view. You've done such a great job of getting inside his head, people might start to wonder. That is a compliment, by the way. But after all, the guy is an artist, and everybody knows they're flaky. It's part of the job description.'

Another pause, a considering one. Doing mental sums, as it turned out. 'Seriously, this book is brilliant. And a first-class commercial proposition: sex and violence, and everybody behaving badly. We should do very well out of it. I mean very, very well.'

On the strength of euphoria, Ged wrote several more chapters. Wrote like a lunatic, stopping only to eat, sleeping only when he literally couldn't keep his eyes open. He had not realized until now how much being unable to write was like suffering from impotence. Not that he ever had, but now he could see such parallels: the loss of that power, the deprivation of that pleasure, the absence of an activity so fundamental to one's sense of self.

Speaking of impotence, it was surely time to have another go at luring Elie back. Living on his own was the pits. Literally the pits, since he had neither inclination nor energy to do the most ordinary housekeeping routines. Elie had always kept the flat as neat and tidy as her own self. But now . . . If he had been able to afford the luxury of a cleaning lady, she would have been leaving him rude notes and threatening to hand in her notice.

But there was no use pretending that he only wanted Elie for her housekeeping abilities. Even if she had been as slobbish as . . . well, as he himself was, he would still have wanted her back. He was now in a position to make the comparison, and had decided that not having Elie in his life was even worse than not being able to write.

He went back to the glass and granite palace off Fleet Street where she had been working when last seen. Instead of asking for her at reception, he sat down on a stone bench by the fountain in the courtyard, where he could watch everybody going home at the end of the day.

Elie didn't come out.

But the security guard did. No sign had been posted about two hour parking limits, but apparently those were the rules, or something like that. 'Can I help you, sir? I noticed you've been here for some time.'

Ged said he was waiting for Elie Rae. Which was true, as far as it went.

'I don't know the lady, sir. I'll go and enquire at reception.'

The bad news was that she didn't work there any more. The good news was . . . well, there wasn't any good news.

He went back to the flat and phoned Valerie.

The good news turned out to be that Valerie had a phone number for Elie. 'She's flat-sharing with a friend, she says. But I have to say I haven't actually set eyes on her since the night you were here.'

'I suppose she's been busy,' Ged muttered, not knowing what else to say. I suppose she doesn't want to see you: there wasn't any point saying that.

He rang the number. A woman answered.

He asked for Elie. She called Elie.

Elie came to the phone and said, Hello?

He said, Elie? and she hung up.

He rang back.

The woman answered again. He asked for Elie again.

This time the woman asked who was calling.

He thought of lying. But there wasn't any point, because Elie would just hang up anyway as soon as she heard his voice. So he told her who was calling, and she said Elie didn't want to speak to him. And then she too hung up.

Along with that failure went all his elation about the book.

He was on his third whisky when the phone rang.

Not Elie. A bright female American voice, with her vowels squashed about as flat as they could go. 'Mr Gerard Hawke? I have Mr Welles calling for you.'

Mr Welles, who the hell was Mr Welles? He was kept in suspense for at least a minute, the unknown Welles evidently having money to burn on sending silence down transatlantic telephone wires.

Finally a man's voice, clipped, but kinder to the letter *a*. 'Brad Welles here. Your father's agent.'

Ged recalled him now. He also recalled that he hadn't heard from Calum for a while. Hadn't really even thought about him much, what with all that murder on his mind. 'I posted that agreement back to you, if that's what you're ringing about.'

'Yes, I received that, thank you. And thanks for putting your confidence in us. We'll do our best to get the best for you. And that's really what I'm calling about. I'm anxious to get those paintings to New York, where I can keep an eye on them. I'm very concerned about the idea of leaving them in that isolated house.'

'My son is there, isn't he? And that girl, the house-keeper.'

'Yes, but frankly, the sooner we get that work safely into storage, the happier I'll be. And you too, I'd imagine, since they're your property. I've already made arrangements to exhibit them in a major gallery in New York. That's to run in tandem with a retrospective at MOMA.' A pause for emphasis. 'That'll be a big, big deal, believe me.'

'Well, great. Brilliant. But what do you want from me?'

'I'd like your permission to get those canvases packed up and on their way.'

Ged tried to focus his alcohol-challenged brain on the situation. There was something slightly fishy about this. Why was Bradford Welles the Fifteenth ringing up out of the blue like this, to put pressure on him to hand over the paintings? What did Welles know that he didn't?

'That might be a good idea,' he allowed, 'but I can't do anything until I talk to Mr Deforte. I don't know what the current legal situation is with the will and the estate. Isn't there something called probate? And I'd better have a word with Calum, to see if he's finished clearing up the studio.'

'That's fine, talk to Rene. Let me know what he says.' Welles cleared his throat. 'You know, I got the impression that Calum is maybe a mite too young to be coping with all that responsibility. I don't think he has fully taken on board how serious this is. Those paintings really are very valuable, and very important in cultural terms, and I'm not sure how much that might have registered with him. You know kids – they can't really take anything seriously, can they?'

Calum was certainly about as unserious as kids came, but Ged didn't see any reason for saying so to this stranger. 'I'll talk to Deforte. And to Calum,' he repeated curtly. 'I'll get back to you.'

The smell of fish, or possibly even rat, was definite now.

He sat and nursed his whisky for a while, wondering exactly what was going on. It was, let's see, three o'clock or thereabouts in Oregon. He was debating whether to ring Deforte or Calum first, when the phone rang again to settle the question for him. Calum.

Not a very coherent Calum. 'Dad, listen. Something weird has come up. Several weird things, in fact. Angie and I think you'd better come out here and see for yourself.'

Angie and I. That sounded pretty matey. 'What exactly is the problem?'

'It's to do with the will. I mean, what Malachy wanted. That's what a will is, isn't it, what you want to happen after you're dead? We've had a few arguments, and, well, I'm not sure what to think.'

That frank admission of uncertainty didn't sound like Our Calum, but the vague explanations surely did. 'Could you possibly be more specific?'

'Not over the phone, I can't. You really need to see this for yourself.'

The last thing Ged wanted to do right now was traipse off to America. He had a novel to finish, at long long last. 'Why don't you ask that lawyer what he thinks? I haven't a clue what you're talking about.'

'I know, I know. Sorry I can't be clearer.' Calum took a deep breath that was audible even half a world away. 'Look, Dad, can you come out right away? I really would prefer it if you were here. The fact is, I don't know what to do.'

Calum saying he needed his father. Calum saying he

didn't know what to do. The world turned upside down, by Christ. The whole thing was undoubtedly some wild goose chase, but . . .

But Calum.

Ged didn't even know if he had enough credit on his cards to buy another air ticket. Some day soon, he was due to be bloody rich. Right now he was still dead broke.

'OK, kid. I'll come as soon as I can.'

It didn't seem right to be flying to the other side of the world without telling somebody he was going. There had to be some human being here in London who cared where he was, or wasn't.

He wouldn't be gone long enough to have to cancel his next night out with Rufus. His mother hardly seemed to know which planet she herself was on, let alone worry about the whereabouts of anyone else. Elie had just made it plain she didn't care if he went to America – or even Mars – and stayed there. And his agent would think he was daft if he rang up to say he was going away for a few days.

He finally used Calum as an excuse to tell Polly.

More precisely, he was using Calum as an excuse to speak to Polly in a context that did not include any recriminations about their last unfortunate meeting. Once they had had an occasion to talk about something else, to get past it, so to speak, then the whole fiasco could be forgotten, or at least ignored in future.

'Polly?' He nearly added *It's Ged*, before he recalled how that had pissed her off before. Not that she needed any excuse for being pissed off with him.

'Oh, Ged.' She sounded faintly flustered. Maybe she'd been expecting a call from someone else. Another man, he hoped. Somebody to take her mind off her troubles. Or at least to give her some different troubles to worry about, for a change. 'Um, how are you?'

'I'm OK. I just rang up to tell you that I'm flying back to America, to wind things up with this will business.

Calum says he's nearly finished sorting out, so he should be home again soon.'

'Oh. Good.' She paused. 'He sent me a postcard.'

'Good for him.'

'It's not like him, though. He's never ever sent me a postcard before. I hope he's all right.'

'I'm sure he's fine. It's likely the influence of Angelina.'

'Who is Angelina?'

'My father's housekeeper. A strong-minded young lady. I expect she has stern views on one's social obligation to send postcards to one's mother.'

'Are you telling me Calum actually has a real girlfriend?'

He hadn't meant to imply any such thing. Angelina seemed the type to regard the reformation of rakes and layabouts as part of her job, but he had no reason to suppose she would get personal about it. She certainly hadn't struck him as likely cannon fodder for Calum's bed.

He backtracked rapidly. 'Polly, I was only joking about the postcard. I don't know anything about his relationship with Angelina. Except that when I spoke to him last night, he made some reference to "Angie and I". You know the way people do.'

'Yeah, I know. I know what you mean. I just wonder what he meant.'

She paused and gave a little cough and said Um again. He had just opened his mouth to say something that would allow him to hang up, when she blurted out, 'Ged, listen. You've got to talk to Lulu.'

He hadn't talked to Louise for three years. She had run out of the room, the last time he saw her. She had refused to speak to him, the last time he phoned her. Three years ago. 'What do you mean, talk to Lulu? I thought she didn't want to talk to me.'

'Maybe she will now. You might have gained some absentee glamour. I'm just her boring old mother who doesn't understand.'

The words came tumbling out faster, the more she said.

And she was saying more than she meant to. 'I've always been understanding with her, haven't I? I've always tried to talk things over with her. I've never been judgemental or heavy-handed. I didn't nag her about schoolwork, or try to discourage her from going out with unsuitable boys. I think I've been exactly the sort of mother I'd have liked to have. It's not as if I've ever given her any reason for treating me like this.'

'Like what?'

'Going off like that. As if I was some kind of ogre she couldn't be expected to put up with. I didn't even yell at her when she said she wasn't going back to school to do her A-levels. It's not like the old days, is it? When you had to get everything right at the right time, or you'd lost your chance for ever. Nowadays kids can decide to take a year out, and then go on to a sixth-form college. So I just said, OK, you take the time and space to think about what you want to do, there's no point jumping into something if you think it's not right for you. Mothers can't get much more understanding than that, can they?'

'That sounds wonderfully understanding, Polly. I don't understand what the problem is.'

'I told you. She's gone off.'

A big fat sob came down the telephone line. His heart sank. Polly hysterical was a Polly he had seldom seen. Even the idea unnerved him.

'She's moved out,' she managed to explain through her tears. 'She said she's sixteen and old enough to live her own life, and there's nothing I can do about it. And there isn't, is there?'

'What do you mean, she's moved out? Where the hell's she gone?'

Polly was sobbing intermittently now, less comprehensible than ever. 'A squat, I think. With Hezekiah. She thinks it's ecological and anti-capitalist and communitarian and all that. I suppose it is, but I think she's too young. If she'd finished school, I wouldn't mind. But I

393

don't know what to do about it. When I tried to talk her out of it, she called me a hypocrite and stormed out, and she hasn't been back here since then.'

Ged didn't know what to do about it either. If Polly, the social worker, the big expert on delinquent teenagers, didn't know what to do when her own daughter began to behave like one of her bloody stupid clients, then how the hell did she expect him to sort things out?

Right now he was more concerned to get Polly to stop crying. 'OK, Polly, listen. Listen, Polly.' He repeated that patiently, waiting until the sobs had subsided to snivels. 'It's just a phase she's going through. With kids it's always one damn phase after another, you know that. Besides, I wasn't a lot older than her when I was hitch-hiking around the world.'

'But you're a man!'

She must have been truly distraught if she could utter such heresy. 'I thought you said this Hezekiah person was a sweet boy. That's what you told me, isn't it?'

'Yes, I suppose he is, but he's also quite a bit older than her. And he's . . . his background . . . it's a street culture, I mean, very peer-group oriented, and they pick up unfortunate attitudes . . .' She floundered into silence. Self-censorship seemed to be making it difficult for her to think, let alone communicate.

'Spit it out, Polly. What is the problem?'

She couldn't say it out loud, she had to whisper. 'Drugs.'

He nearly said Oh Christ, before he remembered that he was supposed to be cheering her up. He didn't think it would cheer her much to remind her that the first time they met, at a party, they had both been stoned. She might even think that was a clinching argument against chemically altered states of consciousness.

There was nothing left but to promise to do whatever it was she wanted him to do.

'OK, Polly. I don't know what the hell to do about all

this either, you know. You always tell me I've been a rotten father, and I can't really argue with you about that. But if you're sure you want me to, I'll try to have a chat with her when I get back from America.'

Assuming Louise would speak to him, of course.

30

The heat of the Willamette valley was not much diminished, though the year had moved on towards the end of September. The skirts of the coastal mountains still wore their cool flounce of sea fog. And the trail around the mountain up to Malachy's house had not grown any less steep.

But Calum, when he came out to greet his father, was a good deal browner. And a lot less hostile. He seemed honestly glad to see Ged.

Maybe Polly could solve her problem by packing Louise off to the coast of Oregon for a month or two.

Her problem. Ged felt guilty for thinking like that. It was his problem too. Louise was his child as much as Polly's. More his child, in a way; Polly and Louise had never been soul mates, whereas he had always regarded his daughter as the child who 'took after' him. But she wasn't around him now, so he didn't have much occasion to think about her. And at the moment, he had more things on his mind than his daughter's adolescent rebellion.

'Why didn't you want me to bring Rene Deforte along?' he asked Calum. 'He's the legal expert, not me.'

'Because I'm not sure if this is a legal problem.'

'Interpreting the will, you said.'

'*His* will, I meant. Malachy's. What he wanted you to do.'

Ged felt the familiar prickle of irritation at Calum's chronic vagueness and apparent inability to make himself understood. 'It was clear enough, wasn't it? I get the house and the paintings, in return for doling out the cash to everyone else.'

'Yeah, but I think—' Calum glanced at Angelina and corrected himself. 'We think he had a very particular reason for setting things up that way.'

Ged noticed that glance, and the *we*. But it was none of his business now, what Calum at nineteen got up to. Even with his grandfather's mistress.

'Show him the other stuff first, Calum,' Angelina urged. 'The notebooks and the pictures. Then we can show him you-know-what.'

She opened a drawer in the desk and brought out a stack of plain brown notebooks, just like the one he had at home. Each one with a date written on the cover.

'They're all here,' she assured Ged, setting them down on the desktop and giving them a proprietary pat. 'I checked them every night after George went home, just in case the temptation got to be too much for him. But everything was always here.' She gave Calum a mysterious look, mysterious to Ged at least. 'I guess Calum put the fear of God into him.'

Ged picked up the first one, *1957*. The second one, that was; he had the first one back in London. He skipped through the brief entries, not for the moment trying to make sense of items like 'Untitled Woman Number 6'.

At a longer entry, he paused. It turned out to be a detailed account of Malachy's seduction of one of his models. Calum had mentioned this peculiarity of the diaries. Ged noted that though the description was fairly frank, it hadn't quite the same brutal and unrelenting physical realism of the entries in the very first diary. And it seemed to be simply sex that Malachy was in search of here, rather than a culturally significant corpse.

Angelina was hovering at his elbow. 'Can I get you some coffee? Or would you rather have a beer?'

Looking up from the diary, Ged glanced through the open patio doors. They framed a fine view of the setting sun, engaged at this very moment in going down with all hands into the sea. The room was filled with solar splendour, setting afire the flesh of everyone it touched. Turning them all into angels. Making them shine with the glory of the Lord.

He had to close his eyes for a moment against that unendurable brightness.

When next he dared to look at the world again, the sun and the sunlight had vanished. They were all mortal once more.

And Angelina was still hovering, still waiting to hear his preference in the matter of refreshment.

'Any chance of a glass of red wine?'

'Sure thing. Calum, can you come and uncork it for me?'

When the two of them had disappeared into the kitchen, Ged set the notebook down and stepped out on to the deck. That great ungainly monster of a dog was in possession of the hammock, but he had no plans for disturbing it.

He leaned over the railing, looking up to heaven and down to the sea. In the wake of the sun's departure, the entire world, air and water both, had melded into a single colour: a pale breathless blue, luminous, numinous. It made his flesh glow, more subtly than sunlight.

The colour of the air was not merely a matter of surroundings, he realized. He was breathing it through his nose, drawing it in through his eyes. It wasn't just *out there*, it was *in here*. The marches of his mortal solitude had been dissolved by this radiant mist, in which he momentarily lived and moved and had his being.

It dawned on him that he knew nothing about the world. Nothing about creation and its creatures. Nothing about himself, or anyone else. Out of the boundless possibilities of infancy he had made an ignorant island, blind and deaf and senseless.

After what seemed an eternity and the wink of an eye, he became aware that Angelina was standing beside him, watching him, with a glass of wine in her hand. He had no idea how long she had been standing there. He seemed to have just returned from the far side of the sun.

He straightened himself, made an effort to bring his head back to where his body was. 'Sorry, Angie, I didn't see you.'

'Are you OK?'

'I'm fine. I was just . . .'

She set his glass of wine on the railing at his elbow. She leaned out companionably alongside him, gazing into the unattainable kingdom of twilight. 'Admiring the evening?'

He took the glass in hand, but not yet to drink. He had an obscurely compelling need to acknowledge, even to himself, what he had just experienced. 'I was just thinking how, living in the city, one forgets what the world really is.'

She turned to look at him. Her eyes held the same pale glory as the sky, but bound and bounded by the delicate dark structure of pupil and iris. 'What is the world really?'

He held the wine out towards the evening. 'Immensity. Astonishment.'

That was true, and yet the kind of thing some poetasting con man might say. He took it back at once. 'But you see this every day. It must seem ordinary to you.'

'Ordinary just means normal and natural. Why shouldn't it grab you by the throat every day of your life, if that's what it's meant to do? We need to be jolted out of our selfishness.' After a pause she confessed, 'I've never lived in a city.'

'They're full of people,' Ged explained dryly. 'So many people that you forget anything else exists.'

'That's the way we're made, I guess. Like dogs wanting to be with other dogs.'

Calum came out on to the deck. He came up behind Angelina, and set a hand to the railing on either side of her.

He wasn't touching her. It needn't have meant anything. Only it did, of course, because it was deliberate. Deliberately staking out his territory. For Angelina's benefit, or his father's? Or maybe just normal masculine behaviour, letting the world in general know that she was his woman.

But where Calum was concerned, there was nothing unremarkable about it. Up until now, he had treated women like tins of beer, to be consumed and discarded. Commitment had been a long word, the length of one night.

He bent over to speak into Angelina's ear. 'Shall we show him the Untitled Women right away, or wait till after dinner?'

She made a face. 'It might put him off his dinner, if he looks at them now.'

'I think his stomach is strong enough to cope.' He moved away from her, towards the studio. 'Dad? Do you want to see them?'

Ged was ready to look at anything that would make sense out of Calum's plea for assistance. He followed his son into the studio and over to the work bench, still unable to imagine what sort of thing he was about to be confronted with.

When he saw the grotesque scenes of butchery, his mind froze.

He's basically a misogynist, isn't he? Out and out, I mean.

Misogyny and murder. Obsession and confession. These drawings and that notebook.

His father's legacy.

He must have stood still too long. He heard Angelina say rather timidly, 'They're only pictures.'

Were they?

It was clear from the notebooks that Malachy had been producing these Untitled Women throughout his career. He had never shown them to anyone, as far as Ged knew; certainly no-one had ever mentioned their existence. A secret obsession, a secret enterprise. Like Turner frantically painting his dreamscapes, abstracted explosions of colour that would have shocked his fellow Academicians. But these works were far more shocking, and for different reasons.

Malachy must have known that. Even if there was no art to find the mind's construction in the face, it was not impossible to find his mind's construction in his art.

And he had known he was dying, had time to prepare. But he hadn't destroyed these witnesses to – what? Callousness? Depravity? Malevolence? Maybe even murder. Drawing from the life. Or the death.

Instead, he had left them to his son. His unknown, once-met son.

Ged made himself move. He reached for the pile of paper, pulled the top one down to look at it. Then the next. And the next. He recalled all the women he had paid to fuck, and the women he had murdered in his mind. He had thought of them in much this manner, not as living creatures but as pieces of sexual flesh, breasts and buttocks and hips and thighs, female meat he was buying for his own use. How great a step from that to this?

Calum and Angelina watched him turn over the papers, Calum with lively interest, Angelina more anxiously. He had to remind himself that they knew nothing: neither what was in that first notebook, nor what was in his own head.

'What do you think?' Calum wanted to know. 'Was he crazy, or what?'

The very thing Ged was asking himself right now, just as he had when reading the *1952* diary. *After all, the guy is an artist, and everybody knows they're flaky. It's part of the job description.*

What did it mean to be mad? People were decreed to be insane if they murdered someone because a voice in their head had told them to, but not if they did it because their wife had told them to. You were expected to understand that murder was wrong, even if someone else said it was all right. But that didn't seem to hold if the someone was a disembodied voice. Of course most people didn't hear voices in their head. Maybe madness was simply a way of describing motives that were incomprehensible to most people.

Ged shrugged. 'He was an artist.'

'So what does that mean?' Calum demanded. 'Artists are sadists? Artists are Martians?'

'It means they have a powerful imagination.' Ged said it slowly, explaining himself as much as his father. 'You could even say they're dominated by their imagination. Obsessed by the need to find some means of expressing it.'

Angelina wasn't having any of this artistic licence nonsense. 'Why couldn't he imagine something nicer? When I was a little kid and had nightmares, my grandma always told me to think about birds and flowers.'

Calum gave her a sardonic glance. 'And did that help?'

'Most of the time. What I mean is, just because it's in your head doesn't mean you have to find a way to put it out there for everyone to see.'

'But art is only an act of the imagination. It doesn't hurt anyone. At least . . .' Remembering 1952, Ged corrected himself. If art moved into life, and life itself became an art form, then any bloody thing was possible. 'You said yourself, Angie, that these are only pictures. Images of ideas. The ideas might be nasty, but they're only pieces of paper.'

'They could still hurt someone, if they put those ideas into someone else's head. Someone who otherwise maybe would never have gotten around to thinking them up.'

'They might give other people nightmares, you mean?'

'Yeah, sure but . . .' She surveyed the obese body parts, the litter of dismembered female corpses. 'For some of those other people, maybe it won't be a nightmare. Maybe it'll be . . . exciting.'

31

After dinner they showed him the last diary. The secret will, as Calum kept calling it. The key passages didn't take long to read.

It took a little while longer to sort out their implications.

'Now let me try to get this straight,' Ged found himself repeating. 'Some of those paintings in the studio, and some other paintings that have already been sold, were actually painted by somebody else, acting on instructions from Malachy. Is that right?'

Calum and Angelina both nodded vigorous agreement.

'But some of the same group of paintings are copies that Malachy made of the paintings that this somebody else, or somebody elses, had done in his style. Is that right too?'

Again they nodded. They had had several days to work all this out.

'And the fact that two paintings may appear to be identical is no proof that one of them is really by somebody else, because he was also in the habit of making copies of his own paintings. Right?'

Another nod. Two nods, that was, one from each of them.

'And in any case, some of the non-Hawke paintings never had any copies made.'

Ged didn't ask for confirmation this time, but they gave it all the same.

Up to that point he had kept his cigarettes out of sight

and out of light, but now he needed something to help him think. He went out on to the deck and lit up out there in the darkness.

He thought of his surroundings as darkness, but the sky was full of stars. Improbably full. Infinitesimal points of light kept popping out of blackness even while he stood and stared, as if he had willed them into existence.

Calum and Angelina came out. Calum leaned back against the wooden rail near his father. He wasn't wearing the lip ring, Ged noticed. Maybe he had given up on it. One small step towards civilization.

'Dad? What do you think?'

'Brad Welles knows all about this, doesn't he? Those pictures, and the faking?'

Calum's face split into a grin. 'Did he ring you up? He said he was going to.'

'He did ring me, but I couldn't quite make out why.'

'What did he say?'

'He claimed to be concerned about security. Said he thought you weren't taking things seriously enough. How did he find out about the diaries?'

'It was an accident,' Angelina explained, with suspicious haste. 'He turned up without any warning, when we were in the middle of sorting out the Untitled Women, and it sort of flustered us, and somebody accidentally let that slip out.'

Somebody being Calum, of course. If Angelina had been the guilty party, she would have said so at once. 'What did he think about it?'

'He didn't believe it.' She paused, then added carefully, 'He was convinced it was a hoax.'

'Maybe it is a hoax. There's nothing to prove that everything Malachy put into those diaries is gospel truth.' And Ged had good reason to hope that some things at least were not.

'But he talks about the faking several times. Seems like he was obsessed by it. And he's very particular about exactly what he did. Besides, why would anyone lie to their own diary?'

'Because he expected someone else to read it, I suppose.'

'Everything else is true, though. The Untitled Women, the Untitled Children, all the paintings he mentions. And if the fakes are real – real fakes, I mean – then someone else knows it. The person who did them.'

'Any idea who that might be?'

Ged had asked out of idle curiosity, because Angelina was as likely as anyone to be able to hazard a reasonable guess. But he was intrigued by the oddly formal phrasing of her reply. 'I wouldn't really like to say.'

'Oh, come on, Angie,' Calum urged. 'You can trust us with your deep dark secret.'

'I really would not like to say,' she insisted, looking more and more uncomfortable. 'I couldn't prove anything, could I? All I can tell you is, it wasn't me. I was always hopeless at art.'

Calum couldn't resist speculation. 'So let's see, it had to be someone artistic, someone with a good motive for keeping their mouth shut . . .'

'Or someone who was unlikely to hear about any resulting controversy.'

Calum wasn't very good at keeping his own mouth shut, not at least when seized by surprise. Jaw ajar, he stared at his father. 'Why'd you say that?'

'It just occurred to me. They might be dead, for instance, or living in another country. Or they might be like Melly.'

'Two coupons short of a pop-up toaster, you mean.'

'I only mean your grandmother never reads the papers.' Ged smoked and thought, and listened with half an ear to the world around him: the monotonous sounds of waves and wind and tide, the irregular noises of living creatures in pursuit of life. 'I take it that Rene Deforte knows nothing about this.'

'I wouldn't have told him,' Calum said indignantly, 'not before talking to you. Absolutely not. I mean, he's a lawyer. Once he knew, he couldn't just forget about it, could he? He'd have to tell.'

A touching belief in the incorruptibility of the legal profession, Ged thought. Maybe Calum wasn't quite as knowing and cynical as he made out. 'How about that odd boy with the motorbike? Jesús.'

'George,' Angelina amended firmly. 'No, he doesn't know. We weren't going to say anything to anyone, because it's your business really, isn't it? Mr Welles only found out by accident, like I said.'

'Jorge is the expert on Malachy's art, isn't he? It might not be a bad idea to find out what he thinks.' Ged finished his cigarette, dropped the stub and crushed it underfoot. 'Let's go back inside. It's getting cold out here.'

As soon as they had settled themselves by the fire, the cats came crowding round, demanding attention. Calum and Angelina each ended up with a lap full of fur. A substantial marmalade tom took up residence on Calum, while Angelina had the luxury of two cats, a delicate long-haired tabby with cream-coloured stockings and extravagant ear tufts, and a fluffy little oatmeal-flavoured kitten.

Seeing Angelina encumbered with cats, Ged poured a glass of duty-free whisky for himself and Calum. Then he invited them to inform him of their thoughts on the matter of the fakery. The Untitled Women didn't call for thought; they had their existence on some deeper, more visceral plane.

Calum and Angelina were happy to oblige. They were both convinced that the diary was not a hoax, and that the fakes were, as Angelina had put it, real. But that was the only way in which they agreed.

Angelina thought the truth was the only important consideration, even if nobody knew exactly what the truth was. Anybody who wanted to buy one of the paintings was entitled to know whatever there was to know, that was her line.

Calum wasn't bothered about truth as the ultimate virtue. He was concerned to carry out Malachy's intentions, whatever they might have been. The punters were only entitled to know whatever Malachy had meant them to know. Calum just hadn't decided what that was.

There was something to be said for each of these viewpoints. But the say-nothing school had an advantage over the tell-all advocates, in that nobody knew what was genuine and what was not, including the diary itself. Ged pointed this out.

'So what?' Angelina retorted 'It's like religion, isn't it? You can say, the Church knows everything and this is what you're supposed to think. Or you can say, Well, this is as much as we know, and this is how we know it, but you'll have to make up your own mind about it, and take the consequences.'

'Angie,' said Calum, surprisingly gently, 'I don't think that's the point here. We're not discussing God and the universe and everything. My father isn't even a free agent. He's supposed to be executing his father's will. So the real question is this one: did old Mal want us to tell everybody what he'd done, or not? That's all we've got to decide.'

Angelina was not in the least intimidated by this intellectual approach. 'Well, he might have wanted your dad to go out and murder someone. Does that mean we should carry out his last wishes?'

'That's just crazy,' Calum told her. 'But I get your point. Maybe what we've really got to decide is whether what he was trying to do is OK or not. Is it OK to deceive people, and even defraud them, if you're doing it because they're buying and selling what shouldn't be bought and sold?'

'You mean it's immoral for people to buy and sell paintings?'

'No, but it's really his name they're trading in. Look, let's say you and your sister are being sold off as slaves. Let's say the auctioneer says the girl on the right is Angelina and the one on the left is Jane, but really it's the other way round. The people who buy you can see what they're buying. Have they got any right to complain, if they discover they've bought Jane instead of Angelina?'

'They have no right to buy either of us,' she said stonily.

'Well, OK, what if they were selling off portraits of you two? What if they mislabelled the pictures? Nobody knows who you are, or who Jane is, so they would be buying the pictures because they liked them. What cause would they have for complaint if years afterwards someone says, That's not Jane, it's Angelina?'

'But what if a picture of Jane turned out to be worth a lot more than a picture of Angelina?'

'Why would it be?'

'Maybe Jane was more famous than Angelina. Or better looking.'

'She couldn't be,' said Calum, laughing. 'Let's suppose they're both pictures of Angelina, painted by two different artists. Suppose they're both sold simply as pictures of Angelina. What's the problem then?'

'People have a right to know who the artist is. Or at least not to be lied to about it.'

They would happily have carried on like this all night, but for Ged the night was already eight hours too long, with an ocean and a continent in between where he was now and where his body thought it was. He dragged himself back from the brink of unconsciousness, tried to make his eyes focus. 'Sorry to interrupt the ethics class, but I'm in desperate need of a bed.'

Angelina jumped up, scattering cats. 'Gee, of course you are. It must be the middle of the night back in England.'

'Worse than that. It's already morning.' He stood up, more slowly than Angelina. His body was stiff, after all those hours on a plane, in a car. Bone-weary, creaking in an alarming way. An elderly way.

At forty-four he was starting to fall apart. Couldn't even stay up all night any more. He headed for the hallway, feeling more decrepit with each step.

Angelina followed him. 'I've put you in Malachy's room again. You know, the door on the right.'

He paused to ask something that was none of his business. 'Where does Calum sleep?'

She blushed. She really did. He hadn't seen a girl do that since he was a child. Maybe she was only the victim of her fair skin, exposed to his stare without any saving veil of cosmetics. But she met his look head-on, with those marvellously clear, light-and-dark eyes. 'I couldn't say for sure where he'll be sleeping tonight.'

Meaning, he supposed, that she wasn't sure whether, with his old man around, Calum would opt for propriety or frankness. Which showed how much she knew about Calum. A young man who had been in the habit of screwing strangers under his parents' roof was hardly likely to worry about upsetting his father by sleeping openly with his grandfather's mistress.

Or was she? Leaving the sex and the age difference out of it, he couldn't see her posing for one of those macabre paintings in the chest. She was too good to be one of Malachy's anonymous victims, he thought. He touched the door to Malachy's room. 'Did you ever sleep in here?'

'No, never.' This time she didn't blush. 'It never occurred to me people might think that, until Calum said . . . well, never mind what Calum said. When I took this job, my grandma told Malachy she'd come around with a shotgun if he even thought about seducing me. She didn't know about all his women, of course, but she claimed that the nobles back in Poland had had a terrible habit of raping their maids.'

'And what did Malachy say to that?'

'Well, he didn't have to say anything. I had to translate for her, so I changed it a little. I told him she said she could see that he was an honourable man who would treat me fair and square.' She looked more regretful than disapproving. 'Maybe I'm the only woman he ever did treat like that.'

*   *   *

The moon was up, and past its prime.

Through the uncurtained window, Ged could make out its bulging outline, neither wedge nor round of cheese. With no man-made competition, even a gibbous moon could drown the darkness in chilly light. It might have been the moon that wakened him.

Malachy liked moonlight, Angelina had said.

That made his father sound improbably romantic. What was there about the moon or its shining that Malachy could have cared for?

For one thing, he realized, looking around the room, it gave objects form without colour. The bold outlines on the Navaho rugs were plainly visible, but showed no sign of the vivid reds and deep-toned yellows that formed those patterns. The squares of remnants and rags that made up his quilt had to compose themselves in shades of grey, instead of every dye imaginable. Was moonlight the only light with this peculiar property? How odd that a painter so famous for his colours should take a fancy to a world without them.

And then, as if he were suddenly looking at the same things through some very different eyes, he understood what his father must have seen.

It was as if he were inside one of Malachy's paintings. When all the world was one colour – whether that colour was grey, or red or yellow or blue – then there could be nothing but shape and form to see. Shapes given form by shadow and light, rather than line or hue.

What Malachy had been doing was using colour to nullify colour.

1971

Once I had the idea I could catch moments, the way I capture things on canvas.

I used to try for the significant moment, the still point, the action outside time, without before and after. I didn't want to sleepwalk my way through life, everything gone as soon as it's here, a future and a past but no present.

I wanted to pin down the present.

Well, it doesn't work like that. We ain't things. We're alive, and we move around. It's the movement that matters.

Because when we stop moving, we're dead.

32

There was an element of lotus-eating about this place. Nothing had urgency, nothing seemed to matter one day more or one day less. Nothing much to do but go for a swim, or doze in the hammock, or maybe take the dog for a walk around the mountain, through forests several hundred feet high. As for cooking and cleaning and boring necessities like that, Angelina did them with such casual competence that they appeared, at least to the onlooker, no chore at all.

Having eaten an excellent breakfast – odd how people who never ate breakfast were happy to do so when someone else was preparing it, and they had leisure to enjoy it – Ged took his coffee out on to the deck, where the still-summery heat of the late September sun was tempered by a seaworthy wind.

The sky this morning was innocently ordinary, betraying no hint of the shining infinities it had shown him last night. Today there were not even clouds to give depth and perspective to heaven; it was simply a flat blue canvas, the sort that had led the ancients to imagine it might be the inside of a dome. Off to the west of the canvas, far out over the sea, someone had painted in the ashes of the moon.

The sounds of this world were rhythmic, the lungs and heart of the earth: rush and recession of waves, gust and gasp of wind. Or the staccato rattle of a woodpecker drilling for his breakfast; the chatter of an angry blue jay; the blissful snores of Charles from under the shade of the hammock.

Another repeated sound was harder to identify. There was wood in it somewhere. Possibly the world's champion batter hitting an endless succession of cricket balls. But this was America, where they had scarcely heard of cricket. Baseball, maybe.

Angelina came out. He asked her about it. She solved the mystery, and set up another one. 'That's Calum chopping wood.'

'*Calum* is chopping wood?'

'Well, firewood doesn't grow on trees, you know.'

Her wide, luminous eyes watched him with a flicker of amusement. She had all the traditional American virtues – frankness, plain dealing, ingenuity, enterprise, and energy – and now he found she was witty as well as wise.

He was amused enough to smile. 'I know where firewood comes from, but as you've just observed, it involves hard work. Work and Calum don't usually get on together.'

She shrugged, with something between a grimace and a smile. 'Everybody works if they have to. If he doesn't chop firewood, we won't have a fire.'

So much for lotus-eating. 'And what should I be doing to earn my keep?'

'Nothing. You're paying *my* keep, aren't you? I'm not doing anything around here that Calum couldn't do for himself.'

'He certainly couldn't have cooked a breakfast like the one I just ate. Not to mention the dinner last night.' Dinner had been simple but delicious: freshly caught crab, accompanied by a cream sauce delicately flavoured with juniper, and new potatoes roasted with white wine and sprigs of rosemary.

Again the glimmer of a smile in her eyes. 'I didn't say he'd do it as well as I do.'

Ged was beginning to think this girl was much too good

413

for his son. But maybe she already knew that. 'Do you fancy him?'

'I'm in love with him, if that's what you mean.'

She said it so . . . not flatly, there was obviously nothing flat about her feelings towards Calum, just the opposite . . . so frankly, that was it, so simply, that he hardly knew how to respond. How to warn her about Calum's attitude towards relationships. 'Are you sure that's wise?'

She shook her head. 'I should think it's pretty foolish.' With a touch of wistfulness she added, 'But it sure is exciting.'

'I thought you said you didn't go in for excitement.'

'I didn't use to. It leads to trouble more often than not. And Calum's no exception.'

'That didn't warn you off him?'

'Well, he likes excitement. It must be catching. Besides,' she added, 'some might think that he'd have been warned off me, what with my having been a nun. Well, almost a nun.'

'What's wrong with being a nun?'

'Nothing's *wrong* with it. It's just that nobody can understand why anyone would want to do it. You can do just about anything nowadays, except give up sex.'

'But you were willing to do it.'

'It seemed like the least part of it, at the time. Why can't women learn to live without men? And I didn't know any man I'd've wanted to marry, or even any man that made me think I might ever want to marry. In the end, what I couldn't take was them wanting me to hand over my soul.'

The Faustian implications of this statement puzzled Ged. 'I thought nuns were the brides of Christ. You make it sound like a pact with the Devil.'

She lowered her voice. To prevent the wind or the woodpecker from hearing her heresy, perhaps, since there was nobody else in sight. 'That's what it is, in a way. Funny how things get turned right around. They say you have to do what the Church says, and believe what it tells you to believe, or else you'll go to Hell. Now how can that

414

be right? We're all of us born with our own soul to save, and you can't do that by taking orders. You have to do it on your own.'

'But if everybody makes up their own mind about morality, how do they know they've guessed right about right? It's easy to justify almost anything, at least to yourself.'

'It's not a question of guessing and justifying, not if your salvation depends on it. You can fool yourself, but you can't fool God. You've got to have a right heart.'

She gave him one of those pure and penetrating glances that he found so disconcerting. It was easy to imagine – to fear – that those lucid eyes could see too clearly all that was not right in his own heart. But instead of denouncing his sins, she said, 'Are you going to talk to Rene Deforte about those fake paintings?'

'I think I've got to. Don't you?'

'I do, yeah. Lawyers have to keep things confidential, don't they? Like priests?'

'Only for their clients, I think.'

'Well, Malachy was his client, and it's Malachy's diary we're asking about. But you'll have to see him anyway, to hand over all the bank statements and savings books and such like that we found. That's what goes to all the rest of his sons, isn't it? We've got a box full of them. There weren't any stocks or shares. That sort of thing was too capitalist for him, seemingly. Which reminds me, did Calum tell you about that Sheila?'

'Sheila who?'

'Some kind of cousin of Malachy's. She turned up here and . . . well, I guess Calum ought to tell you himself.'

Now why did this Sheila woman strike a chord somewhere in his brain? It was the thought of Rene Deforte that made him remember, in the end. She was the only woman mentioned in Malachy's will.

Jesús Jorge arrived before Deforte. He was sporting what Ged presumed was meant to be a beard, though it looked more as if the trimmings from his moustache had somehow stuck to his cheeks and chin.

'Great to see you again,' he greeted Ged warmly, and apparently sincerely. 'We've been having a good time here, winkling out Mal's little secrets. Did they show you all those women?'

'The paintings, you mean? Yes, I've seen them.'

Jorge bounced up and down on his booted toes, unable to restrain his enthusiasm. 'Brilliant stuff, eh?'

'I'm not an art critic, but I found them extremely disturbing.' A calculated understatement, to say the least. In the context of the first diary, Ged had found them the stuff of nightmares. Very personal nightmares. 'Which doesn't prevent them from being brilliant, of course.'

'Course not. Just the opposite. Another fortune for you there, I reckon.'

'So Bradford Welles appeared to think.'

'Yeah, Angie said he was here the other day. Seems like he had some sort of set-to with Cal. Angie said she hoped he wasn't going to sue.'

Ged decided he didn't want to know what that was about. 'He won't do anything like that. Not if he wants the chance to earn any commission from those paintings.'

'That's the spirit. Don't take any shit. Listen, you remember that book I told you I was writing? Have you had any more thoughts about that? When these diaries started turning up, I thought maybe . . .'

Angelina had warned that Jorge already knew about the notebooks and their approximate contents, except for the last one. But he hadn't been allowed to read them.

'Because they're your property,' she explained to Ged. 'And I know he's trying to dig some dirt for that book he's writing. So don't give him anything for free. You could sell those diaries for a lot of money, if you wanted to. I don't think you should, because Malachy was your dad and it's not right to be selling your own father's secrets. I'm just saying you could if you wanted to.'

Ged had been touched by this ingenuous advice. He

didn't bother explaining in return that he was already in the process of selling his father's secrets, only passing them off as his own.

'Speaking of diaries,' he deflected Jorge gently, 'Calum has something to show you. I want you to read it, and tell me what you think.'

Jorge was agog. He could hardly sit still long enough to read the diary. The problem was that Calum wanted him to direct his attention to the bits dealing with the making of the fakes, and Jorge wanted to read the whole damn thing.

'Just do what Calum says and get on with it, George,' Angelina instructed him briskly. 'Rene will be here soon and he has to read it too.'

Jorge peered at the small screen. 'Why didn't you print it out?'

'Because Malachy didn't have a printer.'

'I didn't even know he could type.' He pressed the Page Down button. 'Couldn't spell worth a damn, either.'

'They're probably typos,' Angelina suggested, defending Malachy to the end.

'It's OK, Angie, I wasn't trying to put him down. He never claimed to be an educated man. What would he need an education for, anyway? A Ph.D. wouldn't have helped him to paint any better.'

'Read, George. Never mind philosophizing.'

Jorge read. What he read obviously agitated him. 'This is crazy,' he muttered. And then, 'This is brilliant.'

'But is it real?' Ged wanted to know.

'Is what real?'

'Did he do what he says he did? Brad Welles professed not to believe a word of it.'

'You want to know if he made this stuff up?' Jorge tipped his chair away from the desk and the computer, and linked his hands behind his head, but he kept his eyes on the screen. 'No, I don't think so. It's all of a piece with other things he did. For instance, he'd been making copies of his own work for years, and he didn't make any secret of that. Just the opposite – he made a big deal about it. He was doing it deliberately, to try to diminish the commercial value of his paintings, to take them out of the commercial bear pit.'

'But, George,' Angelina protested, 'there's a big difference between copying your own paintings, and copying other people's paintings. Or getting other people to copy your paintings.'

'Look, Angie, if he did the copies, then they're his paintings, no matter who he was copying. If he was copying somebody else, then the result is a Hawke original. Artists rip each other off all the time. That's what the history of art is all about. Course, they don't call it copying. They call it homage, or referencing, or "in the style of" or "after": that kind of thing. The most frequently imitated artists are the most important ones, in historical terms.' He paused to consider his last remark. 'Maybe Mal was making fun of that too.'

Angelina put her hands up to her head, as if to hold her brains in.

Ged sympathized. Copies and originals, copies and fakes, original copies: it was getting too complicated. Deliberately complicated by Malachy.

Angelina made a stab at trying to simplify things. 'Listen, George, I don't give a darn about history. I just want everybody to do what's right. If Malachy was deliberately trying to defraud the people who buy his paintings, then that's wrong.'

'He wasn't trying to defraud them, Angie. Fraudsters are trying to make money, but Mal was trying to do just the opposite. He was trying to kill the commercial value of his work.'

'That's just what I said,' Calum agreed eagerly. 'I got the impression he was trying to kill the whole idea of an art market.'

'Sure he was. That's what it's all about, that's why he did it.' Jorge turned to Ged. 'And that's why we shouldn't spoil his last joke, by telling anyone about it.'

'Rene, you mean?'

'Well, whoever. Lawyers aren't known for their sense of humour. Neither are agents, for that matter, so it's just as well Brad thought the whole fake thing was a scam.'

'But it is a scam,' Angelina persisted. 'You can't get around that by calling it a joke, because there's money involved. Big money, as Mr Welles keeps pointing out.'

'Well, OK, it's not really a joke,' Jorge amended. 'It's more than a joke. It's too important to be a joke. Why don't we call it a work of art? His last great work of genius. A three-fingered salute to your capitalist art market, conning collectors through their own incorrigible materialism. They buy his stuff for the brand name, and if it's fake, serve them right. It's like Gucci selling fake Gucci. Is it really fake, if Gucci sells it? After all, the paintings look the same, don't they? So from Mal's point of view, anyone who buys them has nothing to complain about, even if they're not his work. They were supposed to be buying a visual experience, not a commercial investment.'

'Now that's nice,' Calum commented. 'I like that idea. But for it to really work, we'd have to flog all this stuff and *then* let the cat out of the bag.'

'Too late for that,' Jorge observed. 'Here comes the lawyer.'

Rene Deforte was hardly the image of hard-line law. His suit, apparently the same one as last time, was even more rumpled, suggesting that he had been wearing it continually ever since. No-one would ever have called him hard-nosed, at least on appearances. Though appearances are proverbially deceiving.

Ged let Calum describe the painting problem to Rene. Let him show the diary to Rene.

Deforte didn't take too much notice of the on-screen evidence. He made it clear that he believed whatever Malachy had put there. 'Mal wasn't into fiction,' he explained. Which made Ged's blood run a little colder.

At Rene's suggestion, they went over to the studio, where he could study the evidence.

'The thing is,' Calum explained, 'that poof – the agent, whatsisname, Welles – claims he doesn't believe any of this. He's planning to sell them all as if they were genuine. And we can't decide if he has any right to do that, partly because no-one can tell which ones are real and which ones aren't.'

Deforte surveyed the paintings on the walls with the same unhurried consideration that he might have given them if he were about to invest his savings in art. 'So some of these things were painted by somebody else. Do we know who?'

'Not a clue,' Calum said confidently.

Angelina didn't look quite as confident, so maybe it was just as well Deforte hadn't asked directly.

Rene persisted in his cross-examination. 'But some of the paintings done by this somebody have already been sold. And the somebody didn't stand up and say, Hey, those are mine, I did those. Is that right?'

'Yeah,' Calum admitted, 'but they might not have known for sure which ones were theirs. Because he also did copies of the ones they painted. Or maybe they were copying paintings he'd already done. Whatever, they might not be able to tell which one was theirs and which one was his.'

'Now let's just hold our horses here, Cal. Let me get this straight. This other person, or people, if there was more than one, painted those pictures the way Mal told them to do it. Is that right?'

'Well, yeah. But they'd have had to, wouldn't they? If it was going to be a convincing Hawke.'

'Well, sure. Stands to reason. But doesn't that make them real Hawkes, after all?'

Calum stared. 'What do you mean? How can they be his, if somebody else painted them?'

Deforte did his famous imitation of a hick lawyer obliged to wrestle with intellectual concepts. 'Well, as I understand it – Dr Bravo here is the art expert, he can correct me if I'm wrong – quite a few artists nowadays don't actually do the work themselves. Sculptors, for instance, they don't chip away on stone like Michelangelo any more, do they? They get a welder to stick some scraps of steel together, on their instructions. Or they get somebody to cast the bronze, or the concrete. I think it's supposed to be the idea that constitutes the art, not the thing itself. Is that so, Dr Bravo?'

'Well, it is, yeah,' Jorge allowed, speaking slowly at first and then with more enthusiasm. 'You're absolutely right. I hadn't thought of Mal as a conceptual artist, but hell, why not?'

He held out his hands in appeal to Ged. 'Don't you get it? If artists can take objects made by other people on the artist's instructions, and exhibit them as their own art, then why can't Mal take other people's paintings, which he had them make, and call them his own art?'

'But in that case, isn't he supposed to tell everybody what he's done?'

'Tell, hell. He would have said it's none of their business. What you see is what you get, as far as Mal was concerned.' Jorge snapped his fingers in sudden illumination. 'Holy shi— moly, it's even better than I thought. He's expropriated the idea of authorship and authenticity, and turned it on its head.

'Well, then, there's no argument,' he announced authoritatively to the rest of them. 'Tell the world, go ahead. Everybody will love the concept. Tell Brad he should publicize this diary. If anything, it'll let him jack the prices up.'

'Wait a minute, wait a minute,' Calum protested. 'Are you telling me that any old thing can be art, just because an artist says it is?'

'Well, sure.' Jorge didn't need to reflect on this concept, it was so deeply instilled in his post-modern psyche. 'It has to be like that, doesn't it? Art is what artists do. What else could it be? It's up to them to define it.'

421

'But who defines the artists?'

'They define themselves. *Creo, ergo artist sum*. That's how it works.'

Calum looked like a man who has just run a marathon in the wrong direction. 'You mean Malachy's last great work of art, as you called it – his deliberate scam against the art market – is going to be co-opted by the cannibals in New York?'

'Looks like it.' Jorge shrugged. 'Tough luck, isn't it? I guess some people just can't help making money, no matter how hard they try.'

33

'I don't get it,' Calum complained to Angelina.

They were on their way down the mountain in the resurrected pick-up truck, on their way to go for a swim. But not in the ocean, which along this coast was too cold to be endured for more than thirty seconds. There was other water, warmer water, sheltered pockets in the little mountain glens. Angelina was taking him to her favourite beaver lake.

Ged had said he was jet-lagged and would rather take a nap. Angelina wasn't really sorry. Every minute alone with Calum counted now, because there were not likely to be many more.

'What don't you get?' she wanted to know.

'How come any old rubbish becomes incredibly valuable, just because some artist says it's art?'

That hadn't made much sense to Angelina either. She had been thinking about it all afternoon, and had come to some conclusions. 'That's how fashion works, isn't it? People go crazy over something because other people say it's the bee's knees. But it's only valuable for as long as people believe that. That's what valuable means: something you value highly.'

'But this isn't just all in the mind. Those paintings are worth real money.'

'What's real about money? It works the same way,

doesn't it? It's just scraps of paper that everybody believes are valuable.'

'Yeah, but at least the government has a hand in that, to make it all official. What I want to know is, if art is what an artist says is art, then what makes an artist an artist? Nobody hands out qualifications, they don't have framed certificates on the wall of their studio, there's no committee to give them the stamp of approval. It sounds to me like anybody can say he's an artist, and then he can say that whatever he does is art.'

'I guess anybody can say whatever they like, but there's no guarantee that people will believe them.'

'So what? Artists are always misunderstood.'

They drove in silence for a few minutes. Only relative silence: there was always the sound of wind in the trees and rushing water and birdsong, not to mention the creak and rattle of the ancient truck on the rutted road, the crunch of gravel under wheel, the resentful slap of hemlock bough on the roof of the cab.

Angelina pulled off on to a patch of grass, just big enough for parking purposes. She turned to Calum, in time to see his brooding countenance split into an enormous grin. Just about the widest smile she had ever seen on his face, and that was saying something. 'What's so funny?'

'Nothing.' He wrenched at the door handle, flung the door open, jumped down to the grass. He stood there, looking up at her, still grinning like a lunatic. 'I just decided I'm going to be an artist.'

'Why is that funny?'

'Well, I think it's funny. Maybe you won't. I even know what my very first work of art will be. I'm going to call it "Homage to Mal".'

She scrambled out of the other side of the truck, still mystified. She could tell just by looking at him that he wasn't going to tell her any more.

They had to cross the beaver dam to get to the far side of the lake. The water in the lake was warm and still. So still that its surroundings reflected on its surface with perfect fidelity: the shadowed green underside of hemlock fronds; birch bark banded in silver-white and creamy-white; deep brown crewcut bulrush heads; the uptilted tail of a dowsing mallard. Calum and Angelina, when they leaned over to admire themselves. Beyond their heads, haloed in sunlight, a scrap of sky had wedged itself under the water, a perfect, peaceful, bottomless blue, like a passage to infinity.

They had come with every intention of swimming. But as soon as they started to take off their clothes, other ideas came into their heads.

Maybe it was the sun. The four-o'clock sun bathed their bodies in the thick and poignant light of September, giving them for that moment the flawless beauty of wood-land godlings, the natural beauty of beasts in the wilderness. The air was heady with sunlight, with the sticky scent of sun on pine. Even Calum, when she kissed his neck, smelt of the sun. Angelina thought she would fly apart with joy.

Afterwards, they swam.

Calum towelled her dry, and combed her hair for her. Mermaid's tresses, he called it, because of the way it fanned out and swirled around her in the water. She wanted that moment of wistful sunlight and solitude, casual caressing and the comfort of his nearness, she wanted that perfect piece of time to last for ever. A classic September moment, so moving precisely because they were coming to the end of all such moments. It was price-less, not valuable.

She spoke to him without turning her head. 'Calum?'

'Yeah?'

'Are you going back home with your dad?'

'I guess I will. Not much point in staying here, is there?'

'No discos, you mean. Ouch!'

'You see what happens when you say nasty things? Your hair gets knotted.' She could hear the grin in his

425

voice. 'What are you going to do? You haven't got a job any more.'

'I think I'd better go back to Sweetwater and help my grandma. She shouldn't have to struggle along on her own any more.'

'She seemed like a pretty tough old bird to me.'

He combed in silence a while.

'Angie?'

'Yeah?'

'Why don't you come back to London with me?'

'They won't let me stay, will they?'

'I don't know. We might be able to sort something out when you get there.'

Sort something out, what did that mean? Did it mean . . . ?

She dithered. Should she tell him now? Should she tell him at all? She wasn't sure about it, was she?

But she was sure, inside herself. She could count, even if he didn't seem able to.

She tried to guess his reaction. She had an awful feeling she already knew what his very first response would be. She couldn't stand to hear him say it. 'What do you mean, sort something out?'

'Get you a visa, or a work permit, or something.'

'Oh.' In spite of her disappointment, she steeled herself to say it. This was her last chance, only chance. 'I thought maybe – I thought you meant something else.'

'Like what?'

It was a good thing she wasn't looking at him, otherwise she never would have gotten it out, out of her head and into the open air. 'Like getting married.'

The comb stopped.

After an eternal minute he smoothed her hair down over her shoulders with his hands. 'I think that's as good as it's going to get. Here's your comb.'

She turned to look at him, to see what he looked like right now. But he had already turned away, heading towards the dam. He didn't look back at her. Not even

426

when he said, 'Nobody gets married, these days.'

'I only meant . . .' That was a lie, it wasn't what she had meant at all. 'I meant I could stay over there, if we were married. Or you could stay here.'

'And live with your gran, I suppose.'

The dry, faintly derisive tone silenced her. She couldn't tell him now. He would think it was just a way of getting what she wanted. And she couldn't stand to hear him say what she knew he would say, if she told him.

She knew what he would say, because he'd said it already, when it was only hypothetical. Back at the beginning of September. The longest, loveliest month of her life.

When they were jouncing and jarring their way back along the dusty track, she thought of another loose end. 'What do you want me to do with your painting? The one you left with my grandma.'

He had to be looking at her, because his head had turned in her direction. But she couldn't make out anything about the expression in his eyes. He had put on his sunglasses against the invasive fire of the lowering sun. 'Do you like it?'

'I like it a lot, yeah. Maybe because I know what it is. The others are too abstract for me.'

He went back to staring at the sun. 'Keep it, then. You can have it.'

'But Calum, it's supposed to be for you. You told me your dad gave it to you, to pay you for the work you've done for him.'

'So what? Now I'm giving it to you for the work you've done for me.'

'You don't have to pay me. Your dad's already paid me.'

'He wasn't paying you to clear up Malachy's mess, was he? Anyway, the old bastard should have left you something in his will.'

'Why should he? I'm no relation of his. And he did give me his horse, when he got too sick to ride any more.' She

427

shifted gear, heading up a steeper incline. 'Calum, that's a crazy idea. You heard Brad Welles say those paintings are worth thousands and thousands of dollars. You can't just throw away something that valuable.'

'Can't I?' He smiled into the sun, at a private joke. 'Just watch me.'

1975

Once upon a time we didn't sell art. We gave it to the gods.

The cave paintings were prayers for good hunting. The Parthenon was an offering to Athene. All art was religious art in the Middle Ages, even in the Renaissance. And my grandfather's people thought art was for making magic, not for making money.

We know better now, don't we? We know there aren't any gods. We know survival is the point of existence. We know everything has a price. We know art is just a commodity. We know so many damn things our stupid ancestors didn't know.

34

The weather comes out of the west.

It always had, and now it was coming again: clouds at the edge of the midnight sea, invisible in darkness, except for the deeper dark they brewed against a skyful of stars. She could smell the prophecy of rain, taste it in the wind, feel it in her bones.

But she had no bones now. Her body was back in bed.

The sea surged below her, rising slowly to the challenge of the wind. The storm winds always outran the speed of the waves they summoned, so that the last of the great breakers only reached shore after the fury and excitement had moved on. Like the lag between the rising of the moon and the turning of the tide. Heaven and earth were doomed to be forever out of sync.

She wasn't flying. She had no need to fly. In this immortal body, the thought was the deed. She made a wish, and it was so. She had to be very, very careful what she thought about and what she wished for, when she was in this state. Calum, for instance: she didn't dare think of him.

Now she tasted something else, overriding the rain. Danger.

She was drawn to it, maybe following the scent, a hot, vivid, searing odour. Drawing her back to the shore, down to the mountain.

To the body in bed.

She opened her eyes and reached out to touch Calum. He wasn't there. Not even traces of his body heat. He was gone.

She sat up in the darkness. The stench of danger clogged her throat. But she couldn't call out, not with Calum's father asleep across the hall.

She went out into the hallway, crept along the house to the living room. The patio door stood open.

Calum was out there, standing on the deck, staring into the studio. Standing there stark naked, like a disoriented ghost.

She could see him clearly, because the studio was not in darkness. A light, all flickers and flares, illuminated the high room.

Firelight. But not in the fireplace.

'Oh, golly!'

Calum spun around. As if the firelight had mesmerized him, and her cry had broken the spell. 'The studio's on fire.'

She had already worked that out for herself. 'Get your dad out of bed. I'll call the rangers.'

Since the house was surrounded by a national forest, the forest rangers were the local fire brigade. She ran into the kitchen, snapped on the light and grabbed the cell phone. She had to step out on to the deck to get a strong enough signal. Communication was chancy, here in the mountains.

Clancy Smith was the duty officer. She recognized his slow, deliberate voice; he used to play poker with Malachy. There was always somebody on duty up there, day and night, because of the danger of forest fires. They wouldn't necessarily care if Malachy's house burnt down, but they wouldn't want it to start a forest fire at the same time.

She told Clancy what was happening.

At some point she realized that she herself had not a stitch on. She was as crazy as Calum. She ran back to her bedroom and turned on the light, surprising the drowsy cats, who were scattered around the counterpane. Seville and Champagne, she noted with one corner of her mind, but no sign of Miss Fudge.

She opened the window, to allow them an escape route if things got desperate. Then she pulled on shirt and jeans, sweater and boots. She jammed the phone into her hip pocket, and grabbed a flashlight from the drawer beside the bed.

Calum came in. He went through the same routine as she had just done, pulling on his clothes, but without any sign of urgency. 'What do you do for a fire brigade around here? You can't get a fire engine up a road like that, can you?'

'I've already called the forest ranger. Where's Charles?'

'I suppose he's in the kitchen. That's where you put him every night, isn't it? What the hell do you want him for? He's a bloody big hound, but he can't put the fire out by pissing on it.'

'I just wanted to make sure he was out of the way. I don't want him to get hurt.'

When she came out on the deck again, she could smell the smoke. She could have smelled it before, if she hadn't been in such a panic. It was pouring from the studio chimney, thickening the air.

Calum's father came out, wearing jeans and a sweater. He surveyed the studio, surprisingly calm for a man whose inheritance was going up in flames.

'I'll get the key,' Angelina told him. 'We might be able to rescue some of those paintings.'

He glanced at her, an oddly abstracted look, as if he had forgotten about her. 'You stay out of there. It's not worth risking your life, even for the Mona Lisa. Have you got an outside tap and a garden hose?'

'Around the back of the house, by the kitchen door. We'll have to run it right through the kitchen.'

Ged followed her into the kitchen. She was so grateful for him. Calum was wandering around like a zombie, if a zombie could trip on speed, but his father was being

432

purposeful and helpful. It just went to show that you couldn't inherit common sense.

'Let me get the key to the studio for you, just in case.' She reached for the hook beside the back door, where the key always hung. But it wasn't there. 'Where's it gone? I'm sure I put it away before supper.'

Ged hustled her through the door. 'Never mind the bloody key. Let's get that hose-pipe rigged up and working.'

The wind was rising dramatically. Any fire fed by that would be out of control in no time. But the rain was coming too. She could smell it even through the smoke. Hurry, hurry, she prayed to the weather. Wind, bring rain. Let it bucket down.

But they couldn't rely on the arrival of the rain. 'We'll have to soak the deck,' she pointed out. 'Otherwise the fire will burn right across to the house.'

'I know, I know.' In the windy, roaring, starless darkness, Ged was wrestling with the hose, trying to marry it to the tap, while she held the flashlight for him. 'Where's my idiot son? Tell him to get his arse out here.'

She handed him the light and left him to grapple with the hose, while she ran around to the deck, to find Calum and see what was happening.

Fire was happening. The walls were all ablaze by now. Oil on canvas makes good tinder. She could see the chest with the Untitled Women in it, not far from the door. But she couldn't open the door to rescue it, because that would let in the wind.

Not that she necessarily felt like rescuing those pictures, even if they would have made Calum's father rich. Fire was maybe the best place for them.

And the fakes – or at least the non-Hawkes, whichever ones those were – they were making fodder for the flames as well. The art market wouldn't get a chance to spoil Malachy's last joke, or work of art, or whatever it was. Maybe Malachy would even have approved this accident.

Accident? If Malachy had set fire to his own studio,

Jorge would probably have called it another work of art. Performance art. Art that couldn't be bought or sold. Art that just was. The kind of thing that Malachy had always wanted his paintings to be.

Calum was standing on the deck, mesmerized by the flames. She grabbed his arm. 'Calum, your dad wants you to help him with the hose.'

He turned his head, a slow, dreamy expression on his face. 'Angie, this is fantastic. A fortune going up in smoke, it isn't every day you get to watch a thing like that.'

'Don't be so cheerful. That's your dad's fortune.'

'No, it's Mal's. He's taking it with him.'

He was laughing. He seemed to have gone crazy. She shook his arm and shouted at him over the wind. 'For the Lord's sake, Calum, get around to the back and help your dad. We'll all be sleeping in a tent if we can't keep it from spreading to the house. And if it jumps over to the trees, the whole mountain will catch fire.'

He went off, laughing to himself. Maybe he really had flipped. She stood a moment, staring through the wall of windows. Watching all that was left of Malachy's life going up in flames.

And then she saw Miss Fudge.

The tabby was asleep on the near end of the big bench, curled up on top of one of the Untitled Women.

Angelina ran to the door and wrenched at the handle. Where the heck had that key got to? She pounded on the glass, trying to rouse the cat. 'Fudge! Wake up! Fudgie, please!'

'Angie, if you open up that door, the wind will get in and the fire will destroy the lot.'

Calum stood behind her, unbelievably cool. He must have come back when she started shouting.

'We have to get her out!' She turned on him in a fury of grief. 'How did she get in there? She was eating supper in the kitchen, along with the others, after I locked this door.'

He shrugged. 'Cats get everywhere.'

434

Angelina pressed herself up against the glass, torn between two mutually exclusive rescues. There was no doubt in her heart that the little cat was worth any amount of art. Only it wasn't *her* art that would be destroyed, if she let in the wind. She rapped on the glass again. If she could only manage to attract Miss Fudge over to the door . . .

The glass began to crack.

First in one place, then another and another, collapsing outwards, upwards, downwards, like the mirror in 'The Lady of Shalott' when the curse was come upon her. Sensing victory, the wind hammered with unseen fists in a renewed fury, demanding to be let inside.

The window fell inwards piecemeal. The wind swept through the gap, with a dark shriek of triumph.

The fire exploded.

Things got very confused after that. Angelina had a vague memory of falling backwards against the rail, and of Calum dragging her across the deck, as the flames began to bite at the boards. He hauled her down the steps, into the night that was no longer dark.

She became aware of other noises. The biggest noise was a racket of revving and grinding and shouting, as if an army was assaulting the mountain, tanks and all.

'I think the cavalry have arrived,' Calum remarked. 'The rangers, I mean.'

Angelina held up an open hand to heaven. She had heard other, subtler sounds beneath the din of wind and flame and full-frontal fire-fighting technology. Sounds of hiss and spatter, rhythmic sounds, natural sounds.

Now she could feel it, too. Great soft drops, exploding on her seared skin, washing away the pain and the tears.

Summer was over. The first rain of winter had arrived.

35

Malachy was saying something, but she couldn't hear him. In this disembodied state she didn't hear with her ears, but right now she couldn't even hear his thoughts. Couldn't even think. It felt like she had a gale blowing inside her head.

He held up his hands. She saw the smears of paint on his fingers, red, blue, yellow. She reached out to catch his hand.

He was further away than she thought. She couldn't touch him. He held out his hands to her. The rich colours faded, turned to shades of ashy grey. And still she couldn't reach him, however hard she willed to . . .

It was a shock to open her eyes and see Calum. She had already given up on him, already reconciled herself to life on her own. Or maybe that was only the future getting confused with the present. They tended to get tangled, when she was out of her body.

Calum looked different.

'Angie? Are you OK?'

The anxiety in his voice was gratifying. She put up her hands to her face, and realized that her hands were bandaged.

Which meant she couldn't tell what shape her face was in. She could have looked at herself when she came back from travelling, but she hadn't thought of it. Maybe she had been too scared of the possibilities.

'What's my face like?'

'I can't tell. I can't see much of it.' Calum grinned. 'You look like something from *The Mummy's Curse*.'

She patted herself with the useless hands. 'Do I really?'

'Just kidding. Your hair's a bit singed, and your forehead and nose, but that's about all. The backs of your hands are the worst, they said. You must have put up your hands to protect your face.'

She finally cottoned on to what was odd about his appearance. The dreadlocks had disappeared. He looked like a little kid just back from the barber's with his annual summer haircut. But beautiful all the same, mind you. 'What happened to your hair?'

'It caught fire, didn't it? My dad managed to put it out with the hose, so I didn't get burnt much. He gave you a douse with the hose, too. Otherwise you might have been a lot worse off.' He took hold of her burnt hand. A mitt, in its present state. 'Are you OK?'

'I guess I'll be OK, one way or another. Lord knows what I look like, though.'

'You look fine to me. And the doctors say you'll be OK.'

'What about the house?'

'It survived. The rangers knocked the deck apart. They were more het up about the trees than the house. Then that rain came barrelling down and drenched everything.'

Angelina cast her mind back to the fire. 'What happened to Miss Fudge?'

'What do you think? We were outside, and look what happened to us.'

His flat, edgy tone struck at her grief like flint to tinder. She burst into tears and a rage all at once. 'How can you talk like that? What did she do to deserve getting burnt to death?'

'Angie, for Christ's sake, she was just a cat.'

'What do you mean, just a cat? Cats are as good as any other creature on earth. I hope you come back as a stray, and have to scavenge for a living.'

Calum just looked at her as if she had gone crazy.

She *had* gone crazy. Not about Miss Fudge, but about Calum. She was crazy about Calum, and he was about to do something terrible to her.

She tried to pull herself together. 'I didn't mean to yell at you. You must have saved my life.'

'That's OK. It was my fault anyway. I mean,' he added with curious haste and confusion, 'you came up on the deck to tell me to get out of there. Otherwise you'd have been round the back with my father when it exploded.'

'But then you'd have been burnt, instead of me.'

'Well, it would have been my own fault, wouldn't it?' He found an unswathed spot in the centre of her palm and stroked it with his fingertip. 'As it is, it's my fault you got hurt. I feel really bad about that.'

He took hold of the bandaged hand in both of his and brought it to his mouth. The bare patch wasn't wide enough for him to kiss, but he touched it with his tongue.

She pulled her hand away, not because she didn't like what he was doing, but because she did like it. She couldn't do what he was going to want to do in another minute. Not when she was all bandaged up and lying in a hospital bed.

He was looking down at her, his greeny-browny eyes alight with . . . what? Sympathy? Sexual hankerings? The Lord alone knew what was going on in his soul. She didn't reckon it added up to love.

But she had to tell him anyway.

She hadn't intended to tell him at all, but somehow the fire had changed things. He had to be told, had to make his own decisions and take the consequences. That would open her up to certain rejection, but it wasn't fair not to give him the chance. Not after he had saved her. And also saved . . .

'Calum, listen. I'm going to have a baby.'

Just at first he was full of astonishment, leaving no room for anything else. How a man who had been making love to a woman every day and night for the better part of a month could be so amazed to hear that he had made a

438

baby in her, she didn't know. To her it sounded like a recipe for getting pregnant. Especially when the condoms had featured only off and on. Maybe all those Saturday night flings back in London had let him forget what sex was basically all about.

'You're kidding.'

'Of course I'm not.'

'No, of course you're not.' He went on staring, still not taking it all on board. 'I told you to go to the doctor and take that pill.'

'And what did we do on the way back?'

'So what? This wouldn't have happened, if you'd taken the fucking pill like I told you to.'

Incredulity had already given way to blame. Neither made a jot of difference to the reality, so she didn't bother to answer.

'So what do you want me to do about it?'

'It's not what I want you to do. It's what you want to do.'

He rubbed his hand across his face, sideways and up and down, staring at her the whole time. Maybe it helped his brain to work. 'Well, I . . . I'm going to go home. I told you that. And like I said, if you want to come with me, we can try to get you a visa.'

She had to say it, because it was the only thing she could say. Not that it was any use. 'If we got married, there wouldn't be any problem with a visa.'

'But I don't want to get married.'

To his credit, he had to turn away from her to say it. He paced the small room, lifting and lowering his gaze, looking everywhere but at her. 'It's not that I don't want you around, but this is . . . well, bloody hell, I'm just not ready to be a father. I feel like I'm still a kid myself, actually. Don't you?'

'No.' She waited for him to look at her before she added to that. 'I'm old enough to have a baby, and old enough to work and vote, so I don't guess I can call myself a kid any more. And you're old enough to father a child, and old enough to join the army and maybe die in a war. So I don't guess you're really a kid any more either.'

He looked distraught, hunted, defiant, a long way from breaking out the champagne. Not the way anybody would want their father to look, in response to the news of their impending existence. 'But, Angie, listen. I don't know what I want to do. With my life, I mean. And whatever it is, I haven't even started to do it.'

Angelina couldn't help sighing, because she understood. Boy, did she ever understand. She hadn't made even the first start at the job she was here on earth to do, and the baby would make things much harder. 'I haven't done any of those things either, Calum. So what? It doesn't change the facts. I'm pregnant, and you're the father. I've got this baby in me, and it's going to grow into a real person, just like you and me. And it's going to need its father.'

She took a deep breath. 'You told me how much you hated it when your dad went off with that girl. You know how your dad feels about the way Malachy treated him. So are you going to do that to your own kid?'

'I haven't got any kid yet,' he said sulkily. 'For God's sake, Angie, this isn't the Middle Ages. Why don't you just get an abortion?'

'Do you have any idea what that means?'

'It means the bloody baby won't be born.'

'It means that your child won't be born. It means my child won't be born, *our* child won't be born. Something will be missing from the world for ever, and maybe the world won't even notice. But you and I will know.'

'Know what? That something that might have happened, didn't happen? Life is full of possibilities.'

'In this case, it's quite a lot more than a possibility.' She caught his hand with her bandaged mitts and laid it on top of the sheet over her belly, to try to make him understand what she could not help but know with every element of her being. 'It's here, inside me. It's part of you, and part of me. It's not *it*. It's a he or a she. It's your baby.'

'It's not a baby, it's a microscopic blob,' he growled. 'Why should I have to suffer for your loony Catholic conscience?'

'This has nothing to do with the Church. I told you, I'm not a Catholic any more. And why do you call it suffering?'

'Because I don't want a fucking kid around my neck at nineteen, that's why. If you had any sense, you wouldn't either.'

'I'm not nineteen, I'm twenty, and what a heck of a difference a year makes. If you really, truly didn't want to be a father, you shouldn't have been doing what makes babies.'

He reacted with incredulous anger to what seemed to her to be a plain statement of fact. 'Angie, you are really truly crazy. Because you were a nun, you think I should be a monk?'

Angelina had meant to be calm and cool about this. It wasn't as if she hadn't known what kind of response to expect. But she was trembling all over by now, and they were both shouting. So much for true love.

She lay back and turned herself away from him.

'Never mind, it doesn't matter.' She forced herself to speak quietly. In the end it wasn't hard, because her voice came out rusted by tears. 'I knew what you'd say. I was just hoping you wouldn't say it.'

Calum went quiet as well. She could sense him shifting uneasily. A bad conscience was better than nothing, but it wasn't at all the same thing as doing what your conscience said you should do. 'So if you . . . insist on having this kid . . . what are you going to do with it?'

'I'll go home to my grandma. She needs looking after anyway.'

'She won't be very happy about the baby, will she?'

'She'll be happy about the baby. She won't be very happy about you.'

'She must be used to disappointment by now, an old lady like her.' She could hear the half-ashamed shadow of a grin in his voice. 'Well, you've got that painting to keep you going financially. The art shark should be able to get a few bob out of it for you.'

'I'm not going to sell it.'

'Why not?'

'I don't need the money. Not yet, anyway. I saved up just about all of my salary while I was working for Malachy, since I didn't have to pay rent or buy food or anything.' In a less practical vein she added, 'Besides, it's Malachy's painting, isn't it? I saw him make it. And I've never owned a real work of art before.'

Again he shifted. 'Well, that's . . . well, I suppose it's up to you, what you do with it. I gave it to you before I knew about this baby business, anyway.'

He put his hand out to stroke what remained of her frazzled hair, where it lay crumpled on the pillow. He did it in a distracted way, as if he hadn't noticed what his hand was doing. What was his hand doing? Touching her without really touching.

'I think my dad is intending to fly home tomorrow. He thinks I'm going with him.'

'Are you?'

'Well, I am, yeah.' He gave her a defiant look. 'I told you, didn't I? Before all this other stuff came up, the fire and the baby and all. And there's not a lot I can do for you right now, is there?'

'I guess not.' She swallowed. Bitter disappointment was hard to digest, however far off you had seen it coming. 'Besides, there's not much excitement around here.'

'Hey, that's not fair. This baby business is all your idea.'

By now his edgy movements were more like squirming than shifting. Maybe he wasn't entirely convinced by his own claims to blamelessness.

'Listen, Angie, you're not going to be able to drive for a while, with your hands wrapped up like that. If they let you out today, I can pack your gear for you, and take you over to your gran's place with the pick-up. And Charles and the cats, of course.'

Angelina cleared her throat of tears. Her voice came

out cool and steady. If it was underpinned by irony, he didn't appear to notice. 'That would be real nice of you, Calum.'

For once, on the drive to the airport, Calum didn't bother to insulate his brain from the outside world with a private wall of sound. He slumped in the passenger seat, staring out at the alien plain with nothing but sunglasses for defence. He was not in a chatty mood.

Neither was Ged. Malachy's house had survived, and the rangers had prevented the fire from spreading to the forest, but that was the end of the good news. The paintings hadn't been insured, of course. From Malachy's point of view, that would have been selling out to the enemy.

Calum spoke without turning his head. 'What did Brad Welles say when you told him?'

'Several words that Angelina wouldn't have approved of.'

Calum grinned behind his glasses. 'Anything else?'

'He pointed out, not very diplomatically, that this wouldn't have happened if I'd let him take the paintings away when he wanted to. He implied that leaving you in charge of them was courting disaster.'

The grin vanished. 'I hope you told him to go screw himself.'

'Something like that.' Ged jammed the lighter in. A heavy dose of tar and nicotine was just what he needed right now. 'He did retract a little when he found out that I'd been on site when disaster struck. How did you two get to be so friendly?'

'He said something really rotten to Angie. So I punched him out.'

Ged was wrestling single-handed with the cigarette packet, trying to remove one without driving the car into the ditch. In his distracted state, this confession, if you could call it that when delivered in a flat, off-hand manner like a verbal shrug, took a minute to sink in.

He took another minute to decide how to respond. On the one hand, assault was a criminal offence. On the other hand, a smarmy git like Bradford Welles the Fourth was virtually inviting a punch on the nose. On the third hand, it wouldn't do to encourage Calum in this sort of bad behaviour; punching people out had already got him thrown out of school and hauled into court.

'Did Angie appreciate your gallant gesture?'

This time the shrug was visible. 'She ticked me off, of course. She'd think that was her duty, wouldn't she?'

She would, yes. Angelina took her morality seriously. She would have no truck with ethical relativism or the sensitivities of sinners. Once upon a time, surely, it must have been regarded as an admirable thing to speak up for virtue, to speak out against wrong. That would have been in a time when people were more confident of wherein virtue lay, and more persuaded of the possibility of damnation. Some less sophisticated time than now.

What did a girl like that make of Calum? Aside from being totally smitten, of course. It made him think better of his son, the fact that Angelina could fall in love with him.

For that matter, what did Calum make of Angelina? 'What's happening with you and her?'

Calum's face took on a look of pugnacious petulance, a familiar expression that he used to assume as a child whenever he felt himself to be maligned and misunderstood. 'What d'you mean, what's happening? Why should anything be happening?'

'You were sleeping with her, weren't you?'

'So what? That doesn't mean I'm going to marry her or anything.'

At this point, for some reason, not even the dark glasses were sufficient protection from his father's regard. He swung his head away, to give the fire-scarred fields of stubble the benefit of his scrutiny. He muttered something inaudible. Talking to the cornfields, maybe.

'What?'

444

'I said' – still a mumble, just barely comprehensible – 'I asked her if she wanted to come to London, but she didn't.'

'Why not?'

Calum contemplated the scenery for some moments before answering. 'Something about staying with her gran. She thinks the old bag is getting too feeble to look after herself. Only right now, her gran is having to look after her, of course.'

So it was enough of an affair for Calum to ask her to come home with him, but not enough for Angelina to abandon her grandmother.

Not that Calum had anything very pressing on his plate in London. 'Why don't you stay with her for a while? The old lady lives on a farm, didn't she say? They could probably do with some help.'

'She didn't ask me, did she?' Calum said curtly. 'Anyway, that place is absolutely the back of bloody beyond.'

The scenario made Ged feel obscurely guilty. 'Malachy should have left her something in his will.'

'He did, in the end. Sort of.' A pause, possibly significant. 'You know that painting? The one you gave me?'

'That was burnt along with the rest of them. Wasn't it?'

'No. I took it to her gran's place. I didn't want Mr Slime the Fourth taking it off to New York by mistake.' Another long pause. 'I told her she could have it.'

'Why did you do that?'

Calum lifted the shoulder nearest to Ged, the one that wasn't propped against the door. 'She said she'd seen him paint it, so we knew it couldn't be one of the fakes. And it had, like, sentimental value for her.'

'That was very . . . generous of you.' Ged glanced at his son's close-cropped head, but Calum's thought processes did not display themselves. He couldn't begin to guess what would motivate Calum to give such a valuable gift to a girl he was leaving behind.

'Speaking of the fakes, I've got something for you.'

Calum leaned forward to shove his hand into the rear pocket of his jeans. He pulled it out again, to study the results of the trawl: a key and a floppy disk. He held up the disk. 'This belongs to you, doesn't it?'

Ged only needed one glance to recognize it. The label said *1988*, with Malachy's signature below the date.

The last of the diaries. The one with the history of the fakes in it. Most of those paintings were ashes now, but according to the diary, some of them had already been sold. So Malachy's last joke, or whatever it was, hadn't quite ended up a damp squib.

And most of the Untitled Women still existed in a ghostly afterlife, on Jorge's film. Jorge should be able to get a scoop out of them, at least, for his book. But Ged wouldn't see a penny from it.

Calum lowered his window a couple of inches, to let him throw away the key that had been in his pocket along with the disk. 'That belonged to you too, I guess, but you won't be needing it now.'

'What is it? I mean, what *was* it?'

'It *was* the key to the studio.'

'What were you doing with that?'

'I was going to give it to the lawyer, before we left. But I decided there wasn't much point, seeing there's no lock, no door, and no studio.'

An unarguable conclusion. 'All the other diaries were in there, you know. I'd taken them over so I could look at the paintings while I was reading them.'

'Angie told me. I think she thought it was divine providence, making sure that Jesus couldn't get his hands on them for unholy purposes. And that reminds me, what are you going to do about Sheila and the ashes?'

It was Ged's turn to shrug. The urn with Malachy's ashes was almost the only thing to survive the fire, the urn and the bust of Alexander. Unsurprising, perhaps, since the ashes had already been once through the fire. 'I'll let her have them, I suppose. I certainly don't have any plans for them, and Malachy didn't leave any particular

446

nstructions, except that he was to be cremated. If they're
mportant to her, she might as well take them.'

He thought about that for a little while longer.

Thought about the unknown place where Malachy had
been born, the unknown culture he had been raised in.
The tribe he had thought himself a full member of, until
his grandfather told him different. The inheritance he
had rejected, even while he carried it in his veins and
passed it on to his sons and grandsons. The blood of that
unknown people, which made an octoroon of Ged
himself.

He couldn't simply instruct Rene to ship his father's
mortal remains off to some distant cousin. Not under the
circumstances. This Sheila person seemed to regard them
as some kind of sacred cultural relic.

'I think I'd better hand them over to her myself. Go to
Montana, I mean. After Rene's sold the house and I've
got the money from that.'

Calum turned to face him for the first time. With the
heel of his hand he pushed his sunglasses up into his hair,
forgetting that he no longer had any hair to hold them.
When they slipped down again, he slung them on to the
dashboard. 'Are you really going to do that?'

'Why not?'

'No reason. No reason at all.' Calum was looking ahead
now, down the road to Portland. And to Montana. But
right now, the road back to London. 'Can I come with you
when you go?'

447

36

They please themselves in the children of strangers.

It was raining in Fulham.

Ged came out into the real world, after spending the night in the belly of a transatlantic jet, and a dozy hour on the tube from Heathrow. The real world was littered with abandoned sweet wrappers and runaway crisp packets, the rattle of vacant pop tins, the sullen, sodden fag ends of tobacco addiction. In the real world it was cold, dark, windy and wet, hardly morning at all. As if the real world couldn't be bothered to get up today.

He didn't have an umbrella, of course. It never rained, this time of year, not where he had come from. Never till now.

By the time he got back to the flat, he was as soggy as the cigarette butts on the pavement. And too tired to notice, as he stepped inside, that the doormat was littered with mail.

Bloody bills, he thought, slamming the door and fumbling to retrieve his post. Whatever his foot hadn't scattered had been strewn about by an uninvited gust of wind. The only envelope still lying on the mat had his wet footprint plastered across it.

They were all bills, at a cursory glance and guess. Except for his bank statement, which was not good news either. When he last went out the door, he had thought he was going to be rich. Now he was back home, and broker than ever.

He threw all the mail into the waste paper basket. A childish gesture of defiance, which made him feel better. Then he lit himself a cigarette and thought about going to bed. He hadn't slept on the plane. Hadn't slept since . . . he was too tired to work it out.

The phone rang. He thought about not answering it. Then he thought it might be Elie.

He always thought it might be Elie. He tried very hard, every time, not to think that. But not trying to think something was the same as thinking it, because you had to think about it in order to deliberately not think about it.

Maybe *think* was too strong a word for what went on in his head. An inarticulate mental mumble, that might be more like it.

The phone was still ringing. He decided to answer it, if only to stop it ringing.

It wasn't Elie, of course.

It took him a moment to recognize his agent's voice. 'Didn't you get my letter?'

'What letter?'

'I sent you a letter. I left a message on your machine, but when you didn't get back to me I thought maybe it wasn't working, so I wrote instead. You should have got it by now.'

Ged glanced across the room at the bill-filled basket. 'Maybe I did. I just got in. I've been away.' He rubbed his forehead with the heel of his hand, trying not to set fire to his hair with the cigarette. No, no fear of that. Trying not to extinguish the cigarette in his rain-drenched hair. 'What was it about?'

He could hardly hear what the agent was saying. It didn't seem to make sense. Especially not the figures. 'What do you mean, a quarter of a million?'

'Dollars, not pounds. But that's on top of the hundred thousand pounds for UK rights . . . film rights . . . Frankfurt book fair . . .'

449

Ged let him rave. He wasn't going to believe any of this until he saw it written on a cheque.

Then his agent said something that brought him right down to reality. 'They want a two-book deal.'

'What? What for?'

He could hear the shrug in the agent's voice. 'If they're going to hype you, they won't want somebody else getting the benefit of their efforts.'

And they were going to want another book just like this one. But he didn't have another diary up his sleeve. He might not even have another book of any sort in him. Signing the contract would be making promises under false pretences, then waiting for the day of reckoning. Was the money worth the possibility, the probability, of being exposed as a fraud and a failure?

He told himself he didn't have any choice. He had all those bills to pay, not to mention keeping a roof over his head. Even thinking about money – the money he needed and didn't have – sent his pulse rate into hyper-drive, and probably his blood pressure along with it.

All he had to do was say yes.

So he was going to be rich after all. Another god-damned legacy from Malachy.

Only this was a secret one. His father's secret life. He didn't know if that was a fantasy life or a real one. He told himself that nobody would know, could know, now. Like the fake Hawkes.

But according to Jorge and Rene, those fakes weren't really fakes. In the visual arts, it would appear, nobody cared if you got other people to do your painting for you, as long as it came with your name. Whereas people were definitely sniffy about ghost writers, and plagiarism was a fighting word. In literary circles, you had to be who you said you were, and do what you said you'd done.

Where did inspiration end and stealing words begin? He would have to add a lot more words of his own, to make the story the length of a novel. But adding another chapter to *War and Peace* didn't give you the right to put your name on the title page.

He could try telling the truth. Not all the truth, just about the existence of the diary. Famous painter's son bases novel on father's secret life. That would get him a huge amount of publicity for the book, help the sales enormously. His agent could probably screw an even bigger advance out of the publishers. If they wanted to see the diary, he could say it had been in the studio when it burnt down; all the others had met that fate, after all. These days, you had to sell yourself to sell your books. And he had his father to sell.

Did he want his father to be branded as a murderer?

Malachy had deliberately bequeathed him whatever tangible evidence existed of the state of his soul, not excluding the darkest corners of it. Had left his honour and reputation in his son's hands. Maybe it was all some kind of test. Was blood thicker than water, or at least thicker than money? Was it thicker even when it was the blood of a stranger?

No, he couldn't tell, not about anything. Not for ten times the advance. And especially not to salve his own professional conscience. He had said once that he wouldn't let the old bastard buy him. Well, he wasn't going to be tempted into selling him, either.

But Calum might guess the truth. Calum had read the diaries, knew that Ged had had the first one. Calum would almost certainly recognize his grandfather's eccentric style of writing. Might well recognize his obsessions too, recognize Miss Right as one of the Untitled Women.

Maybe, by sparing Malachy, he himself was leaving his honour and reputation in his son's hands.

Well, he couldn't help it now. The novel had to be completed, sold, published. Malachy's words were stuck in his head, and when he sat down to write, it was Malachy's style that came out. Even if the first diary had gone up in flames with the rest, it would have been too late to take things back.

Even if it had gone up in flames . . .

He got the notebook out of his desk drawer. He took it into the kitchen and tore out the pages, one by one. He held each one over the sink, and brought the flame of his cigarette lighter up to a corner; held it until the flames came too close to his fingers, and only then dropped it into the sink.

He weighed the computer disk on the palm of his hand. Did he want to destroy it? No need, surely. It could be reused, unlike paper. Nowadays history could always be rewritten.

Then he went into the bedroom and stretched out face down across the double bed, not even noticing that he hadn't yet taken off his wet shoes. Or the rest of his damp clothes, for that matter. He didn't have time to notice, before he fell asleep.

It was dark when he woke up. And still raining.

He ached all over from sleeping in his wet clothes. Rheumatism, probably. People started suffering from things like that, didn't they, once they got past forty?

He found a pizza in the freezer, and bunged it in to the oven to bake, while he peeled off his stiff and sticky clothing. Then he placed himself under the hottest shower he could bear, letting the stinging heat of the water pummel his body back into working order. Afterwards he wolfed down the pizza, by now so hot it burned his mouth.

Then he dug out some dry clothes. Not necessarily clean clothes, since he wasn't sure what was clean and what was not. Everything tended to end up in a heap on the floor, or mixed up in the laundry basket. The drawer where his socks and underwear ought to live was empty. His clothing had got entirely out of hand, all over the place, a total muddle. Just like the rest of his life.

While he was searching for a pair of matching socks – a perfectionist fantasy, under the circumstances – he came across the scrap of paper with Elie's phone number on it.

He left off the search for socks, and phoned Elie instead.

This time it was a man who answered. A man who turned aside and spoke to Elie. A man who came back to tell him that Elie didn't want to speak to him.

A man. Her man? Had she left him for another man? For some reason the thought had never occurred to him before. Dumb egotism, he supposed.

Maybe this guy was rich. Another Ben.

He was rich too, or going to be. He hadn't had a chance to tell her that. Maybe she would come back if she knew. He could buy her back. He knew she was for sale.

God help him, he was hopelessly in love with a whore.

He grabbed a couple of socks – one black and one navy, but what the hell – and went through all his jacket pockets until he found his car keys. If a whore was what he wanted, then he would go out and find himself one.

A young one. A green girl, too timid to resist whatever he would demand of her. He had had enough of brazen women and their public parts.

He went to King's Cross. He had never gone there before, because he had an idea that the police were more likely to be prowling around, but it was easy to find a dark place for parking. For fucking.

For killing.

The rain had dwindled to a mist by now, the visible breath of autumn in the air. Everything had a halo, the street-lamps, the traffic lights, even the girl who came over when he stopped alongside her. Beads of mist glowed at the fringes of her long blond hair.

Her face was shadowed by the hair, but he could see as much as he needed to as she stood shivering in her skimpy little skirt and thin tight sweater. A young one, with slim thighs and high girlish breasts, and a waist he could have put his hands around. The hair was bleached, of course, it always was. A visible symbol of adulteration, to contradict the natural innocence of her slight young figure. A 'For Sale' sign.

He said two words and she said two words, and then

453

she got into the car. Neither of them spoke again, all the way to the dark place.

She stared out of the side window, or down at her hands and knees, even after the car had stopped. He guessed she hadn't been long on the game. Not long enough to reconcile herself to becoming the property of strangers.

His property, now.

No matter what bargain she might have thought she'd struck, he had bought her. She was only an Untitled Woman. Body parts, not a person. He could do what he liked with her. Make her do whatever he wanted. Fuck her to death.

He put his hand on her thigh, pushed it up under her skirt.

He felt her flinch at his touch. He heard a quick indrawn breath, a whimper on the edge of tears. Heard her whisper something terrible.

'*Daddy, don't . . .*'

He took his hand away. That was instinct, not understanding. There wasn't any way he could have understood what she had said.

She was staring at him now. Just enough random urban light to see her face, for the first time. To see her staring at him in horror. Reflecting his own expression, maybe.

Her left hand was fumbling for the door latch. Found it, pulled it up, fell out as the door fell open. She was trying to run, tottering on the too-high heels, fettered by the too-tight skirt. Stumbling over stones in the night. Falling down and getting up again.

The rest of the world stood still while he watched her.

If he let her go, she would almost certainly never tell anyone, because she had her own secret to hide.

If he let her go, he would never see her again. She hadn't wanted to see him before, and she never would want to now.

Can you talk to her, Polly had said.

Polly had been in tears. Something about drugs.

Something about moving out, living in a squat or some such thing. He had forgotten, in all the dramas and disappointments that had made up his life since then. Forgotten that he had said he would try to have a chat with her. Have a chat. Jesus bloody Christ.

He flung open his own door, and went after her.

It was hard to see in the darkness, but her hair caught the light for him. A peroxide halo. That was what had betrayed him, the fraudulent blond hair. It had taken away her individuality and made a type of her.

He caught up to her quite easily, caught her by the wrist. The thought went through him that he might have been someone else, some stranger after her with other intentions, some other man with murder on his mind. Some other man, who could have caught her just as easily.

For that instant, to his eyes, the barren ground was littered with images. Paintings of faceless, dismembered women.

'Don't touch me!' She tried to wrench free of his hand. She was sobbing and shaking violently. 'Don't you touch me. Take your hand off me.'

He let go. 'I'm not going to touch you, Lu. Calm down.'

She stumbled and fell, literally fell off her high heels. She landed with one foot under her and the other stuck out in front of her, a graceless, childish pose. She sat like that on the damp ground, weeping, not trying to run any more.

He hunkered down beside her. When she had been a little girl, crying because she had hurt herself, he used to give her a cuddle for comfort; but he couldn't do that now. Not because she was too big, but because she might misunderstand. *Take your hand off me.* He didn't dare touch her.

'Lulu, did you hurt yourself?'

A burst of sobs. 'I think I broke my heel.'

'Your heel? You mean your ankle?'

'The shoe.'

She wrenched it out from under her. The heel had

snapped right off. He took the broken shoe and its high chunky heel, and flung them into the darkness. Her other shoe had come off too, in the tumble. He sent it after its mate.

She was sitting up in surprise, staring at him, no longer crying. Her eyes were huge. Even in the dim light he could see the tearful trails of mascara down her cheeks, like a clown's make-up. 'Daddy, what are you doing?'

'You don't need them any more, do you?'

She looked up at him, then down at herself. She made a few quite pointless efforts to tug the hem of her skirt down and loosen her jumper.

Giving up on that, she wrapped her arms around herself and gazed at the ground. 'Did you really not know it was me?'

'Of course I didn't know.'

Her voice trembled. 'How could you not know?'

How could he have done to her what his father had done to him? How could he have turned himself into a stranger?

'Well, for one thing, you've gone blonde,' he said slowly, to himself as much as to her. 'And you're thinner than . . . than when I last saw you. And wearing all that make-up. And it's dark.' He trailed off, coming to the end of his excuses. 'But you didn't know it was me, did you?'

A quick, emphatic shake of the head. 'Not till you . . . leaned towards me, and I could see your face close up.' A painful pause. 'I haven't got my contacts in. One of them got lost.'

Christ. No wonder she hadn't had much luck in getting away from him. He thought of her standing at the kerb-side in the shivery mist, half blind, half naked, waiting for some man to pay her twenty pounds to rape her. Stupid child.

His child.

He said as matter-of-factly as he could, 'Come on, Lu, you'd better get up. You'll catch your death of cold, sitting there like that.'

She was trembling all over. Not surprising that her voice was shaking too. 'What are you . . . what're you going to do?'

'Take you home.'

'I can't go home like this.' She started crying again. 'I can't let Mummy see me looking like a— like this.'

Like a tart, he thought brutally. But he didn't say it. He didn't have the right to say it. 'I meant home to my place. Just for a chat.'

'*She'll* be there.'

'She's not there.' He added for the sake of honesty, 'She's not there any more.'

That surprised her out of her tears again. 'You mean you've dumped her?'

'I mean she walked out on me.'

He reached down a hand to his daughter, waited to see if she would take it. If she would let him touch her.

She looked from his face to his hand. 'I haven't got any shoes. You threw them away.'

It would have been simplest to pick her up and carry her back to the car. But he couldn't do that now. All he could do was offer her his hand. And wait.

She brushed the side of her fist across the mascara trails, leaving a smudge like a huge bruise along her cheekbone. She went on staring at his hand.

Finally she struggled to her feet, on her own. She limped alongside him, refusing his help, all the way to the car.

He slid into the driver's seat and slammed the door. He glanced at her and saw she was shivering violently. 'Do you want my jacket?'

She shuddered. With cold, he hoped. 'I'll be OK.'

He started the motor, turned the heat on full blast.

She mumbled, 'Maybe you better just take me back to where you picked me up.'

'Why?'

She was gazing out the far window again, just as she had done all the way here. 'Then we could forget about . . . forget all this.'

He stared at her. The fact that they had both survived that calamitous encounter didn't change anything. Didn't change what he had done, what she was doing. 'What is it you want us to forget? What I was buying and you were selling?'

'Don't, Daddy!' She crossed her legs as well as her arms. She was crying again, but quietly this time. 'I can't just go home. It's not . . . not that simple.'

He hadn't had time to wonder about why. But now that he did, the answer came at once. From what he knew, from what Polly had said. He leaned forward to check the traffic before turning into the main road. 'You know what they say? If you want to break a habit, you should change your friends.'

She pulled a tissue out of her sleeve and wiped her nose. 'H— how did you know?'

He said in exasperation, 'Why else would you be doing this?'

She sniffled a few more times, mopped her eyes with the back of her hand. By now her elaborate make-up had been so smeared about that she looked like a child who had got into her mother's cosmetics drawer. 'What about you?' she demanded. 'Why were you doing it?'

'Well, it's not the same thing, is it?'

'Why not? Because I'm a woman and you're a man, I suppose, or some such sexist thing.'

'We were talking about motivation, not morality. I might enjoy having a meal at a restaurant, but you're unlikely to get much pleasure out of waiting on me.' He observed her fingers digging into her arms, and decided to turn the screw. 'Or do you enjoy renting out your body for any passing stranger?'

'Don't,' she whispered. She hunched away from him, curled herself into a ball. 'It made me sick, the first time. I couldn't do it, I was sick. They make me sick. How can they . . . ? How could you?' She turned her head along her shoulder, fixing him with great accusing eyes. 'You'd have done it to me too, if I wasn't your daughter.'

458

The thought made her shudder visibly. Not, he guessed, the unthinkable thought of sex with her father, but the thought of her father behaving like other men. Behaving like a man instead of a father. But of course that was just what he had been doing all along, ever since he left her for Elie.

'Have you done it before?' she demanded.

He couldn't bring himself to say so. He just nodded.

'Lots of times?'

It was important not to lie to her, any more than to Calum. Another nod, slow and reluctant.

'Why?'

He shrugged. He couldn't think of any defence that he felt able to offer her. *Because I like fucking slags* was not likely to explain the problem. Anyway, he didn't want her to know that he liked fucking slags.

And maybe he didn't, any more.

Louise looked away again, out the window, out at anywhere else. 'I can't stand it,' she said, and started to cry.

37

He took her back to the flat and sent her into the bathroom. She came out a long time later, wrapped in his
dressing gown, her face scrubbed clean, the artificial glow
of her hair dampened down by the shower.

He found another pair of unmatched but relatively
clean socks to keep her feet warm, and a plaid rug to cover
her legs. Then he gave her a cup of tea with a tot of whisky
in it, to warm her up inside. He poured himself tea as well,
but took his whisky neat alongside.

Louise sat in the corner of the sofa, her feet tucked
under her and the rug tucked around her. She surveyed
the tiny sitting room. He had lived there for three years,
and his daughter had never seen it before.

She was not seeing it at its best just now. 'Wow, what a
tip. It makes our squat look tidy.' She sipped at her forti-
fied tea. 'How long since she, um, left?'

'I can't remember,' he lied. 'Months ago.'

She gazed around the room again, while he watched
her. Her face was no longer the softly rounded, half-
childish one that had run out of the room three years ago.
It was thinner and sharper, with a subtly exotic flavour
that the new-found knowledge of his own past allowed
him to identify as the influence of Malachy's Cheyenne
blood. But aside from that, without the make-up, with the
yellow hair subdued and combed back, she looked almost
as if the last three years had never happened.

Some such thoughts, but in a different context, must have been going through her head. 'You know, Mummy doesn't have a boyfriend or anything.'

How easy and pleasant everybody else's life would be, if they only did what we want them to do. How easy, if he could turn the clock back to the days before he discovered whores. And Elie.

Had he been happy then? He couldn't recall. Perhaps he had only been not quite so unhappy.

'I've already heard about the state of your mother's love life. Calum told me.'

'Calum? Is he back?'

'He came home this morning. With me.'

'It feels like I haven't seen him for ages.' She shifted uncomfortably, coiled herself up even more tightly. 'I've been living with Hez.'

It took another cup of tea to get the story out of her, not very coherent, and undoubtedly highly censored. All about Hezekiah and his brother Ichabod. Two sternly Biblical names for a couple of social casualties.

She didn't actually have a habit, she said. It wasn't a real habit, as long as you only smoked. Everybody said that. Anyway, needles were gory, and dangerous on account of Aids, whereas smoking was cool. Everybody did it. It made you feel really cool. And she didn't smoke every day. Hez did, but she didn't. Just to make sure she didn't really get a habit.

The money was the problem. Icky said that Hez owed him money, and he was going to get him beaten up if he didn't pay. And he would, too. He'd done it to other people. Hez told her what Icky had done to other people. But Hez couldn't pay, he didn't have the money. He wanted her to help him out. But she didn't have any money either. She was too young to sign on.

It was Icky who talked her into going on the street. It was easy money, he said. Just a job like any other, he said. And she had to learn to pay her way some time, he said. Drugs weren't free, and neither was food.

She thought at first she might not mind too much. Sex was just an ordinary biological function like anything else, wasn't it? It was no big deal, just a bit of fun. Lots of people did it with strangers. Calum, for instance, had sex with all sorts of girls, people he hardly knew the names of. So why shouldn't she do it with strangers? What difference did money make?

But when it came down to it, it wasn't the same at all.

And Hez didn't seem to mind. How could he love her, if he didn't mind that other men were doing that to her? He said it didn't count, if it was only for money.

But the money made it worse. Smoking made her feel good, but the other thing made her feel so bad she couldn't stand it. It disgusted her, it made her sick. She couldn't stand to look at herself in the mirror, when she was dressed up to go out to work.

And Hez didn't love her. He had got her to dye her hair by saying he liked it better blonde. Then she heard Icky say that blonde was better for working the street, and she knew that was why Hez had said that.

She couldn't stand to think of anyone knowing about all that. She couldn't stand it.

She wept, scrunched up into the smallest possible space in the corner of the sofa, with her head in her arms and her badly bleached hair strewn around her shoulders. Ged hovered helplessly, stroking her hair where she wouldn't know what he was doing, where it lapped over the back of the sofa. He didn't know what else to do.

Have a chat with her, Polly had said.

'Lulu, listen. You don't have to do those things.'

'I know,' she sobbed. 'I just don't know how to . . . change everything around. I feel hopeless and horrible.'

'You're only sixteen, Lu. No-one can be hopeless at that age.'

'But I'm horrible. My school friends don't know what I've done. With those men. They'd call me a slag if they knew.'

'Everybody does things they wish they hadn't done.'

Christ, didn't they just. 'Things they don't want anyone to find out about. That doesn't mean everybody's horrible.'

She lifted her head to look at him. He took his hand from her hair, a little too quickly, as if he had been engaged in some guiltily furtive activity. Stroking his daughter's hair.

She looked at his hand, and then at his face. 'Do you think I'm a slag?'

'No.'

'Why not?'

Because you're only a silly little girl, he thought. Because it's my fault as much as yours. Because you're my daughter. 'Because you're not going to do that any more. Are you?'

'What if I did?' She had a way of looking, straight and unevadable, that made him feel he was up for judgement as much as her. 'Would you still say I'm not a slag?'

He took a deep breath and dodged the question. 'Look, Lu, I want you to be happy. If you were happy doing what you're doing, then I suppose I'd have to say OK, if that's what you want. But it sounds like you're not happy at all. Maybe you should be doing something else, something that might make you happier.'

'Like what?'

'Well, for a start, go back home. Find some new friends, ones who don't smoke shit. And start thinking about what you want to do with your life. What you're doing now isn't what you want to be doing five years from now.'

'I can't think that far off. Five years is a long long time. Almost a third of my whole life.'

'It's no time at all, believe me.' Five years ago he had been a happily married man, or at least a faithful one.

Louise relaxed a little, unbundling some of her misery. She tugged at the rug, tucking it around her, making herself cosier. 'What about you? Are you happy or unhappy?'

'Right now I'm unhappy. Not this very minute,' he

added hastily. 'At this moment I am blissfully happy, because you're here with me.'

She giggled. At least things were no longer as tragic as they had seemed half an hour ago. 'Why are you unhappy?'

The whole truth was not possible here. The simple truth would have to do. 'Because of Elie.'

'Why'd she leave you?'

'I don't know.'

Her eyes flew wide. 'She didn't tell you?'

'Not a word.'

'She sounds like a slag.' Louise giggled again. Then she sobered. 'Daddy? You know you said you just wanted me to be happy? Like that was the only reason you minded . . . well, you know.'

'Yes, I know. What about it?'

'Well, do you really think all those girls you've been picking up were happy about what you did to them?'

He gave this question careful consideration. Not because he really cared for a moment whether any of those tarts had suffered even a moment's angst from the intrusion of his prick into their anatomy, but because if he gave the wrong answer Louise would never believe that he didn't regard her as one of them. Never believe that he was not like the men who made her sick. That he was not like his own father.

Only, of course, he was.

But this was not the moment to reveal the awful truth. What was needed now was some reasonably honest way of making her think better, or at least not quite so badly, of him.

'What I think,' he said carefully, 'is that I'm not responsible for their happiness. If they don't like doing that, they should be doing something else.'

'But maybe they need the money.'

'So what? Everybody needs money. Most people have to do something they'd rather not be doing, in order to get it. But most people don't stand on street corners, inviting strangers to screw them.'

That must have been the wrong answer, because she shifted herself away from him. 'Daddy, are you saying that you really do think it's OK for men to pay women to have sex with them?'

That was only partly a challenge. The other part was a child asking her father a serious question, asking because she wanted to know the answer. And what the hell did he know about it? Never mind the right answers, he simply didn't have a clue.

'Christ, Lulu, I don't know what's OK. I'm certainly not saying that what I did was OK. All I know is we decide what we want to do, and take the consequences. After all,' he added, remembering something Angelina had said, 'in the end we're responsible for our own salvation.'

'What about yourself?' she demanded. 'If it's not making you happy, why are you doing it? You're not even making money from it, you're throwing money away. You're as crazy as me.'

He shrugged. Maybe screwing up your life was heredi- tary, a genetic form of original sin. Or maybe it was a disease, with which each generation infected the next. Was there any cure for a curse?

Louise impinged her presence on his thoughts. 'Daddy?'

'Yes, Lu?'

'You're not going to do it any more, are you?'

Louise was adamant that she wouldn't go home to Polly. Not yet, anyway. She said it would be too completely crushing, and she wanted some time to get herself sorted without her mother going on at her.

'You know how she goes on,' she explained, unnecessar- ily because Ged knew very well what she was talking about. 'Whenever she wants to talk about something important, she starts to speak in this really phoney voice, like I'm still

465

a little kid. I bet that's how she talks to her clients. No wonder they don't take any notice of what she says.'

There were other reasons for not going home, which she might have considered but didn't mention. Change your friends, he had told her. Keeping her away from Hezekiah and heroin wouldn't be a bad start.

In the end he took her to stay with Melissa. His mother's flat was very small, but life with her was never boring. It probably wouldn't be drug-free either, but people didn't end up working the streets as a result of smoking grass.

Besides, this arrangement would provide a minder for Melissa, as well as giving Louise someone else to worry about for a change. She might even decide that saving trees was going to be part of her new five-year life plan.

That left him with two little chores: fetching her gear, and telling Polly. They could both be done at the same time, since most of her clothing had never left home.

He went to Notting Hill right after dropping off Louise at his mother's place in Camden Town. It was Saturday morning, but there was no car in the paved-over garden. His spirits rose with craven relief. Louise had given him her front-door key; he could simply go in and get what she wanted, and ring Polly later to explain. Explanations were so much easier when you had the ultimate option of hanging up.

Since it wasn't his house any more, he went through the routine of ringing the doorbell. When nothing happened, he unlocked the door and stepped into the hall. He leaned against the door to shut it, and heard a sound on the staircase.

Polly. Coming down.

Her eyes were focused on the stairs below her, so she didn't see him right away. When she did look down towards the door, she gave a visible start and her foot missed the next step. She grabbed the banister to stop herself from falling down the stairs, then stared over it in resentful surprise.

'God, you scared me. I nearly broke my neck. How did you get in?'

'I didn't think you were home. The car's not here.'

'Calum has it.' Recovering her balance and her poise, she came down the rest of the way to confront him on level ground. 'He's taking some old clothes round to Oxfam for me.'

'That's surprisingly helpful of him. I didn't think he'd even be awake. It's not noon yet.'

'He's still jet-lagged, I suppose.' She cast a significant glance at the key he was still holding. 'Where did you get that?'

He too glanced at the key, before putting it away in his pocket. 'It's Louise's. I came over to collect some clothes for her.'

Polly stuck her hands into the front pockets of her jeans and stood with her feet apart, chin up, staring at him. It was probably no accident that she was standing in the middle of the hall, in front of the stairway, physically barring him from entering her house. 'You always start your stories in the middle, don't you?'

Ged lifted one shoulder. 'You wanted me to talk to her, didn't you?'

'But not to help her move out. How did you find her, anyway? I'm not even sure where she's living.'

'I just happened to bump into her, that's all.' Which was true, as far as it went. The last thing he had had in mind at the time was meeting his daughter. 'It seems the squat thing hasn't worked out too well, but for the sake of her dignity she doesn't want to come back just yet.'

'Where is she? Why does she all of a sudden want her clothes? She must have been living in the same jumper and jeans since she walked out of here.'

Louise had made him promise not to tell Polly where she was. That would have amounted to much the same thing as taking her home, since there would have been no possibility of preventing Polly from heading for

467

Camden Town at once. 'Let's just say she's in a safe place. She said she'd ring you later.'

Polly's eyes narrowed. 'She's staying with you?'

'No, she's not. Look, Polly, she'll tell you herself, when she wants you to know.'

'I'm her mother, and she's still a child. I've a right to know where she is.'

'But I don't have the right to tell you. I promised her I wouldn't.'

'That's preposterous. Why would you make a promise like that?'

'Because if I hadn't, she would have disappeared again.'

Out of his life, he meant. Making that promise, and keeping it, was the only way he could even begin to win Louise's trust again. It meant that he was accepting her as a person, with the right to make her own choices. And also, paradoxically, that he was taking responsibility for her, instead of fobbing her off on to Polly.

As for the other promise, it was all but implicit.

As she had got out of the car – the same car she had fled from, twelve hours before – he said to her, 'Don't forget to think about what you want to do with your life.' And she leaned down on the pavement to look at him, much as she had done at the kerbside by King's Cross. Only this time she said, 'I will if you will.'

Which meant, in the context of the night before, I won't if you don't.

Polly knew nothing of all that, of course. But she was growing more, not less, agitated. By now she was all but blaming him for Louise's disappearance, rather than being grateful for her rescue.

There was no point arguing; that would start a row that he didn't want to get into. He had only come to collect Louise's clothes, not to be reminded of all his sins and shortcomings. 'Polly, I promise you, Louise will be all right. She said she'd ring you, and she will. Now will you let me get what she wanted?'

Polly stood aside to let him up the stairs. From the

corner of his eye, as he passed her, he saw her set a hand on the newel post. Heard footsteps on the stairs behind him.

'Promises, promises,' she hissed at his back. 'Twenty years ago this month, you promised to love me till the day you died.'

1982

When I was young I was so god-damned brave, I wasn't scared of dying. I was only scared of dying before I'd had the chance to do all there was in me to do.

But now I know there's never going to be enough chances. I'm going to die still undone.

38

Wisdom is as good as an inheritance.

Life went on in Hyde Park.

The sun had returned, the ripe, evocative sun of October, tugging at the memory, brooding on the past. Old women sat in sunny sheltered corners, overdressed just as they had been in July; perhaps long experience had led them always to expect the worst of the weather. Young men romped with dogs across the broad lawns. There were mothers with children, nannies with children, perambulating or congregating. And one optimistic ice-cream seller, the last of the season. His mates must have flown south with the swallows, leaving him to trundle on unregarded, the ghost of summer past.

Ged was simply walking. He was trying not to think about anything. Thinking hurt. He didn't even know how to think about the things that were shouting for attention in his head.

He had gained and lost an unexpected fortune. Lost a fortune and regained a son. Broken his writer's block by stealing from a dead man and lying about it, lying with silence. Lost and found his daughter: the most painful and humiliating thing that had ever happened to him, and entirely his own fault. No wonder he couldn't think.

He stopped by the duck pond to light a cigarette. He blew smoke into the bright air, polluting the world just by breathing. No, polluting the world by smoking. Do what you want and take the consequences.

The leaves were starting to rust. Those of a more flamboyant nature had flushed bright red. Others would simply turn brown and blow away, or crumble quietly together in a soggy heap. Some had already parted from their parent tree and were skittering past him, gaily coloured and falsely full of life, running away like the gingerbread man from a fate that would catch them up and eat them up, no matter what they did.

Were human beings like those leaves, or more like the trees that begat them? Trees have presence. They endure. They have ancestors, and descendants. But a leaf has less significance or durability than the grass that withers, the flower that fades.

Right now he was voting for the leaves. There was some perverse comfort in the idea that nothing one did had any moral significance or temporal resonance. So the fact that he was a complete shit and a failure in pretty well all respects might not matter very much.

He decided to spare the ducks an extra dose of carbon monoxide and tar. He turned away from the pond and wandered down the path towards Hyde Park Corner.

The benches were more crowded here. It must be lunch-time. The wage slaves were escaping for an hour, drawn out by the sunshine like wasps to a picnic. He eyed the legs on a couple of shopgirls, but his libido wasn't really in it. Hadn't been, since the night he discovered he had turned his daughter into a whore. Maybe he was impotent now, as a punishment for his sins.

He was coming to the bench where Elie used to sit. Where they had sat together one night. Where he had . . . she had . . .

Well, it looked like he wasn't impotent after all. The mere thought of Elie had cured him.

A woman was sitting on the bench, reading one of those trashy romances Elie had been so fond of. An odd coincidence, he thought.

She set the book down and lifted her head to gaze across the park, with the abstracted look of the mind's eye.

His first thought was that she'd done something to her hair. Cut it short, sort of punkish, curt, inelegant. And she was wearing a frumpy, shapeless, muddy-coloured dress. She never used to wear clothes like that.

He dropped his cigarette and ground it out. He fumbled for another one, the last one in the packet, as he walked up to her. He held it out in front of him like the key to some secret garden. 'You wouldn't happen to have a light, would you?'

Slowly she turned her gaze on him. Her face was thinner. She wasn't wearing make-up. He had never seen her without make-up before, except in bed. But her eyes were as amazing as ever. He watched them widen as she took him in.

And her voice was still that same breathless semi-whisper, as if she hadn't the right to speak out loud and maybe interrupt the rest of the world. 'Sorry. I've given up smoking.'

'Have you really? Or are you just saying that to make me feel bad?'

She smiled. It was true what he used to think, she would have been beautiful even bald, even wearing a flour sack. 'No, I really have. They say it's bad for the baby.'

He had been about to sit down on the far end of the bench. He did sit down, but it was more of a collapse. He had to stare at her for at least a minute before his eyes obliged him to believe his ears. Then he had to calm himself, by lighting the cigarette, before he could make his voice work.

'Christ! Elie, why didn't you tell me?'

She wasn't smiling now. 'You said you didn't want it.'

'That was just hypothetical, for God's sake.'

'But I asked you,' she reminded him. She spoke patiently, not accusing or bitter. Not the way most women would sound right now. Elie had never expected much of her men. 'I asked you what if I got pregnant accidentally,

473

and you said – well, you know what you said.'

He tried to recall what he had said, what he had said to drive her away. Something about not believing in accidents, and how they could always be amended. It was so hard to remember his own words, so hard to forget the look on her face when he had said them. 'You thought I'd make you have an abortion?'

'Wouldn't you?' She let the question hang, just long enough to let him hang himself on it. 'And I knew you'd think I was a liar. That I'd done it on purpose, when I knew you didn't want it.'

He wanted to shout at her, shake her, demand how she could have been so stupid as to put him through this for that. Why hadn't she told him? And how could she have thought . . .

But multitudes of men, since the world began, had walked out for that very reason: because they had got their woman pregnant, and they didn't want a child. And he had said – she had asked and he had said – exactly what she had feared. So what else was she supposed to think?

And why shouldn't she have chosen to leave, before he could abandon her? She had chosen him in the first place, she had told him. And now she had left him. Not the simple, passive creature he had once taken her for.

Would he really have thought she had done it on purpose?

Of course he would.

He didn't think so now. Which didn't necessarily mean her pregnancy was an accident. Accidents were not quite the same as mistakes or miscalculations. But he believed her anyway, because he had to. Because she had left him over that. Because he was in love with her.

Since he couldn't deny what she had said, he had no idea how to answer her. Maybe there wasn't any answer.

He wanted to ask her about the haircut and the dress and the absence of make-up, but he didn't know how to put it. You look terrible, what's going on? was hardly the way to win her back.

'Your face is thinner.'

So were her arms, he realized. She was built with fine bones, and now they were showing. But at the same time her body had grown bulky. Christ, she really was pregnant. He hadn't seen her for almost five months, so she must be six or even seven months along.

And he had known nothing.

'I've lost weight.' She looked down at her hands in her lap. 'I'm supposed to be putting it on, but I've been sick the whole time. It's hard to force myself to eat, even though I know I've got to. And going to work wears me out, but I can't afford not to work. Well, it does give me something to do, I suppose.' She put her hand up to her head, and unexpectedly giggled. 'I had my hair cut really short, to save myself trouble. How's that for lazy?'

'When is it due?'

'The end of December.'

Closer to seven months, then.

It, it. His baby in her. That thought made him want to take her home and fuck her senseless, take her home and take care of her. He wanted her so badly, in every, in any sense. But three times she had refused to see him. Or even to speak to him.

He looked at his own hands, clenched with useless passion. He didn't know what to do. He really did not know.

She rose, with only a trace of her former grace. She looked heavy and awkward, thin and frail. 'I've got to get back to work.'

'Wait.' He threw away his cigarette, his last one. He stood up and grabbed her hand. 'Where are you working?'

'Over there.' She waved a hand towards Knightsbridge. That familiar ghost of a smile flickered around her mouth. 'Not selling perfume, though. Pregnant women don't have the right image.'

The mannequins who sold perfume were supposed to be *soignée*, sophisticated, sexy. But what could be sexier than Elie's body, big with the child he had

475

started in her? 'Will you meet me after work?'

She looked down at her hand in his as if it were unconnected to her. 'What good will that do, if you don't want the baby?'

He hadn't got round to thinking about that, about what he thought about the baby. He had believed that a baby was the last thing he wanted. Now he looked at her and thought he must have been mad. The only thing that would make him happier than living with Elie was living with Elie and her baby. His baby.

'I didn't say I didn't want it. I mean, I know I said I didn't want a baby, but I didn't mean this baby.'

'What's different about this one?'

'It's in you.'

They were not alone. There were people passing on either side of them, people variously pushing a pram, cursing a dog, encouraging a child, leaning on a walking stick, ransacking a packet of crisps, muttering to themselves. Not alone, even beyond that, since the park was in the heart of London. They were surrounded by millions of people, all of them deep in the mess and muddle of their lives, saints and shits alike, in a world that refused to order itself by ten commandments and a few quadratic equations.

Elie looked at his hand again, the hand that was holding hers. She came up close to him, making a private place between them, in spite of all the people around them. She took his hand and set it flat across her swollen abdomen, low down near the bottom of the curve.

He could feel the chill of her fingers on his hand, and the warmth of her body beneath it. And then he could feel the movement of the baby in her.

He stroked the place where the baby was. Stroked Elie and child at once. And just for an unobservable instant, he moved his hand lower.

Elie uttered a small breathless laugh before she pushed him away.

Now she was searching for something in her bag. A pen.

She scribbled in the front of her stereotyped love story, and handed the book to him.

There was no point not waiting until she had gone, before reading what she had written. Either he had won her back or he had lost her for ever, and nothing now could change whichever it was.

He let her go, watched her go, in something close to panic. What if he never saw her again? His life would be broken, half of it elsewhere.

When she was out of sight, he looked at the book. A He with black hair, he noticed, and a She of the same colour. One of the rare ones, she had said.

He opened the cover of the book. He recognized her neat, rather childish handwriting, with its air of deliberateness, as if she had never quite mastered joined-up writing. The first time he had seen it, he had taken its simplicity for evidence of simpleness. But since then he had come to understand that in Elie, as in all the practical arts, simplicity was the soul of sophistication.

Now the sight of her familiar script induced a violent pang of loss and longing, almost strong enough to bring him to his knees. It was as if he could only now let himself suffer them, now that they were images on a canvas coloured hope.

And all she had written was one word. *Tomorrow.*

THE END

DADDY'S GIRL
by Janet Inglis

'A story of tremendous power'
Literary Review

Olivia, almost fifteen, feels like a piece of unwanted baggage left over from her parents' broken marriage. Daddy is about to marry one of his former students, who is young enough to be his daughter; Mummy's men friends sometimes stay the night. Her parents have turned into strangers, and neither of them seems to have room for her any more. She feels a burden to everyone she loves.

Then Nick enters her life: Nick, her mother's lover, an amoral, street-wise photographer with an insolent, assessing gaze. Nick violates the sanctuary of Olivia's home by moving in with her mother, and before long he has violated Olivia as well, causing her to become hopelessly addicted to him as he teaches her the meaning of desire. At last she comes to the shocking solution that will change forever her life and the lives of those who have denied her love.

'In this arresting first novel Janet Inglis's writing is wonderfully, brutally and perceptively honest, and poses questions that need answering'
Maureen Owen, *Daily Mail*

'Janet Inglis writes extremely well, with speakable dialogue and imaginable descriptions . . . I believed it was all happening, and very much wished it wasn't'
Jessica Mann, *Sunday Telegraph*

'Few contemporary novels have dealt so thoroughly with the destructive power of sex'
Vogue

0 552 14207 7

FATHER OF LIES
by Janet Inglis

It was her mother's fault; if she had grown up with them, as by rights she should have done, they would be like cousins or brothers, no more, no less. As it was, they had come into her life as strangers, adult males, potential lovers.

When Georgie Payne knocks on the door of her grand.-father's house, she has crossed the Atlantic alone to solve a mystery. Her mother Olivia has had no contact with her parents, Georgie's grandparents, for nearly twenty years. Georgie has never met them and knows nothing about them. How did this situation come about? Georgie has come to England to find out.

To her surprise and delight, she quickly discovers two gorgeous half-uncles, both her own age. There is Matthew, graceful and ambiguous, her grandfather's son by his second marriage. And there is big, blond, shaggy Luke, her grandmother's son from her marriage to Nick, the enigmatic photographer who seems to know more than he will tell about the events of the past. But the more Georgie discovers, the more entangled she herself becomes in the consequences of what happened long ago, as her sudden reappearance breaks the silence of decades.

'It is rare to find a book which affects you sensually and affects your mind'
Maureen Owen, *The Times*

0 552 14208 5

A SELECTED LIST OF FINE NOVELS AVAILABLE FROM CORGI BOOKS

14060 0	MERSEY BLUES	Lyn Andrews	£4.99
14453 3	THE DARK ARCHES	Aileen Armitage	£5.99
14049 X	THE JERICHO YEARS	Aileen Armitage	£5.99
14514 9	BLONDE WITH ATTITUDE	Virginia Blackburn	£5.99
14323 5	APPASSIONATA	Jilly Cooper	£6.99
13313 2	CATCH THE WIND	Frances Donnelly	£5.99
14261 1	INTIMATE	Elizabeth Gage	£4.99
14442 8	JUST LIKE A WOMAN	Jill Gascoine	£5.99
14096 1	THE WILD SEED	Iris Gower	£4.99
14537 8	APPLE BLOSSOM TIME	Kathryn Haig	£5.99
14385 5	THE BELLS OF SCOTLAND ROAD		
		Ruth Hamilton	£5.99
14622 6	A MIND TO KILL	Andrea Hart	£5.99
14529 7	LEAVES FROM THE VALLEY	Caroline Harvey	£5.99
14486 X	MARSH LIGHT	Kate Hatfield	£6.99
14207 7	DADDY'S GIRL	Janet Inglis	£5.99
14208 5	FATHER OF LIES	Janet Inglis	£5.99
14397 9	THE BLACK BOOK	Sara Keays	£5.99
14333 2	SOME OLD LOVER'S GHOST	Judith Lennox	£5.99
14320 0	MARGUERITE	Elisabeth Luard	£5.99
13910 6	BLUEBIRDS	Margaret Mayhew	£3.99
14498 3	MORE INNOCENT TIMES	Imogen Parker	£5.99
10375 6	CSARDAS	Diane Pearson	£5.99
14125 9	CORONATION SUMMER	Margaret Pemberton	£5.99
08930 3	STORY OF O	Pauline Reage	£4.99
14400 2	THE MOUNTAIN	Elvi Rhodes	£5.99
14549 1	CHOICES	Susan Sallis	£5.99
14548 3	THE GHOST OF WHITECHAPEL		
		Mary Jane Staples	£5.99
14378 2	FIVE DAYS IN PARIS	Danielle Steel	£5.99
14476 2	CHILDREN OF THE TIDE	Valerie Wood	£5.99